Translating Trans Identity

This book explores the ways in which translation deals with sexual and textual undecidability, adopting an interdisciplinary approach bridging translation, transgender studies, and queer studies in analyzing the translations of six texts in English, French, and Spanish labelled as 'trans.'

Rose draws on experimental translation methods, such as the use of the palimpsest, and builds on theory from areas such as philosophy, linguistics, queer studies, and transgender studies and the work of such thinkers as Derrida and Deleuze to encourage critical thinking around how all texts and trans texts specifically work to be queer and how queerness in translation might be celebrated. These texts illustrate the ways in which authors play language games and how these can be translated between languages that use gender in different ways and the subsequent implications for our understanding of the act of translation and how we present our gender identity or identities.

In showing what translation and transgender identity can learn from one another, Rose lays the foundation for future directions for research into the translation of trans identity, making this book key reading for scholars in translation studies, transgender studies, and queer studies.

Emily Rose finished her PhD in Translating Trans Identity at the University of East Anglia in 2018. Her work has been published in *Transgender Studies Quarterly* (volume 3 (3-4) and volume 6 (3)), *Queer in Translation* and *Untranslatability: An Interdisciplinary Perspective*, a volume she also co-edited. She currently teaches MFL at a preparatory school in Norfolk.

Routledge Studies in Literary Translation

Series Editors: Jacob Blakesley and Duncan Large

Routledge Studies in Literary Translation highlights pioneering research in literary translation, exploring emerging developments, new voices, and key issues of relevance in core literary genres. The series questions the definition of literary translation as a sub-discipline in its own right with its own particular methodological and theoretical considerations as well as the extent to which its study extends to genres beyond the traditional categories of fiction, poetry, and drama. The series extends its scope beyond Anglophone literary traditions to feature research on translated literary works across a range of languages as well as the interface between literary translation and such topics as multilingual literature, literary canons, publishing markets, classics, and digital humanities. With its dedicated focus on literary translation, this series will appeal to students and scholars interested in the interface of translation studies and literary studies, as well as those in related disciplines such as comparative literature, literary criticism, sociology, and media studies.

Translating Trans Identity
(Re)Writing Undecidable Texts and Bodies
Emily Rose

For more information about the series, please visit: https://www.routledge.com/Routledge-Studies-in-Literary-Translation/book-series/RRSLT

Translating Trans Identity

(Re)Writing Undecidable Texts and Bodies

Emily Rose

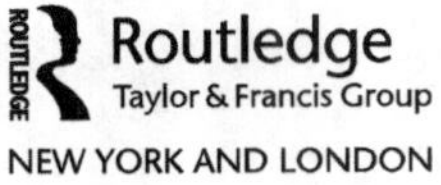

NEW YORK AND LONDON

First published 2021
by Routledge
52 Vanderbilt Avenue, New York, NY 10017

and by Routledge
2 Park Square, Milton Park, Abingdon, Oxon, OX14 4RN

Routledge is an imprint of the Taylor & Francis Group, an informa business

Library of Congress Cataloging-in-Publication Data
A catalog record for this title has been requested

ISBN: 978-0-367-36996-5 (hbk)
ISBN: 978-0-367-74474-8 (pbk)
ISBN: 978-0-367-36997-2 (ebk)

Typeset in Sabon
by MPS Limited, Dehradun

Contents

Illustrations

Figures

Tables

Preface

The work of Derrida and other theorists such as Deleuze and Benjamin, translated to English, will be quoted in this book in the interests of space. These translations have been checked against a careful reading of the originals to ensure that no misunderstandings and no mistaken interpretations occur.

Acknowledgements

Thank you firstly to my PhD supervisors, Professor Duncan Large and Dr Clare Connors at the University of East Anglia, for their advice and support for the three years it took to craft my thesis. Thank you to the Consortium for the Humanities and Arts South East England who funded my PhD from my second year and gave me the opportunity to dedicate (nearly) all my time to research. Thank you to Professor William Spurlin and Professor Clive Scott, my viva examiners; it was their encouragement and enthusiasm for my project that led me to create this book. Thank you to my editors at Routledge Elysse Preposi and Helena Parkinson, to the two anonymous reviewers of my book proposal and to Duncan Large and Jacob Blakesley as series editors who all gave very valuable advice. Thank you to Jamie Clarke for creating my "gendered" font (twice). Thank you to Professor Joseph Harris at Royal Holloway for running a module on transgression in the early modern age which included Choisy's text; without it I may never have discovered Choisy and the other amazing "trans warriors" in this book. Thank you to Romy and Philip for our conversations about translation, literature, philosophy and everything in between. Thank you to my friends for believing in me and building me up every time I wobbled: Gem, Lizzie, Zuleika, Gilly, Lizzie, Susie, Lucy and Merry. Joe: thank you for always listening to me and always knowing exactly what to say. Lastly, and most importantly, thank you to my family – Mum, Dad, Oli and Daisy – for supporting me throughout everything I do, but mostly for being there through my PhD and the process of writing this book which was not always easy.

Emily Rose, Norwich, January 2020

Permissions

Full details of all works used can be found in the Bibliography. The author and publishers are grateful to copy-right holders of the following material for permission to reprint extracts:

Éditions Grasset & Fasquelle, for the extracts from *Sphinx* by Anne Garréta; copyright © 1986.

Éditions Gallimard, for the extracts from Alexina Barbin dite Alexina B by Michel Foucault; copyright © 2014.

Excerpts from MIDDLESEX by Jeffrey Eugenides, Copyright © 2002 by Jeffrey Eugenides. Reprinted by permission of Farrar, Straus and Giroux.

HarperCollins Publishers Ltd, for the extracts from *Middlesex* by Jeffrey Eugenides; copyright © 2003.

Jonathan Cape, for the extracts from *Written on the Body* by Jeanette Winterson. Reprinted by permission of The Random House Group Limited; copyright © 1992 Jeanette Winterson.

Éditions de l'Olivier, *Points*, for the extracts from *Middlesex* by Jeffrey Eugenides, translated by Marc Cholodenko; copyright © 2004.

Great Moments Ltd, for the excerpts from *Written on the Body* by Jeanette Winterson, Reprinted by permission of Vintage Canada/Alfred A. Knopf Canada, a division of Penguin Random House Canada Limited. All rights reserved; copyright © 1992.

Penguin Random House USA, for the excerpts from *Written on the Body* by Jeanette Winterson; copyright ©1992.

The Johns Hopkins University Press, for excerpts from *The Maiden of Tonnerre: The Vicissitudes of the Chevalier and the Chevalière d'Eon* by Charles d'Eon de Beaumont (pp. ix; x; xx; xvi; xxi; xxiii-xxiv, 8; 10; 29) translated and edited by Roland A. Champagne, Nina Ekstein, and Gary Kates, reprinted with permission of Johns Hopkins University Press; copyright ©2001.

Penguin Random House, for the excerpts from *Herculine Barbin*, introduced by Michel Foucault, translated by Richard MacDougall (pp. xii-xvi) © 1980

Libella, for extracts from *Dominique* by Cookie Allez; copyright © 2015

Deep Vellum Publishers, for the extracts from *Sphinx* by Anne Garréta, translated by Emma Ramadan; copyright © 2015.

Beacon press, for the extracts from *The Lieutenant Nun: memoir of a Basque transvestite in the New World* by Catalina de Erauso, translated by Michele and Gabriel Stepto; copyright © 1996.

Special Collections, University of Leeds Brotherton Library, for extracts from *Grande Epitre Historique de la Chevaliere D'Eon En 1785 A Madame La Duchesse De Montmorenci-Bouteville A Paris* by Charles D'Eon de Beaumont, BC MS Chevalier d'Eon/01; copyright © 1785.

Special Collections, University of Leeds Brotherton Library, for images from *Grande Epitre Historique de la Chevaliere D'Eon En 1785 A Madame La Duchesse De Montmorenci-Bouteville A Paris* by Charles D'Eon de Beaumont, BC MS Chevalier d'Eon/01; copyright © 1785.

Cathedral Archive of the Colombina Institute (el Archivo de la Catedral de Sevilla (ACS)), for images from *Copia manuscrita de la autobiografía de la monja Catalina de Erauso* [manuscript] Sección Fondo Historíco General, 34; copyright © 1646.

Every effort has been made to contact copyright-holders. Please advise the publisher of any errors or omissions, and these will be corrected in subsequent editions.

Introduction

This book grew out of the translation challenges posed by one particular text: the *Mémoires de l'abbé de Choisy habillé en femme* [memoirs of the Abbot de Choisy dressed as a woman]. It is made challenging by the voice of its author-narrator, the seventeenth-century priest François-Timoléon de Choisy (1995, 17), who explains that, after his mother died:

> Je n'étais donc contraint de personne, et je m'abandonnai à mon penchant. Il arriva même que madame de La Fayette, que je voyais fort souvent, me voyant toujours fort ajusté avec des pendants d'oreilles et des mouches, me dit en bonne amie que ce n'était point la mode pour les hommes, et que je ferais bien mieux de m'habiller en femme. Sur une si grande autorité, je me fis couper les cheveux pour être mieux coiffée.
>
> I was therefore constrained by no one and I abandoned myself to my inclination. It just so happened that Madame de La Fayette, who I saw very often, seeing me often accessorized with earrings and beauty spots, told me as a friend that this was not the fashion for men and that I would do better to dress as a woman. On such authority, I had my hair cut to be better coiffed (my translation).

Before the exchange with Madame de La Fayette, Choisy uses masculine gender on "contraint" [constrained] and "ajusté" [literally: adjusted; accessorized]. Once Choisy takes Madame de La Fayette's advice, "coiffée" [coiffed] is written in the feminine. Choisy does not just dress as a woman, he becomes one in the language he uses. Choisy can write as both a man and a woman because French marks gender on adjectives, nouns, and past participles, not just in third person subject pronouns. The general premise is that those assigned the male sex at birth use masculine grammatical gender while those assigned female the feminine. Translating a text into English whose author breaks these rules is challenging, because English only marks gender on third person pronouns (he or she) and possessive adjectives (his or hers).

A specific translation conundrum began this research: how does a translator deal with shifting linguistic gender identity when translating into a language, such as English, which does not use gender in the same way? This led to a much more far-reaching question: What does considering how to translate this shift, instead of putting it down as a regrettable but inevitable translation loss, reveal about the act of translation and/or about gender and how we present our gender identity (or identities) to the world?

For the purpose of this book, I describe protagonists who use shifting linguistic gender as trans. Throughout this book I take "trans" to be "an umbrella term to describe people whose gender is not the same as, or does not sit comfortably with, the sex they were assigned at birth" (Stonewall 2017). In contrast, I define a "transgender" person as "a person whose identity does not conform unambiguously to conventions of male or female gender, but combines or moves between these" (Oxford 2017); transgender is therefore one type of trans identity. Transgender men and transgender women (or trans men and trans women) are often described as people who are assigned one sex at birth but who live and identify as the other sex (see Stonewall 2017; Tate, Hagai, and Crosby 2020, 6). This is important but here I want to focus on the idea of the transgender person as not conforming to one sex or another despite seeming to have "crossed the border" between one sex and another. Like the Abbé de Choisy, who becomes a woman and who I have argued elsewhere was transgender (see Rose 2017), any trans protagonist goes through such a process of becoming and unbecoming. This constant becoming and unbecoming makes these protagonists undecidable.

Undecidability

I use the term "undecidable" in preference to "ambiguous" or "undefined" because it makes apparent the important readerly and textual nature of the problem I am addressing. It situates my work within the fields of literary criticism and postmodernism, and specifically aligns it with the work of Jacques Derrida. The concept was first introduced by Kurt Gödel in 1931; it "proposed that in any formal system, that is, any system constructed by rules, there would be certain propositions that could neither be proved nor refuted by finite logical procedures, while still remaining meaningful. Such proposals were called 'undecidables'" (Froneman 2010, 294). According to Derrida, a reading of a text can only take place if undecidability is maintained, where there is an aporia, "where to make a choice is to cheat the text, cheat meaning" (Dick and Wolfreys 2013, 300).

Any text is undecidable but I argue that trans texts are quintessentially undecidable texts. The main question this book asks is how translation can deal with sexual and textual undecidability that represents the impossibility of knowing or pinning down a fixed meaning. I begin with the premise that undecidability is an inherent characteristic of texts written by or about trans people and that translation is the best place to explore and represent it. This undecidability, or becoming, is best conveyed in translation as it is not a simple transfer of meaning from one text to another where the end result is fixed. I investigate the idea that this textual and sexual undecidability, which is revealed and celebrated in the translation of trans identity, is actually present in all texts and bodies, whether "trans" or not.

To investigate undecidability and its translation in trans texts I decided to look at authors and texts that approached the question of being "trans" and that of "becoming" from a variety of perspectives. One could make an argument that if trans is a trans-historical phenomenon there is no need to historisize early texts. I contend that early-modern texts can be labeled "trans" (even though this category was not available to the writers themselves at the time). I see this as a new way of describing something that has existed for centuries but which has only recently been given a name. Furthermore, in this book, I look to Walter Benjamin's ([1924] 2012) theory that translation is the source text's afterlife to show that translations affect their sources, therefore a queer translation makes its source retrospectively queer. For me, a queer translation is one that allows the translator and the reader to explore and question what happens when we accept gender fluidity and what the placing of human beings into discrete, incontrovertible categories has cost those individuals who could not fit (see Tate, Hagai, and Crosby 2020). As a term, "queer" connotes elasticity and indeterminacy and it "ceaselessly interrogat[es] both the preconditions of identity and its effects" (Jagose 1996, 1). I do look at early-modern conceptualizations of gender, however, to suggest that while it has always been possible to be trans, what it means to be trans and the consequences of publicly identifying as "different" change over time. My early-modern texts are trans but I also acknowledge that this is perhaps a different kind of "trans" (that all kinds of "trans" are in some ways individual). This acknowledgement is queer: "Attention to these very transgressions, these slippages of signification, these differences, when we work across languages and cultures is, in effect, a comparatively queer praxis" (Spurlin 2017, 173).

When choosing the "trans" texts to work on, it was important to include memoirs written by trans people themselves (even if they could not identify as trans in their own time) because, according to Catherine Baker (2017): "The stories of what it means to be trans are even more disproportionately told by cis creators, and keep coming round to the same tropes that fascinate people who aren't trans". I have included stories written by cisgender authors as well – these texts, whether we like it or not, tend to reach a wider audience and, most importantly, are translated.[1]

Undecidable Texts

My final selection of texts was made very carefully to fit with a structure based on the translation of different kinds of trans identity. I begin with the early-modern memoirs of the Chevalier d'Eon and Catalina de Erauso, two protagonists who appear to "become" the "opposite" sex permanently but whose writing belies this permanence. The Chevalier/Chevalière d'Eon demonstrates how this process of movement is inevitable but also transgressive – he tells his eighteenth-century readers that he becomes a woman despite himself, that he is powerless to resist crossing the gender divide, in order to lessen his transgression (Champagne, Ekstein, and Kates 2001, 3).[2] The lives of d'Eon and Erauso have been examined by researchers interested in history, autobiography, sexology and sexuality, among other things. They have not, however, been extensively discussed by translators or translation scholars; the translation challenges of these memoirs are discussed by their English translators, but with little attention paid to the "trans" aspect. These "trans" aspects and the difficulties they present for translation into English will be discussed here where the two texts are brought together for the first time. Their juxtaposition reveals the importance of maintaining the "trans" aspect in translations of texts whose writers specifically use writing to show their shifting gender identity when no other means were at their disposal. And, indeed, I argue that the creativity needed to overcome the linguistic challenges these texts present for translation only serves to enhance the original transgression these writers practised by writing "trans" memoirs intended for public consumption.

Because of this oscillation I need a way to refer to the protagonists that does not force them to be definitively masculine or feminine. Since the Middle Ages, English has dealt with the need for ambiguous pronouns by using "they" or "he or she" (see Baranowski 2002, 378). Many object to these, however, because "they" should not be used in the singular, being a plural pronoun and "he or she" is awkward (ibid.).[3] Other options have included creating neologisms, and, while Dennis Baron (2010) claims epicene pronouns are the "words that failed," they are becoming more widely used and recognized. No one set of epicene pronouns is uniformly used by everyone (see Chak 2015) but the set I use in this book are "ze" (he or she), "hir" (him or her) and "hirself" (himself or herself) (see Robinson 2020 who uses "ze", Chak 2015 and Holmes 2008 who uses "hir").

I continue with the French memoir of Herculine Barbin, one of the most famous "hermaphrodites" of the nineteenth century (Dreger 1998, 51). I compare it to the fictional *Middlesex* whose protagonist, Calliope, constantly becomes and unbecomes both male and female and this is shown in the name I use – masculine "Cal" and feminine "Callie" become "Cal/lie". These two texts are rarely read together (see Holmes 2008 for an exception) despite the fact that *Middlesex* is a good fit for comparison with Barbin's *Mes Memoires*, because Cal/lie is supposedly inspired to write after having read it. Many critics and researchers ignore the undecidable aspect of both texts and struggle to label the protagonists as male or female rather than both or neither and I offer a rare argument for undecidability in these texts. Barbin's life and memoir have been examined by many, including Judith Butler (2006), and *Middlesex* has received much critical attention which is unsurprising for a Pulitzer-prize-winning novel. However, neither their translations (into English for *Mes Memoires* and into French and Spanish for *Middlesex*), nor the very specific issues they create for translation, have been profoundly probed thus far. By providing such a probing here I aim to show that translation, and, more specifically, digital translation, is an appropriate medium through which to transmit texts which are made undecidable by, among other things, layers of both intertext and paratext because translations themselves are layers added to the source text.

I close by looking at *Sphinx* and *Written on the Body* whose narrators are neither male nor female and so whose "becoming" brings up questions of identity and existence; the unnamed narrator of *Written on the Body* becomes "less present" the more we try to pin down their sex. These are two texts which have been studied relatively extensively both in the original and, in the case of *Written on the Body*, in translation; again many readers ignore the undecidable aspects of the texts, looking to label the protagonists by clutching at textual clues. The English translation of *Sphinx* was only published in 2015 and so while many theorists and critics have considered the French text, far fewer focus on its translation. The materiality and "constructedness" of the text and the body are highlighted by these highly unconventional texts which erase both sex and gender. I maintain that because translation requires such close reading at the level of the text and because it brings up questions of linguistic gender, it is more illuminating to look at translations of texts with no gender than it is to look at the "original" texts alone. By reading these texts alongside each other I am offering a new angle on the critical analysis of *Written on the Body*, a field which would appear to have become saturated with studies claiming to have deduced the narrator's gender identity, and am offering a new approach to translating undecidability.

Despite the fact that some of these texts are well known and well researched they have all been undervalued as texts which tell the reader about, or help the reader to question, what it is to be trans and, by extension, what it is to be human. Here I develop a way of reading these texts which not only counteracts this undervaluing but restores value through translation. While trans people are still subject to violence and persecution, a discussion of how to educate people about trans lives and how to promote trans rights will always be important. By exploring the relationship between translation and trans identity, I aim to bring trans writing and lives to the fore across cultures. By bringing translation and trans-gender issues together I seek to take account of undecidable identity by shining a light on trans texts and bodies.

Theoretical Context: (Trans)gender

Transgender theory is concerned with questioning norms and exposes the myth that one's gender follows naturally from one's sex. Sex and gender are different: "sex refers to the biological and reproductive classification of an organism – male or female. Gender [...] refers to the cultural aspect of sex – how we come to know ourselves as social beings that are male or female" (Franklin 2012, 1). Though, of course, in the remainder of this book I shall prove that there are not only two choices. Some trans people see their sex and gender as being totally separate while others do not and I am moving away from using "transgender" as an umbrella term because not all transgender people view (the concept of) identity in the same way or have the same goals (see Robinson 2019, xv). Transgender people do not necessarily view their (own sense of) identity in the same way as intersex and transsexual people even though "transgender" can be used as a term to refer to all three. Indeed, one's gender identity does not even have to match the way one expresses one's gender, the clothes one wears or the things one does to present oneself to others (see Baker 2017). For these reasons I use "trans" as an umbrella term to denote the people with whom transgender theory is concerned.

The disparity between people who identify as trans and yet who believe different things about their sex or gender reveals a central tension at work amongst trans people and activists. There is at once a usefulness and force in the appeal to essentialism, the idea that one feels one's gender both spiritually and physically, and an equal usefulness to anti-essentialist arguments that permit gender mobility and play. That gender is not a core was an idea propounded as early as the 1940s by theorists such as Simone de Beauvoir ([1949] 2009, 295) who famously wrote that "one is not born, but rather becomes a woman." This idea was taken up by Judith Butler (2006, xv-xvi) who demonstrated in a 1999 preface included in the 2006 Routledge Classics edition of *Gender Trouble* that gender is not essential:

> the view that gender is performative sought to show that what we take to be an internal essence of gender is manufactured through a sustained set of acts, posited through the gendered stylization of the body. In this way, it showed that what we take to be an "internal" feature of ourselves is one that we anticipate and produce through certain bodily acts.

Butler's (2006, 10) innovation, however, was the argument that sex is also a construct, that there is no distinction between sex and gender or nature and culture: "gender ought not to be conceived merely as the cultural inscription of meaning on a pregiven sex (a juridical conception); gender must also designate the very apparatus of production whereby the sexes themselves are established." If both sex and gender are perceived as discursive products of society, then being male or female is as complicated as being masculine or feminine.

Butler claims that trans people prove the performativity of gender (and intersex people prove the performativity of sex) though she is not saying that all gender is drag; drag is an example of performativity, not a model for it (Butler 1994, 32). In her 2004 work *Undoing Gender*, Butler argues that we should take this revelation and use it to question all gender. Butler (2004c, 27–28) claims that if trans people were seen as normal, instead of "abnormal", the instability of all gender would be exposed and norms would become unsettled. Judith Halberstam (2005, 57–58) also believes that "cisgender" identities are just as strange as "transgender" ones: "Eccentric, double, duplicitous, deceptive, odd, self-hating: all of these judgements swirl around [...] the self-defined transgender person, as if other lives – gender normative lives – were not odd, nor duplicitous, not doubled and contradictory at every turn." In this view, trans people and cis people all struggle with gender and this suggests that gender is not essential, because it is not easy to do. For Butler (2006), gender is something we "do", not something we are.

Many trans people, however, want to "pass" as men and women and do not wish to draw attention to their "transness". While Butler's work repudiated the idea of a core, some transsexuals believe that they were "born in the wrong body" (Wilchins 2002a, 23–24) and that sex reassignment realigns their outer appearance with their inner "core". We cannot entirely do without essentialist thought – as Diana Fuss (1989, 104) says: "Fictions of identity, importantly, are no less powerful for being fictions." A gender core may be a fiction but it is too powerful, too entrenched in many people's consciousness, for it to be wholly denied out of hand. Both sides of the essentialist/constructivist argument must be kept open. Rather than denying essentialism, we can instead question it: the questioning of the core becomes even more radical because so many believe it to be "sacrosanct". Constructionism and essentialism are not mutually opposing categories; indeed, even though constructionism is based on the social and essentialism on the natural, the social can be essentialist and the natural constructionist (4–6) (the prime example being doctors assigning babies with "a gender" based only on the genitals they can "see").

Essentialism can be deployed effectively in the interests of a group to appeal to the collective consciousness of that group (Spivak 1988, 13). To group people by class or gender is not irrational, even if there are many differences among the same people in one group. The unification of a group can be used to undo the power wielded by that very unification, to reveal that power as illusory: "Class-consciousness on the *descriptive* level is itself a strategic and artificial rallying awareness which, on the *transformative* level, seeks to destroy the mechanics which come to construct the outlines of the very class of which a collective consciousness has been situationally developed" (Spivak, 14). Strategic essentialism, for example, is useful in the fight for the visibility of women in language carried out by Francophone feminists in particular (see De Lotbinière-Harwood 1991; Yaguello 2002). This is despite the fact that, usually, trying to appeal to the concept of "women" as a whole is decried as impossible because all women are different. Feminists need a concept of woman as essential to claim an autonomous female voice (see Fuss 1989, 2). I am claiming an autonomous trans voice here to bring trans issues to the fore, but I am also acknowledging the heteroglossic nature of that voice, given the evidence that many trans people do not see eye to eye on what it means to be trans.

My aim is not to set up a debate between trans people, or to claim that those who do draw attention to their transness are more transgressive and are therefore more deserving of theoretical attention. And neither was this Butler's aim; *Gender Trouble* was not arguing that we can pick and choose what gender we will "do" on a daily basis, that being trans is a conscious choice (Butler 2014), despite many mistakenly enlisting it to argue for precisely that (see Butler 1994; Prosser 2006). The revelation that gender is not determined by biology, genitals, or chromosomes allows individuals to declare what their gender is or to deny the sex they are assigned at birth. Gender is not binary; acknowledging this does not preclude the idea that somebody "knows" they are a woman even if they were assigned the male sex at birth. And it is the revelation that gender does not follow from sex, that it is not determined by genitals, which makes it possible for these seemingly incompatible positions to co-exist.

For Butler (2014, n.p.), identity politics is necessary because "sometimes we do need a language that refers to a basic, fundamental, enduring, and necessary dimension of who we are." Her 2014 ideas suggest that if somebody wants to see their gender as essential, this would not be "wrong" but neither would it be wrong to conceive of one's gender as fluid. On this point I follow Butler's (ibid.) proclamation: "No matter whether one feels one's gendered and sexed reality to be firmly fixed or less so, every person should have the right to determine the legal and linguistic terms of their embodied lives." This view is important in a world where trans people experience their identities in very varied ways.

What I wish to take from Butler's views on trans identity and the foregoing discussion of the paradox of essentialism is that these different, yet equally valid, positions on sex and gender can be explored through trans literature and the representation of transness in writing. Furthermore, the notion of a "core", of originality, of passing, and of "interpreting" meaning (of making assumptions based on what we "see," be that a body or a text) are all notions that concern translation scholars. Gender is stable yet fluid, dichotomous yet multiple, conservative yet radical, and, because of these contradictions, is queer. Translation is all of these things too, and it is the juxtaposition of trans embodiment and translation that helps us to see that translation is fluid, multiple, radical, and queer. In transgenderism, something initially taken as "x" experiences itself as "y" as is similarly in translation. A text "x" becomes expressed as "y". The "trans" in translation and transness is this crossing between "x" and "y" and it is the translator's job to both express "x" as "y" textually (remembering that "y" can never be the same as "x") and, in translating transness itself, to respect the fact that "x" has become "y" sexually (acknowledging the fact that "y" might go back to "x" or even become "z").

Theoretical Context: Translation

Translation studies have been concerned with the translation of gender for many decades now but this has largely been in relation to the translation of women and to the figuration of the translator (see Castro and Ergun 2017; De Lotbinière-Harwood 1991; Federici and Leonardi 2013; Simon 1996; Von Flotow 1997, 2011, 2013). Both translation and women have traditionally been seen as secondary, derivative and inferior to men and original writing. For Lori Chamberlain (2012, 254) there is a gendered distinction between writing and translation: writing is masculine because it is original, translation is feminine because it is derivative. Though the translation is female, the translator, in their role as "usurper of the author", is "figured as male, the text itself is figured as a female whose chastity must be protected" (256). In this view, masculinity is authoritative and active, femininity is submissive and passive; by extension, women cannot be translators.

Translation has also long been seen as a dressing up of one text in different clothes to make another text, those clothes being made from the target language and covering the body of the source (see Van Wyke 2010, 18). This is a pertinent metaphor for my particular study. James St. André (2010a) shows that translation has long been conceptualized in terms of gender and clothing because both translation and cross-dressing have been seen as the act of changing an external appearance to (mis) represent an internal "truth". A cross-dresser covers and conceals their physical body with clothing and, according to this metaphor, a translation covers and conceals the original textual body with a new text. In 1790, Alexander Fraser Tytler (1992, 130) wrote that a translator must "be ever so thoroughly master of the sense of his author" because if the translator is not, "he will present him through a distorting medium, or exhibit him often in a garb that is unsuitable to his character."

This metaphor of translation as clothing suggests that the truth is something that is concealed under layers (St. André 2010a, 9). Translation has long grappled with this notion of a "core" meaning at the centre of the text. For centuries, it was believed that the translator should uncover the essential core that the author created for the text and then re-cover it in a new language; this must be done while usurping the author but at the same time preserving "his" character. When it proves impossible to reproduce the text's core, as it always does, the translator is accused of betraying the source text. In 1683, Pierre Daniel Huet (1992, 88) was of the opinion that a translation that departs from the original is a deception: "Who would not burn with anger when he feels that his face has been ill represented? [...] an adulterated translation is most like [...] a woman's face plastered with cosmetics." This quotation reveals the extent to which translation has been linked to women and, with its misogynistic tones, the extent to which both have been maligned over the centuries. Not only is translation deceitful like a woman but it is also, in both the translation-as-betrayal and translation-as-clothing metaphors, a concealing or masking of the "truth" behind layers.

The fact that translation is always a betrayal demonstrates that meaning is not inherently there in the text waiting to be discovered. Roland Barthes' (1977) notion of the "death of the author" was largely taken to mean that meaning is in the hands of the reader, that the reader usurps the author's place as the authority on the text's meanings. However, for Barthes, the "reader" is the place in which all of a text's multiple meanings gather (Connors 2010, 77). What Barthes' theory does not take into account is the fact that readers do select meanings for a text from the multiple choices available. We cannot follow every thread and thus we sacrifice the ones we do not pursue: "Writing does not simply weave several threads into a single term in such a way that one might end up unravelling all the 'contents' just by pulling a few strings" (Derrida 2004, 384). In other words, the reader can never unravel the whole text but only the meanings which emerge from the strings they choose to pull. Taking it one step further than Barthes does, we can see that "if signifiers do point to other, absent, signifiers, then it follows that a text is a force-field which itself pushes some meanings to the fore by excluding others from its terrain" (Connors 2010, 77).

For Derrida (2001a, 8), meaning is always both relational and dynamic. It does not inhere in single units but arises from this dynamism: meanings jostle with each other, "preventing each other's emergence" but "provoking each other too, unforeseeably". Any reading of a text can "uncover" the author's intention but it can also "uncover" elements that are in tension with that intention (see Connors 2010) and this is how the author can be both alive and dead. There is also a tension between play and presence: "Play is the disruption of presence. The presence of an element is always a signifying and substitutive reference inscribed in a system of differences and the movement of a chain" (Derrida 2001a, 369). The notion of innumerable paths and a play of identity is formalized by Derrida as "*différance*", where "*différance*" is both "to differ" and "to defer," where a word's many meanings are always out of reach (see Johnson 2004, ix). It is not simply that one word never has only one meaning, it is that each different meaning a word could have can itself be understood in various ways. Derrida differentiates Barthes' (1970) notion of polysemy from his own concept of dissemination.

Derrida (2004) describes that dissemination "endlessly opens up a *snag* in writing that can no longer be mended, a spot where neither meaning, however plural, nor *any form of presence* can pin/pen down [agrapher] the trace" (22). Dissemination entails countless possible paths of meaning but these paths, while always present, can never all be "interpreted" by one reader and one meaning is made at the expense of these countless others.

There is a difficulty with the concept of "interpretation" which goes back to the idea of essentialism – it suggests that there is something essential in a text to be perceived and then found by the reader, that what we interpret is the core. However, just as we need the concept of an essential core for some types of gender identity, we need the concept of interpretation. According to Nietzsche, we need interpretation precisely because the "truth" is an illusion (Nietzsche 1967, 47); truth only exists because society agrees upon what is true, and things in themselves are not inherently "true". Everything has to be an interpretation: "Against that positivism which stops before phenomena, saying 'there are only facts,' I should say: no, it is precisely facts that do not exist, only *interpretations*" (458). There are no truths because there are no originals. Nietzsche (46) uses leaves to demonstrate this:

> No leaf ever wholly equals another, and the concept 'leaf' is formed through an arbitrary abstraction from these individual differences, through forgetting the distinctness; and now it gives rise to the idea that in nature there might be something besides the leaves which would be "leaf" – some kind of original form after which all leaves have been woven.

In this book I demonstrate that the same applies to both texts and bodies.

Transgender Translation

Having explored the tenets of Transgender and Translation Studies that have influenced my research, I shall now bring together the two contexts to demonstrate how the two fields have much in common and how a combination of the two undermines the dominant ideology surrounding "original" writing and "original" gender. The work of Feminist Translation Studies is by no means over, as Luise von Flotow (2013, 163) states: "This topic will not go away." Questions are still being asked about women in translation, women as translators, and women as authors. However, recent work on the topic of gender and translation has also turned its attention towards the "other genders, or perhaps other gender positions, that humans can be seen to enjoy, perform, choose, interchange, and translate" (164). I am following this new turn which moves away from, but is in many ways parallel to, feminist translation theory by looking at the translation of trans-gender. To do this I am drawing on the feminist translation theories that have prepared this ground. Furthermore, I also use poststructuralist philosophy and literary criticism.

In 2010, St. André (2010b, 276) suggested a metaphor for translation inspired by cross-dressing: "Translation as cross-identity performance." He states that with this metaphor, our knowledge of the cross-identifying performer is put into question along with the translator's knowledge of the source text. He also compares the skills needed to mimic a gender performance to the skills needed to mimic the performance of a text (281). One of the most important points of this book is that translation and trans identity can learn from each other in several different ways. What St André's metaphor throws into sharp relief is that translation and the trans person have traditionally had to hide but, in revealing themselves, they show that the things they masquerade as "normal" gender and "original" writing are themselves masquerades. Trans people reveal the performative aspect of all genders while they sometimes attempt to pass as cisgender in heteronormative surroundings; translations reveal the performative aspect of all writing while sometimes attempting to pass as original writing in literary surroundings.

In 2011, Von Flotow (2011, 3) claimed that "the much discussed performative aspects of gender, which would seem to fit nicely with the performative aspects of translation, have hardly been explored or developed." And she stands by this position in 2013 stating that "while the theorizing around gender continues to be intense and highly political, actual studies of its impact in and upon translation in many different societies still needs to be explored and studied" (von Flotow 2013, 164). It is true that the subject of the transgender writer or translator or protagonist has yet to fully emerge within Translation Studies. A recent notable exception is the 2016 special translation issue of the journal *Transgender Studies Quarterly* (TSQ). Two collections on Queer translation published by Routledge for their Advances in Translation and Interpreting Studies series also followed in 2017: *Queer in Translation* (Epstein and Gillett 2017) and *Queering Translation, Translating the Queer* (Baer and Kaindl 2017). As if to demonstrate the sense of urgency currently surrounding studies in this field, the latter was published only seven months after the former. These texts complement my work and my work also complements these texts (I contributed articles to both the *TSQ* edition (Rose E. 2016) and to *Queer in Translation* (Rose 2017)). Finally, in January 2019, Douglas Robinson brought out a new book called *Transgender, Translation, Translingual Address* in which he puts cisgender and transgender people into dialogue. He does what Von Flotow called for in 2013 and argues for a relationship between transgender and translation where: "The '*oscillation or indeterminacy of personality in translation*' translates as the '*oscillation or indeterminacy of gender in transgender*'" (Robinson 2019, xiv).

Some of the questions I am asking here are beginning to be asked all over the world. The special issue of *TSQ*, entitled "Translating Transgender", published in November 2016, asks: "What do transgender subjectivities – in and around language – contribute to our knowledge of translation practice?" (Gramling and Dutta 2016, 339) and "What particular contingencies attend the task of translating texts that themselves narrate transgender subjectivities?" (347). I ask similar questions here as well: What can being trans or writing a trans text tell us about the act of writing or the act of translation? And what can the act of translation tell us about being trans or about being human? My book is born in the thick of a proliferating discussion of queer and trans identity in translation. What it brings to the field is a close examination of trans texts which allows us to consider trans lives, and the translation of trans lives, more fruitfully. It also allows us to expose the gender masquerade (that we all have one and that it is always only one of two choices) and the masquerade of original writing (that writers are in control of their texts and originate all the words and ideas they use).

I am also concerned with how the notion of originality can be challenged in both translation and transgender studies. Subversive performances show that the gender core is a fiction (Salih 2004, 93); translation can also be seen as a subversive performance which emphasizes the fiction of an "original" text or a "genius" author. Just as the concepts of a "core" and of "interpretation" are complicated, so too is that of "originality". "Original" can "mean 'from the beginning, former, ancient' […] *and* it can mean 'fresh, new, novel, unexpected'" (Pope 2005, 57). The source text is the origin (the beginning) for the translation but that translation can still originate something in its own right (59). Furthermore, the source text's supposed originality (in the sense of innovation) cannot spring from nothing (64). Translation is creative where "creative" means to celebrate the potentialities in every text.

Translation as a creative act entails more than a simple transfer of meaning: "The translated text no longer forms a dependency on the original text, but actually transforms it, subverting radically the binary between original and copy. This […] calls attention to the *performativity* of translation" (Spurlin 2014, 206). Or, put another way, the performativity of both gender and translation leads us to reconsider the idea of an "original" text or body. For Butler (2004a, 127), gender is "*a kind of imitation for which there is no original*; in fact, it is a kind of imitation that produces the very notion of the original as an *effect* and consequence of the imitation itself." The trans person reveals that gender is a product of previous acts which it needs to stay alive. This idea can be directly linked to translation and to Walter Benjamin's ([1924] 2012, 76) ideas on the afterlife of translation: that the translation continues the life of the source text. It is through acts of translation that the "original" text remains available, but the idea of the original is a myth; translation is not a copy of an original but a copy of a text which is also copied from former texts. Derrida (2001b, 199) takes the idea of translation as both prolonged life and life after death for the source text one step further: "Doesn't it guarantee these *two* survivals by losing the flesh during a process of conversion [*change*]? By elevating the signifier to its meaning or value, all the while preserving the mournful and debt-laden memory of the singular body, the first body, the unique body that translation thus elevates, preserves and negates [*relève*]?"

Derrida's use of the body metaphor for translation demonstrates that, conceptually, translation and the body are linked as multiple and mobile. A recurring theme of this book will be the haunting of the text, and especially translation, by earlier texts and the haunting of the body, and especially the trans body, by earlier bodies. Many trans people may reject this comparison, as the trans body *preserves* and negates the 'first' body when they wish only to negate it. Yet to be openly trans is to acknowledge that something, no matter how unwanted, came before. I will discuss further in chapter eight how texts which remove gender have an *Aufhebung* of gender where gender is, as with Derrida's notion of *relève*, preserved and deleted.[4] For Hegel (2010, 80), "becoming is the unseparatedness of being and nothing [...] being and nothing are each unseparated from its other, *each is not*. In this unity, therefore, *they are*, but as vanishing, only as sublated." "To sublate" is the English translation of the German "aufheben" which "has a twofold meaning in the language: it equally means 'to keep,' to 'preserve,' and 'to cause to cease,' 'to put an end to'" (Hegel 2010, 81–82). Being and becoming is contradictory and never pure. Like the "original" that is both old and new in Pope's definition, the trans body, too, is both old and new; indeed, to be trans is to be in between. The earlier versions are not lost, they are the ghosts that make the text and the body what they are and they guarantee that the text and the body are in a constant evolution of becoming and unbecoming.

The notions of becoming and unbecoming are taken from Gilles Deleuze (1990, 3) for whom there is a "simultaneity of a becoming whose characteristic is to elude the present, becoming does not tolerate the separation or the distinction of before and after, or of past and future. It pertains to the essence of becoming to move and to pull in both directions at once." Deleuze looks to Plato to explain, stating that this is "a subterranean dualism between that which receives the action of the Idea and that which eludes this action. It is not the distinction between the Model and the copy but rather between copies and simulacra" (4).

Pure becoming "contests *both* model *and* copy at once" (ibid.). That there is no model (or original) and no copy, but that both are simply two "ends" (ends which are never finished or finite) of the same process of becoming, is how I see the relationship between source text and target text or the different gender identities that can be held by the same person.

What is important for my study is that Deleuze rejects binary terms. The conception of binary terms as different actualizations of one and the same duration could be applied to the notions of "cisgender" and "transgender" and of "writing" and "translation," all four made up of continuous acts or performances and therefore undecidable. Deleuze is influenced by Henri Bergson whose method of "intuition" works "to restore the complexity of undecidability to the real. It reveals and makes explicit the fine threads within and between objects (including living beings) that always makes them more than themselves, always propels them in a mode of becoming" (Grosz 2005, 9). The complexity of undecidability can be restored through language because "it is language which fixes the limits [...] but it is language as well which transcends the limits and restores them to the infinite equivalence of an unlimited becoming" (Deleuze 1990, 4). Here, I am examining how people who experience an "unlimited becoming" can articulate this state of movement, this undecidability, through language.

Outline

This book offers a critical analysis of texts which I label "trans" because they are either written by or about trans people. For these fictional and non-fictional trans people, writing is central to the performance of their gender identity and they all deliberately play with language to express themselves. They are all solecists in that they defy convention but the three memoirists, Catalina de Erauso, the Chevalier d'Eon, and Herculine Barbin, also deliberately misuse the conventions of French and Spanish grammar. The three novelists, Jeffrey Eugenides, Anne Garréta, and Jeanette Winterson, do not break linguistic rules but every word they use has been thought and re-thought over and chosen very carefully, anticipating the translator's task before it has even begun.

Close textual analysis is especially important for these texts which have all been translated before because they all benefit from a "rereading." This act of rereading gives the texts back their undecidability and the idea that this undecidability comes from the reader is important. According to Scott (2014a, 50), we must imagine the source text "as something living into its own multiplicity and undecidability. [It] does not already have this multiplicity; it is invested with a multiplicity by its reader/translator, and this in turn generates an increasing undecidability." Following Scott's notion of the text as multiple, then the translator who attempts to put down a definitive version of a text on paper works to immobilize the text and undo the text's undecidability. The translator who attempts to put down a definitive version of a trans person does the same in that they immobilize the body and undo the body's undecidability.

The immobilization of both the body and the text can be out-witted with a kind of translation that is experimental. These techniques can achieve a kind of mobility; through experimental translation the protagonists of these source texts can be seen as being in a perpetual process of becoming, of movement, of self-differentiation (Scott 2014a, 217). With experimental translation we can suggest that the text and the body are multiple, are old and new. Because of my focus on experiment and creativity, I am not necessarily suggesting translation methods which could be adopted for the translation of every trans narrative, or which would be readily accepted by many publishers. My aim, instead, is to encourage the translator-reader to think about how texts are read and how meaning is derived: the text and the trans identity within are written anew with every reading. This makes any translation and any reading of that translation one layer in the manifold layers that make up any body of text or any body in text. This, in turn, means that any one translation never has to be a definitive representation of one text or one body, not least because there is no "one" text or body to be represented.

I carry out multiple experiments to show that the body and the text are multiple and these trans texts and bodies are the perfect variables for this experimentation because they are, in and of themselves, variable. Trans bodies are variable because they are queer and they are uncertain. This uncertainty can be celebrated in experimentation. Des Fitzgerald and Felicity Callard (2014, 17) specifically "direct attention to spaces of experimentation in which the intersections between scientific 'objects,' instruments [...] and experimenters still quiver with uncertainty." To acknowledge this uncertainty, I follow a transdisciplinary methodology. This methodology is "issue- or problem-centred [...] Methodologically, transdisciplinary research follows responsive or iterative methodologies and requires innovation, creativity, and flexibility" (Leavy 2011, 9). I explore innovative, creative and flexible ways to consider the "problem" of how to translate trans source texts. Considering a transdisciplinary approach is a new direction for translation studies that look at gender and it is apt because I am bringing together translation theory, transgender theory, gender theory, literary theory, philosophy, poststructuralism, and queer theory to create a "trans" theory that informs my translation of trans identity.

My first section deals with Erauso and d'Eon, who could be called transgender by today's standards, despite writing centuries before the term was first used. These case studies allow me to consider how gender was conceptualized in a time very different from our own, and to argue that we cannot see these texts in a cultural vacuum but that they are products of their time. In these chapters I introduce the idea that translation is an active intrusion on the source text and this is a view

I shall develop throughout the book. The theme of textual and sexual haunting is also introduced here and shown in translation through the palimpsest.

My second section acts as a bridge between the first section which looks at memoirs and the third which look at novels by examining Barbin's intersex memoir and Eugenides' intersex novel written three centuries apart. I define an intersex person as someone who is born with 'a physical and/or chromosomal set of possibilities in which the features usually understood as belonging distinctly to either the male or female sex are combined in a single body" (Holmes 2008, 32). The gap in time between my two source texts offers an opportunity to explore the history of intersex and how it has been treated by the medical establishment over time. Like Erauso and d'Eon's texts, these two texts also blur the lines between memoir and fiction because both are intertextual and neither offer a completely "truthful" portrait of the subject who writes. Autobiography does not "discover" the subject just as the medical establishment does not "discover" the intersex child; both are created by the very thing that claims to be at their disposal. What makes these intersex texts difficult to translate are things all of my texts have in common: confused genres, intertextuality, divided narrative voices, open endings. The haunting of the body and the text by previous bodies and texts and their undecidability is represented in translation here by the hypertext.

My last section looks at Garréta and Winterson's twentieth-century novels whose narrators are agender (someone who has "an absence of gender identification or expression" (Huston 2015)) and explores how to keep such seemingly important character traits out of translation. I consider how the undecidability of these characters has been viewed as a gimmick by some critics and as something to be solved by others. At this juncture it will be clear that trans texts are undecidable and that my aim is to queer them through translation so that no definitive conclusion can be reached on who their writers or protagonists "really" are. These chapters also centre on the themes of freedom and constraint, that there is a freedom of potentiality and multiplicity in the constraints of language (which is exploited by our writers), in the way that translation is always constrained. Here my translation method is influenced by erasure and fragmentation, it comes full circle back to the palimpsest but this time to a perverse palimpsest (Barthes 1986), to a conscious unwriting that demonstrates how translation is always a rewriting. The text and the body are constantly read, written, reread and rewritten and this is why they are undecidable.

Notes

1 A "cis-gender" person is defined by the *Oxford English Dictionary* as someone "whose sense of personal identity and gender corresponds to his or her sex at birth" (Oxford 2017). Though this book aims to suggest that cisgender and transgender people are not as different as these terms would like to suggest

because transgender people reveal such things as binary sex to be fictitious, I use it here as a contrast to “transgender”.

2 This attempt to lessen recrimination through fear can also be seen in Choisy’s work. In the excerpt I quote at the start of this introduction, Choisy uses the authority of a woman, Madame de La Fayette, to justify his dressing as a woman.

3 I choose not to use “they” because I am always analysing two texts and two protagonists – it would become confusing as to whether I was referring to the protagonists (such as Erauso and d’Eon) in the singular or plural.

4 Whilst I link them here because they are both notions which are relevant for my study, Derrida’s notion of *relève* and Hegel’s *Aufhebung* are not the same: “Hegel sets out the immanent self-undermining of pure being, whereas Derrida points to, among many other things, the play of unresolvable differences that (he thinks) make possible and render impossible and idea of pure becoming […] The two philosophers do, however, share a common belief that the idea of pure being is problematic” (Houlgate 2006, 303).

1 The History of (Trans)gender

The abbé François-Timoléon de Choisy (1995, 81) wrote hir seventeenth-century memoirs in the form of a letter to hir friend the marquise de Lambert who wanted to hear of hir racy life – ze promises her that she cannot even begin to imagine it. In hir writing, Choisy mixed masculine and feminine gender markers to refer to hirself: "Every time I ruined myself and I wanted to quit gambling, I fell back into my old weaknesses and became a woman again" (82, my translation). All of the past participles take the masculine gender in French including the last: "et suis redevenu femme". And ze was not the only early-modern memoirist to leave behind an account of what could now be considered a transgender life.

Around twenty years before Choisy was born, Catalina de Erauso was writing (or possibly dictating) an account of hir "transgender" life. Erauso was born in 1592 in the Basque region of Spain. Following three of hir sisters, ze joined a convent at just four years old. The conventional part of hir life ended at fifteen, however: ze escaped the convent disguised as a man, worked in northern Spain as a page, and traveled to the Americas as a soldier. When ze was discovered to be a biological woman ze became known as the "Lieutenant Nun". Ze was given a soldier's pension by King Philip IV for distinguished military service in the Americas and was allowed to continue dressing as a man thanks to a dispensation from Pope Urban VIII.

Four years after Choisy's death, Charles Geneviève Louis Auguste André Timothée d'Eon de Beaumont, known as the Chevalier or Chevalière d'Eon, was born on October 5, 1728 in Tonnerre, France. In 1771, while d'Eon was in London, ostensibly in the diplomatic service but also spying for the French king, a rumor began to spread that ze was "really" a woman. When ze decided to return to France from England, one of the conditions of hir return was that ze wear women's clothing again, suggesting that d'Eon had been falsely dressing as a man (Conlin 2010). D'Eon's memoir is the fictional story of a woman who dresses as a man who is forced to return to her "natural" state of womanhood, penned by someone who lives the first half of hir life as a man and the second half as a woman. D'Eon's contemporaries believed ze was a cross-dressing woman until hir death in 1810 (see Kates 1995).

The two writers that bookend Choisy's life, as well as Choisy hirself, have voices which are not normally represented in literature but are omitted from traditional discourse (see Harris 2010, 177). I consider their voices to be transgender and this to be transgender writing because the authors are explicitly undecidable: in their memoirs they shift between a feminine and masculine gender identity through the medium of grammatical gender. In this chapter I will look at how gender was conceptualized in the seventeenth and eighteenth centuries, looking back to theorisations from antiquity. I discuss how Catalina de Erauso and the Chevalier/Chevalière d'Eon have previously been categorised to argue that this categorisation is, ultimately, futile.

Early-Modern (Trans)gender

"Transgender" as a term was first used as an adjective in 1974 and a noun in 1987 (Oxford 2017). Clearly, neither Erauso nor d'Eon would have ever thought of themselves as "transgender" but they were seen as violating the gender rules of their time. However, what these gender rules actually were is a matter of some debate, a debate I examine in this chapter in order to prove that firstly, Erauso and d'Eon were transgressive and, secondly, to demonstrate that the translator has the power to maximize or minimize this transgression.

Following his ideas on the death of the author, Roland Barthes might claim that what was or was not seen as transgressive in Erauso's or d'Eon's time is of no consequence because it is the reader's context that matters: he states that the author "is born simultaneously with the text, is in no way equipped with a being preceding or exceeding the writing" (Barthes 1977, 145). While this may work for contemporary texts, there has to be a different way of looking at texts from the distant past. We should not just look at Erauso's, or d'Eon's, texts in the here and now without considering the then of their lives because we can attempt to excavate the historical ontology of early modern texts and this excavation has implications for translation choices. Understanding the gender system operative during Erauso or d'Eon's times is important background work for any translation, not that my goal is to 'understand' Erauso or d'Eon's behavior. This chapter aims to show that because of these conceptualisations, Erauso and d'Eon would have been seen as transgressive and therefore had limited means to present their identities to the world around them, making their writing central to their performances. This call to examine or reconstruct the past is complicated, however, by conflicting opinions on what the gender systems of the seventeenth and eighteenth centuries actually were.

I shall now take a look at some of these opinions to show how I come to my own conclusions regarding early-modern gender; they are conflicting because during the sixteenth and seventeenth centuries theories of gender and how the body worked "were drawn not only from experimental anatomy but also from earlier medieval and classical belief systems" (Gilbert 2002, 35). Thanks to these classical belief systems, sex was conceptualized in two ways: the first was based on Hippocrates' writings from the fifth century BC. In this position, which was taken up in the early medieval period, male and female were seen as on a continuum, they were not binary opposites. It espoused a fluid system of sexual differentiation based on a "one-sex" model. Following the Hippocratic position, Thomas Laqueur (2012, 802) states that "before the eighteenth century men and women were regarded not as two opposite and distinct sexes but rather as hierarchically ranked versions of each other". This meant that, according to Laqueur (802), "there was a time before what we now call gender (a set of prescribed behaviors, legal standings, social arrangements, and much more) was grounded in what we now call sex." Gary Kates sides with Laqueur; he claims that "d'Eon conceived of the distinctions among the sexes as fluid, mutable, and elastic" (Kates 1991, 185–86). Nerea Aresti (2007, 406) also appears to buy into the one-sex model, saying that, in Erauso's time: "The female body was unstable and deficient, but might change towards the masculine form under the influence of extreme physical effort."

This theory is backed up by Eva Mendieta (2009, 172-3): "The body was seen as something less fixed, more mutable, and thus made the transformation from one sex to another appear to be plausible. If the body of a woman was a natural transvestite, containing male organs within it, was not transvestism only a natural social extension of 'the myth of mobility' intrinsic to this sliding scale?". Cross-dressing, however, was illegal. Though it would appear that a woman could escape prosecution if her cross-dressing was for the purpose of bettering herself (in the image of Christ) and not for usurping a male role: Erauso was protected from punishment despite hir participation in the exclusively masculine activity of warfare because of hir virginity (Mendieta 2009, 167; see also Rex 2016, 40) and, because of hir fame. Readers of Erauso's biography can see hir masculine identity as a kind of fiction: "even as her readers are following along with Erauso's very macho adventures as an agent of empire, the foreknowledge of her subject position as a virginal nun prevents her audience from [...] buying into her performance of *lo masculino* as a natural, fixed identity" (Rex 2016, 37).

The idea that Erauso was somehow going against hir "essential" female self made hir a natural rarity in hir time to be collected by the royal court (along with hermaphrodites, dwarfs and eunuchs). Indeed, Aresti (2007, 405), who espouses the anti-essentialist position seen above, claims that "the real reason for [Erauso's] eventual popularity and recognition was precisely the difficulty of categorizing her in terms of the binary oppositions that underpinned that particular society."

While the Hippocratic, the one-sex model represents a continuum and men and women were still opposed: men were at the top, women, the biological inverse of men, were at the bottom while hermaphrodites were in the middle (see Lester 2017). However, binary oppositions are much more pronounced in the two-sex model.

The one-sex model did eventually give way to a two-sex model; doubt, however, surrounds the question of when this took place. Some believe, like Laqueuer above (2012), that it was in the eighteenth century (see also Lester 2017, 74–75 and Mendieta 2009, 172). Others believe it was much earlier: studies carried out by Ruth Gilbert on the early-modern period and Robin Headlam Wells on the Elizabethan period challenge the idea that Erauso and d'Eon's gender fluidity would have been considered natural, or a product of biology, at the time. Gilbert (2002, 40) argues that in the thirteenth century, many returned to Aristotle's fourth-century BC declaration that male and female were fundamentally binarized based upon their essential oppositions. The Hippocratic position became popular again in the sixteenth century but, despite this, it "intersected still with elements of the Aristotelian tradition" (Gilbert 2002, 36). Gerald Callahan (2009, 19) believes that the one-sex model gave way to the two-sex model after the discovery of the clitoris in the fourteenth century: "It seemed to contradict the one-sex hypothesis then popular [...] How could a woman have 'two penises' and still be the perfect homologue of and basically the same as a man? That rattled the foundations of then-current thought [...]. Where certainty had ruled for nearly two thousand years, a seed of doubt began to sprout."

Headlam-Wells (2005, 6) also disproves the popular belief that in the sixteenth century "Shakespeare and his contemporaries were anti-essentialists. That is to say, Elizabethans are thought to have had no general theory of humankind as a species: human beings had no existential 'center'; they lacked any kind of unifying essence." According to Headlam-Wells, there is no evidence that the Elizabethans felt this way.

Erauso and d'Eon presented themselves in a manner which contradicted their biological makeup (they were either rejecting their "essential" centers or these centers were out of kilter) and this made them unusual. The overriding impression we get of how Erauso and d'Eon were seen by their contemporaries is that they were both curious spectacles. The question of d'Eon's "true" gender caused such a sensation in 1771 that bets were taken on the London Stock Exchange "in the form of life insurance policies that paid out (or not) depending on whether d'Eon was found to be of one or other gender" (Conlin 2010, 50). After Erauso had been discovered to be a woman, ze could not walk the streets for people wanting to see hir: "We entered Lima after nightfall, but nonetheless there were more people than we could cope with, all curious to see the Lieutenant Nun" (Erauso 1992, 113, my translation). D'Eon knows that the renegotiation of hir character is transgressive which is perhaps why, as we have seen, ze claims to have been forced to dress a certain way by hir parents in hir memoir. Choisy also hopes to diminish and explain hir transgression by seeing hir identity as rooted in the fact that hir mother dressed hir as a girl in childhood; ze portrays hir penchant for the feminine as a "weakness" ze is powerless to resist, as can be seen at the start of the chapter.

While we can assess the contexts in which Erauso and d'Eon were writing, problems arise when attempting to *portray* these contexts as they were because reading is subjective: we read from where we are. However, just because we read from our own position does not mean that we cannot grasp the historical or cultural position of someone from the past. Though, of course, we can never wholly grasp that past, as demonstrated by the ongoing debate surrounding early-modern sex and gender. The reader's modern knowledge must be taken into consideration as well and in this book I ask, along with William Spurlin (2014, 205): "How do we work with translating terms for naming genders and sexualities in comparing texts and cultures of the past which may not be translatable to modern understandings of gender or to contemporary understandings of gay, lesbian, bisexual or queer difference?" As proved by Michel Foucault in his volumes on *The History of Sexuality*, sex is much more than a biological "fact". What sex has been in the past directly feeds into what sex is (and consequently how we see ourselves as gendered beings) now: "in the space of a few centuries, a certain inclination has led us to direct the question of what we are, to sex. Not so much to sex as representing nature, but to sex as history, as signification and discourse" (Foucault 1978, 78).

I assert that the past is translatable to modern understandings if we see the translation of very old source texts as a rewriting of the past; indeed, this helps us to see that all translation, no matter how old the source, is a rewriting of the past: the source text is not a historical artefact but a living body of words. Through translation, the source text can be "reinserted into a vivid here and now as an active intrusion" (Scott 2014a, 29). The translator is an intruder on the source text who can rewrite an original from any perspective they choose. Is it, however, going too far to rewrite a text written in a time when "transgender" and "queer" did not exist as terms, from a transgender perspective, or with a queer agenda?[1] Feminist translation theorist Sherry Simon (1996, 15) asks, "what would be the result of a translation which blatantly redirected the intention of the original text, consciously contravening its intentions?" She goes on to state that "feminist translation implies extending and developing the intention of the original text, not deforming it" (Simon 1996, 16).

However, translation is always a "deforming" of the original text as it can never be wholly "faithful" to it. As Venuti (2000, 469) has said, every translation – however foreignizing – is domesticating as well, since there is no way to provide a completely foreignizing translation. Translation is a political act; a manipulation. Comparatively, we can appropriate texts through translation for political agendas. A re-translation of Erauso's or d'Eon's texts can counter the fossilization of seventeenth- or eighteenth-century gender identifications but can also be a locus of trans engagement today by allowing past conceptualizations of gender to engage with modern ones. A translation with a queer agenda is not about "faithfully" portraying the source text but about using that text and appropriating its content to influence how people see gender today. To use d'Eon and Erauso to shine a light upon gender today, it is necessary to look more closely at their own gender identifications in their writing and how they used their writing as part of their identification.

Early-Modern Transgender Writers

I propose that Erauso and d'Eon are transgender because they oscillate. They are undecidable – this is a fresh take on a debate over how to label them.[2] This debate on how to label Erauso and d'Eon has lasted for centuries; to argue that this debate is both sterile and unnecessary, I shall elucidate some of the conclusions that have been drawn on why Erauso and d'Eon crossed the gender divide by those who have come before me.

One of d'Eon's biographers, Frédéric Gaillardet (1970, vii), wants to know what led d'Eon to cross-dress. Unsurprisingly, Gaillardet has no watertight answer to this question. Robert Baldick (1970, xix) tries to explain d'Eon's change of gender with two ideas: the first is that d'Eon became a woman on orders from Versailles so that ze could not take part in what would be a scandalous duel with the son of a French Ambassador called Guerchy whom d'Eon had insulted. Baldick (ibid.) himself, however, describes how being dressed as a woman did not prevent d'Eon from dueling in England. That d'Eon dressed as a woman out of necessity does not explain why ze took on a feminine voice in hir writing.

The second of Baldick's (xiv) ideas is that d'Eon was a transvestite (or at least that ze was afraid to be perceived as one) and to avoid this label, ze claimed to really be a girl forced by "her" parents to dress as a boy (despite the fact that many people from hir home town knew ze had been assigned the male sex at birth). D'Eon did use hir dress as an important part of the renegotiation of hir gender, despite some arguments that d'Eon dressed as a woman reluctantly. Kimberley Chrisman-Campbell has made a specific study of d'Eon's dress, examining what clothes ze purchased. She claims that in d'Eon's account books "there is evidence that d'Eon voluntarily wore at least some items of women's clothing (particularly corsets) long before he was compelled to do so" (Chrisman-Campbell 2010, 98). Chrisman-Campbell's discovery proves that d'Eon's identity vacillated, that ze wore corsets while ostensibly a man, but it does not prove that d'Eon was a transvestite. Havelock Ellis (1928) certainly thought ze was, however, and perhaps thanks to Ellis' research, "since the eighteenth century, he has been known as one of the most famous transvestites in history" (Champagne, Ekstein and Kates 2001, ix). Marjorie Garber (1992, 259) also considers d'Eon to be a transvestite, referring to hir as "the most famous transvestite in Western history".

There are many biographies of d'Eon. Some of their writers, and those who in turn reference them, seem to have been unwilling or unable to consult d'Eon's own papers. Magnus Hirschfeld, for example, is duped by Gaillardet. Hirschfeld (1991, 334) considers d'Eon to have had a very weak sex drive; though he does write of relationships d'Eon had with women based, presumably, on Gaillardet's largely fictional account of d'Eon's life in which ze is supposed to have taken many lovers before becoming engaged to the playwright de Beaumarchais and fathering the English king George IV (see Gaillardet 1970, vii; Burrows, Conlin, Goulbourne and Mainz 2010, 2). Burrows et al. (2010, 2) believe that Gaillardet's portrait of d'Eon as a man who dressed as a woman to seduce other women was taken by so many to be true because of the "precedent" of Choisy's memoirs in which Choisy does seduce girls dressed as a woman. I have argued elsewhere, however, that while Choisy did seduce young women, that is not the reason ze cross-dressed (Rose 2017).

I see Choisy as a precedent because for me, both Choisy and d'Eon are transgender. Though Choisy did not live as a woman for as long as d'Eon, in hir memoirs ze does claim to successfully pass as the Countess des Barres for quite some time. However, according to Gary Kates (1995, 562), "the story of a public figure successfully assuming a female identity every day for over thirty years is something without precedent." He is convinced that d'Eon's behavior is a mystery but goes on to offer an explanation, claiming that d'Eon's crossing was for political reasons: "the evidence reveals that d'Eon's gender transformation must be seen as part of a midlife moral and spiritual crisis brought on by his political status as an exile in London" (592). I find this argument unlikely. By ascribing d'Eon's transformation to a "midlife crisis", Kates inserts a twentieth-century trope into an eighteenth-century context in which the idea of "autobiography" as a genre that tackled ideas of modern self-identity and subjectivity was not yet fully developed. This is also a striking departure from the position Kates held in a 1991 article in which, as already indicated above, he seemed to follow Hippocrates' one-sex model of gender fluidity. There, he intimated that d'Eon was neither out for publicity, trying to rehabilitate a failed career, nor mad, but dreamed of "a world where someone's biological sex might not predetermine their gender identity; a world in which gender identity might be considered fluid and malleable" (Kates 1991, 189). This wording suggests that Kates believes that the world d'Eon lived in did *not* consider gender to be fluid or malleable. Kates (178) does not go so far as to consider d'Eon transgender but in this article he gives more time to the idea that d'Eon wanted to become a woman on hir own terms.

Demonstrating how difficult it is to pin d'Eon down, Kates, as one of d'Eon's translators, along with Champagne and Ekstein, departs again from his previous ideas and describes d'Eon's memoir as "certainly the story of a transgendered person; but it narrates the journey of a supposed male-to-female transvestite, when the actual situation involved male-to-female transgendered life" (Champagne, Ekstein and Kates 2001, x). They claim that "his autobiography thus bears witness to his profound ambivalence concerning gender. While forced by society to be either a man (1728–77) or a woman (1777–1810), d'Eon's natural state seems to have been far more indeterminate and unstable" (xx). What suggests a transgender experience is that while d'Eon was a man ze wore women's corsets and while ze was a woman ze wore both hir Dragoon's uniform and hir Cross of Saint-Louis on hir female clothes, both vestiges of hir life as a soldier. The only thing that is clear is that there is no "right" reading to be made of d'Eon.

As we have seen with d'Eon, it would appear that the most popular twentieth-century label for those who transgressed gender boundaries in the early-modern period was "transvestite". The title of the Steptos' translation of Erauso's memoir is *The Lieutenant Nun: Memoir of a Basque Transvestite in the New World* (a title obviously never chosen by Erauso). It suggests that they, or their publishers, see Erauso as a sensationalist cross-dresser. It is highly likely that the addition of this term in the title is to attract the reader's attention, in much the same way that Choisy's memoirs, originally called *Memoires de l'abbé de Choisy habillé en femme* [memoirs of the abbot de Choisy dressed as a woman] were translated with the less subtle and more sensationalist title of *The Transvestite Memoirs* (Scott [1973] 2008). In her foreword to the Steptos' translation, Marjorie Garber makes reference to her book *Vested Interests* (1992) to explain "a 'category crisis' and a related manifestation I call the 'transvestite effect'. A category crisis is a failure of definitional distinction, a borderline that becomes permeable, permitting border crossings from one apparently distinct category to another" (Garber 1996, xiv). She talks of crossing borders only in one direction, there is no vacillation. Encarnación Juárez Almendros (2006, 130, my translation) also sees Erauso as a transvestite but she highlights hir hybridity: "despite hir man's suit and having obtained official permission to live in such, hir autobiography is a different and hybrid work, because in reality what is narrated within is the life of a man and a woman." Eva Mendieta (2009, 19) additionally considers that Erauso and hir work are hybrid and, like Almendros, she also labels Erauso a transvestite (166). Nevertheless, she then argues that Erauso was, in fact, a transsexual (194). It is true that when Erauso returned to the Americas with hir dispensation from the Pope, ze lived the last twenty years of hir life as a mule driver called Antonio de Erauso.

Mendieta finds proof for Erauso's transsexualism in a letter of 1626, written by Pedro de la Valle: "She has no more breasts than a girl. She told me that she had used some sort of remedy to make them disappear. [...] it hurt a great deal, but the effect was very much to her liking" (in Stepto 1996, xxxiv). Indeed, other theorists also make reference to this letter to show Erauso's quest for total masculinity. Chloe Rutter-Jensen (2007, 87) uses it to argue for transsexualism: she refers to Erauso in the masculine and claims that "despite the fact that throughout the narration he rarely recognizes his feminine sex, the story concludes (as it starts) with a specific allusion to his masculinity" (89, my translation). This allusion is subtle – Erauso threatens to stab some passing women (and herein lies the masculinity we must assume) – because they refer to hir as "Señora Catalina".

In my analysis of the source text in chapter two, I will show that Erauso frequently recognizes hir feminine sex in grammatical gender throughout the text. Rutter-Jensen (91) spends much of her article claiming that Erauso is exclusively a transsexual and refuses to see hir as undecidable. However, she says that: "Even though he changes to a different gender, his feminine past is constantly invoked as a reminder. He is not Antonio de Erauso, more appropriately he is Antonio de Erauso and the Lieutenant Nun [...] His feminine birth and status as a monk are constantly added to his new name" (92, my translation). If Erauso's feminine gender is always there as a reminder and ze is always both a nun and a lieutenant, then ze must be undecidable. In a similar vein to Rutter-Jensen, Sandy Stone (2006, 222) uses the Chevalier d'Eon as an example of a historic transsexual and goes on to say about hir and similar accounts that "the authors also reinforce a binary, oppositional mode of gender identification. They go from being unambiguous men, albeit unhappy men, to unambiguous women. There is no territory between" (225). On closer inspection, for me, neither d'Eon nor Erauso are ever unambiguous men or women.

Conclusions

As we have seen, for centuries theorists have fought over how to categorize both d'Eon and Erauso, who have variously been appropriated as proponents of or precedents for transvestism and transsexualism. Some might think that I go too far in claiming d'Eon and Erauso as "transgender" by today's standards, but like Leslie Feinberg (1996, 85) I consider Erauso to be an early "transgender warrior". A close analysis of both Erauso and d'Eon's lives and works reveals that they were undecidable. Any translation of their texts needs to be aware of such undecidability. Indeed, the translation of undecidability is important because Erauso and d'Eon used their writing as an important outlet to express their shifting gender at a time when they had to outwardly present themselves as one sex or another and appear to make a definitive choice.

Notes

1 As we have already seen, according to the *Oxford English Dictionary* (Oxford 2017), "transgender" as a term was first used as an adjective in 1974 and a noun in 1987 (it was being used to indicate a middle ground between the sexes in the 1990s) and "queer" was first used as a derogatory term in 1894 to mean "(male) homosexual" and then was reclaimed as a positive term in the 1980s.

2 In naming Erauso and d'Eon "transgender" and "undecidable" I am, of course, labeling them. These are two terms that I try to leave as open to doubt as possible – they themselves connote uncertainty.

2 Close Readings of Transgender Texts

I have shown that Erauso and d'Eon are undecidable and in this chapter I wish to take the idea of undecidability further by applying it not just to what they wrote, but to how they wrote their life stories. I shall discuss how the nature of the two memoirs, and any memoir, is part fact, part fiction and how this makes them, in and of themselves, undecidable. I shall then analyze published translations of both texts – *The Lieutenant Nun: Memoir of a Basque Transvestite* (1996) by Michele and Gabriel Stepto and *The Maiden of Tonnerre: The Vicissitudes of the Chevalier/Chevalière d'Eon* (2001) by Roland Champagne, Nina Ekstein, and Gary Kates – to see whether this undecidability is acknowledged by the translators or whether it is written out.

Two Undecidable Transgender Memoirs

The genre of all texts is "trans": all genre is "trans-genre" because nobody can follow Derrida's (1980, 55) call that "genres are not to be mixed," not even Derrida himself. It is impossible not to mix genres and no text can stay within the boundaries of any one recognizable genre, even if most texts are "pigeonholed" by publishers, reviewers, libraries and book stores. Derrida (56) argues that "as soon as the word 'genre' is sounded […] as soon as one attempts to conceive it, a limit is drawn." Once that limit is drawn, restrictions abound: "One must not cross a line of demarcation, one must not risk impurity, anomaly, or monstrosity" (57).

In some senses, what trans-lation and trans-gender do is highlight the fact that all writing and all gender cross that line of demarcation for both textual and biological genre. They both risk monstrosity because they are necessarily hybrid, multiple, and in-between and I will return to the idea of the monstrous in-between in Chapter 4. Just as texts are mixtures, so too are bodies: "Mixtures are in bodies, and in the depth of bodies: a body penetrates another and coexists with it in all of its parts, like a drop of wine in the ocean, or fire in iron" (Deleuze 1990, 5–6). That bodies are mixtures of other, past, and future bodies (reflecting the idea that texts are mixtures of other texts) is something I will return to when I look at Derrida's concept of the specter.

Erauso and d'Eon both use autobiographical and fictional genres in their writing. According to Frow (2006, 2), "genres create effects of reality and truth, authority and plausibility" but texts "do not 'belong' to genres but are, rather, uses of them." Even though, as briefly mentioned in Chapter 1, the concept of the autobiography was not fully formed while Erauso and d'Eon were writing, I use the term here as the easiest way to speak of "self-writing"; I also use the terms "autobiography" and "memoir" interchangeably to mean "an account of a person's life given by himself or herself, esp. one published in book form" (Oxford, 2017). But, contrary to what this suggests, autobiography is not a straightforward art form that shows us the true thoughts and feelings of the writer:

> We assume that life *produces* the autobiography as an act produces its consequences, but can we not suggest, with equal justice, that the autobiographical project may itself produce and determine the life and that whatever the writer does is in fact governed by the technical demands of self-portraiture and thus determined, in all its aspects, by the resources of this medium?
>
> (De Man 1984, 69)

When one scrutinizes the autobiographical genre, one comes to see that the author does not have the authority over the text they presumed they had. This denial of the author does not make him or her entirely superfluous. However, because the reader looks to the author while simultaneously rejecting them, "the author will reappear as a desire of the readers, a specter spirited back into existence by the critic himself." This return cannot happen without a death and the author "must continue to be dead though he has returned" (Burke 1998, 30). The presence of the author as a specter needs closer examination and will be briefly discussed later in this chapter and in the following chapters. Here we are interested in the idea that the author can only come back "on the condition that his life is discontinuous, fictive" (31); and, paradoxically, nowhere is the author's life more fictive than in autobiography. The speaking subject is never whole and the narrator is never quite the same person as the author. This means that in autobiography, the person who writes and the person who lived the life written about are not the same. As a genre, "self-writing" creates the effect of reality and truth but that effect is itself taken from fiction.

Both Erauso and d'Eon wrote with full knowledge of the self-fashioning power of writing because they both manipulate their texts to portray the life story they wanted others to attribute to them. They self-fashion themselves through the use of particular narrative styles. Erauso's autobiography, for example, borrows from various narrative forms: the soldier's journal, the picaresque novel, and the religious autobiography (Almendros 2006, 131; see also Stepto 1996, xxxiv for the influence of the picaresque tradition).

Both Erasuso and d'Eon looked to those who had written confessions. Erauso's predecessor was Teresa de Ávila and d'Eon, whose contemporary was Jean-Jacques Rousseau, took inspirations from Saint Augustine (Champagne et al. 2001, xi). The person who confesses believes they are writing down or saying out loud their inner-most thoughts, confessing "the truth", for absolution. Jeremy Tambling (1990, 194) asks: "Is not the confessant the actor above all? Yet confession as acting means also, of course, self-fashioning, and implies the presence of metonymic displacements and a glossing of the (textual) self." Those making confession believe that they are confessing to acts they had control over (and therefore that is why they need absolution). According to Butler (2006, 195), however, we are not autonomous subjects, responsible for our acts because, as she states in *Gender Trouble*, taking her lead from Nietzsche's *On the Genealogy of Morals*, "there need not be a 'doer behind the deed,' but [...] 'the doer is variably constructed in and through the deed'."

The idea that there is no doer behind the deed would seem to preclude the idea of "self-fashioning". While it does, there is a paradox at work here which is brilliantly summed up by Stephen Greenblatt in his study on self-fashioning in Renaissance England. He notes that during his study, "the human subject itself began to seem remarkably unfree, the ideological product of the relations of power in a particular society" (Greenblatt 2005, 256). However, what we also have to understand is that "in our culture, to abandon self-fashioning is to abandon the craving for freedom, and to let go of one's stubborn hold upon selfhood, even selfhood conceived as fiction, is to die" (257). This echoes Diana Fuss' (1989, 104) statement that "fictions of identity, importantly, are no less powerful for being fictions." Selfhood is fictional but we cling to it to live. As Butler would say, following her reformulated ideas on performativity given in her 2016 talk on gender in translation, to find our own identity is a kind of freedom. But we can only be free if society accepts our choices: "We are all ethically bound to recognize another person's declared or enacted sense of sex and/or gender. We do not have to agree upon the 'origins' of that sense of self to agree that it is ethically obligatory to support and recognize sexed and gendered modes of being that are crucial to a person's well-being" (Butler 2014, n.p.).

For Butler, seeing gender as performative does not preclude the belief that gender is essential. She does not argue against the language of ontology but believes that laying claim to an essential self is performative; saying "this is who I am" is the deed, the performative moment (Butler 2016b, n.p.). In the early-modern period and in a society that followed the two-sex model, there were "few possibilities for the expression of intermediate or shifting positions in sexual definition" (Gilbert 2002, 40); one of those possibilities must have been to express oneself, or perhaps "one's selves", through writing.

Undecidable Source Texts

Even if society as a whole believed that each person had an essential sense of self, it does not preclude the idea that this core could be complex or divided. Erauso as an author is both complex and divided. Ze is not just divided in hir own writing but is actively divided by others because the original manuscript of hir autobiography no longer exists. According to Stepto, the original manuscript was kept by the Urbizu family of Seville (descendants of Erauso's first patron Juan de Urquiza) for a century after it was written. In the eighteenth century this manuscript was copied by Cándido María Trigueros and then this version was again copied by Juan Bautista Muñoz in 1784 (Stepto 1996, xlv). There are now three versions of Erauso's autobiography available – there is one manuscript held in the Madrid Royal Academy of History (Bautista Muñoz's transcription) and two manuscripts are held in Seville Cathedral (transcriber and date of transcription unknown). The title of the manuscript in Madrid claims that it was "written by herself [Catarina de Araujo] on the 18th of September 1646 on returning from the Indies to Spain [...] arriving in Cadiz on the 18th November 1646" (1784, 206v, my translation). This is potential proof that it was not written by Erauso hirself because there is irrefutable evidence that Erauso arrived in Cadiz in 1624. While this could have been a mistake in transcription it certainly adds to the feeling that what we have in front of us, in the Madrid manuscript, is significantly removed from Erauso's hand, perhaps so much so that we cannot really call it *Erauso's* memoir at all. While the text might be embellished in places and simply wrong in others, Erauso did exist, ze did pen, dictate or inspire a written account of hir life and according to Rima de Vallbona (1992, 2). It is even said that Erauso hirself handed the manuscript to the editor Bernardino de Guzmán in 1625. The three extant manuscripts are, however, all we have to go on.

Two copies of Erauso's text have been published based on the Madrid manuscript; the first, *La Historia de la Monja Alférez, doña Catalina de Erauso escrita por ella misma* [the story of the lieutenant nun, Miss Catalina de Erauso written by herself], was transcribed by Joaquín María Ferrer in 1829. Ferrer claims to have transcribed his version from a text held by his friend Felipe Bauzá called *Vida y sucesos de la Monja Alferez Doña Catalina de Araujo, doncella natural de San Sebastian de Guipuzcoa, escrita por ella misma* [Life and Events of the Lieutenant Nun, Miss Catalina de Araujo, Natural Maiden of San Sebastian de Guipuzcoa, Written by Herself] which itself was copied from Bautista Muñoz's manuscript; that version being copied in Seville from various papers in the possession of the poet María Trigueros (Ferrer 1829, xvii).

The manuscript currently in the Madrid Royal Academy of History has a very similar title but it is much longer so this would seem to confirm that, as indicated by Ferrer himself, his version is not taken straight from Muñoz's transcription but from a copy of that. He claims that the copyist made mistakes with place names, character names, and dates which he corrected by comparing authentic documents (Ferrer 1829, xxiii). Ferrer's publication also departs from the manuscript by dividing the story into twenty-six chapters when the Madrid manuscript has only twenty.

The second version of Erauso's text based on the Madrid manuscript is entitled *Vida i sucesos de la monja alférez, Autobiografía atribuida a Doña Catalina de Erauso* [Life and Events of the Lieutenant Nun, Autobiography Attributed to Miss Catalina de Erauso] and my investigations have confirmed that this text, edited by Rima de Vallbona, was faithfully transcribed from the manuscript currently held in the Madrid Royal Academy, as Vallbona (1992, 3) asserts. That Vallbona's title claims that what we are reading is the autobiography "attributed" to Erauso in contrast to the title of the Madrid manuscript (and also Ferrer's text) which assures us that what is in front of us is "written by [Erauso] herself" will become more and more germane as my discussion of the text's authorship develops.

In the 1990s Pedro Rubio Merino discovered two more manuscripts purporting to be Erauso's autobiographies in the Santa Iglesia Cathedral of Seville. Rubio Merino's version is entitled *La Monja Alférez: Doña Catalina de Erauso, Dos Manuscritos inéditos de su autobiografía conservados en el Archivo de la Santa Iglesia Catedral de Sevilla* [The Lieutenant Nun: Doña Catalina de Erauso, Two Unedited Manuscripts of her Autobiography Kept in the Archive of the Holy Cathedral of Seville]. The first Seville manuscript is entitled *Vida y sucesos de la Monja Alférez, Da Catharina de Erauso* [Life and Events of the Lieutenant Nun, Miss Catharina de Erauso]; the second is untitled. I shall henceforth refer to them as Seville M-1 and Seville M-2.[1] Rubio Merino (1995, 18, my translation) believes that the two manuscripts, which were found at different times and in different locations, were copied by the same amanuensis even though the variations are "notable and frequent". Having seen the Seville manuscripts myself I can attest to the fact that they appear to have been written by the same hand, though the handwriting of M-1 is neater (see appendix I).

Although both Seville M-1 and M-2 vary from each other, the stories contained in each are similar and it is possible that a previous manuscript was the source for both copies. Like Vallbona, Rubio Merino (1995, 46, my translation) assures his reader that "the edition which we make today of the two autobiographical manuscripts of the Lieutenant Nun aims to maintain maximum fidelity to the original text." Though, of course, the term "original text" must be used with some caution, as there is no "original" text to be faithful to. What Rubio Merino's publication is faithful to is the two manuscripts he discovered, not to Erauso's "original text", wherever that might be. The complicated textual history of the memoir makes it difficult to come to any definitive conclusions about the text and aptly mirrors the difficulty of coming to definitive conclusions about the identity found within. And the fact that this identity is hard to define is caused *by* the various manuscripts: gender usage is not only inconsistent within the texts but is also inconsistent between the texts. This is something I shall address in more detail in the following section with a close reading of Erauso's texts.

Before I move on to a close analysis of Erauso's text, however, it will serve my argument that all texts are inherently multiple to investigate how a text with a clear origin such as d'Eon's can still be unclear in its genre.

D'Eon's text, unlike Erauso's, is available in its original form. As was found to be the case with Erauso though, it would be more appropriate to talk of d'Eon's texts, as hir memoir is made up of various writings and letters. These writings are kept in the archives of the Brotherton Library at the University of Leeds and, according to Champagne et al. (2001, ix) they are what d'Eon originally planned to include in hir memoir.[2] D'Eon had organized a publisher, had paid an advance, and hired an English translator but, somehow, the publication never came to be (ibid.). The title of the 2001 English translation, *The Maiden of Tonnerre: The Vicissitudes of the Chevalier/Chevalière d'Eon* is a direct translation of d'Eon's intended title for hir memoir: *La Pucelle de Tonnerre: Les Vicissitudes du Chevalier et Chevalière d'Eon*. The translation includes *La Grande Epître Historique de la Chevalière d'Eon en 1785* [the great historical epistle of the chevalier d'Eon in 1785] addressed to the Duchess of Montmorenci-Bouteville, a collection of d'Eon's correspondence and a manuscript describing the lives of those who could be seen as "religious precedents". These precedents were women who dressed as men for varying reasons and were subsequently sainted. We can already see d'Eon's memoirs slipping from the category of autobiography here as they merge with those of correspondence and biography, seen in this final chapter called the "Pious Metamorphoses".

The "Pious Metamorphoses" section details the lives of women who were sainted despite gender transgressions. D'Eon identifies with these women and sees them as mavericks (Champagne et al. 2001, 141). While d'Eon did not include Joan of Arc amongst these historical precedents it is clear that she was hir main inspiration, ze explicitly references Joan in the title ze chose for hir unpublished work: *La Pucelle de Tonnerre* [the maid of Tonnerre], echoes Joan of Arc's "Pucelle d'Orléans" [maid/virgin of Orléans], and the idea of both as characterized by their virginity. Joan herself could well have been inspired by the same women as d'Eon. In her day, Guillaume Bouille, an adviser to Charles VII "justified a woman wearing men's clothing if undertaken from the perspective of modesty [...] Moreover, she could wear male clothing if asked to do so by divine revelation, as other female saints had done" (Harris 2013, 7). We see the same attitude to Erauso's cross-dressing, though Joan of Arc paid the ultimate price for her participation in warfare, something Erauso avoided.

To align hirself with Joan of Arc "d'Eon invented at least four major myths about himself" (Champagne et al. 2001, xvi): D'Eon claims that hir parents raised hir as a boy after they lost their only male heir; ze claims that in Russia ze dressed as a woman in the service of the Empress Elizabeth; ze claims that while in England ze was discovered to be a biological female and a trial was carried out to verify this; and ze presents correspondence between hirself and hir mother in which she corroborates the fact that d'Eon was born female. D'Eon specifically chose these myths to fashion hir narrative identity. D'Eon also presents hirself as the innocent virginal woman by never writing about desire or love, coming across as almost asexual. It would appear that it was their statuses as virgins that saved both Erauso and d'Eon, their female virginity a virtue preventing them from being suspected of perversion.

By becoming a virtuous woman, d'Eon could keep the same sort of status in society that ze had enjoyed as a diplomat and a soldier in receipt of the Cross of Saint-Louis. However, to the modern-day reader, d'Eon's gender deception is made clear by the fact that after hir death ze was identified as a man; in fact, no reader of d'Eon's papers would have ever thought they were reading the "truth" as hir memoirs were never made available in hir lifetime, only after hir death and the revelation of hir "male" sex. We have a situation where deceit is revealed: "The person who is crossing intends to deceive her or his immediate audience, although in fiction the reader is typically apprised of the 'real' identity of the character" (St. André 2010b, 278). Although with both d'Eon and Erauso I would suggest that while the deception is revealed, the reader is never appraised of their "real" characters, whatever they may be.

No matter how hard we look, Erauso and d'Eon's texts only ever have an "implied author"; each text points to a figure "who is outside and precedes it" (Foucault 1979, 14). The figures of Erauso and d'Eon are caught up with the scholarly investigation of their texts: all those who come to Erauso and d'Eon believe they can somehow "know" them via their texts but they will only ever be the implied authors. All scholars (myself included) who look at Erauso and d'Eon construct their identities to make them into the authors of the texts they are reading. This is unavoidable: "These aspects of an individual, which we designate as an author [...] are projections, in terms always more or less psychological, of our way of handling texts" (21). We can never "know" a d'Eon or an Erauso free of mediation. Any "interpretation" of Erauso and d'Eon is always them "plus interpreter," and, as we have seen in the discussion of how Erauso and d'Eon have been labeled, the outcome of any investigation depends on what the interpreter feels is pertinent or should be excluded. This has a bearing on translation.

What emerges from this consideration of confession and self-writing as self-fashioning are discussions of the originality of Erauso's and d'Eon's texts and their authorities as authors. The writer constructs an identity in writing but the reader also constructs one in reading. The translator, as both reader and re-writer, does the same. In the next section I shall consider how the translators of these two texts have read and re-written these identities.

Translating Erauso

Erauso's memoirs were translated by mother and son duo, Michele and Gabriel Stepto, in 1996.[3] Their translation is largely taken from Ferrer's edition of the Madrid manuscript, *La Historia de la Monja Alférez* though they claim to have "also consulted Muñoz's *Vida y sucesos*, recently made available in an excellent edition edited by Rima de Vallbona" (Stepto 1996, xlvi). Despite this assurance that Vallbona's text was consulted, there is no evidence in the translation for this consultation. The Steptos even follow Ferrer's chapter divisions. The "implied author" of the Steptos' translation is necessarily different from the "implied author" of the "original" texts and they made exclusions with their choice of source text even before the translation proper began.

The translation includes a foreword by Marjorie Garber and an introduction by Michele Stepto. As mentioned in chapter one, in her foreword, Garber (1996, xvi) is very interested in Erauso's "border crossings," hir crossing of the border between Spain and the Basque country, between the old world and the new: "The disruptive gender identities (marked in the text by 'male' and 'female' pronouns) and geographical wandering between Spain and Peru are undertaken by a figure already exceptional and transgressive." The reader is therefore made aware in the paratextual material of the translation that Erauso was a transgressive figure; however, it is hard to tell if "the text" Garber refers to is the Spanish source or the English translation. In the Spanish text, male and female pronouns are non-existent, not only because this is a first-person account but also because subject pronouns are rarely used in the Spanish, the ending of the verb already denoting the subject (but not their gender). In the English translation, the gender-neutral *I* is prevalent, but where third-person pronouns are used for Erauso, they are always made "female".

Erauso's gender is marked on adjectives, not pronouns. Readers cannot directly access a sense of Erauso's unusual use of grammatical gender in the English text, something Michele Stepto (1996, xlvi) readily admits:

> There are several challenges facing the translator who would render Catalina's memoir in English. One, at least, is insurmountable – there is no English equivalent for the gender inflections of the Spanish adjective, which make a primary, grammatical notation of gender

> with practically every sentence, thus setting up a drumbeat of sexual self-identification that reverberates from one end of the text to the other. The fact that Catalina almost invariably uses masculine endings to describe herself is lost in English, as are those rare moments when she chooses a feminine ending.

Stepto is clearly aware of how important this grammatical use of gender is and yet she marks it down as an inevitable loss in English. After openly discussing this loss from the original which she and her son took no steps to compensate for, she goes on to say that "it has always seemed to us that the best translations were those that hued [*sic*] most closely to the original text [...]. For this reason, nothing has been added here, *nothing left out*" (xlvii, my emphasis). Stepto openly admits they accrued translation losses and then claims that nothing has been "left out" but the Steptos' removal of grammatical gender (which is important by their own admission) cannot really be called hewing "most closely to the original text".

The back cover of the paperback version of the translation includes a quotation from Roberto González Echevarría who states that the Steptos manage to turn the memoir into a compelling English text while also avoiding betraying the original (Stepto and Stepto 1996). We can see that translation is still being discussed in terms of betrayals and originals. González Echevarría, like theorists centuries before him, is of the opinion that it is possible not to betray the original text or author (and that this should be the ultimate goal of any translator). But, betrayal is inevitable and that becomes acceptable because the source text is not "original" in the way Echevarría or the Steptos suggest. The translators had to omit (or betray) something, and I do not criticize them for that, but in my opinion they chose to omit exactly what makes this memoir so compelling.

In order to demonstrate why this memoir is so compelling I shall now analyze in detail some key moments where Erauso's use of grammatical gender is unusual and see how the Steptos have dealt with it in translation. I have taken quotations from *La Historia de la Monja Alférez, Vida i sucesos de la monja alférez* and both of the Seville manuscripts. *La Historia de la Monja Alférez* will be used as the main source because this is the text the Steptos used for their translation.[4] In the Spanish quotations, the gendered words are underlined, while the gender used shall be indicated in parentheses after the appropriate word in my English translation in square brackets.[5] Stepto and Stepto's English translation will come after the Spanish example.

In Chapter One, Erauso introduces hirself variously as "Doña Catalina de Erauso" in Ferrer's text (Erauso 1829, 1), "Dª Catalina de Araujo" in both the Madrid manuscript and Vallbona's text (Erauso 1992, 33), "el Alferez Cathalina de Erausso" in Seville M-1 and Rubio Merino's text

(Erauso 1995, 53) and "el Alferez D. Cathar[a] de Erausso" in Seville M-2 and again in Rubio Merino's transcription (Erauso 1995, 95). Ze describes what happened when ze left the convent aged fifteen:

> eché no sé por dónde, y fui calando caminos y pasando lugares por me alejar, y vine a dar a Vitoria, que dista de San Sebastián cerca de veinte leguas, a pie y cansada.
>
> (Erauso 1829, 5)
>
> [I moved out not knowing where I was going and I went treading paths and passing places to distance myself, and I came to Vitoria which is almost twenty leagues from San Sebastian, on foot and tired(f)].
>
> I set off without knowing where I was going, threading my way down roads and passing villages, until I came to the town of Vitoria, some twenty leagues from San Sebastian, on foot, tired.
>
> (Stepto and Stepto 1996, 4)

The feminine gender is also presented in Vallbona's text and she adds a note to indicate that: "The feminine is employed in the manuscript as in the Ferrer edition" (Vallbona in Erauso 1992, 36, my translation). Both Seville manuscripts also use the feminine gender here (Erauso 1995, 54, 96). At this point Erauso has fashioned shorts, a short jacket and leggings out of the dress ze wore in the convent and ze has cut hir hair short. While ze has yet to fashion for hirself a male persona with an alias,ze is, to all intents and purposes, dressed as a man. However, ze still uses feminine grammatical gender and this shows that it is not simply a change of clothes which indicates a change of gender. Erauso does take up the male name of Francisco de Loyola when ze moves to Valladolid which ze keeps when ze then moves on to Estella:

> Entré en Estella, donde me acomodé por paje de don Carlos de Arellano, del hábito de Santiago, en cuya casa y servicio estuve dos años, bien tratado y vestido.
>
> (Erauso 1829, 9)
>
> [I entered Estella where I settled in as a page to don Carlos de Arellano, an inhabitant of Santiago, in whose house and service I stayed for two years, well treated(m) and dressed(m)].
>
> I headed for Estella in the province of Navarre, which must be about twenty leagues off. I found work there as a page to don Carlos de Arellano, a native of Santiago, and remained in his house and employment for two years, well-fed and well-clothed.
>
> (Stepto and Stepto 1996, 6)

In *Vida i sucesos* (Erauso 1992, 38) the two past participles are feminine: "Tratada" and "vestida". Why the gender is different in Ferrer is only something we can guess at; it is possible that Ferrer's edition of Erauso's work (or the work he transcribed from) does not take full account of the gendered aspects of the text. We know that Vallbona's version is more accurate than Ferrer's as it is taken directly from the Madrid manuscript so Erauso is still using the feminine gender despite hir change in costume.[6] Despite Ferrer's seemingly erroneous interpretation of the Madrid manuscript, Seville M-2 also uses masculine endings on "tratado" and "vestido" (Erauso 1995, 97).[7] Furthermore, this next excerpt somewhat weakens the hypothesis that Ferrer may have been changing grammatical endings on purpose as we have a clear example, in both Ferrer's and Vallbona's (Erauso 1992, 98) versions, of Erauso using the feminine gender while dressed as a man. Erauso has stolen a horse and has been caught:

> Rodeáronme ministros, y dijo el alcalde: «¿Qué hemos de hacer en esto?». Yo cogida de repente, no sabía qué decir; vacilante y confusa, que parecería delincuente.
>
> (Erauso 1829, 83)

> [The ministers surrounded me and the mayor said: "What do we have here?" I was caught(f) so suddenly I didn't know what to say; so unsteady and confused(f) that I looked like a criminal].

> The deputies surrounded me and the mayor said, "Well, what do we have here?" The whole thing was so sudden that I didn't know what to say, and there I stood, confounded and stammering, the very picture of guilt.
>
> (Stepto and Stepto 1996, 53)

The suggestion here could be that as Erauso has been caught off-guard in a moment of weakness ze reverts to the feminine gender. Rubio Merino claims that there are moments in the Seville manuscripts where Erauso is "betrayed by her feminine sentiments" (Erauso 1995, 30, my translation). In chapter seven of M-1 (Erauso 1995, 67) and chapter eight (Erauso 1995, 111) of M-2, Erauso describes being completely alone in the desert after hir two companions have died of the cold along with their horses, ze is completely lost and:

> tan cansada, aflixida y lastimada de dos pies [...] arrimándome a un árbol, comencé a llorar, cosa que no hice después que estube en las Indias.
>
> (Erauso 1995, 67)

> [so tired(f), sorrowful(f) and wounded(f) in both feet [...] leaning against a tree, I began to cry, something I hadn't done since I was in the Indies].
>
> You can imagine my wretched state, dead tired, barefoot, my feet in shreds. I propped myself against a tree and wept – for what I think was the first time in my life.
>
> (Stepto and Stepto 1996, 27)

The wording of M-2 is different but the three gendered participles used as adjectives are exactly the same. In both Ferrer (Erauso 1829, 40) and Vallbona (Erauso 1992, 69), the feminine gender is also used. That Rubio Merino thinks that Erauso is "betrayed" by "her" feminine sentiments suggests that he thinks that ze is inherently feminine and this femininity slips out when ze cannot help it, that ze is playing at being a man. However, Erauso does not exclusively use the feminine grammatical gender in moments of high emotion. There is no obvious reason why Erauso switches and the switches can be used as evidence of Erauso's vacillating, and undecidable, gender identity; ze is inherently both masculine and feminine.

In order to prove the above it is necessary to do some quantitative research. I have looked through the four texts and counted each instance of feminine and masculine gender markers (shown in Table 2.1):[8]

We can see from this that the Madrid manuscript includes a predominance of masculine pronouns while one Seville manuscript includes more feminine pronouns. We can only refer to M-1 here: because M-2 is unfinished it cannot be used to argue for a predominance of masculine markers. That there are more masculine markers than feminine in the majority of the texts is not something I, or anyone else, can fully explain.

In a footnote provided by Vallbona, Roslyn M. Frank (in Erauso 1992, 35) affirms that the use of gender in the Basque language, Euskara, is problematic because no grammatical gender exists. Adjectives did not take masculine or feminine suffixes and the only time gender was observed was on verbs in dialogue which indicated the listener's gender not the speaker's. According to Frank (ibid.), it was not uncommon for a Basque woman to refer to herself in the masculine in a monologue with no unusual sexual connotation. This is not a satisfactory explanation for Erauso's appropriation of masculine gender though, because the manuscript is written in Castilian Spanish and it is certain that Erauso would have learnt Castilian Spanish during hir time in the convent (Mendieta 2009, 35). Mendieta (42) looks into the idea that Euskara may have interfered in Erauso's use of Castilian syntax and she concludes that it does not. For her, as for me, because it is only Erauso's gender that oscillates and Erauso

Table 2.1 Instances of gender markers appearing in Erauso's texts

Manuscript	*Feminine markers*	*Masculine markers*
Madrid: Ferrer	22	87
Madrid: Vallbona	33	76
Seville: M-1	40	36
Seville: M-2	16	48

is a clearly undecidable character, this oscillation must indicate that Erauso cannot be labeled, that a decision cannot be made on hir gender.

The only conclusion we can take from this data is that the two grammatical genders are constantly mixed. When Erauso admits that ze is a woman in confession to a bishop ze starts using only feminine gender markers in Seville M-1 (Erauso 1995, 86). For example, "me asentaron en un libro por ciudadana Romana" (91) [they settled me in a book as a Roman(f) citizen(f)] and "estuve tentada de cortarles las caras" (92) [I was tempted(f) to cut their faces]. However, in three versions of the story there are actually two confession scenes.[9] When ze is first injured ze confesses to a priest in the Madrid manuscript: this is just "declaré mi estado" (Erauso 1992, 102) [I declared my status]. Vallbona replicates Ferrer's note: "As this declaration was made in confession, it was not divulged and did not cause the admiration it subsequently caused in Guamanga when Erauso revealed the secret ze had guarded so well for so many years to the bishop of the diocese" (Vallbona in Erauso 1992, 102, my translation). In Seville M-1 this scene is more explicit: "declaré que era mujer" (Erauso 1995, 82) [I declared I was a woman] but hir secret is still kept and ze uses masculine gender markers until the confession to the bishop when feminine markers take over.

The idea that confession has the power to reveal what is within, or force the confessant to live by the "truth" they have admitted, is complicated here. It is only Erauso's later confession to the bishop that leads to hir exclusive adoption of feminine gender markers in Seville M-1: "He took me by the hand and asked me softly and closely if I was a woman. I answered him yes" (Erauso 1995, 86, my translation). It is also revealing that in the first confession Erauso speaks the words – "declare" [I declared] – but in this later confession it is the bishop who uses the word "woman," Erauso merely agrees. Ze does not own the title of "woman" out loud. Furthermore, Erauso uses the masculine gender in Ferrer and Vallbona after ze has confessed; Vallbona (in Erauso 1992, 111) even notes that one would expect Erauso to use feminine gender markers exclusively from the revelation of hir femaleness onwards but ze does not. The above example from Seville M-1 describing Erauso's time with the Roman senate is in the masculine in Vallbona: "me asentaron en un libro por Ciudadano Romano" (Erauso 1992, 123) [they entered me in a book as a Roman (m) citizen(m)] and in Ferrer (Erauso 1829, 117).

Despite the predominance of masculine markers in Ferrer, and even after the "confession scene," chapter headings always use the feminine gender. However, they are also, for the most part, in the third person and so it is possible that they were not chosen by Erauso hirself but were added later:

> Capítolo XVIII. Mata en el Cuzco al Nuevo Cid, quedando herida. (Erauso 1829, 85) (same gender in Erauso 1992: 101)
>
> [Chapter XVII. S/he kills the New Cid in Cuzco, being left injured(f)].
>
> Chapter 18 – In Cuzco, she kills the New Cid and is herself wounded.
>
> (Stepto and Stepto 1996, 55)

Because subject pronouns are rarely used with verbs in Spanish, "mata" [he/she kills] could be either masculine or feminine. The Steptos chose to make it "she kills," adding a gender marker. Their choice of the feminine gender in this example is most likely dictated by the fact that "herida" [injured] is feminine. In contrast, the chapter headings of Seville M-2 use the masculine gender whenever a gendered word must be used:

> Cap. 15 Dánle una comissión. [...] Mata en la ciudad de la Paz a un criado del Corregidor y, sentenciado a horca, se libra.
>
> (Erauso 1995, 124)
>
> [Chapter 15. They give her/him a commission. [...] S/he kills a servant of the magistrate in the city of La Paz and, sentenced(m) to the gallows, frees him/herself].

In Ferrer (Erauso 1829, 73) and Vallbona (Erauso 1992, 93) the chapter heading is much shorter and carries no gender at all, but the Steptos select the feminine gender again:

> Chapter 15 – She travels to La Paz and murders a man.
>
> (Stepto and Stepto 1996, 40)

These titles still need to be treated with care in translation because it is possible that Erauso did have a hand in them: they are not all written in the third person. In the Madrid manuscript the narrator uses the first-person singular in the subheading for the final chapter. Vallbona's *Vida i sucesos* has "Embarquéme i pasé a Cartagena" (Erauso 1992, 115) [I enlisted myself (on a ship) and passed to Cartagena]. Ferrer's version, however, has the title in the third person and he uses "embarcase" (Erauso 1829, 106) [he/she embarks]. Because of this, Stepto and Stepto's translation is: "She embarks in Tenerife and sails to Cartagena and from there leaves with the fleet for Spain" (Stepto and Stepto 1996, 71). Up to this point the chapter titles have seemed like paratextual material, given the use of the third person, as previously mentioned, it could be assumed they were added later. However, here we have an indication that Erauso did write at least one chapter heading. It could be that in the original manuscript, or in the transfer from one version to another, first-person headings for other chapters were lost. With the use of the first person, the narrator and the protagonist briefly become one (see also Pérez-Villanueva 2014, 38). This adds weight to the argument that Erauso was both writer and narrator, not just a narrative voice used by another writer entirely, and that ze chose the grammatical gender of hir words.

What this close reading of Erauso's source texts has shown is that we will never definitively know Erauso or how much Erauso really switched because we cannot be sure which of the versions we have left are most like the text ze wrote, or why ze switched. The reasons why ze switched, or the causes of transgender identity, is not something that should concern the translator of Erauso's text and nor is it the translator's job to find the autobiographical subject's "true" self (as if it could ever exist) and then represent this in translation. However, the Anglophone reader deserves to be aware that the Erauso of these stories switches gender.

Translating D'Eon

It should be clear by now that we are dealing with at least one complicated source text which makes its translation challenging; I shall now look at d'Eon's memoir in more detail to show how hir text is also complicated and to see how hir translators have dealt with such a nebulous source text. The question is whether they too believe that translating grammatical gender is an "insurmountable" problem like the Steptos.

What d'Eon's shifting grammatical gender does is compound the ambiguity of hir text. Just as Erauso's text is unreliable (we get hir story at least third hand if we consider that we have to go through the original amanuensis and Juan Bautista Muñoz before we get to Ferrer/Vallbona) so is d'Eon's; in both texts, "the writing subject endlessly disappears" (Foucault 1979, 15). In order to see how d'Eon "endlessly disappears" in hir own writing I will now turn my attention to the source text and its translation. As mentioned above, Roland A. Champagne, Nina Ekstein and Gary Kates' 2001 translation of d'Eon's writings comprises various correspondences currently kept in the Leeds Brotherton Library but *La Grande Epître Historique* will be the only part of the translation examined in detail here. In their introduction, in contrast to the Steptos, the translators explain how important d'Eon's gender shifts are and they explain how they have translated these shifts into English: "To give the reader a sense of the ambivalence with which d'Eon 'marked' his own gender, we the translators indicate each instance with an *m* or an *f*" (Champagne et al. 2001, xxi).

The French quotations below are my own transcriptions from the manuscript which I consulted in the Brotherton Library Collection (d'Eon 1785).[10] Again, I have underlined the gendered words and used parentheses in my translation. D'Eon begins by describing how ze was educated as a boy (though here ze is claiming to be a girl who was raised as a boy). Ze claims to have had two personalities and was therefore confused when having to choose a career; ze took refuge with the Dragoons:

> Je me conduis de façon que personne ne peut dire si je suis fille ou garçon. Si je suis blessée, je ne serai pas deshonorée pour avoir été à la guerre. Si je suis tuée je serai couverte de la poussière de la gloire militaire.
>
> (d'Eon 1785)

> [I conduct myself so as nobody can say whether I am a girl or a boy. If I am injured(f), I will not be dishonoured(f) for having been to the war. If I am killed(f) I will be covered(f) in the dust of military glory].

> During the day I will act in such a way that no one will be able to tell whether I am a girl or a boy. If I am wounded^{f} I will not be dishonored^{f} in having been a warrior. If I am killed^{f} I will be shrouded^{f} with the dust of military glory.
>
> (Champagne et al. 2001, 8)

That d'Eon should use the feminine gender in a passage which describes hir time as a soldier could well have been hir way of emphasizing to the reader that ze was a girl dressed up as, and acting like, a soldier. Further on in this passage, d'Eon talks about how ze will be able to hide among the officers because they sleep alone. The original French has "je n'y entrerai que comme officier, ainsi que couchant seule il ne sera pas facile de me decouvrir" (d'Eon 1785) [I will only enter as an officer, so sleeping alone, it will not be easy to discover me].

One problem caused by the handwritten form of the manuscript centers around the word "seule" [alone] which is in the feminine but is my decipherment of the handwriting. The word "seule" is written underneath

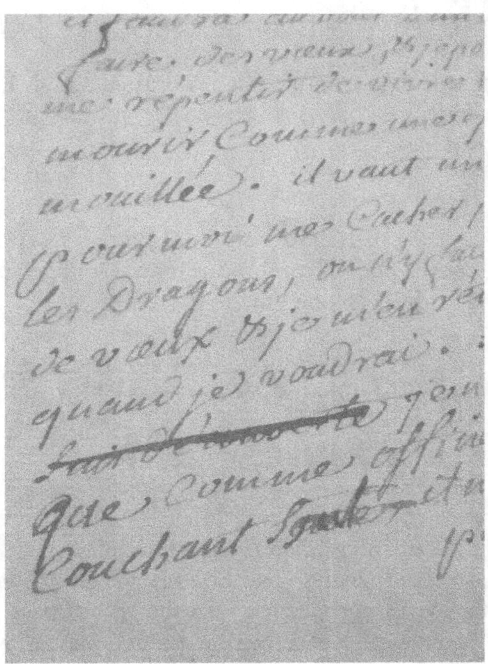

Figure 2.1 La Grande Epître Historique de la Chevalier d'Eon en 1785, page 5 recto, BC MS Chevalier d'Eon/01. Reproduced with the permission of Special Collections, Leeds University Library.

other letters which had been written over the top in a different colored pen. It is possible that what was added was "eul" to make the feminine "seule" a masculine "seul" (see Figure 2.1).

I have worked from the same manuscripts as Champagne, Ekstein and Kates and it seems that maybe to avoid this transcription challenge, they have opted to translate the sentence as "I will serve only as an officer; given the way they bed down at night" (Champagne et al. 2001, 8), thus avoiding any need to choose a gender for "alone". This translation, however, "loses" the idea of discovery, that d'Eon is afraid of being discovered, of being seen to be a woman, that what is "underneath" the Dragoon uniform is hir true identity. This idea of being seen, that what we see with our eyes must be the truth, especially pertaining to anatomy, is something I will return to. Here, d'Eon wants what is "underneath," what is "real," to be hir femaleness and this is legitimized by hir fear that others might see it and this would confirm it as "true".

When d'Eon uses different grammatical genders in the same sentence, ze could well be indicating the undecidable nature of hir identity. D'Eon is in conversation with Dom Bernard (hir Uncle's friend and confessor) and explains who hir own confessor is:

> «C'est l'abbé Lebel Docteur de Sorbonne – je le connois depuis longtems, c'est un homme savant et pieux. J'irai le voir, je lui parlerai» m'en étant donc allé contente.[11]
>
> (d'Eon 1785)

> "It is the Abbé Lebel, Doctor of the Sorbonne – I have known him for a long time, he is a knowledgeable and pious man. I will go to see him, I will talk to him" so having gone(m) there happy(f)].

> "The Abbé Lebel, a doctor of the Sorbonne. I have known him for a long time. He is knowledgeable and pious. I will go see him and talk to him." And so I left^{m} contented^{f}.
>
> (Champagne et al. 2001, 10)

A short examination of grammatical agreements in early-modern French will show that agreement between subjects and past participles used with *être* was not inconsistent in d'Eon's time despite d'Eon's own inconsistency. It is therefore very likely that by using the extra *e* on the end of past participles with *être,* ze was deliberately breaking the rules of, and playing with, standardized grammar. The most common way to form the past tense is to use the verb *avoir* as an auxiliary with a past participle; in today's usage the participle only ever agrees with preceding direct objects and only in three particular cases. The past tense can also be formed using *être* as an auxiliary: today, in these cases, the past participle always agrees in number and gender with the subject. Nathalie Fournier's (1998, 316) *Grammaire du français classique* describes grammatical changes made to classical French during the seventeenth century; agreement of the past participle with the subject takes place with passive verbs and with transitive verbs. In his *Remarques sur la langue française,* Vaugelas (1647, 178, my translation) declared that "the participle in the passive preterit not being indeclinable takes the number and gender of the nouns which precede and follow it". In fact, the only real debate over agreements with *être* centers on the use of a verb of movement before an infinitive – here the "participle could agree with the subject (which is the norm with the verb *être*) or could remain invariable" (Fournier 1998, 317, my translation). In the eighteenth century there was always agreement between subjects and past participles taking *être* (Champagne et al. 2001, xxi).[12] D'Eon might therefore genuinely be indicating the undecidable nature of hir identity by combining the masculine "allé" with the feminine "contente".

In another passage in which d'Eon is with Dom Boudier, ze has gone to stay at the St. Denis Abbey where ze is served dinner and ze is:

Reconnoissante et confuse à l'exces d'etre traité en uniforme comme une mère d'enfans, je voulais partir après le caffe. (d'Eon 1785)

[Excessively grateful(f) and confused(f) at being treated(m) in uniform like a mother of children, I wanted to leave after the coffee].

Appreciative^{f} and yet painfully embarrassed^{f} at being treated^{m} like a mother while in uniform, I wanted to leave after the coffee.
(Champagne et al. 2001, 29)

Here d'Eon is evidently dressed as a man in uniform because ze describes being confused at being treated like a woman while wearing male clothes. To begin with, ze uses the feminine gender and then when ze talks of hir uniform ze uses the masculine gender. The fact that ze uses the feminine gender while dressed as a man aligns with those instances in which Erauso's gender does not match hir clothes and suggests more than conventional transvestism. However, we must remember d'Eon's constant double-bluff, ze is trying to make hir reader think that ze really *is* a woman. Furthermore, d'Eon's fiction is trying to make the reader think that in this scene ze is dressed as a man but is really a woman underneath, something hir fellow diners are apparently aware of (this scene occurs after d'Eon has been discovered to be a 'real' woman. Ze is on hir way to Paris where ze will be forced to dress as a woman but is still wearing male traveling clothes). That ze is being treated like a mother and trying to convince the reader ze is a woman but uses the masculine gender on "traité" intimates a vacillating gender identity.

In a conversation with Madame Louise (the former king's daughter), in which d'Eon is claiming that the king asked hir to carry out espionage by cross-dressing, ze remarks:

J'ai été elevée ainsi, votre Auguste père le savoit et s'est servi de moi. Mais maintenant qu'il est mort, je suis devenu une servante inutile.
(d'Eon 1785)

servant(f) useless(f)

[I was brought up(f) this way, your noble father knew it and took advantage of me. But now that he is dead, I have become(m) a useless(f) servant(f)].

I was raised^{f} like this. Your illustrious father knew it and made use of me. But now that he is dead, I have become^{m} a useless servant^{f}.
(Champagne et al. 2001, 29)[13]

Here d'Eon uses the feminine gender throughout, except for "devenu" which is masculine. D'Eon uses the masculine gender on the verb "become" which is, I argue, a "trans" verb of transition. In the epigraph of chapter one, Choisy (1995, 82) also uses the past participle "became" in the masculine directly before a feminine noun: "et suis redevenu femme" [and I became again(m) a woman] – D'Eon (1785) hirself says "je suis devenu fille malgré moi" [I became(m) a girl despite myself]. D'Eon constantly claims to be fighting an internal dualism, but this is a Platonic dualism: "It is not at all the dualism of the intelligible and the sensible, of Idea and matter, or of Ideas and bodies. It is a more profound and secret dualism hidden in sensible and material bodies themselves" (Deleuze 1990, 2).

This dualism is hidden but, like the undecidable, it is not a concealment that can ever be uncovered. It is a "pure becoming" that "moves in both directions at once. It always eludes the present, causing future and past, more and less, too much and not enough to coincide in the simultaneity of a rebellious matter" (Deleuze 1990, 2). This usage of the verb "become" therefore hints to undecidability because it suggests that before this becoming d'Eon was female but ze does not fully become male because the gender on "servant" remains feminine – ze has become both masculine and feminine.

Throughout, d'Eon is in an in-between state. Hir constant double use of gender markers show just how difficult it is to pull apart these two selves: "as d'Eon revealed an affiliation with one gender, then the self's alliance with the other gender was both concealed and implied in the same affirmation, and vice versa" (Champagne et al. 2001, xxiii-xxiv).

Conclusions

Just as we cannot know precisely why Erauso uses different grammatical genders at certain times, we cannot be entirely sure why d'Eon does either. When and how often both d'Eon and Erauso choose to use the feminine grammatical form (or the masculine) could, of course, be entirely capricious and a product of free-form playfulness. Erauso, d'Eon and even Choisy use grammar; indeed, it would be more appropriate to say that they deliberately misuse it. What all of these writers have are memoirs which "prolong, supplement and even supplant the various gender performances that characterized their lives" (Harris 2010, 179). While both d'Eon and Erauso spend a good deal of their lives living as only one gender (d'Eon as the Chevalière in England and Erauso as Antonio in the New World), it is their autobiographies that make them undecidable. As Champagne et al. (2001, xxiv) say, "while the Chevalière claimed several times to have buried his dragoon self, the autobiography literally resurrects him. And the d'Eon who is resurrected is beyond the categories of male and female." The same can be said for Erauso: hir undecidability is played out in the autobiography as it cannot be anywhere else, not even in life. My in-depth examination of these transgender texts has proven that because their writers specifically choose to play only with grammatical gender, they had an undecidable gender identity, even if that identity would not have been called "transgender" in their times. The question now is how to represent that undecidability in translation.

Notes

1 The manuscripts themselves are labeled M-1 and M-2. I have added "Seville" to avoid any confusion with the Madrid manuscript.

2 Other writings, which shall not be examined here as they were not intended by d'Eon for hir memoir, and not included in the English translation, can be found in the Paris National Archives and municipal archives in Tonnerre.

3 A previous translation was carried out by James Fitzmaurice-Kelly in 1908 entitled *The Nun Ensign*, which can be found as an appendix in Vallbona's text (Fitzmaurice-Kelly 1992). It will not be consulted here in the interests of space.

4 There are more differences between the four sources than grammatical gender, for example *Vida i sucesos* and the Seville manuscripts use Basque spelling. However, as the main focus of this book is grammatical gender, those differences will not be remarked upon.

5 I use my own translations instead of a gloss so the source text is easier to read. My English translations aim to give the non-specialist reader a general idea of the Spanish or the French and are not to be taken as finished products (the possibility of which this book would argue against anyway).

6 We must also always bear in mind that the Madrid manuscript itself is open to question, Vallbona's text might be an accurate transcription of the Madrid manuscript, but how much was the Madrid manuscript itself an accurate transcription of the original?

7 This passage is not mentioned in Seville M-1.

8 In gathering this data, I took note of gendered adjectives, past participles used as adjectives and gendered nouns. I only counted adjectives or past participles used to refer to multiple persons when Erauso is referring to hirself and one woman. For example, Erauso and hir charge María Dávalos are "consolados" [consoled] (Erauso 1992, 90), in the masculine despite both being "biological" women. I did not count those where other men were present as the masculine form would dominate no matter Erauso's gender identification at the time. Furthermore, where the gender marker was repeated, as in "ciudadano Romano" or "buena christiana" I only counted one marker as the gender of the second word is redundant being given already in the first.

9 Seville M-2 is cut off before Erauso has confessed.

10 I transcribed the text to the best of my ability, maintaining d'Eon's spelling and use of accents (ze misses accents on many words which need them in modern-day usage).

11 There are no speech marks in the original but I have added them here to make the passage clearer.

12 Whether past participles should agree with preceding direct objects or not has been the subject of much debate; they often did not agree (agreement is now obligatory in Modern French) (see Rickard 1989: 74; Petitjean 1991; Fournier 1998). However, these past participles agree with objects and not

subjects and reveal nothing about d'Eon's gender identity so in this book I am only interested in past participles that agree with the subject (and therefore the auxiliary *être*).

13 This passage forms part of a myth created by d'Eon suggesting that ze dressed as a woman to spy in Russia, something which is thought to be untrue (Champagne et al. 2001, xvi).

3 The Palimpsest

As we have seen in chapter two, we are dealing with undecidability on many levels, not just on the level of the language used by the protagonists. What I am searching for is an extra-linguistic translation process that attempts to show not only Erauso's and d'Eon's multiple source texts, but to highlight the multiplicity of every text and body. Every text is unstable, not just a translated text and every body is undecidable, not just a transgender body. They are undecidable because they are constantly becoming, always formed of their past, present and future selves; because of this we could see transgender identity as formed of layers of different bodies and identities the way that translation is often considered to be formed of layers of (inter)text. Derrida (2004, 389) claims that "to write means to graft. It's the same word". If we take "graft" here to mean "attach layers" we can directly compare this to how Jean Bobby Noble (2006, 84) sees "transed bodies as grafted where one materialization is haunted by the other, as opposed to crossing or exiting". In this chapter I will look at the idea of the graft and at Benjamin's concept of the afterlife to think about the fragility of the "original". I also discuss the first of my experimental translation solutions: the palimpsest. The second half of this chapter will center on a demonstration of my own palimpsestuous translation of sections of Erauso's texts.

The Graft

With the graft we can help to eliminate ideas of an "original" or "right" gender or text (Derrida 2004, 389) because "each grafted text continues to radiate back toward the site of its removal, transforming that, too, as it affects the new territory" (390). The translation transforms the original as in Walter Benjamin's (2012: 77) concept of the afterlife: "In [translations] the original's life achieves its constantly renewed, latest and most comprehensive development". The "first" text or body is not exited or passed up but transformed by the new text or body, subsumed but not forgotten: "The apparently 'present' statement is not the statement of any present, not even of any past present, of any past defined as having taken place, as having been present. Far from any essence, you are straightway plunged by the imperfect into the already opened thickness of another text" (Derrida 2004: 372). As soon as you start to try to analyze the text you are looking at you have immediately called forth a different, new text that is related to, but can never be the same as, the text you were looking at.

It is helpful to see transgender identity as a graft too because we can challenge the idea that transgender people or translation should "pass" and instead emphasize the idea that transgender people and translations that refuse to pass are celebrating their statuses as texts and bodies that have been born of a specific combination of multiple other texts and bodies. The concept of passing in terms of (trans)gender can be paralleled with the concept of passing in terms of translation with illuminating consequences for both. As gender performances involve clothes, make-up, hair-style, gait and speech, performances of texts in translation involve style, format, punctuation and words. As transsexuals and cross-dressers reveal the performative aspect of all gender while they attempt to pass in heteronormative surroundings, translations reveal the performative aspect of writing while sometimes attempting to pass as original writing in literary surroundings. When people pass they reinforce the idea of binary gender and the idea that one must choose between one of only two genders. In this binary system, being undecidable is impossible: the concept of the transgender person becomes invisible just as passing a target text off as an original work encourages the invisibility of the translator. With the graft, the "first" body (the rejected body) and the "first" text (the source text) are proven never to have been "first" and are made visible as a trace residing beneath the surface of the new body or text. The text and the body are shown to be in a continual process of becoming in which resides "the paradox of infinite identity (the infinite identity of both directions or senses at the same time – of future and past)" (Deleuze 1990, 2). Because this identity is infinite, is both future and past, it is undecidable.

Erauso and d'Eon shift between a feminine and masculine gender identity. Neither identity is ever entirely forgotten just as the source text of a translation and a translation's influences and intertexts are always residing beneath the surface, haunting the text. Both d'Eon and Erauso indicate in their memoirs that they experienced an oscillation between the masculine and the feminine. Consequently there is an oscillation between source text and target text that goes both ways because the source text influences the translation but the translation also modifies the source text. This sexual and textual fluidity can be exemplified by the palimpsest.

The Palimpsest

Palimpsests were created as early as Egyptian times when a shortage of paper was dealt with by erasing text from used parchment or papyrus to make room for new texts. They were used on a domestic scale by the ancient Greeks and the Romans and the practice came to an end in the fifteenth century with the increased availability of paper (Dillon 2007, 13). The erasures were imperfect and the old text would reappear centuries later underneath the new text. The old text could be mathematical and the new text religious as with the Archimedes Palimpsest: in the thirteenth century a tenth-century manuscript written by Archimedes was erased to make room for a book of orthodox Christian prayers. Both texts are now visible (see Dillon 2007; Easton and Noel 2010).

The Archimedes palimpsest is a demonstration of how the palimpsest is "an involuted phenomenon where otherwise unrelated texts are involved and entangled, intricately interwoven, interrupting and inhabiting each other" (Dillon 2007, 4). The texts we are interested in here – the source, the target and their intertexts – however, are not unrelated. The texts underneath influence and inspire the text on the surface and so they are even more entangled – one cannot exist without the other. For example, d'Eon's text is heavily influenced by an existing narrative tradition; hir text includes the pre-texts of Joan of Arc, Pope Joan and Saint Paul (Champagne et al. 2001, xi). And we saw in the previous chapter that Erauso was influenced by picaresque texts, religious autobiographies and soldier's journals. Parts of d'Eon's and Erauso's texts, therefore, are palimpsestuous even before we come to a translation. I use the term "palimpsestuos" as synonymous with "intertextual" following Gérard Genette's definition of intertextuality which he sees as one type of transtextuality: "a relationship of copresence between two texts or among several texts: that is to say, eidetically and typically as the actual presence of one text within another" (Genette 1997: 1–2). In the palimpsest one text is literally present beneath another.[1]

This idea of purposefully flagging up the intertextual nature of the source texts in a translation, which itself would be doubly intertextual given the translator's influences are added to the author's, works well with these particular texts because any translation carried out today would have to be a retranslation: "Because retranslations are designed to challenge a previous version of the source text, they are likely to construct a more dense and complex intertextuality so as to signify and call attention to their competing interpretation" (Venuti 2013, 104). Re-translations always hold previous translations within them, even if the translator never consulted one when translating.

This palimpsestuous nature is visible in d'Eon's physical text as well because some parts of the text are crossed out but what is underneath is still legible and, as mentioned in the previous chapter, some words, like "seule" are written over in a different pen. Because these texts are handwritten, they feature crossings out and re-writings; this is the physical evidence that the texts are worked on multiple times, see Figure 3.1 for an example of how d'Eon's text has clearly been worked and

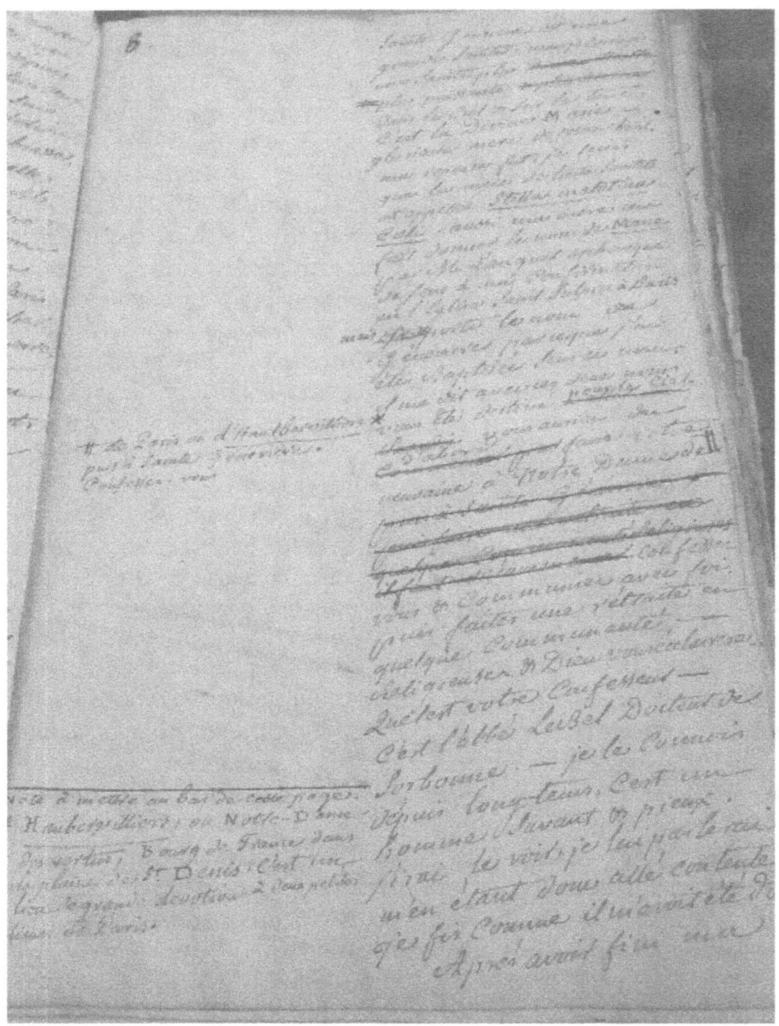

Figure 3.1 Page 8 of d'Eon's manuscript which involves both crossings-out and annotations. Reproduced with the permission of Special Collections, Leeds University Library.

re-worked. A previous draft is a text that has come before and helped shape the text that we see.

These translations are not only retranslations but they are translations of memoirs in which the self has been written and re-written over a substantial period of time. The possibility of retranslations refutes the notion that there can be one fixed or definitive translation of any source text.

Erauso hirself may not have written all the versions of hir autobiography but both hir text and d'Eon's have been constantly revised; there is no definitive, "original" version as shown in chapter two. The palimpsest is the perfect embodiment of the layering we find in the graft, and it can dispel notions of the "originality" and "authority" of all writing because: "A text is not a line of words releasing a single 'theological' meaning (the 'message' of the Author-God) but a multi-dimensional space in which a variety of writings, none of them original, blend and clash. The text is a tissue of quotations drawn from the innumerable centers of culture" (Barthes 1977, 146).

There is no omnipotent author who controls all, he or she has become one voice among many. In Foucault's work on "Self Writing" he contrasts the writings of the *hupomnēmata* with epistolary writing to show how multivocality is present in all texts. The former is not intended to reveal what is hidden within the writer but "to capture the already-said, to collect what one has managed to hear or read" (Foucault 1994, 211). We are dealing with memoirs that both capture what has already been said by the author but also by others. While Foucault makes it clear that the *hupomnēmata* are not what we would now think of as an intimate journal in which the author confesses their deepest feelings and bares their soul, we can use the analogy of the *hupomnēmata* to better understand how all writing is a mixture of voices as Bakhtin (1981, 262) has argued. Foucault (1994, 214) uses the analogy of the chorus to show how many voices make the whole. The *hupomnēmata* and epistolary writing are both forms of self writing that help us to get a clearer understanding of what is happening with the memoirs we are examining here because neither form is "a decipherment of the self by the self" (217). The self is never alone and all texts contain within them a mixture of genres, of forms and of voices; they are never singular in any way.

The Genotext and Phenotext

Multivocality is highlighted in the palimpsest because the texts which comprise the palimpsest cannot be ordered in a hierarchy; the texts cannot even be separated. But they are also "not the essential attributes of the palimpsest" (Dillon 2007, 43). If this is the case, the palimpsest could help to dispel notions of the "essentiality" of gender, or highlight the idea that any essence is complex and undecidable. According to Dillon (92), the palimpsest "serves as the hymen that holds the masculine pheno-text and the feminine geno-text together and apart." The terms phenotext and genotext were coined by Julia Kristeva; the genotext is "a process, which tends to articulate structures that are ephemeral (unstable, threatened by drive changes, 'quanta' rather than 'marks') and nonsignifying (devices that do not have a double articulation)" (Kristeva 1984, 86). The phenotext denotes "language that serves to communicate," it is "a structure [...that] obeys the rules of communication" (87). The genotext is not interested in "meaning-making" or in communicating to an addressee, it "moves through zones that have relative and transitory borders and constitutes a *path* that is not restricted to the two poles of univocal information between two full-fledged subjects" (ibid.). The genotext and the phenotext can never be separated, however, and the presence of the genotext in every phenotext means that no text is ever final or can ever "encompass the infinite totality of that [signifying] process" (87–88). The two texts, one in constant motion, one a seemingly stable structure (that the process of the genotext constantly undermines) are held together and apart by a membrane: they are both fused together and forever separated meaning that the palimpsest represents an in-between state (Dillon 2007, 97).

Trans experience could be the "between of bodies," a between that is characterized by queer notions of identity as unstable. The genotext and the trans body have much in common: they are infinite, unstable, transitory and ever crossing borders. We can return to the graft here and the concept of passing as well if we think of the phenotext as representing the body that is presented to the world, which is always mediated by other identities beneath the surface which make that very surface possible. Homi Bhabha's (2004, 56) Third Space is based on a similar hybrid status, it is "the 'inter' – the cutting edge of translation and renegotiation, the *inbetween* space – that carries the burden of the meaning of culture." Bhabha (ibid.) then claims that by "exploring this Third Space, we may elude the politics of polarity and emerge as the others of our selves." We can reject binary notions of gender and embrace the others of ourselves (those others haunting us beneath the grafts of new bodies) by allowing identity as queer, as multiple.

The palimpsest has a role in the queering of textuality, writing, reading and identity because it represents the idea of the subject as a specter, it shows that identity and writing are both involuted (Dillon 2007, 124–25). The palimpsest is a powerful, uncanny object because it brings back to life the murdered texts and identities from former ages. Indeed, it shows that these texts and the bodies they narrate never really passed beyond the veil. Where translation is concerned, the author and all their past (and future) lives and the source text and all its past (and future) iterations haunt the translated text. Chapter six will develop these ideas of the author as specter and the haunted text by looking at Derrida's *Specters of Marx* ([1994] 2006).

Impossible Translation

Derrida's (2001b) concept of a "relevant" translation is also prescient here: translation itself is involuted because everything is translatable and also untranslatable, or, to put it another way, nothing is translatable or untranslatable (178). As Benjamin (2012, 77) has it in "The Translator's

Task," everything is untranslatable because as soon as a text is translated the "original" is changed. The "original" can never be fully represented in another language (not least because there is no equivalence in language) because once translation has taken place the original is no longer the text one was trying to represent because it has gone through this very process of representation. At the same time, translation is always already there as a possibility: for any text to be properly called a text, it must always, and from the very start, be translatable. This means that translation is in every text whether it has been translated or not and therefore the translation does not come after the source (see Butler 2016a, xxi).

If every text is both translatable and untranslatable and both requires and rejects its translation, it has at its heart a double bind which is exemplified by the hymen: the understanding of the language of the other (what is strange and foreign), "interrupt[s] the *hymen* even as it consummates it" (Derrida 1979, 150). The hymen is an apt analogy because of what it signifies as both the Greek God of marriage and the symbol of virginity. Derrida (2001b) suggests that translation is equally contradictory in that it signifies both original writing and derivative writing. The Greek god Hymen also suggests the idea of the palimpsest/translation and suggests the double bind of translation as both an enlightenment and an obfuscation of the source text as the God is represented "as a young man carrying a torch and veil" (Oxford 2017). Translation acts as another veil placed on the source text. So by adding veils the translation adds to the source text: the word hymen was perhaps chosen for the God of marriage because, etymologically, it has links with the verb "sew" meaning "join together with thread" (Oxford, 2003). The hymen joins the source text and the target text together so that, as we saw above, the source text changes, becomes different to itself and lives on and survives in this altered form (see Benjamin 2012, 76).

The translation of a source text is an impossible task because as soon as you try to "uncover" it you inadvertently but inevitably "cover" it further but this does not mean it should never be undertaken. Translation could, therefore, literally show its divisions, its multiplicities. This would be a total departure from seeing translation as a betrayal of the source text because it acknowledges that the translation can never represent the source text and never should. The translation becomes a new text in its own right and the source text is one of its many genotexts but it is not the only one. Venuti (1992, 12) describes translation as never having one single identity but "always a lack and a supplement, and it can never be a transparent re-presentation, only an interpretative transformation that exposes multiple and divided meanings in the foreign text and displaces it with another set of meanings, equally multiple and divided." In exposing these internal contradictions, the translation can point to the multiplicities of the characters it represents. Translators can write themselves into their translations instead of trying to hide. This idea brings to mind Sandy Stone's (2006, 232) call to transsexuals to become "posttranssexual", "to be consciously 'read,' to read oneself aloud – and by this troubling and productive reading, to begin to write oneself into the discourses by which one has been written." A translator could also write themselves into textual discourse by allowing their status as translator to be consciously "read".[2]

To expose the contradictions inherent to the text, the author and the translator, experimental methods could be used. Translation can actually help us to move beyond ideas that an experimental text or body is counter to the traditional text or body:

> For too long traditional and experimental forms of writing have been seen as separate currents, mistrustful of one another; literary translation [...] suggests a more intimate and constructive fusion of the rearguard and the avant-garde, a fusion which has implications for the very making of translational texts: translation [...] calls for the harnessing of new kinds of paratext, or hypertext, new communicational channels.
>
> (Scott 2014b, xi)

As mentioned in the introduction, a transdisciplinary, or "entangled" approach can bring this experimentation. And what I want to take from the idea of experimentation is the re-running of experiments, doing things repetitively, changing one element every time to see what results you get. Fitzgerald and Callard (2014, 17–18) explain this thus: "It is not our desire for control that undergirds our positive turn to experiment. Quite the opposite: we are compelled by the promise of digressions, transgressions, mistakes and the subterranean existence of not-as-yet-played-out narratives." A scientific stance on experimentation, the idea of constantly repeating the experiment, suggests the palimpsest if every layer we try is not discarded but kept underneath. The difference here is that we are not repeating to find the perfect solution, we are repeating precisely to create some of the possible not-as-yet-played-out-narratives the text holds within. Translating the text multiple times in multiple ways is an enactment of the fact that all writing is a game. The author plays with writings that have come before: "the writer can only imitate a gesture that is always anterior, never original. His only power is *to mix writings*, to counter the ones with the others, in such a way as never to rest on any one of them" (Barthes 1977, 146, my emphasis). I am aiming to make my translations ludic manipulations of the undecidability of these trans texts.

Palimpsestuous Translations

In this section I will discuss my own translation strategies for dealing with transgender undecidability, looking firstly at linguistic strategies that focus around a new "gendered" font and then extra-linguistic strategies that focus around the palimpsest.

I look at linguistic strategies because the specific instances of shifting gender markers do have to be dealt with in translation: ignoring these, as the Steptos do, impoverishes such non-normative texts. Using an "m" and an "f" in superscript, as Champagne, Ekstein and Kates do, is one way to translate the phenomenon of an extra "e" in French and would also work for Spanish words that end in "o" (masculine) or "a" (feminine). This strategy works well for an academic rendering or annotation of the memoirs. However, I want my solution to stretch the English language, to be ludic to resist translation norms and gender norms. To that end, I have designed a new font which uses the symbols of Mars and Venus on certain letters to indicate if a word was originally masculine or feminine. With this font, the masculinity or femininity of a word is not given in an after-thought but becomes part of the word itself as in the French and Spanish. The font was created for me by a professional typographer who put the symbol of Mars on letters with a curve at the top (a, c, e, g, o, p, q, n, m, s) and the symbol of Venus on letters with a curve at the bottom (a, b, c, d, e, o, s, u, v) (see Figure 3.2).

The limited number of letters does restrict translation choices but there is no reason why many more, if not all twenty-six, letters could not be "gendered" in the future.

Concurrent with finding this solution for translating the "trans" appropriation of grammatical gender is my consideration of how to translate "trans texts" as a whole and this is where I look to the palimpsest as something that challenges the reader. Butler (1994, 38) warns against challenges that become legible as they are "readily recuperable." What subversive practices have to do is "overwhelm the capacity to read, challenge conventions of reading, and demand new possibilities of reading" (ibid.). The way we read both bodies and texts need to be challenged. The reluctance to give a definitive portrait is queer. Queer theory allows theorists, and translators, to go to extremes,

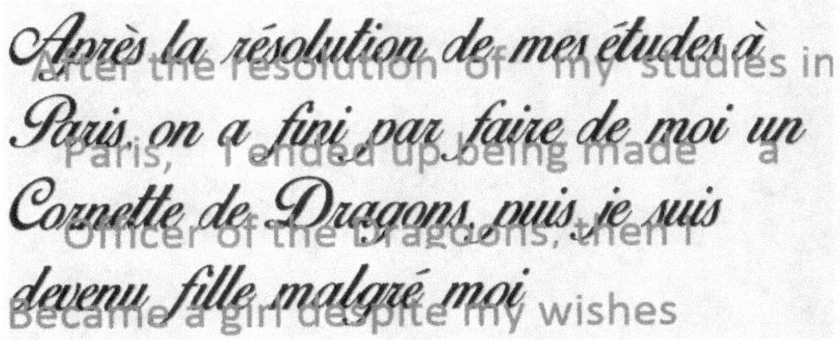

Figure 3.2 An excerpt from *La Grande Epitre* with the translation in color.

Noreen Giffney (2009, 9) talks of theorists writing about queer theory, but the same could apply to translators translating with queer theory: "There is a valuing of difficulty because of the concerted effort made by theorists not to make things easy or palatable but to challenge the reader to work through concepts with the same expenditure of energy exerted by the writer." However, it is important to make a distinction between what is challenging in the sense of being difficult and what is challenging in the sense of being incomprehensible.

Following my transdisciplinary methodology, any translation must be iterative, creative and innovative. The experiment should be repeated many times with different variables. In the spirit of experimentation, I began with the simplest method I could think of: a method that superimposed the translation straight above the source text, in the vein of a genuine palimpsest. I started with a translation by hand (Figure 3.3):

In a concession to readability I wrote the source text in a different color but it is still difficult to read; it is not impossible but while I want my text to be "writerly" I also want Erauso's story to be read. I then tried a similar technique using different fonts and colors in Microsoft Word (Figures 3.4 and 3.5):

These different versions show that the translation is easier to read in black and this is a method that does work, especially with d'Eon's text but the more layers you add, the more illegible it becomes. This method certainly represents the complexity of the palimpsest and of every text. Erauso's text, for example, has multiple source texts: the Madrid manuscript, Ferrer's version of the Madrid manuscript, Vallbona's version, Seville M-1 and M-2. And because of these multiple source texts, you can also have multiple translations because you will get a different translation depending on which source you use. You could have as many translations as sources and therefore many more layers. Indeed, if we wanted to acknowledge that this is a retranslation, we could even include the Steptos' translation (Figure 3.6):

With only three layers the palimpsest starts as fairly readable (Figure 3.7):

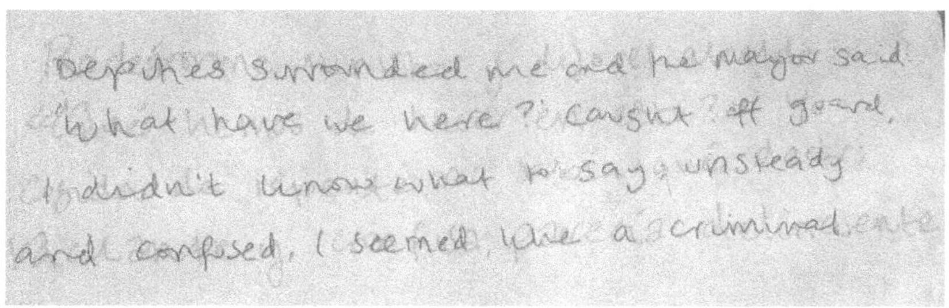

Figure 3.3 My first palimpsestuous translation of an excerpt of Erauso's text.

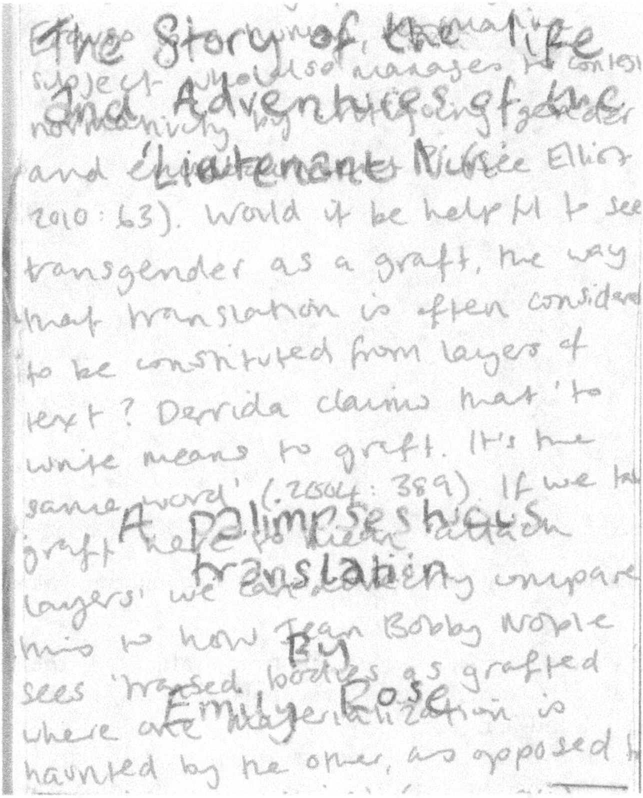

Figure 3.4 The front page of my first attempt at a physical palimpsestuous translation.

But when all layers are added, only certain words can be picked out (Figure 3.8):

While this demonstrates how many layers Erauso's text is made up of and how many layers my translation of hir texts is made up of, all residing beneath the surface, the next stage of my experimentation was to find a translation that could show layers but was also easier to read. Furthermore, in my first attempts above (Figure 3.3, 3.4, and 3.5) I did not incorporate my new gendered font to tackle the issue of linguistic gender. To create a readable experimental translation that shows Erauso's switches I decided to make a physical palimpsest. My first try involved, once again, writing by hand on tracing paper. I titled it *The Story of the Life and Adventures of the Lieutenant Nun*. It can be seen in Figures 3.9 and 3.10.

The layers I chose to incorporate were Ferrer's version of the Madrid manuscript, Vallbona's version of the Madrid manuscript, and my notes

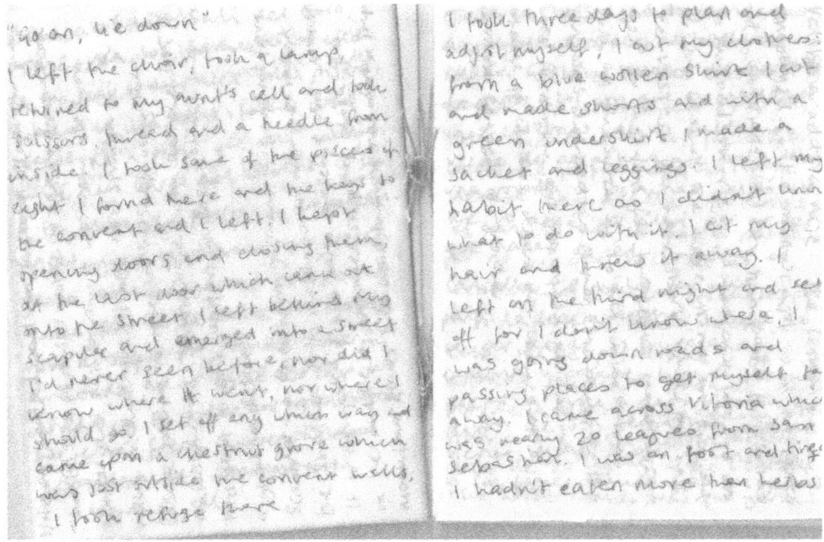
"Go on, lie down"
I left the chair, took a lamp,
returned to my aunt's cell and took
scissors, thread and a needle from
inside. I took some of the pieces of
eight I found there and the keys to
the convent and I left. I kept
opening doors and closing them,
at the last door which came out
into the street I left behind my
scapular and emerged into a street
I'd never seen before, nor did I
know where it went, nor where I
should go. I set off any which way and
came upon a chestnut grove which
was just outside the convent walls,
I took refuge there

I took three days to plan and
adjust myself, I cut my clothes:
from a blue woollen skirt I cut
and made shorts and with a
green undershirt I made a
jacket and leggings. I left my
habit there as I didn't know
what to do with it. I cut my
hair and threw it away. I
left on the third night and set
off for I don't know where, I
was going down roads and
passing places to get myself fa
away. I came across Vitoria which
was nearly 20 leagues from San
Sebastian. I was on foot and tire
I hadn't eaten more than herbs

Figure 3.5 The inside pages of my first attempt at a palimpsestuous translation.

on the text which were a mixture of comments from drafts of my thesis and explanations of early-modern Spanish vocabulary, all of which can be seen in Figures 3.4 and 3.5.

While this certainly works as a palimpsest and is readable, it is a fragile object (held together by string) and certainly would not work for mass production (though this is not the main aim of the exercise). My second attempt was more sophisticated and involved layers of text made from acetate paper, which were properly bound with a comb. My translation is entitled *The Life and Adventures of Catalina de Erauso: "The Lieutenant Nun"* incorporating the titles given to the work by Bautista Muñoz and Ferrer, Vallbona and the Steptos.

The first layer is Vallbona's "supposedly" seventeenth-century reading (supposedly, on the basis that the Madrid manuscript was actually transcribed in the eighteenth century). The second layer is Ferrer's nineteenth-century transcription. The third layer is made up of my translation notes distinguished by being in red font and the fourth layer is my twenty-first-century translation (see Figure 3.11). Each "page" of my translation therefore actually comprises four pages altogether. The order in which my translation layers are placed can be varied: the translation does not have to be on top, it could even come between the source texts. Because Ferrer and Vallbona's versions of the story are so similar it is possible to have each page of the source texts and the translation map roughly on top of each other by using different fonts and

Ferrer/Madrid: Entrado en Valladolid, donde estaba entonces la corte, me acomodé en breve por page de D. Juan de Idiaquez, secretario del rey, el cual me vistió luego bien, y lláméme Francisco de Loyola, y estuve allí bien hallado siete meses (1829: 6-7).

Translation: Having entered Valladolid, where the court was staying at the time, I briefly settled as the page of D. Juan de Idiaquez, secretary of the king, who soon dressed me well and I called myself Francisco de Loyola, and I was well situated for seven months.

Vallbona/Madrid: Entrada en Valladolid, donde estava entonces la Corte, me acomodé luego en breve por page de D. Juan de Ydiaquez, secretario del Rey, el qual me vistió luego bien, i lláméme allí Francisco de Loyola, i estuve allí bien hallado siete meses (1992: 36-37).

Translation: Having entered Valladolid, where the court was staying at the time, I soon settled briefly as the page of D. Juan de Ydiaquez, secretary of the king, who soon dressed me well, and I called myself Francisco de Loyola here, and I was well situated for seven months.

Seville M-1: Fúyme a Valladolid y me acomodé con Don Juan Idiáquez, Secretario del Rey, por page suyo, llamándome Francisco de Loyola. Vistióme muy bien y muy galán. Estuve con él siete meses (1995: 54).

Translation: I went to Valladolid and settled with Don Juan Idiáquez, secretary of the king, as his page, calling myself Francisco de Loyola. He dressed me very well and very handsomely. I was with him seven months.

Seville M-2: Legada a Valladolid, me acomodé por page de D. Juan de Idiáquez, Secretario del Rey, llamándome Francisco de Loyola, el qual me vistió muy bien y me tuvo consigo cosa de siete meses (1995 : 96).

Translation: Having arrived at Valladolid, calling myself Francisco de Loyola, I settled as the page of D. Juan de Idiáquez, secretary of the king, who dressed me very well and I was with him a matter of seven months.

Stepto and Stepto: The Court was in Valladolid at the time, and it wasn't long before I found work as a page with the king's secretary, don Juan de Idiáquez, who immediately dressed me up in a fine new set of clothes. There I went by the name of Francisco Loyola, and for seven months I did very well for myself (1996: 5).

Figure 3.6 Translations of the same section in all of Erauso's texts.

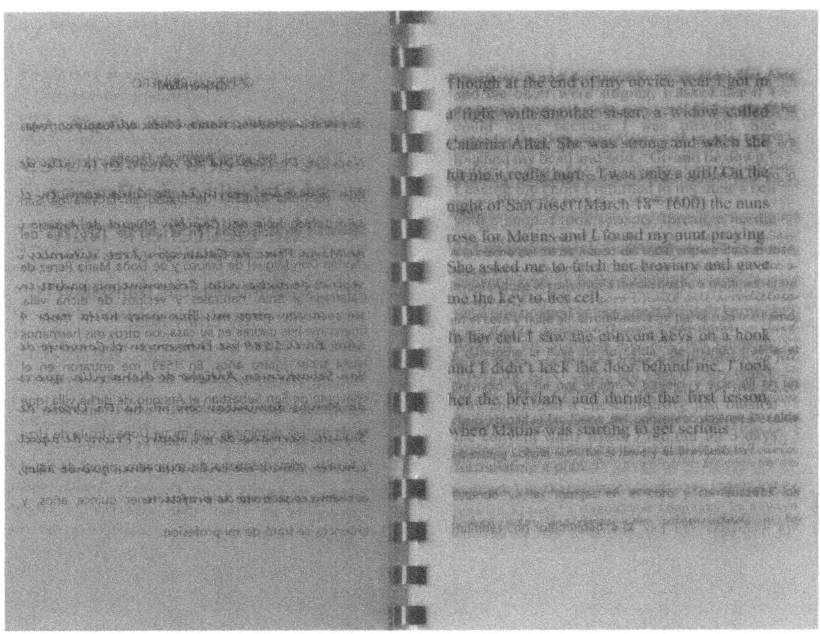

Figure 3.7 My palimpsest of Erauso's texts.

The Court was in Valladolid at the time, and it wasn't long before I found work as a page
Having arrived at Valladolid, calling myself Francisco de Loyola, I settled as the page of
Legada a Valladolid, me acomodé por page de D. Juan de Idiaquez, Secretario del Rey,
with the king's secretary, don Juan de Idiaquez, who immediately dressed me up in a
D. Juan de Idiaquez, secretary of the king, who dressed me very well and I was with him
llamándome Francisco de Loyola, el qual me vistió muy bien y me tuvo consigo cosa de
fine new set of clothes. There I went by the name of Francisco Loyola, and for seven
a matter of seven months.
siete meses.
months I did very well for myself.

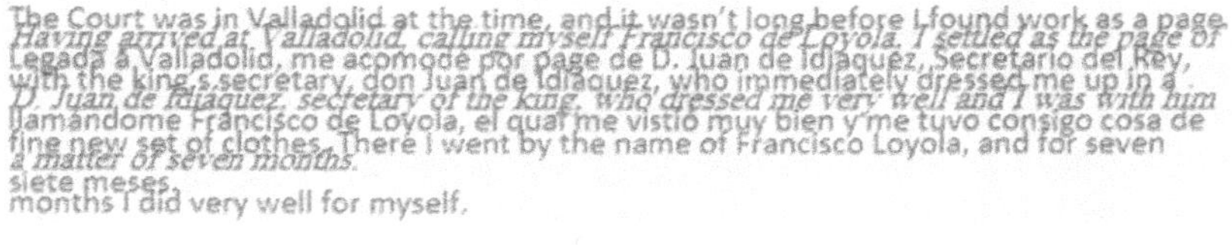

Figure 3.8 Palimpsest of Erauso's texts and translations involving only three layers.

font sizes. For example, each page of the first four-page section ends in Erauso mentioning hir profession as a nun: "i entonces se trató de profesión" (Vallbona), "y entonces se trató de mi profesión" (Ferrer), "and then I was meant to become a nun!" (my translation). There is an extra, invisible, layer to the translation as well because the ultimate layer of any text always belongs to the reader and the text and the trans identity are written anew with every reading.

I have also created a digital version of this palimpsest (see Figure 3.11). Here the palimpsest is suggested more than shown and I have experimented with slightly different layers: the first (bottom) layer is

After the resolution of my studies in Paris, I ended up being made an Officer of the Dragoons, then I became a girl despite my wishes

Après la résolution de mes Etudes à Paris, on a fini Par faire de moi un Cornette de Dragons, puis je suis devenu une fille malgré moi

Figure 3.9 My translation of the same extract from *La Grande Epitre* with the source text in color.

♂	a	e	c	s	q	p	g	n	m
♀	a	e	ç	s	u	d	y	b	

Figure 3.10 The masculine and feminine gendered characters of my font based on Baskerville, created by Jamie Clarke.

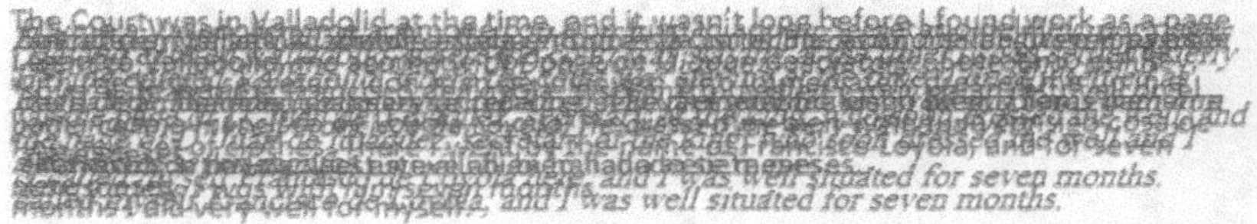

Figure 3.11 Palimpsest of Erauso's texts and translations involving all layers.

Vallbona's version of the source text, the second layer is Ferrer's, the third layer is my first translation draft and the top layer is my "final" translation. I was inspired by an image I stumbled across of the Talmud and the idea of text as not being conventionally written from the left hand side all the way to the right and from the top of the page all the way to the bottom. The Talmud has boxes of text in the middle of the page, surrounded by two columns of text on either side. This also brought to mind the idea of marginalia and d'Eon's text which has notes in the margins: D'Eon's text is covered in crossings out, and several pages have

Capítulo I

Su patria, padres, nacimiento, educación, fuga

CAPITULO PRIMERO

Su patria, padres, nacimiento, educación, fuga y correrías por varias partes

Chapter One

Hir homeland, parents, birth, upbringing, escape

My name is Catalina de Erauso and I was born in San Sebastian in 1585. My parents, who are both from San Sebastian, raised me at home with my siblings until I was four when I went away to a convent. The convent of San Sebastian caters for Dominican nuns and is run by my aunt, Doña Ursola de Sarastre. I was educated at the convent until I was 15 and then I was meant to become a nun! At the end of my novice year I got in a fight with another sister though, a widow called Caterina Alizi. She was strong and when she hit me it really hurt – I was only a girl! On the night of San Josef (March 15th 1600) the nuns rose for Matins and I found my aunt praying. She asked me to fetch her breviary and gave me the key to her cell. In her cell I noticed the convent keys on a hook and I didn't lock the door behind me. I took her the breviary and during the first lesson, when Matins was starting to get serious and the choir were singing, I asked her if I could leave because I was unwell she touched my head and said, "Go and lie down."

said, "Go on, lie down."

tía, tocándome con la mano en la cabeza, me dijo: anda acuéstate.

– *Anda acuéstate.*

Figure 3.12 A digital translation of the beginning of Chapter One in Ferrer (1829, 1–5) and Vallbona (1992, 33–35).

annotations as can be seen in Figure 3.1 For me, the act of writing in the margins is another in-between activity: in-between the act of reading and writing. The reader is making a commentary on what they have read, in the same way that a translation is a commentary on the source text. It is active reading: "the margins are sites of engagement and disagreement: between text and reader [...] From Talmudic studies to legal amendments, margins have been the places where texts have been kept alive — alive because they've been read and responded to" (Brent Plate 2015). All of my translation attempts are keeping Erauso's texts alive because they engage with them, they add layers or veils, bringing the translation both back to the source and at the same time taking it further away. My digital palimpsest does not strictly have any marginalia but because you can only see the entirety of the top layer which is the smallest layer, the only readable parts of the layers below are to the sides of the top layer which are, effectively the margins. This translation, therefore, hints to the idea of the translator as a commentator but it also shows the text's multiplicities, not only in its sources but also in my translation drafts, to point to the multiplicity of the character it (re)presents and also to the idea that no work that gets put down on paper is ever really "final", even once it has been published and it can never be, therefore, decidable.

Conclusions

What makes Erauso and d'Eon hard to "read" is the transdisciplinary stance needed to try to understand and (re)present or (re)produce their lives. This transdisciplinarity is, like translation itself, an act of violence and is something that is embodied in the palimpsest. As well as being a figure for the specter, the palimpsest is a figure for transdisciplinarity, "for the productive violence of the involvement, entanglement, interruption and inhabitation of disciplines in and on each other" (Dillon 2007, 2). If we want to acknowledge the violence of translation and of openly identifying as transgender (the violent revelation that both writing and gender are products of effort not of creative genius or biology) then we can play with transgender identity in translation. The translator can replicate Erauso and d'Eon's gender play in a translation that is itself playful. In their writings Erauso and d'Eon make everyone, including the reader, question the stability of gender; in writing down transgender experiences, implicit lived performances become explicit literary performances and the stability of all gender is brought into question.

I am not trying to get to the "truth" of d'Eon's or Eraso's identities. Gaillardet (1970, xi) claims that his biography of d'Eon aims to "reveal the truth, to catch nature as it were in the act, to strip the man and show him, as much as possible, in a state of physical or moral nakedness which leaves the eye in no doubt." Aside from the fact that much of Gaillardet's biography was complete fiction and therefore could not possibly "reveal the truth," the purpose of any work on d'Eon or Erauso, biography or translation, should not attempt to leave the reader "in no doubt". By writing Erauso's and d'Eon's texts *as* palimpsests, I am exemplifying the fact that I am adding another layer, or another veil, to the many texts that make up both their past and their future. Any biographer or translator of the two figures cannot possibly hope to represent them fully, unequivocally or to reveal their "true" identity. They can only add to the layers of identity that Erauso and d'Eon created for themselves and that other biographers or translators have added before them.

What I have shown through the palimpsestuous translation of transgender identities is that we can expose all gender as complex. And we can also expose the unoriginality of any writing: the palimpsest does not rest on any of the translation's sources as being definitive or authoritative but is constantly moving between writings, demonstrating that nothing comes first, not even the source text. If we create a true palimpsest of translation over source text, then we can place an early-modern and twenty-first-century reading together; we can create something recognizable and yet incomprehensible, normative and yet non-normative, multiple and yet unified, masculine and yet feminine, foreign and yet domestic. Through experiment and risk we can expose all writing and all gender as always already queer.

Chapter four considers how, despite queer arguments against the idea of an essential identity or gender, intersex children are still assigned by doctors what is presumed to be their "correct" sex, without their consent. Harris (2010, 182) looks to d'Eon's constant switching between worlds, one masculine and associated with war, blood and duty to the king, the other feminine and associated with religion, purity and duty to God and sees "a sense of metaphysical rootlessness not unlike that which we find in the hermaphrodite Herculine Barbin's memoirs in the nineteenth century." I explore the translation of intersex identity through the translation of Barbin's memoirs and the 2002 novel *Middlesex* by Jeffrey Eugenides. The chapter will continue to focus on the translation of textual undecidability and will also consider how to deal with sexual undecidability.

Notes

1 I choose to use the term "palimpsestuous" over the term "intertextual" to align my source texts more fully with my translation technique which involves creating palimpsests.

2 Of course, we must add the caveat that being "consciously" read suggests that we can make other people see us as we wish to be seen, something we can never really do because clothes, texts, embodiments are always interpreted differently by different people.

4 The History of Intersex

In *Annabel*, the intersex protagonist Wayne Blake wishes that more people were like him and regrets the fact that "he" lives in a world where everyone else feels certain that they are either a man or a woman (Winter 2011, 414). Wayne's sense of the world is rather over-simplified, however. As we saw in chapter one, people have been experiencing doubt about whether they are a "woman" or a "man" or both, and writing about this doubt, for centuries. Despite this, books that tackle the question of what it means to be intersex are still relatively rare (see D'Erasmo 2011 and Holmes 2008, 116; D'Erasmo 2011).

Intersexuality "refers to a physical and/or chromosomal set of possibilities in which the features usually understood as belonging distinctly to either the male or female sex are combined in a single body" (Holmes 2008, 32). It seems to have first become a subject to be fictionalized in the nineteenth century: Julia Ward Howe wrote *The Hermaphrodite* in 1846 and Herculine Barbin's memoirs were first published in a medical journal in 1874. But after this the subject disappeared for more than a century until Alain Roger wrote a French novel of the same name, *L'Hermaphrodite* in 1977 and Foucault re-published Barbin's memoirs in 1978. The twenty-first century, however, has seen a proliferation of English-language texts exploring intersexuality: *Middlesex* by Jeffrey Eugenides (2002), *Annabel* by Kathleen Winter (2011), *Golden Boy* by Abigail Tarttelin (2013), *Alex as Well* by Alyssa Brugman (2013), *Double Exposure* by Bridget Birdsall (2014), *None of the Above* by I.W. Gregorio (2015), *Lum* by Libby Ware (2015), two memoirs called *Intersex: A Memoir* by Aaron Apps (2015a) and *Born Both: An Intersex Life* by Hilda Viloria (2017) and a collection of poetry entitled *Dear Herculine* also by Aaron Apps (2015b).[1] In this chapter I shall continue the work of chapter one to look at how gender was conceptualized in the early-modern period to see whether hermaphroditism was feared or accepted. To do this I return to Aristotle and Hippocrates. I look at how intersexuality has been treated from Barbin's time to the present day in order that later in this book I can consider how my intersex texts were viewed and translated in the past and how they could be translated today.

Early-Modern Hermaphroditism

Looking at Barbin's nineteenth century novel and Eugenides' twenty-first century novel allows me to discuss the medical management of intersex both past and present in more detail. Given the wide gap in time between my primary sources in this chapter I will start by discussing how hermaphroditism has been seen over the past two centuries, starting before Barbin's time and ending today.

Whilst fiction and autobiography relating to sexual undecidability may be rare compared to texts about cis-gender characters, intersex has been recognized for centuries (though not under the name "intersex") and case reports abound, especially in Ruth Gilbert's *Early Modern Hermaphrodites: Sex and Other Stories*. In the early-modern period, hermaphroditism "told [...] stories: about order, knowledge, nature and culture; about what it meant to be an outsider and what it meant to be human" (Gilbert 2002, 1). Intersex can still tell us those things today despite the change of name and of attitudes towards the "condition" which have changed dramatically over the years.[2] It is important to look at the history of intersex because "intersex, contrary to the dominant medical story currently in play, is an historical phenomenon and not a neutral biological fact" (Holmes 2008, 31). I am attempting to expose intersex as a construction and to do this we have to understand that it is a construction with a long and complicated history which works very hard to hide its constructedness.

In chapter one I argued against the popular idea that many people followed a one-sex model in the early-modern period. This model supposedly meant that "early medical practitioners, who understood sex and gender to fall along a continuum and not into the discrete categories we use today, were not fazed by hermaphrodites" (Fausto-Sterling 2000: 32). However, while this is definitely not the case when we get to Barbin's time, it would appear that it was not the case before hir time either: "Sexual ambiguity, whether embodied or enacted, anatomical or erotic, has always generated confused responses" (Gilbert 2002: 3). My research into opinions on early-modern sex and gender in chapter one revealed that it is debateable that people still followed Hippocrates' one-sex model in the early-modern period. I briefly return to a questioning of the one-sex model here to consider the early-modern treatment of intersex.

According to Dreger (1998, 32), by the early-modern period people were following Aristotle who encouraged people to imagine "hermaphrodites to be doubly sexed beings. That tradition specifically held that hermaphrodites had extra sex (genital) parts added on to their single 'true' sexes." While the Aristotelian position allowed for genital doubling, this made no difference at all to the body's single sex, which was determined "by the heat of the heart and, regardless of corporeal morphology, was always decisively determined as male or female" (Tidd 2000, 76).

This meant that binary notions of sex were unharmed by hermaphroditism. Aristotle studied under Plato (Callahan 2009, 10) and the idea of binary sex follows Plato's fourth-century BC ideas in *The Symposium* (2008): he writes, through Aristophanes, that there used to be three types of human: male (offspring of the Sun), female (offspring of the Earth) and androgynous (offspring of the Moon). To control these beings (and invent heterosexuality), Zeus had them all cut in half, effectively destroying the category of the androgynous. These half-beings now roam the Earth looking for their other half, be that male or female. Plato certainly does not argue against homosexual love but he does argue for binary sex that is only ever male or female. Binary sex is a postlapsarian idea: "For some of the early Fathers [...] the difference between human nature before the Fall (prelapsarian) and human nature after the Fall (postlapsarian) was expressed through sexual difference: prelapsarian humanity was virginal; postlapsarian humanity was sexual" (Bernau 2012, 73). After Adam and Eve had been tainted by "original sin," Christians had to decide whether to live spiritually or carnally, and Christ and the saints were the models for a spiritual life (models that both Erauso and d'Eon followed to transcend sexuality and the gender binary); an unwavering devotion to a spiritual life was hard, however, because of the indelible mark of original sin (ibid.). Heterosexuality, and the gender binary that upholds heterosexuality as the norm, are postlapsarian consequences of original sin. And people have followed the idea of a gender binary for centuries, including, I argue, in the years leading up to and including when Barbin was alive – as we shall see below, in Barbin's time, and for a long time afterwards, hermaphrodites, once discovered to be in-between, were forced to make a decision or had that decision made for them.

Hermaphroditism from Barbin to Now

From 1870 to 1915, a period which Alice Domurat Dreger calls the "Age of Gonads," the hermaphrodite could be controlled, could be made to fit into society's categories of male and female because the medical establishment agreed that everybody and every body had a true sex and that this "true" sex could be distinguished by one thing and one thing only: "The anatomical nature of the gonadal tissue as either ovarian or testicular" (Dreger 1998, 29). This agreement suppressed the troubling discovery that sex was open to doubt.

Nevertheless, this "suppression" was not universally agreed upon by all who studied or were involved in the treatment of intersex. In 1910 Magnus Hirschfeld, considered a founder of sexology along with Richard von Krafft-Ebing (see Wolff 1986), wrote, in *Transvestites: The Erotic Drive to Cross Dress*, of "sexual intermediaries" by which "we understand manly formed women and womanly formed men at every possible stage, or, in other words, men with womanly characteristics and women with manly characteristics" (Hirschfeld 1991, 18). Hirschfeld cites Otto Weininger's 1903 work *Sex and Character* as a forerunner for texts about sexual intermediaries. In *Sex and Character* Weininger argues that all people are a mixture of the male and the female. He asks: "Is it really the case that all 'men' and all 'women' are totally different from each other, and that all those on either side of the divide, men on the one hand, women on the other, are completely alike in a number of respects?" (Weininger 2005, 10). Both Hirschfeld's and Weininger's work demonstrate that by the beginning of the twentieth century, men and women were considered different but they were also considered similar and, furthermore, it was acknowledged that no two women or men were the same. Gender was beginning to be seen on a spectrum: "It must be assumed from the outset that there are not only extreme males with the smallest residues of femininity on the one hand, extreme females with totally reduced masculinity on the other hand, and a concentration of those hermaphroditic forms in the middle, with nothing but empty spaces between these three points" (Weininger 2005, 13). Despite new ideas about the instability of sex and gender, medical practitioners clung to their rigid categorizations to contain the hermaphroditic body.

The late nineteenth century seems to be the location of a calcification of medical opinions on sex which lasted for some decades. These opinions were shared by many because ideas were constantly being exchanged across borders (Dreger 1998, 75). The medical discourse of truth was being used to keep people in their proper places and to maintain heterosexuality as the norm. However, these authors and doctors who agreed that there must be one true sex could not agree on which traits indicated that a person should be classified as male or female (83). This must have meant that an intersex person who was classified as "male" by one doctor could have just as easily been classified as "female" by another if they differed on what made up a man or a woman.

Today, in the wake of feminist and queer theory the interrelation between the terms "gender" and "sexuality" has come under theoretical and political scrutiny, but in the past it was believed that sex, gender and sexuality all had characteristics that fitted together to make heterosexual masculine men and heterosexual feminine women. This belief was not disrupted by the fact that some people broke these rules (see Dreger 1998, 89). The study of intersex and other trans identities has helped to uncover sex and gender as separate categories (though both cultural) because, as Butler (2006, 152) argues, "it does not follow that to be a given sex is to become a given gender." Butler's (2004b, 344) point is that exceptional cases like cross-dressers or drag artists expose the workings of the gender paradigm to us. However, Andrea Rossi (2013, 189) claims that Barbin cannot be a paradigm because ze is too exceptional. Rossi (ibid.) goes on to say that "our society has since produced far more flexible mechanisms to deal with 'abnormal selves'. This is undeniable." It is true that the treatment of intersexuals has changed since Barbin's time but it is not "undeniable" that treatment is more "flexible".

We have seen that intersexuals were firstly seen as having two sexes in the same body. One sex was seen to prevail and that was the sex they were made to live as. It was then considered that there was always only one "true" sex (and that intersexuals could, therefore, not have two sexes). Gender assignment was carried out by doctors who used their expertise to decide which sex was "true". The third phase of the "treatment" of intersexuals changes tack from a "true" sex to a "best" sex: this is whichever sex doctors deem is most appropriate (see Hird and Germon 2001, 163–164).

While the search for a "best" sex would appear to consider the best interests of the child, using evidence gleaned from *Middlesex* which I shall examine in more detail later, I propose that "best" really refers to the sex that society can most easily accommodate, especially the sex which would lead to a heterosexual relationship. "Best," therefore, is still a normative term and it could be argued that a "best" sex is simply a "true" sex under another name. In both the nineteenth and twentieth centuries intersex children were operated on according to which sex doctors chose for them. Typically, doctors who advocated corrective surgery excluded the parents from any decision being made about the sex of their child (Callahan 2009, 7). In the early 1900s, however, the benefits of surgery were being questioned and parents started becoming more involved, gaining access to more information and support online and in hospitals. This led to corrective surgery being delayed or refused entirely (see Creighton 2001; Shapiro 2010, 169; Clune-Taylor 2019, 692).

In 2006 the "Disorders of Sex Development" [DSD] treatment model was instituted to replace the "Optimal Gender of Rearing" model introduced by John Money and Joan and John Hampson which had been in place since the 1950s. The "Consensus Statement on Management of Intersex Disorders" published by the American and European pediatric endocrine associations stated that surgery should only be performed in "cases of severe virilization" because although it is felt that surgery "relieves parental distress and improves attachment between the child and the parents; the systematic evidence for this belief is lacking" (Lee et al. 2006, 491). However, Catherine Clune-Taylor brings together evidence that proves that "it is now clear that DSD has not brought about a reduction in the frequency with which genital normalizing surgeries are performed on infants unable to provide informed consent," in actual fact, surgery "is performed as frequently as it was before, and may even have increased" (Clune-Taylor 2019, 694). For Clune-Taylor, "DSD aims at securing a specifically cisgendered future for the intersex patient, and is thus, practically speaking, a suite of medical interventions aimed at the clinical production of cisgendered lives" (2019, 690).

Though the medical establishment seems to be going backwards, changing attitudes to intersexuality are helping to pick apart the concept of binary sex because intersex babies reveal invaluable information about "non-intersex" babies: all babies are *made to* fit into the categories of male and female. No baby fits naturally. What all intersex people demonstrate is Butler's point from *Gender Trouble* that sex is as cultural as gender, it is not "natural": "the cultural construction of 'sex' is made all too apparent in the medical management of intersex bodies" (Carroll 2010, 191). This construction becomes "all too apparent" when one focuses on Barbin's and Cal/lie's texts.

Intersex Writers

These debates over how hermaphrodites were seen in the early-modern period are important not just for how these texts could be translated today but for how they were viewed and translated in the past. An adherence to the one-sex model has fed directly into the reception of my first text, Barbin's memoir. David Glover and Cora Kaplan (2009, xiv-xv) state that, according to prevailing medical discourse, it is possible to classify everyone as male or female, "yet, if one looks at 'sex' from the long-term historical perspective recommended by Foucault, the fate of Herculine Barbin suggests that to define identity like this is also to close down some of the options that once had been available to those who felt themselves to be 'different'." They suggest that in Barbin's time people were not made to fit into the labels male or female, a label that was chosen for them. However, while Foucault makes it clear in his introduction to Barbin's memoir that a hermaphrodite was free to choose whichever sex he or she wanted, he also makes it clear that this decision had to be final: "When the time came to marry, the hermaphrodite was free to decide for themselves if they wanted to forever be the sex they had been assigned, or if they preferred the other. The only imperative: to never change" (Foucault 2014, 10, my translation).

Foucault's reading of Barbin and of intersex history is unique compared to the readings made by Glover and Kaplan, by Gilbert or by theorists I will look at in chapter five because it was his reading of the memoir which gave rise to much of the theory through which intersex is discussed. Foucault is not one in a long list but the one at the forefront of research into theories of sex. The imperative that a sex must be chosen demonstrates the fear felt by the medical establishment surrounding these figures: if someone was free to choose a sex it suggests that no sex could be forced upon them, perhaps because one could not be medically "proven" to prevail, but it is equally clear that the hermaphrodite could not be allowed to remain "undecidable". In the late nineteenth century, when Barbin was writing, sex was open to doubt but this was stringently covered up.

What Barbin's memoir and hir treatment show is that the nineteenth-century medical management of intersex bodies was established around the idea that desire revealed "the truth" of the intersex body. Barbin's memoir, *Mes souvenirs* (1874) [My Memoirs], helped make hir the most famous "hermaphrodite" of the nineteenth century (see Dreger 1998) and ze is seen almost as the "original" textual hermaphrodite who started the textual exploration of intersexuality by writing a memoir which "provided the model: speak instead of being spoken about" (Fassin 2014, 241, my translation). Because it is seen as a precedent I choose to explore *Mes souvenirs* as my first intersex text. I read this alongside the 2002 novel *Middlesex*, whose author, Jeffrey Eugenides also draws intertextual inspiration from Barbin's memoir.

Eugenides found Barbin's memoir disappointing: "I expected the memoir to be fascinating, wildly dramatic, as well as revelatory about experiences I myself had no clue about. Unfortunately, Herculine Barbin wrote very much like the convent schoolgirl she was" (Eugenides 2007a). He has his narrator, Calliope Stephanides, find them disappointing too; they "make unsatisfactory reading, and it was after finishing them years ago that I first got the idea to write my own" (Eugenides 2002, 19). Despite this connection, *Mes souvenirs* and *Middlesex* are rarely studied together. One exception can be found in *Intersex: A Perilous Difference* (2008), in which Morgan Holmes uses both Barbin's and Eugenides' texts as case studies for her exploration of the treatment of intersexuals both in history and in fiction. Holmes (2008, 91) criticizes Eugenides for adhering to the idea that desire reveals the truth of the intersex body in *Middlesex*, an idea that, according to her, was still prevalent when she wrote her book in 2008. My reading takes up and advances Holmes' comparison. Arne De Boever (2012) also reads *Middlesex* alongside Foucault's introduction to Barbin's memoir though he does not mention Barbin's own text and he does not consider their translations. These two texts, written centuries apart, both have protagonists who problematize the idea that sex is natural and this in itself causes problems for translation.

To consider why these texts are difficult to translate, I will begin by taking a closer look at each in turn. *Mes souvenirs* was first published by Ambroise Tardieu in 1874 in a medical journal. It then fell into obscurity until the 1970s when it became a cornerstone of much queer theory with its rediscovery by Michel Foucault. He republished the story under the name *Herculine Barbin dite Alexina B* (2014 [1978]) [Herculine Barbin called Alexina B].[3] Barbin was assigned the female sex at birth; however, in hir early twenties ze was declared, by a doctor, to be biologically male. Ze was forced to give up hir job as a teacher and move to Paris to live and work as a man on the railway. There ze wrote hir memoirs until hir suicide. As will already have been apparent, I continue to use epicene pronouns to refer to my protagonists in this chapter. Holmes (2008, 169) also uses epicene pronouns to refer to Barbin, explaining that "my use of 'hir' in such cases is not intended to decide for hir that s/he is transgendered or transsexed, but to allow the recognition of multiple sex and gender identifications." Barbin can definitely be said to have a multiple gender identity because throughout the text ze switches between masculine and feminine gender markers.

While Holmes' case study of Barbin's memoirs touches on the issues involved in translating intersex, her case study of Eugenides' *Middlesex* typifies research into the novel: it completely ignores the translation challenges it engenders. This is quite possibly because *Middlesex* is already in English and translations out of English are not always of primary interest in the anglocentric discipline of transgender studies. The text's protagonist, Cal/lie, like Barbin, is assigned the female sex at birth but does not menstruate during puberty or develop breasts; ze tries to hide this fact for as long as possible but is eventually taken to a doctor who declares hir to be intersex. The doctor offers Cal/lie surgery to become a "proper" girl but ze refuses and therefore never has "corrective" surgery. Cal/lie, therefore, like Barbin, also has a gender identity that is multiple and undecidable.

Conclusions

I argue that one of the ways we can move on from the rigid and binary categorization of babies is to think of intersex people as undecidable, and to see this undecidability as something positive. The search for a "best" sex continues today and has its basis in the nineteenth-century idea of the one-body-one-sex rule, a rule which was created to keep males and females as separate categories (see Dreger 1998, 197; Holmes 2008, 36). These rules forced all human beings to be "decidable" in terms of sex and, preferably heterosexual, in terms of sexuality. My texts involve protagonists who break these rules, who are undecidable in terms of sex and are undecidable in terms of gender and sexuality and my research considers how to make sure that any translation of these texts can continue to break the rules and be faithful to undecidability.

This turn to undecidability is a move away from the use of "ambiguity" to describe intersex people. When describing genitals it seems to mean "not one of two" (the prefix "ambi" points to "two" rather than "more than two"). This, according to the Intersex Society of North America (no date) is not true: "Saying someone has an intersex condition isn't the same as saying she or he was born with 'ambiguous genitalia,' because some people with intersex conditions have genitalia that look pretty typically masculine or feminine." Some intersex people are born with genitalia that would traditionally be called female and then during puberty develop traits which are typically aligned with the masculine sex (this is what happens to Cal/lie). More importantly, Cal/lie is not ambiguous in the sense that ze is a mixture of two genders. Ze is undecidable because ze is an embodiment of the ways in which all human beings are complex.

What is important in the medical management of intersex for my research is that, firstly, surgery seems to demand a binary decision on the part of the surgeon and, secondly, translation into certain languages would seem to demand similar moments of decision by the translator over such elements as gendered pronouns. Thirdly, though, both language and translation can experience and reinvent and, in reinventing, can suggest more flexible and less binary positions and identities. I use the case studies of Barbin and Cal/lie to consider how the surgical decision manifests itself in texts and the treatment of these texts by critics, readers and translators and to consider how we can use translation to think about other, less permanent, options for new-born babies.

In chapter five I shall consider how Barbin and Cal/lie are undecidable medically and how their texts mirror this undecidability by shifting between genres. Most critics short-circuit undecidability and I will read the source texts for specific instances where translation can maintain it. Undecidability can and will be found to affect sex, gender, texts (both fictitious and not), hypertexts, intertexts, translation and transness. As transness is a trope of undecidability so too is undecidability, along with all these other concepts, a trope of transness. Both *Mes souvenirs* and *Middlesex* are undecidable texts about undecidable protagonists and I ask here how translation can deal with both sexual and textual undecidability.

Notes

1 This list is not exhaustive but serves to give an idea of the recent outpouring of literature, both fictional and non-fictional involving intersex characters.

2 Until the early twentieth century intersexuality was known as hermaphroditism but "hermaphroditism in fact retains little purchase outside of myth, since in its most literal sense (the dual possession of full male and female sexual reproductive organs) it has never been known to occur in humans" (Hsu 2011, 91) (see also Intersex Society of North America, no date). "Intersex" was first used in 1901 by German Scientist Richard Goldschmidt (See Intersex Human Rights Australia 2012).

3 Although most commonly known as Herculine, Barbin was christened Adélaïde Herculine Barbin but was known to hir family and friends as Alexina. When ze became a man ze was known as Abel. Throughout the memoir, Barbin uses the pseudonym Camille (which is unisex in French).

5 Close Readings of Intersex Texts

In this chapter I continue to prove that Barbin and Cal/lie are undecidable by carrying out a close reading of their texts. Before I analyze my two source texts in detail and examine linguistic examples of undecidability, a consideration of how the protagonists are undecidable both medically and textually allows me to argue that sexual undecidability is reflected in textual undecidability; and to argue that this is something the translators of these texts should be aware of, and when they are not, the potential for a queer text to be given new life in translation is lost.

Undecidable Intersex Bodies

Here I will examine in more detail the ways in which Barbin and Cal/lie have unreliable and undecidable bodies. In an attempt to explain away Barbin's condition, medical practitioners of the time claimed ze was no hermaphrodite at all: ze was a boy who had been mistaken for a girl; it was thought that Barbin suffered from hypospadias. This was a condition where one is born male but the penis is deformed (see Dreger 1998). The medical reports which were published alongside the memoir tell a slightly different story. The medical journal in which Barbin's memoir was originally published was titled: "La question medico-légale de l'identité dans les rapports avec les vices de conformation des organes sexuels" [The Medical-Legal Issue of Identity in Relation to Irregular Formation of the Sexual Organs] and included all of Barbin's medical reports. Dr Chesnet, a doctor examining Barbin in 1860 (when the intersex condition was first discovered), notes that: she has a small penis or an enlarged clitoris which can become erect but which can only be erect for a limited time; she has only one descended testicle, the left one being higher but able to be produced when pressed; she has a vulva, labia, a feminine urethra independent of an imperforated penis and a short vagina but has never menstruated. He concludes that Alexina is undoubtedly a hermaphrodite, though he then categorizes hir as a man because the masculine sex is dominant (Chesnet 2014, 148–150).

Dr Goujon (2014, 153–158), whose examination comes in 1869 and was carried out post-mortem, reports that "the individual" could play the man or the woman during sex but "he" was sterile in both cases. "He" had an imperforated penis susceptible to erection which could attain the same size as a penis belonging to a regularly formed individual (5 centimetres in length or 2.5 when flaccid);[1] however, this organ was more of an enlarged clitoris than a penis as sometimes in a woman a clitoris could reach the volume of the index finger. He also had a vagina (depth of 6.5 centimetres) ending in a cul-de-sac which would admit the index finger without resistance. Goujon (2014, 159) concludes that after his study it is readily evident that while it may be hard to categorize a child at birth and give him or her a true sex, this becomes much easier once he or she reaches puberty.

The medical discourse of both Chesnet and Goujon serves to demonstrate the determinedness of the medical establishment to find a "true sex" in the face of staggering evidence that one does not exist. To drive home the idea that every person has a "true" sex Goujon (2014, 160) goes so far as to note that men cannot be hermaphrodites. It is a strange position to take after such a clear description of a human being with hermaphroditism, but Goujon evidently thinks that the diagnosis of Barbin as "truly" male effectively "cures" hir of hir hermaphroditism. We saw in chapter four that doctors could not agree on what characteristics made a man or a woman and in Tardieu's journal it is clear that there was no consensus between doctors as to what counted as definitive markers of the female or male sex. Tardieu notes a disagreement between himself and a M. Gallard who attaches "far too much importance to the necessary existence of a protruding penis of several centimetres as a constant sign of the masculine sex" (Tardieu 1874, 40, my translation). Despite these differences of opinion, Barbin was made to become legally male.

Regardless of these medical conclusions, in his introduction to the memoir, Michel Foucault refers to Barbin with both masculine and feminine pronouns.[2] Holmes (2008, 85) criticizes Foucault's introduction because she thinks he accepts Barbin's "true" sex as male following the medical reports. However, Foucault switches between using feminine and masculine gender to refer to Barbin on pages 14–16 and he ultimately believes that "it is clear that it is not from the point of view of the sex finally discovered, or rediscovered, that she writes. It is not the man who finally writes" (Foucault 2014, 17, my translation).

Foucault (ibid.) believes that Barbin is "always for herself without a certain sex" and this is where his introduction can be criticized – in his insistence that Barbin actually has no sex at all. Foucault's mistake is that he believes Barbin lives in a world where sexual identity, as a category, does not exist, that ze has no sex because ze is somehow not regulated, like the rest of humanity, by relations of power. Foucault contradicts his theory of sexuality developed in *The History of Sexuality, Volume I*, as also noted by Butler (2006, 127): she makes it very clear that Foucault's introduction is a misreading because: "Whether 'before' the law as a multiplicitous sexuality or 'outside' the law as an unnatural transgression, those positionings are invariably 'inside' a discourse which produces sexuality and then conceals that production" (134).[3] Butler objects to the notion that there can be a "self-relation" before power; even if we did suppose that Barbin had no identity, Butler's point is that a "non-identity" is still situated in relation to the structures which create identity. Foucault undermines his later argument that while the individual can never escape power, he or she can find ways to subvert it. And, in subverting power the individual can find a position where he or she might otherwise have been excluded.

Within the memoir Barbin is known as Camille, though in reality ze was Herculine when "female" and Abel when "male;" Eugenides' novel tells the story of Calliope, or both Callie and Cal, who is also considered to be intersex but unequivocally male by the medical characters that come into contact with hir. Despite this, and in opposition to Barbin's actual treatment, Cal/lie is offered surgery to continue living as a female. Ze is referred to Dr Luce of the Sexual Disorders and Gender Identity Clinic of New York Hospital whose report on Cal/lie reads thus:

> At birth, somatic appearance was of a penis so small as to appear to be a clitoris. The subject's XY karyotype was not discovered until puberty, when she began to virilise [...]. During examination, undescended testes could be palpated. The "penis" was slightly hypospadic [...] Blood tests confirmed an XY chromosomal status. In addition, blood tests revealed that the subject was suffering from 5-alpha-reductase deficiency syndrome.
>
> (Eugenides 2002, 434–435)

Here, Eugenides is replicating medical discourse, not only by using medical terms but also by putting "penis" in quotation marks. He is ironising the ideology of "true" sex within medical discourse; Dr Luce believes Cal/lie's true sex to be male but because hir "best" sex is actually female, the "penis" is not really a penis. Because Cal/lie is a girl in Dr Luce's eyes ze is characterized by a lack even when ze is not actually lacking: "[women's] lot is that of 'lack,' 'atrophy' (of the sexual organ), and 'penis envy,' the penis being the only sexual organ of recognized value" (Irigaray 1985, 23). 5-alpha-reductase deficiency from which Cal/lie suffers is a form of male pseudohermaphroditism which leads to children who seem like "perfect" girls becoming male during puberty. It can sometimes be caused by genetics and Eugenides bases Cal/lie's deficiency on an incestuous relationship between hir grandparents who are a brother and sister who married on the crossing from Greece to America.

The recommendation that Cal/lie have surgery to become female is made on the basis that ze has been a successful girl up to the age of fourteen (Eugenides 2002, 437). It is also made on the basis of Cal/lie's answer when asked if ze is attracted to boys or girls. Ze makes strategic use of heteronormative assumptions and tells Dr Luce that ze likes boys (ibid.), even though ze spends hir school years in love with a girl known only as "The Obscure Object". Dr Luce tells Cal/lie that ze is a girl but that ze needs surgery. Hbelieves he knows best and, given Eugenides' use of the "speaking name" "Luce" which means "light" in Italian, the reader is meant to assume that the doctor is (that all doctors are) enlightened and therefore correct.

In hir appointments with Dr Luce, Cal/lie is surrounded by an imperative to make a decision about hir sex and as we shall see from a close analysis of *Middlesex* below, Cal/lie can never make such a decision. As Dr Goujon (2014, 159) claimed that it is easy to "know" someone's sex from puberty (the implication being that we then know which sex they desire), Dr Luce feels that Cal/lie should live as a woman because ze said ze was attracted to men. However, Cal/lie thinks ze should live as a man because ze is attracted to women. Cal/lie makes a confession to Dr Luce which is actually a lie, ze is saying what ze thinks Dr Luce wants to hear and is following a (heterosexual) script. This mirrors the way that many transsexuals, when applying to doctors for permission to have surgery, would say what they knew their doctors needed to hear as opposed to what they really felt (see Shapiro 2010, 103).

Cal/lie is being incited to tell "the truth" about hir sexual desires: through confession the subject owns their "core" sexual identity which is then monitored and controlled. Despite what he writes in his introduction to Barbin's text, according to Foucault (1978, 101), discourses of knowledge (telling the truth) and power (controlling the subject), are productive as well as constraining. These discourses limit what we can do but they also open up new ways of thinking about ourselves. Because Cal/lie is confused about how to remain heterosexual in the eyes of society, ze runs from the discourse of power which tries to control hir, to categorize hir, and ze ultimately remains intersex and undecidable. Holmes (2008, 91) criticizes Eugenides for his assumption, popular in Barbin's time, that "desire reveals something innate, and inherently true, about one's sex." However, just as Eugenides mimics medical discourse in Dr Luce's report, he could also be parodying the medical management of sex here to shine a light on the fact that desire still plays a big role in decisions about sex. According to Arne De Boever (2012, 56), "*Middlesex* [...] reflects Judith Butler's critique of Michel Foucault – the fact that Foucault, in his introduction to Herculine Barbin's memoirs, appears to present hermaphroditism as a sex outside of power." Cal/lie does not exist outside of power (in the same way that Barbin cannot) as we see with

Dr Luce's attempts to categorize hir. Barbin and Cal/lie present the reader with a decision that cannot be made. They both subvert the discourses of power: neither is made decidable through surgery and both make their undecidability manifest by writing it down.

What Barbin does is use the binary gender system to create a place for hirself with linguistic gender, a place which is not completely destroyed by prevailing medical discourse because it appears in hir memoir. Barbin uses the linguistic binary, which could be said to preclude hir undecidability, to hir advantage, as Erauso and d'Eon do. Both Barbin and Cal/lie need ways to express gender fluidity because they have bodies which do not fit the norm and, after an examination of their texts' undecidability, I will demonstrate that translation can provide them with these ways.

Undecidable Intersex Texts

I have been considering the bodies represented in these texts as "undecidable" and now I want to show that the texts themselves participate in, and add to, this undecidability. When Tardieu reproduced Barbin's memoir in his journal he did not leave it unedited; in a footnote on the first page he writes "I reproduce here the text almost in its entirety as it was transmitted to me. I remove only the passages which prolong the story without adding any interest" (Tardieu 1874, 63, my translation). When Barbin starts hir new life in Paris, he inserts a comment in square brackets:

> Here ends the truly interesting part of the memoirs of the young B … […] from this day on, his sad life is consumed with bitter reflections on his fate. He stays 5 years in the Company offices and spreads recriminations on everything and everyone […] His journal is nothing but a parade of complaints and contradictory declamations.
>
> (159, my translation)

This is not a footnote but an aside in the main text; the reader cannot miss it. Tardieu does not explicitly state here that he has cut parts of the following pages of the memoir but we can perhaps deduce from his tone and his early editorial note that he did cut some of the more repetitive and self-indulgent passages, of which we can assume there were a few.

According to Andrea Rossi (2013, 187), when the journal was first published in French it was "without any commentary accompanied only by a number of archival materials […] documenting the cultural and scientific resonance of the story in the nineteenth century: a critical gaze deliberately leaving an interrogative mark over the ambiguity of the text." Given that, along with these archival materials, Tardieu included his own introduction to Barbin's text and annotated the memoir, it is hard to see how the journal comes "without any commentary." However, these extra materials certainly do add to the undecidability of the text. By including these extra texts Tardieu almost changes the genre of Barbin's work from memoir to case history. He moves it from the singular to the exemplary, a move that is linked to the work of power and categorization. Through his intervention, Barbin's text is now, and will always be, pervaded with medical discourse. And Tardieu's introduction certainly did not leave an interrogative mark over Barbin's ambiguity but attempted to eradicate it entirely. In the introduction, Tardieu (1874, 62) assumes that there is a true sex, that it can be discovered, and that, in Barbin's case, it is male.

Foucault republished the memoir in 1978 with its new title (*Herculine Barbin dite Alexina B.*) and despite Tardieu's assurance that Barbin is male, he uses the feminine in "dite" [called], emphasizing what he tells us in his preface. Foucault's publication, republished by Gallimard in 1994 and 2014, frames the memoir with paratexts: before the memoir comes a preface by Foucault himself and after the memoir comes a dossier which includes Tardieu's introduction, the medical reports that were made on Herculine pre- and post-mortem, legal documents pertaining to Herculine's change of name and hir birth certificate, a story written by Oscar Panizza called "A Scandal in the Convent" which was loosely based on Herculine's story and a postface by Eric Fassin. An extra frame is also added due to the fact that it was Foucault that rediscovered this text and without his intervention it would not be widely available today. The front cover of the English translation actually gives the impression that Foucault is the sole author of the text (see also Gomolka 2012, 63 who sees Foucault's interference as presenting more of a "biography" than an autobiography).[4] Foucault's entire *oeuvre* thus frames the memoir as does all the criticism of Foucault's preface discussed above.

The addition of paratexts to Barbin's work moves the text even further away from the genre of "memoir". However, just because Barbin originally titled hir work "My Memoirs" it does not mean that its "true" genre is that of memoir (or that "memoir" is a singular genre). As discussed in chapter one, as with any life-writing, the narrative is not a simple retelling of the "truth," as GT Couser (2012, 9) states: "Especially in life writing [...] genre is not about mere literary form, it's about force – what a narrative's purpose is, what impact it seeks to have on the world." The purpose of Barbin's narrative is, I would argue, to tell hir story in hir own words; as Fassin (2014, 250, my translation) says, "Barbin is not 'called,' she (or he) calls hirself." This is a nod to Foucault's title and an acknowledgment of the fact that Barbin constructs hir story, like any writer. There is, as in all texts, a double structure of "story" and "discourse" (Bennett and Royle 2004, 55), the telling of the actions versus the way they are told. These two levels are always present in both fiction and life-writing and this means that it is sometimes hard to tell whether a text is a novel or a memoir, given that they share many narrative techniques. Memoir is simply another way of constructing a self, an identity, a "sex". There is no true genre, just as there is no true sex, no matter how hard we study the "internal evidence".

In what is a common trope of life writing, Barbin (2014, 58, my translation) declares that hir memoir is stranger than fiction:

> When I return to this distant past, I believe myself dreaming!!! Only memories of this sort crowd my imagination!!! If I were to write a novel, I could, on interrogating these memories, provide more dramatic and striking pages than were ever created by an A. Dumas, a Paul Féval!!!

In a similar vein to Erauso and d'Eon, Barbin writes a persona which masks hir "true" self, and part of hir inspiration could in fact have been what also inspired d'Eon in hir autobiography, namely Rousseau's *Confessions* (Tidd 2000, 77). But just as we discovered that d'Eon's and Erauso's texts-as-confessions (and Erauso's actual confessions) were not necessarily a revelation of who they really were, Barbin cannot possibly communicate the "truth" and there is no "true" self and certainly no singular self. We can hear Abel's voice in Camille's story at a time when the Camille of the story should not know of Abel's forthcoming existence: narrator and writer are conflated. As we saw in chapter one, memoir is not without an agenda: the act of writing a memoir does not put down on paper a life that pre-existed the writing, it actually creates that life; it is the record of a new becoming. This reflects the medical establishment's "creation" of intersex: just as the self is not discovered but created by writing, the intersex person is not discovered but created by the medical establishment. Identity is created; it is not already there.

Barbin frequently uses the literary device of pathetic fallacy to allude to hir future. For example, when a storm arrives: "Était-ce un présage de l'avenir sombre et menaçant qui m'attendait? […] ce fougueux orage n'était que le prélude de ceux qui m'assaillirent depuis!!!" (Barbin 2014, 36–37) [was it a presage of the sombre and menacing future which awaited me? […] This explosive storm was only the prelude to those which assailed me afterwards]. In what Butler (2006, 135) calls a "kind of confessional production of the self," Barbin creates a character who is more melodramatic than the Barbin who lived, ze can do this because of the blurring of genres between the autobiography and the novel. Barbin precisely chooses the parts of hir life to include and those to exclude, and those to embellish, and which order to put them in.

According to Couser (2012, 57), "fiction can go where memoir cannot, even when – perhaps *especially* when – it *simulates* memoir." Jeffrey Eugenides' 2002 novel *Middlesex* does exactly that and his "memoiristic" fiction makes for an interesting comparison with Barbin's fictional memoir. It is the undecidable genre of the text that marks the undecidability we perceived in Cal/lie's life in the preceding section. This is something that De Boever (2012, 43) notes as well: "it is only this indeterminate hovering between two realms of signification – fact and fiction – that can do justice to the ambiguity of Cal's life." The literary experimentation found in *Middlesex* complicates the relation between what is true, primary, original, natural and what is deviant, secondary, belated, cultural; these relations are further complicated in the trans body and in translation.

Cal/lie's self-discovery begins with the clinical report written by Dr Luce, a report that represents intersex medical intervention. Barbin is also interpellated by the medical apparatus and this begins hir process of self-actualization and self-fashioning. Barbin's text makes clear how writing makes the autobiographical subject and Eugenides makes clear how the medical establishment makes the intersex subject. Cal/lie writes a "Psychological Narrative" (Eugenides 2002, 417) for Dr Luce; like Barbin's narrative, it is a confession in which the confessant is the actor, but an actor who cannot act without hindsight nor outside of the prevailing discourses:

> Sing, Muse, how cunning Calliope wrote on that battered Smith Corona! Sing how the typewriter hummed and trembled at her psychiatric revelations! […] On that new-fangled but soon-to-be obsolete machine I wrote not so much like a kid from the Midwest as a minister's daughter from Shropshire […]. Half the time I wrote like bad George Eliot, the other half like bad Salinger.
>
> (417–418)

This excerpt is also a good example of Eugenides' constant use of intertextuality and mythological references. "Sing, Muse, how cunning Calliope …" references the fact that Calliope, meaning "fair voice," is one of the nine Greek Muses; she is the Muse of epic poetry and also the mother of Orpheus. As the Muse of epic poetry it is possible that Calliope is the Muse of the opening line of Homer's *The Odyssey:* "Tell me, Muse, the story of …" (Homer 2003, 3; see Freely 2014, 101). However, Homer never mentions the Muse by name. This all points to Eugenides' desire to have the novel read like a "comic epic" (Eugenides 2007a).

Cal/lie writes for Dr Luce, for a specific audience. In this *mise-en-abîme* plot device, Eugenides has Cal, the narrator, write an autobiography (*Middlesex* as a whole) in which Callie, the narrator's "past" self, also writes an autobiography. This use of the autobiographical genre brings us back to the point that life writing is self-invention, that, as we have already seen, the discourse of autobiography produces the subject it seeks to know. Because Callie admits to fictionalising hir "psychological narrative," doubt is thrown onto Cal's framing autobiography – Cal/lie's first attempt at writing is a pretence but it is "crucially, performative in that it serves to produce an identity contingent on the needs of a specific moment" (Carroll 2010, 194; see also De Boever 2012, 64). Eugenides is explicitly commenting on the process of writing autobiography which is always performative. Indeed, Eugenides wanted to perform Barbin's memoir again; when asked in an interview where his inspiration for *Middlesex* came from, Eugenides (2007a) answered that it was after reading *Herculine Barbin: Memoir of a 19th Century French Hermaphrodite*: "The memoir frustrated my readerly expectation. I thought to myself, rather hubristically, that I'd like to write the story myself."

In making a direct comparison between *Middlesex* and *Mes souvenirs*, Eugenides points back to the fictional nature of Barbin's text but also to the fact that Barbin uses narrative power from a marginal position as a way of speaking instead of being spoken about. Cal/lie's story, however, has to be different from Barbin's because of the narrative voice. Fiction enables the voice to be complex and incomplete; it puts voice (which implies many things, including sex) on the stage. Not only is Cal/lie an omniscient narrator, comprehensively relating the story of hir grandparents' migration from Greece to America during a time when ze was not even alive, but ze is also an Anglophone voice which uses different, less gendered linguistic gender than French (or Spanish). What makes both *Middlesex* and *Mes souvenirs* difficult to translate are the narrative techniques employed by both Eugenides and Barbin that make the texts and their protagonists undecidable, especially in relation to narrative voice which only adds to this undecidability. In the next section I will look at the translation challenges posed by these two texts in close detail.

Translating Barbin

Herculine Barbin dite Alexina B was translated by Richard MacDougall in 1980 and given the English title *Herculine Barbin, Being the Recently Discovered Memoirs of a Nineteenth-Century French Hermaphrodite*. In the same way that the translators of Erauso's text chose a more sensationalist title for their translation, MacDougall's can also be seen as varying quite significantly, not only from Foucault's choice of title, but also from Barbin's. The new title removes ownership of the text from Barbin hirself: they are no longer "my" memoirs but the memoirs of "a French hermaphrodite". As Fassin (2014, 250) has noted, the memoir gives Barbin a chance to speak instead of being spoken about, but this title removes that agency. Furthermore, this new title labels Barbin as intersex from the beginning.

The title is not the only part of the translation to come under fire: MacDougall's translation of the paratexts has also been criticized, especially his translation of Tardieu's introduction which is included in the texts that come after Barbin's memoir. Holmes (2008, 82–83) states that "in the first sentence Tardieu refers to Alexina only in ambiguous third-person pronouns. In the second sentence, however, Tardieu unequivocally declares Alexina to be 'ce pauvre malheureux,' a clearly male subject." MacDougall cannot be as ambiguous as Tardieu in the first instance. In French, possessive pronouns anaphorize the possession and not the possessor so Tardieu (1874, 61) can write "on va voir la victime d'une semblable erreur, après vingt ans passés sous les habits d'un sexe qui n'est pas le sien" [we shall see the victim of a similar error, after twenty years spent in the clothes of a sex which was not his/her own]. The masculinity of "le sien" refers to the fact that "un sexe" is masculine. While English can maintain the ambiguity of "victim," MacDougall had to choose a gender for the pronoun possessing "sex" (or use an epicene pronoun): "We are about to see the victim of such an error, who, after spending twenty years in the clothing of a sex that was not his own [...]" (MacDougall 1980, 122). Holmes (2008, 83) takes this as indicating that MacDougall "papers over Tardieu's initial ambiguity and pronounces Alexina to be male, illustrating rather clearly that the translator apprehended Tardieu's final decision regarding Barbin's sex to be the only relevant decision." MacDougall does pronounce Alexina to be male but it is impossible to tell if Tardieu really meant to be ambiguous in the first instance or if the rules of the French language simply inadvertently produced the ambiguity.

When it comes to the memoir itself, MacDougall does not show Barbin's switches between masculine and feminine grammatical gender. He merely makes a note in his translation of Foucault's preface:

> In the English translation of the text, it is difficult to render the play of the masculine and feminine adjectives which Alexina applies to herself [...] The editors of the English-language edition have followed Herculine's system wherever possible, italicizing the feminine nouns which she used in referring to herself.
>
> (MacDougall 1980, xiii-xiv)

This system of italicising follows Foucault who, in turn, follows Tardieu. On the first page of *Mes souvenirs*, Tardieu (1874, 63, my translation) writes in a footnote: "the words marked here in italics are underlined in the manuscript, because the author has introduced the visible affectation of speaking of themselves sometimes in the masculine, and sometimes in the feminine." Italics are only used for the feminine gender, masculine gender being "unmarked," with one exception which we shall come to in the first example. For Tardieu, this underlining is merely an "affectation" and says nothing about the truth of Barbin's gender. Foucault does not mention it at all, as his focus is the medical aspect of the text and not literary criticism, though I am arguing here that the literary invention present in the text is precisely what encourages us not to medically categorize Barbin (or at least to categorize hir as "undecidable").

Following on from the fact that Foucault's preface appeared in the American version before the French, Fassin (2014, 253) thinks that the American version has covered over the French in terms of the gender play because this play has been completely forgotten, even Butler (2006) does not mention it. It is only on page 58 of the translation that the reader is given a clue to the fact that Camille is referred to with the masculine when ostensibly a woman (though not that ze uses the masculine to refer to hirself): "[Sara] took pleasure in using masculine qualifiers for me, qualifiers which would later suit my official status" (MacDougall 1980, 58). The translation overshadows the source text to the target text reader's detriment. Even though MacDougall does what Foucault does, and in that sense has produced a "faithful" translation, for me, the system of italicising is not enough to replicate the gender play in English.

It could be said that, by failing to replicate the gender play, MacDougall translates in a manner which "neutralizes" or "un-queers" Barbin's text; it places hir back in a binary that hir own text was trying to undo (see also Gomolka 2012, 69). Barbin switches between a masculine and feminine gender identity on the very first page of hir memoir:

> J'ai vingt-cinq ans et quoique jeune encore, j'approche, à n'en pas douter, du terme fatal de mon existence. J'ai beaucoup souffert, et j'ai souffert seul! seul! abandonné de tous! [...] *Soucieux* et rêveur, mon front semblait s'affraisser sous les poids de sombres mélancolies. J'étais *froide*, timide, et en quelque sorte, insensible à toutes ces joies bruyantes et ingénues qui font épanouir un visage d'enfant.
>
> (Barbin 2014, 25)

> [I am twenty-five years old and although young still, I am without doubt approaching the fatal term of my existence. I have suffered much and suffered alone(m)! Alone(m)! Abandoned(m) by everyone. *Worried*(m) and dazed(m), my forehead seemed to cave under the weight of sombre melancholies. I was *cold*(f), shy, and in some way, indifferent to all those noisy and naïve joys which bring smiles to the faces of children].
>
> I am twenty-five years old, and, although I am still young, I am beyond any doubt approaching the hour of my death. I have suffered much, and I have suffered alone! Alone! Forsaken by everyone

[…] Anxious and brooding, my brow seemed to sink beneath the weight of dark melancholic thoughts. I was cold, timid, and, in a way, indifferent to all those boisterous and ingenuous joys that light up the faces of children.

(MacDougall 1980, 3)

From the first page, MacDougall has reneged on his decision to imitate Barbin's use of italics, as "cold" is not italicized to match "*froide*". Furthermore, we can see in the masculine "soucieux" that italics are not just used to feminize words, MacDougall has also failed to italicize this, however.

Barbin can use both masculine and feminine grammatical gender because ze is writing after the discovery of hir intersex status. A common trope of life-writing, is not to begin at the start but at a point in the middle or near the end and then travel back to the beginning to continue to tell the story chronologically (Couser 2012, 64). Starting the narrative at the age of twenty-five instead of at birth may actually be conventional, but in the case of Barbin's memoir it presents quite singular problems as we are forced to attend carefully to the gendering of both the Barbin who writes and the Barbin being written about; though at times the distinction between the two does not hold. According to Livia (2001, 179), "the solipsistic masculine qualifiers *soucieux* and *rêveur* apply equally to the Camille of the time of writing and the Camille of long ago, while the socially oriented feminine *froide* and *timide* apply only to the earlier Camille".[5] Livia's argument suggests that she thinks that the Abel who writes has entirely rejected hir feminine identity but, only a page later she says: "through the use of the French linguistic gender system, Camille lets the reader know of her painful gender ambiguity from the first page of the narrative" (180). The question then becomes whether Camille is always undecidable or whether hir undecidability is an effect of alteration through time.

Whether Barbin really is undecidable throughout the text needs addressing because MacDougall seems to think that hir switch from feminine to masculine grammatical gender is fairly clear cut. In the same footnote in which he notes the difficulty of replicating Barbin's use of adjectives, he states that these adjectives are "for the most part, feminine before she possessed Sara and masculine afterward" (MacDougall 1980, xiii). I shall return to this point in a moment. Barbin has sex with hir lover Sara, daughter of Madame P…, headmistress of the school where Barbin teaches, at almost precisely the mid-point of the memoir. And it is true that here ze uses masculine grammatical gender:

Sara *m'appartenait* désormais!! … *Elle était à moi*!!! … Ce qui, dans l'ordre naturel des choses, devait nous séparer dans le monde nous

> avait unis!!! Qu'on se fasse, s'il est possible, une idée de notre situation à tous deux! Destinés à vivre dans la perpétuelle intimité de deux sœurs [...] Assurément j'étais moins troublé, mais je n'avais pas la force de lever les yeux sur madame P ..., pauvre femme qui ne voyait en moi que *l'amie* de sa fille, tandis que j'étais son amant! ...
>
> (Barbin 2014, 75)
>
> [From then on, Sara *belonged to me*!! ... *She was mine*!!! ... What should, in the natural order of things, separate us in the world had united(m) us!!! That one could have, if it's possible, an idea of the situation we were both(m) in! Destined(m) to live in the perpetual intimacy of two sisters [...] Assuredly I was less troubled(m), but I didn't have the strength to look Madame P in the eyes, poor woman who only saw me as her daughter's *friend*(f), when really I was her lover(m)!]
>
> Henceforth, Sara *belonged to me*!! ... *She was mine*!!! ... What, in the natural order of things, ought to have separated us in the world had united us!!! Try to imagine, if that is possible, what our predicament was for us both! Destined to live in the perpetual intimacy of two sisters, [...] Undoubtedly, I was less disturbed, but I did not have the strength to raise my eyes to Madame P. Poor woman, she saw me only as her daughter's *girlfriend*, while in fact I was her lover!
>
> (MacDougall 1980, 51–52)

In the French Barbin writes "unis," "tous" and "destinés" as masculine plural. Because in French the masculine is seen as the standard and always takes precedence over the feminine, these could refer to one man and one woman or two men but not two women. Barbin's use of the masculine here is a usurpation through language which, according to Butler (2006, 136), shows that Barbin is using the binary categories which would normally be seen as precluding hir undecidability; this also shows "the denaturalized and fluid possibilities of such categories once they are no longer linked causally or expressively to the presumed fixity of sex." Barbin is finding hir voice by using the gender binary against itself.

To ascertain whether Barbin's use of shifting gender identity is as simple as feminine before possession and masculine after possession of Sara, I counted the instances of both masculine and feminine grammatical gender markers before and after the incident, which can be seen in Table 5.1. Does the text have a linear narrative of development: female – sexual encounter – male?

Barbin is not made male by hir sexual dominance of Sara. Though clearly the emphasis does shift, Barbin is not unequivocally female then unequivocally male though MacDougall's translation suggests otherwise.

Table 5.1 Gender markers before and after page 75 of *Herculine Barbin dite Alexina B.* (2014)

	Before possession of Sara	*After possession of Sara*
Feminine gender markers	98	36
Masculine gender markers	15	114

Barbin is indefinite, or, using my terminology, undecidable. To emphasize my point I elucidate some examples of shifting grammatical gender both before and after the "possession" on page 75 of the memoir in Table 5.2.

While Livia (2001: 177) and MacDougall argue for a more or less permanent switching of gender in the scene where Barbin possesses Sara, Wing (2004: 107) argues for that shift when Camille writes in Paris:

> Et maintenant seul! ... seul! ... pour toujours! Abandonnéproscrit au milieu de mes frères! [...] De mon arrivée à Paris, date une nouvelle phase de ma double et bizarre existence. Elevé pendant vingt ans au milieu de jeunes filles, je fus d'abord et pendant deux années, au plus, femme de chambre. À seize ans et demi j'entrais en qualité d'elève-maitresse à l'école normale de ... À dix-neuf ans j'obtins mon brevet d'*institutrice*.
>
> (Barbin 2014: 122)

> [And now alone(m)! ... Alone(m)! ... Forever! Abandoned(m), excluded(m) amongst my brothers! [...] From my arrival(f) in Paris, dates a new phase of my double and bizarre existence. Brought up(m) for twenty years amongst young girls, I was at first and for two years at most, a chamber maid. At sixteen and a half I entered the normal school of ... as a student-teacher(f). At nineteen I obtained my qualification as a teacher(f)].
>
> And now, alone! ... alone ... forever! Forsaken, outlawed in the midst of my brothers! [...] My arrival in Paris marks the beginning of a new phase of my double and bizarre existence. Brought up for twenty years among girls, I was first and for two years at the most a *lady's maid*. When I was sixteen and a half I entered the normal school of ... as a student-teacher. When I was nineteen I obtained my teaching certificate.
>
> (MacDougall 1980: 98)

Table 5.2 Examples of gender markers before and after page 75 of *Herculine Barbin dite Alexina B.* (2014)

Before possession	*After possession*
Page 40: 'heureux' [happy] (masculine)	Page 76: 'fou' [mad] (masculine)
Page 44: 'heureux' [happy] (masculine)	Page 77: 'assis' [seated] (masculine)
Page 49: 'honteux' [ashamed] (masculine)	Page 78: 'arrivé' [arrived] (masculine)
Page 71: 'jalouse' [jealous] (feminine)	Page 79: 'inculpée' [accused] (feminine)
Page 73: 'émue' [moved] (feminine)	Page 80: 'invitée' [invited] (feminine)
Page 74: 'folle' [mad] (feminine)	Page 81: 'seule' [alone] (feminine)

Barbin (2014, 132) does actually use feminine grammatical gender again in a passage where ze indirectly relays what a fellow railway worker has said: "Il croyait tout bonnement que *recherchée* un jour par un jeune homme, je m'étais *rendue* à ses désirs" [he simply thought that I was *sought*(f) one day by a young man to whose desires I *gave*(f) myself]. This use of feminine gender could be a representation of what the man said but given its indirect nature we can never be sure of this.

Once this "turning point" has been reached, Barbin slips into despair and kills hirself. Once ze is legally male ze cannot seem to find a way back to being female except in the writing down of hir past life. Barbin's shifting linguistic gender identity is what makes hir undecidable; in hir time this undecidability is what ultimately killed hir because sexual undecidability was unacceptable. After an exploration of *Middlesex* I ask if there is a way for translation to resurrect undecidability and to eradicate the impasse that shifting identity sometimes engenders.

Translating Cal/lie

Cal/lie Stephanides also has a shifting, anomalous gender identity and it too proves to be an obstacle in translation, not least because some readers cannot see it. Eugenides (2007a) claims that *Middlesex* was intended to "encompass many things aside from this sexual metamorphosis. It would concern all kinds of transformations, national, emotional, intellectual – you name it." Daniel Mendelsohn (2002) believes that these other transformations, especially the transformation of Cal/lie's family from Greek to American, completely overshadow the intersex storyline (cf. De Boever 2012, 5). It is certainly the case that the attempt to incorporate these multiple strands has an effect on the narrative; to tell all of these stories, Eugenides (2007b) had to write the novel from a hybrid perspective: "Gradually I came up with a hybrid voice, well-suited to my theme, that shifted from first- to third-person on a dime." Forty-something Cal/ie is the narrator of the text. This Cal/lie, who lives in Berlin, takes on the third-person voice to tell the story of hir grandparents' emigration from Greece to America and the first-person voice to tell the story of hir childhood, from birth to the age of fifteen. Throughout these two main narrative strands Cal/lie interjects to tell hir "current" story.

Numerous critics of *Middlesex* (Carroll 2010, 196; Cohen 2007, 376; Holmes 2008, 93; Hsu 2011, 92; Merton 2010, 45; Shostak 2008, 408) argue that the shifting, hybrid voice created by Eugenides does not work, and does not even exist. Mendelsohn (2002) thinks that the Cal writing and the Callie being written about are split in two like the book: "one is a fairly ordinary Midwestern girl [...], the other all-too-typically sardonic, post-everything American male. But like the two parts of the novel they inhabit, neither seems to have much to do with the other." This echoes D'Erasmo's criticism of another twenty-first-century intersex novel, *Annabel*. She feels that the two "halves" of the protagonist, Wayne and Annabel, are two separate characters. This comparison shows that not only do writers of intersex novels come under heavy scrutiny for signs of "authenticity" (perhaps more than writers of cis-gender characters) but also that critics seem to be so intent on proving that intersex characters have two distinct identities, one "before discovery" and one "after discovery," that they do not make enough effort to perceive undecidability, they under-read the text. I claim this because there is textual evidence to demonstrate the confusion between Cal and Callie akin to that produced between the textual Camille and the writing Barbin.

Reading *Middlesex* closely, we can argue that it is frequently hard to distinguish when Cal is speaking and when Callie is speaking. At the beginning of chapter five, the narrator reminisces about Detroit and says "I am nine years old and holding my father's meaty, sweaty hand [...] I have come downtown for our annual lunch date. I am wearing a miniskirt and fuchsia tights" (Eugenides 2002, 79). The narrator has digressed from the main narrative and uses the vivid present which makes it clear that this is a memory. But the use of the present tense also complicates the voice: for me this is an example of the voice of Cal/lie, both Cal the narrator and Callie the nine-year-old combined. The present is haunted by the past here to the extent that the past becomes the present; the use of the first-person voice suggests that identity-through-time does not stay the same but that what is past is never truly past but also always present. Eugenides uses the vivid present sporadically throughout the novel:

> Getting to my feet (as we did whenever Miss Barrie entered the room), I hear her ask, "Infants? Can any of you translate this little snippet and give its provenance?"
>
> I raise my hand.
> "Calliope, our muse, will start us off."
> "It's from Ovid. *Metamorphoses.* The story of creation."
> (Eugenides 2002, 198)

Like Barbin's Camille who always includes Abel and vice versa, Cal always includes Callie and vice versa.

I have shown that it is difficult to analyze "the Cal who narrates" and to come to any definitive conclusions about that voice. The complicated narrative voice is tricky for translation into French and Spanish, two languages which must show gender where English does not. Just as with Barbin, Cal/lie narrates knowing hir intersex status. The translator must decide if Cal/lie has made a definitive choice about "his" gender role as male or if it is possible for Cal/lie to be a hybrid voice. This is easier in Spanish as the preterite tense does not show gender unlike the French *passé composé* which, as we have seen, requires gender on the past participle used with the auxiliary être.

I shall now closely analyze the source text and its translations. After each section from the French and/or Spanish translation, I will supply my own back translation in square brackets. The novel begins:

> I was born twice: first as a baby girl, on a remarkably smogless Detroit day in January of 1960; and then again, as a teenage boy, in an emergency room near Petoskey, Michigan, in August of 1974.
> (Eugenides 2002, 3)

> J'ai eu deux naissances. D'abord comme petite fille, à Detroit, par une journée exceptionnellement claire du mois de janvier 1960, puis comme adolescent, au service des urgences d'un hôpital proche de Petoskey, Michigan en août 1974.
> (Cholodenko 2003, 11)

> [I have had two births. First as a little girl, in Detroit, on an exceptionally clear day in the month of January 1960, then as a teenager(m), in the Emergency Room of a hospital close to Petoskey, Michigan in August 1974].

The Spanish translator, Benito Gómez Ibáñez (2003, 11), conceals gender using the preterite: "nací dos veces" [I was born twice], the noun for a teenager is also invariable in Spanish: "adolescente". However, the French translator, Marc Cholodenko, has to use a noun instead of a verb to conceal gender. "I was born twice" would normally be translated into French as "je suis né(e) deux fois" but this requires a choice of gender; Cholodenko chooses "I had two births" instead. The use of the noun (birth) instead of the verb (to be born) is one way to conceal gender in French. On the first page, Cal also gives a small summary of hir life:

> I'm a former field hockey goalie [...] I've been ridiculed by classmates, guinea-pigged by doctors [...].
>
> (Eugenides 2002, 3)

> Je suis un ancien gardien de but de hockey sur gazon [...] J'ai été la risée de mes camarades, le cobaye des médecins [...].
>
> (Cholodenko 2003, 11)

> [I'm a former(m) field hockey goal keeper(m) [...] I was the laughing stock(f) of my classmates, the guinea-pig of doctors [...]].
> He sido guardameta de hockey sobre hierba [...] Fui ridiculizado por mis compañeros de clase, convertido en conejillo de Indios por los médicos.
>
> (Ibáñez 2003, 11)

> I've been a field hockey goalkeeper [...] I was ridiculed(m) by my classmates, converted(m) into a guinea-pig by doctors [...]].

The Spanish text uses the masculine gender where grammatical gender is necessary (despite ending in an "a," "guardameta" is an invariable noun in Spanish). Ibáñez may have chosen masculine gender because Cal is currently narrating, assuming "he" would choose masculine gender markers. Cholodenko, on the other hand, could be choosing gender based on Cal/lie's gender at the time the activity took place: ze was ridiculed at school as a girl. It is arguable that in the Spanish translation, Ibáñez is reinterpreting Callie's early experiences in the light of what he perceives to be Cal's definitively male narrative voice.

Neither of the translators has a consistent strategy for dealing with the first-person aspects of this text which carry no gender in English. Both do attempt to make gender neutral where possible, and this happens more often in the Spanish translation as it is much easier to make the first-person gender-neutral:

> How did Calliope feel about her crocus? [...] On the one hand she liked it [...] The crocus was part of her body after all. [...] But there were times when I felt that something was different about the way I was made.
>
> (Eugenides 2002, 330)

> Quels sentiments ce crocus faisait-il naître en Calliope? [...] D'un côté il lui plaisait [...] Le crocus faisait partie de son corps après tout. [...] Mais parfois, je sentais qu'il y avait quelque chose de différent dans la façon dont j'étais faite.
>
> (Cholodenko 2003, 427)
>
> [What feelings did this crocus give birth to in Calliope? [...] On the one hand it pleased him/her [...] The crocus was part of his/her body after all. [...] But sometimes, I felt that there was something different in the way I was made(f)].
>
> ¿Qué le parecía a Calíope su croco? [...] Por una parte le gustaba. [...] Al fin y al cabo, el croco formaba parte integrante de su cuerpo [...] Pero a veces notaba
> que tenía una constitución algo diferente de la demás.
>
> (Ibáñez 2003, 423–424)
>
> [How did Calliope think of his/her crocus? [...] On the one hand it pleased him/her. [...] At the end of the day, the crocus formed an integral part of his/her body [...] But at times she/he noted that it had a somewhat different constitution from the rest].

Cholodenko chooses to make the narrative voice feminine here, perhaps following on from the use of "she" in the previous paragraph. Ibáñez, on the other hand, avoids gender by using "I had a different constitution from others" instead of "there was something different in the way I was made" (this would need gender on "made" [hecho/a]). And in Spanish, he can even avoid using the third-person possessive adjective because "su" carries no gender and can be "his" or "her". Furthermore, as we saw with Erauso, personal pronouns are not used as they are denoted in the verb. It is clear here that "I felt that something was different about the way I was made" is being said by the narrator and is being made in hindsight and we cannot know if the "female" Callie really did feel different at the time. What is not so clear, however, is that just because the "I" of the present narration is contrasted to the "she" of the past, the narrator must be male. In both French and Spanish the stakes surrounding the narrative voice and whether it should be male, female or in-between become even higher because the translator can – and in the case of the French translation above, does – choose to explicitly gender the narrative voice.

Despite moments where gender is concealed, Cal/lie ends both translations male. Towards the end of the novel Cal/lie's grandmother, Desdemona, asks hir, "Are you a boy now?" and ze replies "more or less" (Eugenides 2002, 528). Desdemona repeatedly calls Cal/lie "honey" (ibid.) after this question and the translations both make this term of endearment masculine – "chéri" (Cholodenko 2003, 665) [dear] and "cariño" (Ibáñez 2003, 671) [dear] – as if Cal/lie's answer were definitive. On the final page, the French text concludes with masculine grammatical gender: "heureux d'être rentré chez moi" (Cholodenko 2003, 667) [happy(m) to have returned home]. The Spanish text is neutral: "feliz de estar en casa" (Ibáñez 2003, 673) [happy(n) to be at home], this could be inadvertently due to the invariability of "feliz," a common Spanish word for "happy," but Ibañez has avoided the gender choice of contento/contenta, another Spanish word meaning happy.

In believing that Cal/lie is not definitively male I am reading textual undecidability where other critics have not.[6] They want Cal to be free to choose a "middle" way but they then claim that the ending is no middle way at all because "he" ends the novel as a man. At the end of the text, when Cal/lie has returned home for hir father's funeral aged fifteen, ze blocks the doorway of the house to prevent hir father's spirit from returning: "It was always a man who did this, and now I qualified" (Eugenides 2002, 529). Sarah Graham (2009, 1–2) sees this as confirming Cal/lie's maleness. However, she also believes that "the novel appears to end with an affirmation of intersexuality, the possibility of being 'both/and' rather than 'either/or'" (1) because Cal/lie describes hirself as having "the face of my grandfather and of the American girl I had once been" (Eugenides 2002, 529). Graham's contradictory opinions show how difficult it is to pin down the narrative voice.

I have already made it clear that Eugenides' appropriation of medical discourse could be seen as a type of parody; *Middlesex*'s ending makes the reader think about how medical discourse treated intersex children twenty years ago. Society at large wants Cal to be male and desire women (or be female and desire men if Dr Luce had his way), but Cal/lie is not "perfectly" male; as ze never underwent "corrective" surgery ze still has a hypospadic penis and undescended testes. Eugenides' critics are looking to the end of the novel for the answers because the ending is traditionally where all the loose ends are tied up. I that the ending of *Middlesex* is not a place of revelation and understanding where answers are provided even though his critics want to make it so.

Again, a comparison with the reception of Kathleen Winter's *Annabel* is telling. According to D'Erasmo (2011), *Annabel* cannot accomplish what it first sets out to achieve which is a truly undecidable character because while "a transgender or intersex character may open up many possibilities, [...] narrative is often anxious for closure, and so are readers." Winter is apparently caught by the gender binary: "Winter is, moreover, working from the same binary model she is purporting to overturn: the idea that Annabel is a 'girl' – and that this means someone softer, sweeter, gentler, more emotional – is given here" (ibid.). Annabel is too stereotypically feminine for D'Erasmo, and Cal could be accused of being too stereotypically masculine, but crucially, hir masculinity is represented as a performance (Eugenides 2002, 41). While D'Erasmo sees it as negative that Winter is working from the same binary she is trying to overturn, she cannot work from outside of this binary in the same way that Barbin cannot work from outside of the binary but must use the binary against itself.

As if to reiterate that doing a gender is a constant struggle, near the end of the text Cal/lie declares that: "I never felt out of place being a girl. I still don't feel entirely at home among men" (Eugenides 2002, 479). It is definitely the present-day Cal/lie who is the narrator here but I do not see that this voice is conclusively male. Indeed, reading the French translation very closely, I have noticed that Cholodenko uses a play on words between the French homonyms "mal" [bad] and "mâle" [male]:

> Je ne me suis jamais senti **mal** dans ma peau de fille. Je ne me sens toujours pas complètement chez moi parmi les hommes.
>
> (Cholodenko 2003, 606)

> [I have never felt bad in my girl's skin. I still don't feel completely at home among men].

By hinting that Callie never felt male when ze was female Cholodenko is undermining Cal/lie's hindsight. It is an admission that the teenage Callie never felt male before discovering ze was intersex. This adds weight to the idea that the adult Cal/lie might still feel female, even if ze performs masculinity on a daily basis. Yes, Cal/lie ostensibly ends the novel as a "conventional" male but ze still has unconventional genitalia, is only "more or less" a boy and does not feel entirely at home among men. There is an aporia and therefore the queering of these texts through translation so that no definitive conclusion can be reached is important.

The text ends with the fifteen-year-old Cal/lie at hir father's funeral: this in itself is not closure because that should come with the forty-something Cal in Berlin, the narrator. The last we hear of the narrator's current life comes on page 520 (nine pages before the end) where Cal says:

> You will want to know: How did we get used to things? What happened to our memories? Did Calliope have to die to make room for Cal? To all these questions I offer the same truism: it's amazing what you can get used to.
>
> (Eugenides 2002, 520)

The truism Cal offers does not really answer the last question, which most critics would answer as "yes" because of their determination not to see the undecidability in the text; instead, "undecidability splits the text, disorders it. *Undecidability dislodges the principle of a single final meaning* in a literary text. It haunts" (Bennett and Royle 2004: 249, my emphasis). Cal/lie goes on to say, "In most ways I remained the person I'd always been" (Eugenides 2002, 520), a rather cryptic phrase because who Cal/lie has always been and whether ze has "always" been the same person forms the basis of the entire debate around Cal/lie's gender. What this phrase does bring to light though, is that there is a "person" underlying sexual difference.

Most telling of all, Cal/lie the narrator sees Callie as part of hir, something that always resides just beneath the surface, like a ghost:

> When Calliope surfaces, she does so like a childhood speech impediment. Suddenly there she is again, doing a hair flip, or checking her nails. It's a little like being possessed. Callie rises up inside me, wearing my skin like a loose robe [...] Calliope's hair tickles the back of my throat.
>
> (Eugenides 2002, 41–42)

Middlesex is haunted by all of its undecidable endings. Every text is haunted by undecidable endings, though the texts I look at here are extreme examples of undecidable texts where undecidability is overdetermined.

Conclusions

I have analyzed the translations of two undecidable texts involving two undecidable protagonists. Ibáñez and Cholodenko do attempt to maintain some of the undecidability of their source texts but fall short of portraying Cal/lie as truly inter-sex. MacDougall, on the other hand, makes no attempt to portray Herculine as anything other than ultimately male. While any text or translation is undecidable when the reader is taken into account, these particular texts work hard to be undecidable. To emphasize this point and to shine a light on the undecidability of all sex and gender, translations of intersex texts should reveal textual and sexual plurality. Gomolka (2012, 80) suggests that one way of capturing Barbin's shifting gender identity in English could be "achieved by betraying form for function and rephrasing h/er story in the third and not the first person." That Barbin's story is written in the first person, however, is crucial to understanding how the text is a self-fashioning over time – what makes the "self" in autobiography is a haunting of "present" by "past" selves and of "past" by "future" selves. In chapter six I will look to the question of how translation can capture this state of constant haunting.

Notes

1 Throughout Tardieu's journal Barbin is never once "named" as Herculine Barbin but is anonymous, it was Foucault who travelled to places Barbin describes in the memoir, found hir school and "gave" hir back hir name (see Fassin 2014).

2 The introduction was first included with the 1980 American translation, it was first published in French in the journal *Arcadie* and was then published in 1994 in a collection entitled *Dits et écrits*. Before being included in the 2014 text, it had never appeared in a French edition of the text (Fassin 2014).
3 See Fassin 2014: 233 for a defense of Foucault's position.
4 As a parallel to the prominence of Foucault in the English text, according to Fassin (2014, 227), the French version was more or less invisible until the 2014 edition was published *because* Foucault removed himself from the text. It appears that the popularity of the text is indelibly linked to Foucault being present as its discoverer, its champion.
5 We should note that "timide" is not actually feminine in French but invariable.
6 De Boever (2012, 11) does read *Middlesex* as an undecidable novel; for him there is an aesthetic decision in the novel but that decision "is not opposed to undecidability but can only claim to decide, precisely if it decides the undecidable." See also Athanassakis (2011, 218) for an argument for Cal/lie as undecidable.

6 The Hypertext

In this chapter I look at how a translation can manifest the multiple ghosts that it both represents and creates through electronic literature, and more specifically, the hypertext. Through a hypertextual translation, a translation that readily shows its influences and its possibilities, textual and sexual plurality can be revealed. I first look at how *Mes Souvenirs* and *Middlesex* and their narrators are haunted and then I explain the origins of the hypertext and discuss its advantages and disadvantages as an experimental translation method. The chapter ends with a demonstration of my own hypertextual translation of parts of Barbin's memoir.

Translating Haunted Texts

Any work, like any person, is haunted; for Derrida (2006, 166) "to be" is to be haunted: "Ego = ghost. Therefore 'I am' would mean 'I am haunted': I am haunted by myself who am (haunted by myself who am haunted by myself who am... and so forth). Wherever there is Ego, *es spukt*, [...] ([...] 'it returns,' 'it ghosts,' 'it specters')." These specters, which are always there, whether past, present or future cannot be pinned down: "The subject that haunts is not identifiable, one cannot see, localize, fix any form, one cannot decide between hallucination and perception, there are only displacements" (169). They are the bodily equivalent of the textual trace that meaning cannot "pin/pen down" (Derrida 2004, 22) in Derrida's conception of dissemination.

There is no core meaning to a body as there is no core meaning to a text. The work or the person is open to interpretation. If we look at "interpretation" in the Nietzschean sense, "to interpret a text is not to give it a (more or less justified, more or less free) meaning, but on the contrary to appreciate what *plural* constitutes it" (Barthes 1970, 5). For Derrida, dissemination, above plurality, is that which extends the concept of text. The search for bodily and textual meaning is ever-present but ever-frustrated: the hunter is always the prey (Derrida 2006, 175). The hunter looks for the "essence" of the body or the text which is always deferred; and narrative, with its temporal extension, dramatizes this particularity. The hunter is always looking and is always prey to deferral. There is no essence because bodies and texts are made of many layers of meanings and intertexts.

Both Barbin's memoir and Eugenides' novel are intertextual. And this intertextuality reflects the multiplicity of the intersex bodies that are writing – Barbin's and Cal/lie's texts are multiple, they have no single source and neither are they the product of isolated "genius" (just as the intersex body is not the product of one all-knowing doctor). Barbin is influenced by Rousseau's *Confessions* and Ovid's *Metamorphoses* and ze references the story of Salmacis and Hermaphroditus; Eugenides is influenced by Barbin, by stories of Greek mythology and by George Eliot and J. D. Salinger; Eugenides (2007b) himself claims that his "aim was to have this ghost literature haunt the book, there for alert, close readers [...] to notice, but not mandatory for understanding or enjoying the book." George Eliot's influence can be seen in the novel's title; it ostensibly refers to the name of the street Cal/lie lives on in Grosse Pointe but also alludes to the idea of the "inter" or the "in-between". Cal/lie uses the street name to refer to the house ze lives in which is described as "futuristic and outdated at the same time" (Eugenides 2002, 258). The place, like the book as a whole, is undecidable.

If we can find a device to represent these layers of text, the intertext of the memoirs themselves, then we can also represent the layers of body (the intertext of intersex). Here we can continue to see identity, like writing, as grafted. This works well with *Middlesex* because Cal explicitly describes Callie as haunting hir new identity as a man. Callie possesses Cal and Derrida's (2006, 165) point would be that they possess each other *permanently*: "Is not to possess a specter to be possessed by it, possessed period?" Callie is a permanent presence in the text; "she" ghosts Cal but Cal also ghosts "her," just as Abel ghosts Camille and vice versa. We are haunted by what we have yet to become. These hauntings proliferate, they do not disappear but linger on:

> Once the ghost is produced by the incarnation of spirit (the automized idea or thought), when this *first* ghost effect has been operated, it is in turn negated, integrated, and incorporated by the very subject of the operation who, claiming the uniqueness of its *own* human body, then becomes [...] the absolute ghost, in fact the ghost of a ghost of the ghost of the Specter-spirit, simulacrum of simulacra without end. (158–9)

We can return here to Derrida's position which sees "first" texts and bodies as subsumed but not forgotten and the "first" is only the start of a series of many, indeed it is not the "start" because it is always a coming back, a return from something that has always already begun (Derrida 2006, 11).

We can use Derrida's ideas on the specter to give Callie and Camille narrative authority – they are both seemingly written out by Cal's and Abel's narratives, but a reader attuned to undecidability can tell they are still there. Intersex bodies are perhaps haunted more than most because they are also haunted by their own medical records and by literature written on the intersex "condition:" Cal/lie reads dictionary entries, hir medical records and also medical textbooks to try and understand hir condition. Part of hir intertext is monstrosity – the dictionary entry Cal/lie looks up for "hermaphrodite" says "see synonyms at MONSTER" (Eugenides 2002, 430). Etymologically, "monster" comes from the Old French *monstre* which was itself borrowed from the Latin *mōnstrum* meaning not just "monster" but "portent" or "sign" and "perhaps related to *monēre* to warn; see" (Chambers 2001, 675). The monster is that which is on display; evil is something so powerful that it makes a visible mark. What I investigate here through textual analysis is that what is visible (be that genitals or the way a person presents themselves to the outside world) does not constitute who a person is and I continue this line of interrogation in chapter eight.

Eugenides is inspired by "monsters" of Greek mythology: Hermaphroditus, the Minotaur and Tiresias (see Eugenides 2007a). Graham (2009, 2) believes Eugenides' reliance on Greek mythology suggests that the intersex person is a tragic monster and that because the novel looks to transgender figures from the past, it suggests that there are no modern or contemporary models for anyone who is intersex, transgender or queer; queer figures from the past are always tragic and therefore she believes this implies that all queer figures are necessarily tragic (Graham 2009, 7). But I argue that the images of these transgender figures are not damaging, they are not restricted to the past and neither do they suggest that the intersex figure in general, or Cal/lie in particular, is tragic. Indeed, when Barbin (2014: 41) references Ovid and the story of Salmacis and Hermaphroditus, even though ze does so for melodramatic effect, it is not to forecast a tragic ending (something ze does in myriad other ways) but to forecast the discovery of hir hermaphroditism.

Cal/lie is cast as Tiresias in a school play: Tiresias "saw two snakes coupling, and killed the female. Promptly, he was turned into a woman, and so remained until at length, once more seeing a pair of coupling snakes, he killed the male, and regained his former sex" (Rose 2005, 161). For Graham (2009, 6) the links between Cal/lie and Tiresias suggest that Cal/lie's hybridity is a form of punishment. But Tiresias is not a tragic figure, he is a figure used by many writers, especially modernist writers, including T.S. Eliot, to explore ideas of sexual indeterminacy and hybridity. Eliot (2013, 51) uses Tiresias in his poem *The Waste Land*. Indeed, Eliot describes Tiresias as all-seeing, a crucial character, the only one who truly "sees" the poem (Eliot 2013, 77).

Virginia Woolf's *Orlando* can be seen as an updating of the Tiresias myth and many avid readers of the 1920s would have associated

Orlando with Eliot's Tiresias (Ziolkowski 2005, 92). And this appropriation of the Tiresias myth was not just practised by modernists; Angela Carter's 1982 *The Passion of New Eve* is also linked to Tiresias – when the central character, Evelyn, is surgically changed to Eve he/she is called 'Tiresias' (Carter 1982, 71). If anything, Tiresias is used by writers as a positive figure of metamorphosis and omniscience. Tiresias is a powerful figure of the in-between. Ed Madden (2008, 21–22) adds a caveat to Tiresias' power stating that "the Tiresian [...] may not ultimately function as a subversive figure, nor is it necessarily liberatory or progressive in its intents or effects, haunted as it is by images of loss, structures of sacrifice, and dynamics of displacement." That the figure of Tiresias is both progressive and not progressive, haunted by the past and what has been lost but not forgotten makes it a highly appropriate figure through which to think about intersex identity.

As I have already discussed, voice is crucial both to these intersex texts and to their translations and "the Tiresian figure foregrounds the importance of *voice* as a literary, symptomatic and sexological category" (22). The Tiresian voice is one that suggests something transitive, something "interior" that does not match what is "exterior," what can be seen. In all of my texts the voice of the protagonists show that what we see with our eyes cannot be the only marker of gender identity. Barbin and Cal/lie only exist to us on the page. It is in their textual voices that we find their subversion of the gender binary and their rejection of an enforced sexual assignment. This rejection can be seen in the explicit haunting of their identities that emerges in Barbin's use of both masculine and feminine grammatical gender and in Cal/lie's use of the vivid present tense to entangle the (masculine?) character narrating and the (feminine?) character narrated.

Cal/lie is also made monstrous, according to Graham (2009, 5), because hir condition is caused by an incestuous relationship. For Graham, the inclusion of Cal/lie's grandparents' relationship undoes any possibility that the intersexuality in the text can be seen as something positive. I do not agree with this, however. While an incestuous relationship is something negative, what results from something negative does not have to also be negative. Desdemona and Lefty subvert the rules but this subversion leads to Cal/lie's birth and eventually leads to hir own subversion of the gendered scripts society gives us. This demonstrates the idea that relations of power can be subverted. Lefty spends his time in America "working on a modern Greek translation of the 'restored' poems of Sappho" (Eugenides 2002, 12). It is fitting that one half of the cause of Cal/lie's intersexuality should be, not only a translator, but a translator of something both fragmented and queer.

Linking Cal/lie's intersexuality to both mythology and incest through intertextuality reflects the fact that all intertext is monstrous. And people are always mutating; becoming and unbecoming. With this examination of monstrosity in *Middlesex* we can argue that Eugenides does court clichés of monstrosity, but he deploys these clichés to question the category of monstrosity itself. Inter-ness – or intertextuality – is revealed as a general, not a singular, condition – and so by implication, is intersexuality.

Uncanny Becomings

As we have now established that Barbin and Cal/lie are both bodily and textually made of layers, or hauntings, I will now turn to finding a way of revealing, in translation, that both bodies and texts are constantly becoming: "neither complete nor incomplete, [they are] caught up, along with both writer and reader, in a state of perpetual movement and becoming" (Scott 2014a, 50). I want to show that Barbin and Cal/lie are complicated by the ghosts of their past and future becomings. Cal/lie is forever in an in-between space, neither here nor there and after the discovery of hir condition the same sort of displacement happens to Barbin: ze is no longer a teacher but not a railway worker either (we see the same with Erauso and d'Eon who are both divided between two categories, never properly belonging to either – nun/soldier and ambassador/virginal woman). These uncanny becomings are revealed in their writings and so must be revealed in translation. We can use translation to embody that which is a stranger to us, "a stranger who is already found within (*das Heimliche-Unheimliche*), more intimate with one than with oneself [...] whose power is singular *and* anonymous (*es spukt*), an unnameable and neutral power, that is, undecidable, neither active nor passive" (Derrida 2006, 217). The stranger is other to the self but both are undecidable and contradictory and as Freud notes, this identification with another allows us to question the idea of a "true" self: "a person may identify himself with another and so become unsure of his true self; or he may substitute the other's self for his own. The self may thus be duplicated, divided and interchanged" (Freud 2003, 142).

Derrida develops Freud who first wrote about the notion of the *Heimliche-Unheimliche*: "*Heimlich* thus becomes increasingly ambivalent, until it finally merges with its antonym *Unheimlich*. The uncanny (*das Unheimliche*, 'the unhomely') is in some ways a species of the familiar (das Heimliche, 'the homely')" (134). The *heimlich* becomes the *un-heimlich* because "this uncanny element is actually nothing new or strange, but something that was long familiar to the psyche and was estranged from it only through being repressed" (148). This idea of repression relates to the idea that the uncanny is to do with what is meant to be hidden or secret but has come into view (132–133, 148). Past becomings that were thought to be forgotten re-emerge in the present and this causes an uncanny effect. These emerging becomings do not reveal a "truth," however. As we have discussed, the truth is not contained in what we can see and, furthermore, that which is truly undecidable can never be "revealed".

I contend that Barbin's and Cal/lie's texts are uncanny in the sense that their irrepresible past and future selves make them both familiar and unfamiliar to themselves, they make them undecidable. Freud (156) argues that fiction can obviate the uncanniness of some things that would be uncanny if they happened in real life. However, when an author chooses to embrace the uncanny, they can "multiply this effect far beyond what is feasible in normal experience" (157). Freud (ibid.) sees this as a trick – we are promised everyday reality but the author surpasses it and we enter the realm of the unreal.

What Barbin and Eugenides do though, through literature, is show that the uncanny, the divided self, is a part of everyday reality; these two intersex narratives are apt for exploring how to combine what appears to be contradictory. And translation itself is contradictory:

> In their plurality, the words of translation organize themselves, they are not dispersed at random. They disorganize themselves as well through the very effect of the specter, because of the Cause that is called the original and that, like all ghosts, addresses same-ly disparate demands, which are more than contradictory.
>
> (Derrida 2006, 21)

The "original" and the translation are concerned with the same text but in different ways; the translation always houses the source text as well as itself, and Derrida (25) asks: "Is it possible to find a rule of cohabitation under such a roof, it being understood that this house will always be haunted rather than inhabited by the meaning of the original?" The house of translation is, therefore, uncanny and haunted. As we have already discussed, translation cannot replicate the "meaning" of the original because the original has no one meaning; the source text haunts the target text so the target text is a form of renewal, a renewal that does not break with the past but carries it forward.

The idea of renewal is something that is explored in intersex texts as well; these texts are open to change and though readers search for closure (as we have seen with Middlesex in particular), they are an exploration of the possibility of a renewal, both historical and cultural of how the intersex person is seen (see Wing 2004, 22). This cultural and historical renewal can best be done through translation which can prolong the (after)life of the source text. In Benjamin's (2012, 71) words: "a translation participates in the 'afterlife' (Überleben) of the source text, enacting an interpretation that is informed by a history of reception." A translation of an intersex text is another specter of the body and the text, a fleeting captivation of specters past, present and future. The specter is both spirit and flesh: "For there to be a ghost, there must be a return to the body, but to a body that is more abstract than ever" (Derrida 2006, 157). The body is the site of becoming but each time the body becomes something new it becomes more abstract. To reflect this abstraction and this process of becoming translation can be practised in the experimental mode.

Electronic Literature and the Hypertext

Now that we have established that translation prolongs the ghostly life of both the body and the source text, this section will outline how a translation can manifest the multiple ghosts that it not only represents but also creates. Both *Mes souvenirs* and *Middlesex* are difficult to translate because they are undecidable; but it is also precisely translation that can best represent these texts' undecidabilities because translation itself is multiple. The kind of text which best exemplifies plurality is electronic. Readers come to electronic literature with the expectations they have gained from print literature; the digital builds on these but also changes them: "In this sense electronic literature is a 'hopeful monster' (as geneticists call adaptive mutations) composed of parts taken from diverse traditions that may not always fit neatly together" (Hayles 2008, 4). Like intersex bodies and translation, electronic literature is hybrid. The ways and means of writing electronic literature change with alacrity in our technological world and the hypertext link is the distinguishing feature of early works; later works move on from the idea of the link but here I am interested in what the hypertext link, though perhaps now considered "basic," can tell us about the hybridity of humans and texts.

While there are more complex forms of electronic literature it is also important to note that fighting to make it clear that gender is something you do and not something you are, making gender trouble, is hard; "the point is not to live perpetually where it is troubling to deal with the body, but to get to a place where there can be some breathing room for difference" (Holmes 2008, 15–16). The same can be said for the text: if the text or the body become too incomprehensible, the reader (of both) will give up. This is potentially why readers of *Middlesex* categorize Cal as male, because an undecidable character with an undecidable ending is not an easy read. That is not to say, though, that we can discard Butler's (1994, 38) call for subversive challenges to the act of reading. An electronic translation based on the hypertext link provides a middle ground which takes up the challenge but gives the body and the text room to breathe.

With the hypertext link we can see the layers that make up the body and the text, the intertextuality that is found within that shows us that bodies and texts are unstable. The multiplicity of technology shows us the multiplicity of the body. The term "hypertext" was first used by Ted Nelson in 1965 when he wrote: "Let me introduce the word 'hypertext' to mean a body of written or pictorial material interconnected in such a complex way that it could not conveniently be presented or represented on paper" (Nelson 1965). The hypertext is the fourth type of transtextuality in Gérard Genette's list which includes intertextuality as the first type (1997, 1–5). For Genette, the hypertextuality is "any relationship uniting a text B (which I shall call the *hypertext*) to an earlier text A (I shall, of course, call it the *hypotext*), upon which it is grafted in a manner that is not that of commentary" (5). In this definition, any text can be a hypertext if it is heavily influenced by a text that came before: "what I call a hypertext, then, is any text derived from a previous text, either through simple transformation [...] or through indirect transformation" (7). Genette's hypertext, therefore, is consciously evolved from a hypotext.

Hypertextuality and intertextuality are not the same, though Genette admits that his five types of transtextuality are not mutually exclusive (7). In this chapter I develop the idea that the digital hypertext is always intertextual. In Genette's vision, *Middlesex* is a hypertext of a hypotext: *Herculine Barbin dite Alexina B*. Despite this, the digital hypertext to which I refer here is not necessarily always one that is heavily based on a hypotext. The translation method this chapter evinces is inspired by Genette's ideas on the hypertext as something that "acts as a commentary" and is "transgeneric" (Genette 1997, 8) and therefore multiple. It is also inspired by Genette's definition of intertextuality – that every text has a relationship with works that have come before and will come after – and by the hypertext as a digital tool to link multiple webpages. In my version, instead of text B being grafted upon text A, text B (the translation) is grafted upon text A (the source text) but also upon texts X, Y and Z (the source author's and the translator's intertexts).

The digital hypertext visually represents intertextuality, this presence of other texts, because it is formed of links which, when clicked on, can take the reader to different places: different pages of a text, images or webpages. With the digital hypertext, the critic (and the translator-as-critic) can see the text as an entangled experiment. Multiple experiments can be produced, never solving the problem but always asking new questions; the hypertext exemplifies the idea that there is no single text to be controlled or understood in its entirety because it has no "entirety" that can be pinned down.

The multiplicty that the hypertext affords can contribute to the "writerly" text, forcing the reader to think about what the text they are reading is trying to do. George P. Landow (2006, 4) goes so far as to suggest that "Barthes' distinction between readerly and writerly texts appears to be essentially a distinction between text based on print technology and electronic hypertext." I would not go this far as print-based books can absolutely be writerly, as we have seen with all of the texts I am analyzing here, though it is true that with the digital text the reader is forced to interact with the material placed in front of him or her, more explicitly perhaps than they would with a print text. It is also not true that digital and print texts are totally different: according to N. Katherine Hayles (2008, 31), print texts could be seen to deal with links too as they have "long also employed analogous technology in such apparati as footnotes, endnotes, cross-reference and so on." Furthermore, the hypertext in Genette's (1997, 286) print-based version of it, "may introduce anachronies (analepses or prolepses) into an initially chronological narrative [...]. Conversely, the hypertext may reorder the anachronies of its hypotext." The ability to change the order of a story that already exists is not simply the purview of digital literature.

The concession that the trajectory of any story, print or electronic, is always ultimately in the writer's control does not necessarily preclude the hypertext's championing of the reader's activity above their passivity. While the reader is not free to "invent" the story, what is illuminating about hypertext fiction is that it is a physical manifestation of the ways that print texts, and all texts, are non-linear. A print text is ostensibly linear and print narrative stages the relation between past and present with a beginning, a middle and an end. However, the beginning, middle and end of a print narrative are not necessarily chronological, as we have seen: Barbin's text begins just before the end. The present is never without the past, something which is heightened in autobiography, both print and electronic. There is no "before" the discovery and "after" the discovery in Barbin's text or in hir identity. What is shown in the text is that hir identity is *always* caught up in a process of being and becoming both male and female. An electronic hypertext can visibly undo a chronological narrative: The narratives of *Middlesex* and *Herculine Barbin dite Alexina B.* could be unraveled in a hypertext translation. In each text, the passage where Barbin and Cal/lie are medically interpellated as intersex could come first. This would make manifest the idea that the authors always know about their intersex status, from the moment they began writing.

Furthermore, while electronic and print literature do share paratexts, the relationship between the main text and the paratext is changed in a digital text because the paratexts – introductions, forwards, prefaces, endnotes – do not come at the end but are mixed with the main text, indeed, the distinction between a "main" text and additional material is brought into question (Landow 2006, 45). In the hypertext there is no binary system because there are multiple texts, none of which are in the "center". In practice, this idea of multiple texts with no hierarchy whatsoever is difficult to implement – it is possible to have the main text and the annotation open in two different windows at once so that neither is "main" but, if the first text includes a link to the annotation, until that link is clicked, the first text is "on top". Having said this, in a translation, the target text becomes what is "on top," if one links to the source text, that is what is below;

the traditional hierarchy of target and source is reversed and the idea of a haunting below the surface is emphasized. The translation becomes the "tissue of innumerable quotations" that Barthes (1977, 146) describes and the notions of origins are dispersed. For example, a hypertext translation of *Middlesex* could emphasize Eugenides' sources by linking the myths of Tiresias, the Minotaur or Hermaphroditus to the translation.

The text itself is used as a tool, it is a means to always defer conclusions through the use of layers that complicate the idea of any text having a "single" meaning. And these multiple layers of meaning present in the hypertext, and every text, are not the product of one author but many. The hypertext embodies the idea of multiple producers and collaboration. Print books are also created through collaboration – they are always brought to being via multiple people: an author, an editor, a publisher, a designer, a printer and so on (see Rettberg 2011, 187). However, this collaboration is covered up so that everyone but the author is invisible. This is reminiscent of both Foucault's work in "What is an Author" (1979), and Pierre Bourdieu's in *The Field of Cultural Production* (1993), where they proclaim the multiple personnel who participate in the production of a text which is then retroactively called original. This is an interesting parallel to the way that men and women, and intersex children who are surgically "corrected," are socialized into gender but consider themselves to have been always such since birth.

The hypertext does not pretend to be the product of a single producer or even author (or translator) because hyperlinks are always intertextual. According to Landow (2006: 353), "actual hypertext, hypertext as an information technology in the form of the World Wide Web, can at least permit individual voices to be heard." But the premise of the hypertext is to be something multivocal, these voices are never individual. What hypertext does for translation is suggest that every piece of writing is a collaboration, especially translation, because the translator works with the author – admittedly the translator sometimes works against the author, but there is a dialogue. Landow (356) himself says that "the value of hypertext as a paradigm exists in its essential multivocality, decentering, and redefinition of edges, borders, identities." The hypertext can provide new ways of thinking generally about both trans issues and translation issues and more specifically about intersex issues.

From Book to Blog

In this book so far I have looked at the study of intersex through a queer lens which brings an acceptance of sex as cultural to the fore. As Butler (2006, 46) says: "No longer believable as an interior 'truth' of dispositions and identity, sex will be shown to be a performatively enacted signification (and hence not 'to be'), one that, released from its naturalized interiority and surface, can occasion the parodic proliferation and subversive play of gendered meanings." Intersex people demonstrate both the fragility of sex as a category (it is not binary) and also disrupt the presumed reciprocity of gender, sex and sexuality. The intersex person has an undecidable sex and, consequently, an undecidable sexuality – undecidability is not just a poststructuralist concept but is something that is actually experienced by human bodies.

In this chapter I have acknowledged that a self or identity is a textual "weave" of past and present, of the self as becoming, the self in process. This idea is in marked contrast to the idea of a "true" self or text – and also to the idea that identity is ever a simple decision, with before-and-after moments. What this raises for translation, then, is not only the question of how to translate pronouns and adjectives – but how to translate changeful, haunted narratives – how to translate narratively-narrated-selves, over time.

Certain types of hypertext fiction can be even more restrictive than the book, which can be opened at any page and read in any order, but there are ways of utilizing the hyperlink that do not place the reader in a repetitive loop. Software used for creating hypertext fiction such as Storyspace has quickly been eclipsed (Hayles 2008, 6) and an easier way to produce hypertextual electronic literature for the purpose of my multiple, experimental translation attempts is to use a blog. What a blog can do is gather together different translation attempts, and it can foster the sense of translation Scott (2014a, 3–4) advocates:

> A form of ongoing daily intercourse with texts, as a form of dialogue with others and with self, of the experimental search for an adequate language. A translation is a formal project, yes, but also a journal of reading, an album of try-outs, an intimate letter to its own readers, which multiplies drafts, sketches, casual snapshots.

I have therefore created a blog called "translating herculine" (accessible at www.translatingherculine.wordpress.com). This is my "album of try-outs" in which I translate excerpts from Barbin's text. A blog is an appropriate medium for translating a memoir because writing a blog is usually an autobiographical act: "we create a reflection of ourselves in a weblog. At the same time, we use our blogs to veil ourselves, not telling all but presenting only certain carefully selected aspects of ourselves to our readers" (Walker Rettberg 2014, 127). This is exactly what Barbin (and Erauso and d'Eon) have done in their memoirs and what Eugenides makes Cal/lie do: they carefully select what information they give to their readers but instead of revealing everything they veil themselves more and more.

I have translated carefully selected excerpts from Barbin's *Mes Souvenirs* chronologically but, by means of a contents page in which none of the posts are numbered, the reader is free to read the posts as they wish; though at the moment the contents page is listed in the order

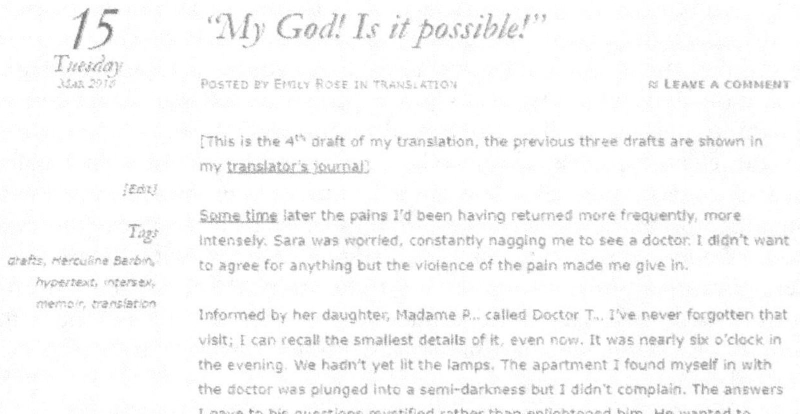
15
Tuesday
Mar 2010

"My God! Is it possible!"

Posted by Emily Rose in Translation

≈ Leave a comment

[This is the 4th draft of my translation, the previous three drafts are shown in my translator's journal]

[Edit]

Tags
drafts, Herculine Barbin, hypertext, intersex, memoir, translation

Some time later the pains I'd been having returned more frequently, more intensely. Sara was worried, constantly nagging me to see a doctor. I didn't want to agree for anything but the violence of the pain made me give in.

Informed by her daughter, Madame P... called Doctor T... I've never forgotten that visit; I can recall the smallest details of it, even now. It was nearly six o'clock in the evening. We hadn't yet lit the lamps. The apartment I found myself in with the doctor was plunged into a semi-darkness but I didn't complain. The answers I gave to his questions mystified rather than enlightened him. He wanted to

Figure 6.1 The fourth draft of my translation of pages 91–94 of *Mes Souvenirs*. When the reader clicks on the link under 'Some time' they can see my drafts (figure 6.2).

each excerpt was translated, that is to say, from the beginning of the text to the end. However, if the reader selects at random they may read of Barbin's discovery of hir intersex status first – a status any reader already knows about when approaching the printed, linear versions anyway, since it cannot be avoided in the title of MacDougal's translation. In many of my posts I try to link the translation to the relevant section of the source text (Tardieu's version) so that the source text is always haunting the translation, residing beneath its surface.[1] Most of my blog posts link my translations with different materials. For example, the post entitled "My God! Is it Possible!" includes my translation drafts: the main blog post is my fourth draft but the previous drafts reside underneath it and can be seen using the hypertext link. (Figures 6.1 and 6.2)

Or, to demonstrate that Barbin's story still causes fascination today, I have included a video clip of the film based on the memoir: *Mystère Alexina* (Féret 1985) [The Mystery of Alexina] in the blog post entitled, "My crime was kissing mademoiselle Sara too often." In the same way that my palimpsest of chapter three is a performance of Erauso's text which has long been taken out of Erauso's hands, my blog is a performance of my reading of Barbin's text which aims to show how both Barbin and hir text are haunted both by texts that came before, but also by texts that have come after hir death.

One of the texts that came before was Ovid's *Metamorphoses*:

> I admit that I was singularly bowled-over on reading Ovid's *Metamorphoses*. Those who know of them will get the idea. This

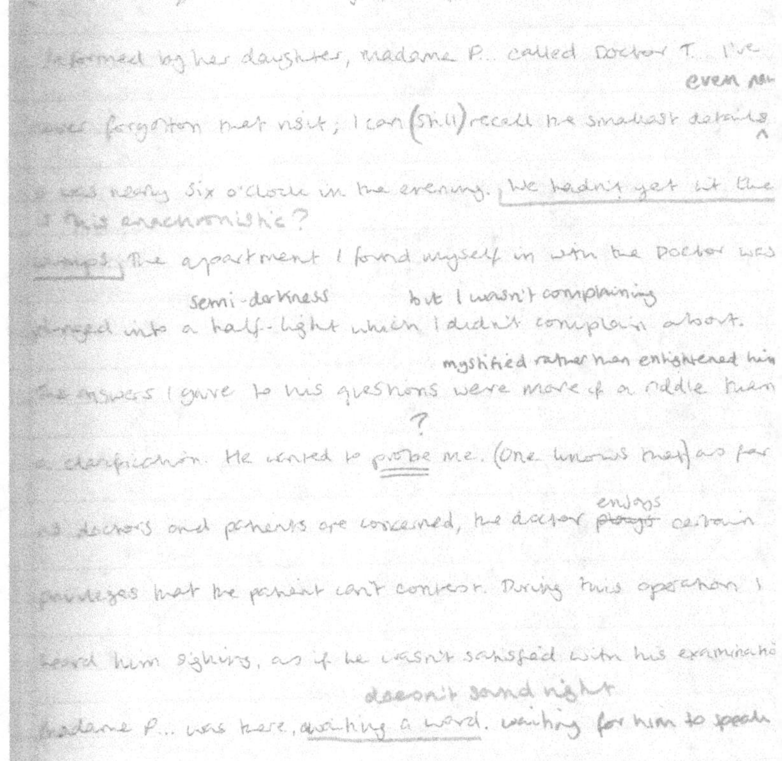

Informed by her daughter, Madame P... called Doctor T... I've
even now
never forgotten that visit; I can (still) recall the smallest details
was nearly six o'clock in the evening. We hadn't yet lit the
Is this anachronistic?
lamps. The apartment I found myself in with the Doctor was
semi-darkness but I wasn't complaining
plunged into a half-light which I didn't complain about.
mystified rather than enlightened him
The answers I gave to his questions were more of a riddle than
?
a clarification. He wanted to probe me. (One knows that) as far
enjoys
as doctors and patients are concerned, the doctor ~~plays~~ certain
privileges that the patient can't contest. During this operation I
heard him sighing, as if he wasn't satisfied with his examination
doesn't sound right
Madame P... was there, awaiting a word. waiting for him to speak

Figure 6.2 My previous drafts of the translation of part of page 91 of *Mes Souvenirs*. Different drafts are indicated by annotations over the first draft.

> find was of a singularity which the rest of my story will unequivocally prove.
>
> (Barbin 1874, 78, my translation)

In my fourth blog post (not including my translator's note), in which the quotation above appears, I attach a link to an online version of *Metamorphoses* (Ovid 2000) so the reader can access, in an English translation, the story of Hermaphroditus and Salmacis to which Barbin is alluding here. An electronic hypertext could also be used to show *Middlesex*'s intertexts and hypotexts, which are numerous. A translation of *Middlesex* could also benefit from the medium of the blog to open up the ending of the text; blog posts are usually written on a weekly or monthly basis and they gain readers who do not have to wait long for their publication. Because of the episodic nature of the blog post, there

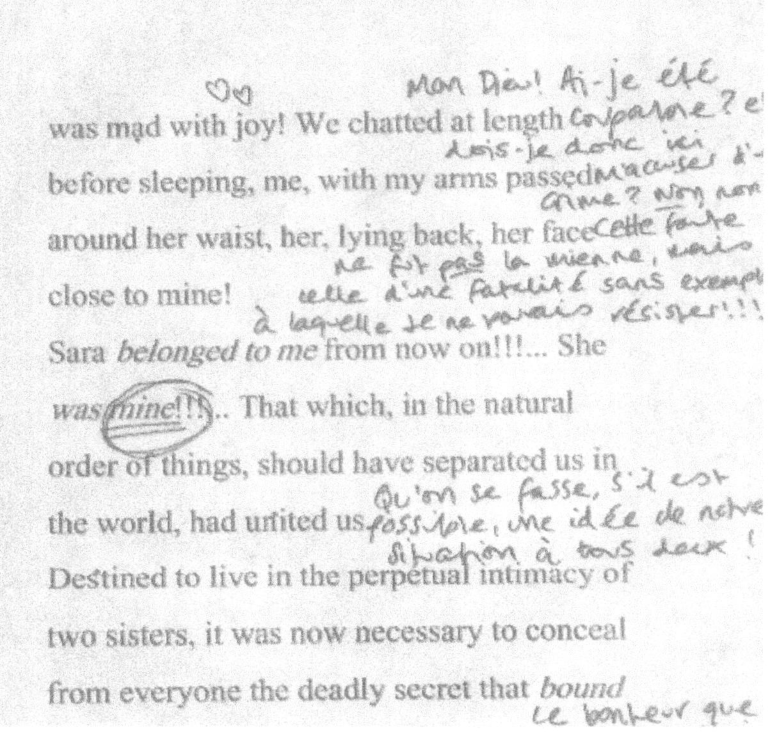
was mad with joy! We chatted at length before sleeping, me, with my arms passed around her waist, her, lying back, her face close to mine!

Sara *belonged to me* from now on!!!... She *was mine!!!*... That which, in the natural order of things, should have separated us in the world, had united us.

Destined to live in the perpetual intimacy of two sisters, it was now necessary to conceal from everyone the deadly secret that *bound*

Figure 6.3 Blog post showing my translation of part of page 110 of *Mes souvenirs* (1874) which experiments with layers.

is no idea of an ending or of closure (see Walker Rettberg 2014, 133). The most recent post on a blog always promises more, in a way that the final page of a book cannot. Despite what I have said is the norm above, I did not write my blog on a weekly or monthly basis: there is a gap of 15 months between my eleventh and twelfth blog posts and this last post was written in January 2018. Just because this is over two years ago, it does not mean that I will never write another post again – it is simply a project in hiatus. Furthermore, it is difficult to archive electronic literature because it is so fluid: books can last for centuries (as we can see with d'Eon's text) but electronic literature may not last more than a decade. My blog is transient because I, as its author, can delete or change what I choose and also because the links I use may become broken. What you read on the blog one day may be different the next and it is, therefore, unstable Figure 6.3.

I can also use the blog to explore the idea that Barbin's authorial persona is always present as part of hir textual persona. In my sixth post

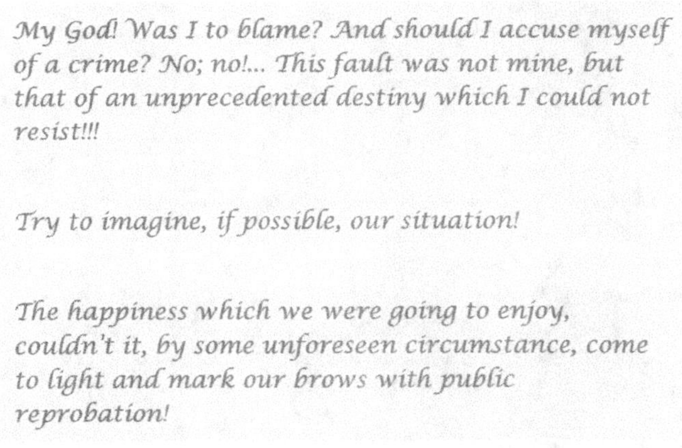

My God! Was I to blame? And should I accuse myself of a crime? No; no!... This fault was not mine, but that of an unprecedented destiny which I could not resist!!!

Try to imagine, if possible, our situation!

The happiness which we were going to enjoy, couldn't it, by some unforeseen circumstance, come to light and mark our brows with public reprobation!

Figure 6.4 The English translation of the French annotations which can be found "underneath" the above excerpt from my blog post.

I took my English translation of pages 109 to 112 of *Mes souvenirs* and removed the instances where you can clearly hear Barbin's authorial voice. I then added them over the text in French in my own handwriting as if ze were annotating hir work, adding these thoughts later as Abel in Paris (see Figure 6.3). This new layer of annotations is literally another layer because instead of writing on the printed paper I wrote on acetate paper, placing the acetate paper over the top of my translation. One could argue that the text without Barbin's later thoughts is an "avant-texte" of the source text which "unfinishes the S[ource]T[ext], multiplies its possibilities of becoming, by introducing into it the passage of time" (Scott 2014a, 51). I have then linked my English translation of these annotations using a hyperlink (see Figure 6.4).

The text is now made up of layers: the first layer is Barbin's narrative voice as if ze had written a diary at the time, the second layer is Barbin's later authorial voice and the third layer is my translator's voice. I add my voice through the use of my own handwriting – a "mode of graphic self-representation [...] which [has] access to the unconscious, to reverie, to the impulses and spontaneities of the reading body, and the harnessing of the languages of text" (Scott 2014a, 2). In a "straight" translation, these voices are merged. Through links I can show the reader my influences and my intertexts and exemplify the idea that Barbin's voice, and the voice of every author, is haunted. The translator's voice haunts the author's voice but is itself always haunted too.

The blog is also a good place to show how Barbin's text is framed by so many others, as I can link the medical examinations carried out both

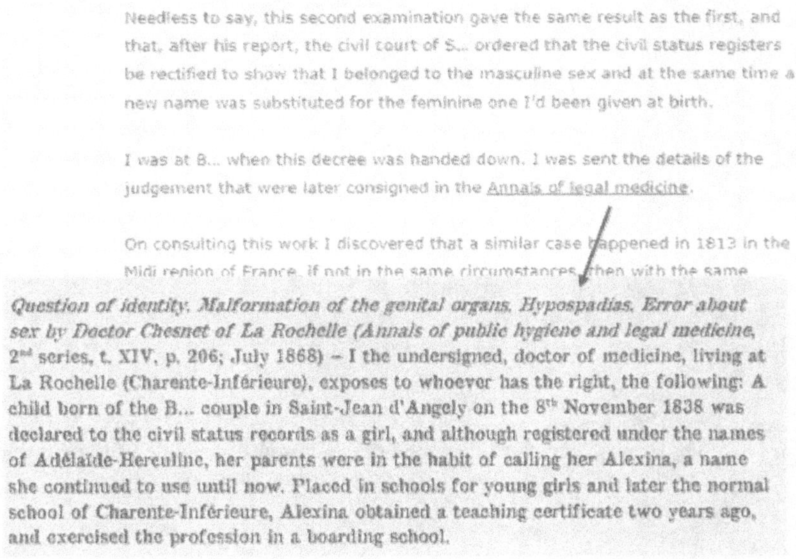

Needless to say, this second examination gave the same result as the first, and that, after his report, the civil court of S... ordered that the civil status registers be rectified to show that I belonged to the masculine sex and at the same time a new name was substituted for the feminine one I'd been given at birth.

I was at B... when this decree was handed down. I was sent the details of the judgement that were later consigned in the Annals of legal medicine.

On consulting this work I discovered that a similar case happened in 1813 in the Midi region of France, if not in the same circumstances, then with the same

Question of identity. Malformation of the genital organs. Hypospadias. Error about sex by Doctor Chesnet of La Rochelle (Annals of public hygiene and legal medicine, **2nd series, t. XIV, p. 206; July 1868) – I the undersigned, doctor of medicine, living at La Rochelle (Charente-Inférieure), exposes to whoever has the right, the following: A child born of the B... couple in Saint-Jean d'Angely on the 8th November 1838 was declared to the civil status records as a girl, and although registered under the names of Adélaïde-Herculine, her parents were in the habit of calling her Alexina, a name she continued to use until now. Placed in schools for young girls and later the normal school of Charente-Inférieure, Alexina obtained a teaching certificate two years ago, and exercised the profession in a boarding school.**

Figure 6.5 Blog post showing an extract of my translation of page 145–148 of *Mes souvenirs* (1874) with a link to my translation of the medical notes taken on Barbin.

pre- and post-mortem on hir body which are included by Tardieu (1874, 146) as a footnote and by Foucault (2014, 147–164) in his dossier (Figures 6.4 and 6.5).

These paratexts are underneath the text and form the layers that create both the text and Barbin's body – both are infused with medical discourse. Barbin's text has been added to by different voices ever since its publication. Barbin's body and text (as all bodies and all texts) are constantly moderated by others and my digital translation experiments with how to represent the many materials that make up Barbin's life, bringing that life to a new audience and shining a light on the textual and sexual plurality, and therefore undecidability, present in every text and every body.

Conclusions

The novels that section three now turns to involve textual collage in the form of fragmentation and erasure because their first-person narrators never reveal their gender. *Written on the Body* by Jeanette Winterson is narrated by an "I" who we never fully know, and *Sphinx* by Anne Garréta not only conceals the gender of the first-person narrator but also the narrator's third-person love interest in French. So far I have been looking at translation methods that use layers to reveal multiplicity. If I am now to move on to methods that can conceal within layers and fragment text, I can take my lead from both the hypertext and the palimpsest. The palimpsest begins life as an erased text, as a layer of text which is removed, and Genette talks of two types of hypertexts, one which amplifies its hypotexts and one which reduces them: for some writers, every reading “brings ever more additions, in the margins, between the lines, on paste-ons and paper strips, even on the galley proofs and, after publication, on the interfoliated blank pages,” but for other writers “every fresh reading calls for more erasures” (Genette 1997, 276). Texts which contain erasure create undecidability and this is crucial in a performance by someone who is agender or who has a total lack of gender identification or expression.

Note

1 For my blog I use Barbin’s 1874 text as my source for reasons of copyright. I use Foucault’s 2014 transcription in my main analysis because this was the source MacDougall used.

7 The History of Agender

In section one I looked at translating identities which move between the poles of male and female. Section two was dedicated to analysing the translation of doubtful (or undecidable) sex because to be intersex is precisely to introduce doubt into the concept of binary sex. I considered how sex as a biological category can (and actually always does) rest in between the binary poles of male and female. Here I want to explore how those binaries can be removed entirely from the equation. A non-binary or agender narrator helps us to look at ways of expressing gender neutrality in languages with an abundance of grammatical gender used by narrators whose becoming constantly puts them at one remove further from a gendered identity.

In Cookie Allez's 2015 novel *Dominique*, Allez describes how France's neighbours believe that her baby, Dominique, has "been born with an unknown sex. A doubtful sex. Not clear" (Allez 2015, 96, my translation). This is not actually the case. Dominique has a clear sex (to the extent that the medical establishment assigns everyone a "clear" sex) but hir parents, France and Gabriel, decide to bring hir up with no sex. Ze therefore has no gender identification or expression. To both hirself and the outside world, Dominique is agender. Dominique does not discover hir sex until the age of seven and does not acknowledge it until the age of eleven but the reader must wait even longer–until the final page–to discover Dominique's sex, and even then hir gender is still a mystery. In this chapter, undecidability is almost exclusively a question of gender, though confusions surrounding sex and gender mean that sex is inevitably included in many of the discussions that follow. This chapter will firstly examine the history of non-binary identity before taking another look at the differences between sex and gender. It will finish by moving on to discuss the two texts I look at in the following chapters: *Sphinx* by Anne Garréta (1986) and *Written on the Body* by Jeanette Winterson (1993). Agender identity has a relatively short theoretical history but I examine some gender identities from around the world which eschew the gender binary, before considering how nonbinary identity has been seen in the past few decades.

Non-Binary Identity

People who attempt to refuse the binary polarity of gender have existed for centuries: Native American "berdaches" were considered neither masculine nor feminine but neuter; the "hijras" of India considered themselves (and still do) as neither men nor women; the Greco-Roman priests of Cybele and Attis, known as "galli" dressed in neither a masculine nor feminine style and were considered "third gender;" and the personnel of temples and palaces in Mesopotamia had the gender identity of neither men nor women (Roscoe 1998, 3, 205–206; for more on hijras see Nanda 1994 and Tate et al. 2020).[1] Furthermore, in Oaxaca region of Mexico muxes are "children identified as male at birth, but who choose at a young age to be raised as female" but "the muxe identity has more in common with being non-binary" (The Guardian 2017). However, current concepts of "nonbinary" or "genderqueer" identity have received little theoretical attention and I hope to begin to redress the dearth of academic writing on the topic here. The two terms are often used to mean the same thing: "Genderqueer" is generally used as an umbrella term along with "nonbinary" for people who feel that they have a gender that is beyond the binary categories of "male" and "female," "man" and "woman" (Huston 2015). Chucky Tate et al. (2020, 7) do make a slight distinction:

> [The] specific labels of agender and genderblended fit into a larger class of experiences that other scholars have labeled *genderqueer* – with queer meaning unexpected or unusual, or not fitting within the gender binary. Currently, scholars also use the label *nonbinary* to indicate people who do not think of themselves as exclusively one of the familiar two categories.

A person who identifies as genderqueer or nonbinary may wish to jettison the categories of masculine and feminine altogether or they may feel they are a mixture of the two.[2] As we can see from these two different possibilities, the "genderqueer" or "non-binary" umbrella can refer to people who may see their gender identity quite differently from each other. This brings us back to the contradiction I addressed in my introduction between trans identities: "genderqueer" can also be used to describe identities which "conflict" with each other. For example, more specific terms, listed by Matt Huston (2015) that come under this umbrella include: "neutrois" ("a neutral gender that is neither male nor female"); "bigender" ("a dual-gender identity, with two sides experienced and expressed either simultaneously or at different times"); "agender" ("an absence of gender identification or expression"); "genderfluid" ("shifting between different gender identities or expressions"); "androgynous/androgyne" ("having both traditionally masculine and feminine characteristics and/or identifying as between male and female").

Finding the right term is important, even if labels can be restrictive. Rikki Wilchins (2002b, 57) takes issue with the term "androgynous" because it suggests that the person who uses it is not both male and female or somewhere in the middle but is actually male: "Man is the default sex; womanhood must continually prove itself by artifice, adornment, and display." The term, with its implications of the male-as-default, must be questioned because of what it suggests about the world as a patriarchy. Since Simone de Beauvoir ([1949] 2009) famously declared that woman is the "second sex," the idea that what is gender-neutral is male, or that man is the universal, has been a constant problem for Francophone feminists; the man is always the unmarked universal in many languages (see Simon 1996, 19; Yaguello 2002, 79 and de Lotbinière-Harwood 1991, 112 for the man as universal in French). Taking this point much further, Monique Wittig (1985, 5) condemns the pronoun "je" as being exclusively male: "Gender is not confined within the third person. Sex, under the name of gender, permeates the whole body of language and forces every locuter, if she belongs to the oppressed sex, to proclaim it in her speech." This is something I shall discuss in the next chapter with regard to attempting to write a genderless first-person text in French and attempting to translate such a text.

Such a variety of terms living together under one label is nothing new. "Trans" as an umbrella term involves many dichotomous identities, including, usually, "genderqueer" itself. This does not mean, however, that all people who identify as "genderqueer" or who use one of its associated terms wish to belong to the trans community. While many who belong to the gender neutral community do associate themselves with the transgender community, they do not identify with the transsexual narrative of being born in the wrong body: on speaking to five people who identify as "neutrois," Rachel White discovered that they all "have no need for masculinity or femininity" (White 2012). Micah (no date, my emphasis), who writes the online blog entitled "Genderqueer Me," writes that "I identify as nonbinary. Since 2010 I've been transitioning – or rather trying to figure out what transition means to me as someone whose gender is *neither female or* [sic] *male*." Micah (2013a) also explains that people who identify as genderqueer do not always take comfort in the same things as those who identify as transgender:

> Transgender people who are binary-identified find comfort on the other side of the spectrum: if they were born male, they see themselves as female, and are at home looking like and being seen as girls or women. However, some trans people find distress or discomfort when putting themselves in the female side as well as the male side. Neither box feels quite right.

It would appear that that some genderqueer people do not wish to belong to the trans community because they feel that being trans involves crossing a border from one gender to another, which they do not do (see Roxie 2011a). While some do not want to belong to the trans community, Micah (2013b) bases a blog post around one reader's comment that, as someone who identifies as non-binary, they do not feel "trans enough," they clearly want to belong to the trans community but feel in some way excluded from it. This may be because being non-binary and stepping away from the gender binary entirely is, or has been, something that is not written about. It is necessary to look to these individual accounts, like Micah's, because of this dearth of research into agender identity.

"Agender," "neutrois," "genderqueer" or any of its associated terms have no theoretical or literary history, according to Marilyn Roxie (2011b): "While 'genderqueer' came into popular use through the late 1990s and early 2000s in the United States, the term had its development in the mid-1990s and implemented [*sic*] far earlier concepts of non-binary identity and expression (e.g. androgyny)." The word "neutrois" is not included in the *Oxford English Dictionary* or the *Collins Dictionary*, though the word has been under review for inclusion according to the latter's website since 2013 (Collins 2020). Identities like "neutrois" and "agender" are much less established than more well-known identities such as transgender, transsexual or even intersex but they are beginning to be noticed. When Maria Munir came out as nonbinary to Barak Obama in 2016 it became clear that even he was unsure of the definition of the term: "It's almost perfect in a way that even the president of the United States isn't fully informed on non-binary issues, because it really puts it home that so many people around the world need to be informed on this" (Khomani 2016). Munir's confession did not only show how little is known about "nonbinary" as an identity but also allowed non-binary issues to become a topic in the British press for several days. Three days after their "outing" Munir wrote an article entitled "Why I came out as non-binary to Barak Obama" in *The Telegraph*. This was Munir's (2016) chance to educate readers: "According to the Non-binary Inclusion Project, there are an estimated 252,728 non-binary people in the UK, so clearly I'm not alone."

In June 2017 a baby born in Canada became the first to be "officially identified as agender" (Jackman 2017a) and in the same month both Washington DC and Oregon allowed its citizens to identify as gender neutral by using an "X" instead of an "M" or "F" on driving licences and ID cards (Jackman 2017b; 2017c). In May 2018, Channel 4 aired a series of programmes called "Genderquake". This included a reality television show which placed 11 trans people in a house together for a week and a live televised debate. A 22-year-old called Saffron who identifies as non-binary took part in the reality show to say that "to those people who say we don't exist, I'm right fucking here" (in Sturges 2018). While the reality show gave a voice to multiple different identities, the debate was less successful: its participants included two trans women, three feminists, a trans man and a genderqueer drag king. However, "talk time was dominated by the two trans women. The trans man and drag king – two perspectives rarely given attention in gender discussions – hardly got to talk at all" (Ditum 2018). While the televised debate was not a success, and perhaps demonstrates the point that some trans identities are still not being listened to, that one of the main terrestrial channels in the UK aired a set of programmes about being trans, and included transgender people, intersex people and non-binary people, opens the way for more off-screen debates and education. Furthermore, in March 2019 the singer Sam Smith came out as non-binary, saying: "I am not male or female" (Fitzpatrick 2019) and in July 2019 Bre Kidman became the first non-binary person to run for the US senate (Parsons 2019). In December 2019, Estrella Vazquez, a muxe appeared on the front cover of Vogue's Mexican and British editions (Wakefield 2019).

As may have become apparent from the preceding discussion, most of what little information there is on genderqueer identity can be found online; it is easier to present an agender identity in writing than in life and it is also easier to present an agender identity online because the visual is missing. The body is invisible and language becomes the site of identification.

Sex vs. Gender in Language

Though I elucidated the differences between sex and gender in the introduction, it will be useful to reconsider the differences between the terms "sex" and "gender" here as these two terms, carry much weight both in the arena of agender identity but also in the language used to represent agender identity.

Whilst it is true that theorists such as Judith Butler (2006, 10) consider there to be no distinction between the two terms because both are culturally produced, it is an important part of being "trans" to have a gender identity that does not "match" what is expected from whichever sex one is assigned at birth. Of course, Butler's point is that there is no need for gender to match sex at all as the latter is simply a category assigned by the medical establishment with the former acting as the policy by which sex is kept in check, but this does not prevent people from believing that gender naturally follows sex. In language, sex and gender are inextricable: "sex-based systems are found in almost all areas where there is gender" (Corbett 2013). Linguistic gender supposedly often matches sex:

> To a linguist, the term *gender* retains its original meaning of 'kind', as in the related words *generic*, *genus*, and *genre*. [...] It just happens that in many European languages the genders correspond to the

> sexes, at least in pronouns. For this reason the linguistic term *gender* has been pressed into service by nonlinguists as a convenient label for sexual dimorphism.
>
> (Pinker 1994, 27–28)

Not all European languages have pronouns that correspond to the sexes, however: English and German have a neuter gender, for example. English assigns gender on a semantic basis (what is male is masculine, female is feminine, inanimate is neuter) while German assigns it on both a semantic and a formal basis (nouns are also assigned a gender according to their form). Mark Twain (2010 [1880], 380) picks up on this peculiarity of the German language: "In German, a young lady has no sex, while a turnip has." A young lady in German is the neuter "ein Mädchen" while a turnip is the feminine "eine Rübe." Here gender is assigned according to morphology and not semantically.

What Twain seems to be suggesting in his diatribe against the "senseless" German language is that how your mother tongue uses grammatical gender influences how you see the world. French and Spanish also have formal gender assignment and it could be argued that this means that French and Spanish speakers see the world as divided by binary gender more than, say, an English speaker. Linguistic relativity, or the idea that the language you speak shapes the way you see the world, has come under much scrutiny over the past eighty years. Peter Sedlmeier, Arun Tipandjan and Anastasia Jänchen (2016, 317–318) cite fourteen studies which argue for linguistic relativity and thirteen that challenge it: they conclude that, on the basis of the evidence, it is unlikely that language controls thought but it can influence it. They then set out to discover if gender is viewed differently by speakers of languages with three genders, the hypothesis being that a mapping between the gender of nouns and sex is easier in languages like French or Spanish which have two genders than it is in languages with three genders like English or German. Their results, however, show that this is not the case and that people who speak a language with three genders still see the world as gendered: there is still a mapping of linguistic gender onto sex (Sedlmeier et al. 2016, 320- 321).

Grammatical gender does influence the way we see the world, even in English. In 2000 Lera Boroditsky and Lauren A. Schmidt carried out an experiment using native English, Spanish and German speakers to determine whether Spanish grammatical gender was universal. They gave English speakers a list of fifty animal names and a list of eighty-five object names and asked them to classify each item as either masculine or feminine: their study found that the English speakers gave the animals and objects gender that correlated highly with Spanish grammatical gender and, indeed, their answers correlated even more highly with German grammatical gender regarding the list of animals. Boroditsky and Schmidt concluded that English has too much in common with Indo-European languages like Spanish and German to test the universality of grammatical gender (Sedlmeier et al. 2016, 321–322). What these studies show is that the division of the world into masculine and feminine binary gender is, in many ways, as much a problem for English speakers as it is for French or Spanish speakers. This would suggest, therefore, that when reading a text with no gender, an English reader might be tempted to fill in gender based on textual clues. This supposition will be tested in chapter eight.

Even though English does not gender such objects as chairs and tables, English speakers are capable of being aware that French, Spanish, German and many other languages do. The concept of gendering inanimate objects is not so far out of their own experience that they cannot grasp it, even if they might not understand why it happens. If they could not grasp it, translation between languages with different systems would not happen: the translator could not hope to translate at all if the source text was beyond his or her understanding, let alone the understanding of his or her readers. This is patently not the case as Jean Boase-Beier (2011, 35) states, "the impossibility of translation [does not] follow from [...] linguistic difference. What does follow is that the translator does not have a straightforward task." All of my texts are queer, and translations with a queer agenda do not shy away from what is hard. Indeed, queer translations of these texts expose grammatical gender as a construct precisely because they show that source languages and target languages can treat it differently; for example, English can conceal gender in the first person quite easily, while to do this in French or Spanish the writer must be creative, avoiding adjectives and certain verbal forms, such as the *passé composé* used with *être* in French. However, in French and Spanish, possessive adjectives are epicene and in English they are not. Furthermore, French and Spanish have gender-invariable nouns which play a vital role in the texts I examine here.

Agender Texts

The writers of *Sphinx* and *Written on the Body*, Anne Garréta and Jeanette Winterson, have their protagonists use language and discourse transgressively to suggest a different kind of gender identity. Their characters' gender transgressions can only be shown through the written word; there is no physical means of "looking," there is no truth in sight (as we saw with Barbin in chapter five, and as I shall discuss in more detail, there is perhaps never truth in sight alone); they only exist in the reader's mind's eye and it is language that creates this image. Fiction can conceal what is often forcibly revealed in lived experience: many people do live as a gender that is neither masculine nor feminine but it is only recently that a third gender has legally become an option, as we saw above with driving licences in some states of America. In countries where this identification is not yet possible those who identify as non-binary are caught by the compulsory regimes which require the body to be a sex or a gender that is always one of only two choices. It is fiction that creates the notion that things can be concealed (see also McAvan 2011, 437); but just as there is no truth behind that which is undecidable, there is no truth behind fiction.

Critics have argued over how to label the narrators from *Sphinx* and *Written on the Body* since their publication but we can never know their sex (and have no pronouns to rely on). Most readers try to glean clues about their sexual identity from their gender presentation (including the discourses they use). We shall see in chapter eight that attention to critical discourse is particularly important but it does not yield any firm answers. Garréta's and Winterson's narrators are variously labelled as male, female, gay, lesbian, straight and trans (see Harris 2000; Livia 2001; Rubinson 2001; Smith 2011). While labels are not always useful, I will argue that it could be enlightening to consider the genderless narrators of both texts, and the genderless love interest of *Sphinx*, as agender to consider how to translate these identities between languages which use grammatical gender to different extents.

Garréta's *Sphinx* involves both a first-person narrator with no gender and a genderless love interest known only as A***. In chapter eight I will carry out a close analysis of *Sphinx* and of Garréta's techniques for concealing gender, but here it will be useful to briefly examine some examples from the text where both *je* and A*** are clearly genderless before we go on to examine the text's reception by critics and academics. *Je* is a theology student who also works as a disc jockey in a nightclub called 'L'Apocryphe'. The club, whose name literally means "apocryphal," is described as "ambiguous" (Garréta 1986, 23, my translation). *Je* says "J'entrais indifféremment dans les boîtes hétéros et les boîtes homos, mâles ou femelles" (29) [I entered indiscriminately into straight and gay clubs and clubs for men or women]. *Je* only uses, or is referred to with, invariable nouns and adjectives: "mon enfant" (15) [my child] and "Il me faut pourtant être juste" (105) [It is, however, necessary for me to be fair]. A*** is a black dancer from New York with a muscular body and a shaved head who is also only ever referred to using invariable adjectives such as "frivole" (54) [frivolous] and "grave" (ibid.) [serious] and invariable nouns: "ce bel animal-là" (56) [that beautiful animal there]. French is a two-sex language and these invariable nouns and adjectives are not strictly neutral in that they are used for both the masculine and the feminine rather than neither, but in doing so they become the perfect recourse for gender-neutral narration.

Winterson's "I" of *Written on the Body* is also often assumed to move between being masculine and feminine from one page to the next, especially as the narrator makes constant references which appear to be gendered: "I shall call myself Alice and play croquet with the flamingos"

(Winterson 1993, 10); "But I'm not a Boy Scout and never was" (58); "I had Mercutio's swagger" (81); "I quivered like a schoolgirl" (82) and "why do I feel like a convent virgin?" (94). These metaphors and similes demonstrate the narrator's identification; Winterson plays with these tropes. They confirm the narrator's identity as agender because they indicate that ze identifies as unstable. Identifying as something is performative and mobile and the use of the simile "like" suggests that we can identify with anything. Identification is made up of a series of acts and processes. It is a dynamic becoming and our identity is a product of these identifications. Winterson's narrator is constituted from multiple identifications: "A subject's identifications viewed as a whole are in no way a coherent relational system. Demands coexist within an agency like the super-ego, for instance, which are diverse, conflicting and disorderly. Similarly, the ego-ideal is composed of identifications with cultural ideals that are not necessarily harmonious" (Laplanche and Pontalis 1988, 208). Identifying with inharmonious characters such as Alice and Mercutio through metaphor or schoolgirls and convent virgins through simile is the narrator's performance of their undecidability.

Conclusions

Like those examined in the preceding chapters, these trans protagonists also go through a process of becoming and unbecoming. Here these becomings bring up questions of existence – the further these characters move from the gender binary (or even a mixing of the binary) the more ghostly they seem to become. This spectrality is not necessarily suggesting that one cannot exist without staking a claim, no matter how temporary, to a masculine or feminine gender presentation. The ghostly endings of these texts, which I shall discuss in the following chapter, are a place of movement and undecidability, the start of an unbecoming before another re-becoming of "agender" identity.

Notes

1 As we saw in chapter one, concepts of gender have differed throughout time and space and so these communities' transcendence of binary gender may not have been judged as transgressive by their contemporaries but it is still useful to consider that the concept of gender, especially as a binary, has always been questioned.

2 While the term "genderqueer" suggests that this identity is specifically concerned with gender and therefore with ideas of masculine and feminine, descriptions of genderqueer people sometimes refer to mixtures between feeling male and female and do not distinguish between concepts of sex and gender. The terms "genderqueer" or "non-binary" are sometimes used by people who feel themselves to be somewhere between male and female, a mixture of both or something entirely different (see Trans Media Watch, no date).

8 Close Readings of Agender Texts

In this chapter I will look at *Sphinx* and *Written on the Body* more closely, examining the sexual undecidability of the three genderless characters and how they have been received by readers. I will also examine the techniques used by both authors to suggest textual undecidability, considering how these techniques involving genre, the texts' endings, intertextuality and voice (techniques we have come across in previous chapters) affect translation. I will then carry out a close analysis of the English translation of *Sphinx* and the French and Spanish translations of *Written on the Body*. I will show that the sexual and textual undecidability in and of these novels, which has often been read out by critics, must be preserved in translation and that translation is a good place to explore problems of gender in language and ideas of the undecidable.

Two Undecidable Agender Texts

I shall now look in closer detail at how *Sphinx* and *Written on the Body* have been received to glean whether these receptions influence their translators. Reviewers and critics generally fall into one of two camps: those who believe the agender characters are decidable and who choose genders for them, and those who believe they were always meant to be, and should remain, undecidable. This examination of the texts' receptions will help me to argue that the characters must be seen as being neither male nor female and neither masculine nor feminine and that it is vital that this undecidability be maintained in translation.

In *Pronoun Envy* (2001), a study with which my work is in near-constant dialogue, Anna Livia carries out a study on the reception of *Sphinx* and she finds that reviewers do make decisions on the characters' gender but they are undecided on what those genders are: *World Literature Today* (spring 1987), sees the narrator as male and A*** as female; the reviewer for *Le Républicain lorrain* (7 March 1986) decides that both the narrator and A*** are male while the reviewer for *Le Canard enchaîné* (March 1986) thinks that they are both female (Livia 2001, 52). Livia (36) herself cannot imagine these characters as gender neutral, she thinks that a decision must be made and the characters must be one sex or the other. She even goes so far as to answer Foucault's (2014, 9) question of "do we truly need a true sex?" in the affirmative: "the narrator and A*** truly need a true sex because we need to know how to refer to them" (Livia 2001, 37). The assumption that readers cannot refer to or imagine a genderless character rather does them a disservice. For many, the function of literature is to defamiliarise, to show us something which is not part of our daily lives; as I shall discuss below in reference to her inclusion in the Oulipo, the aim of Garréta's text is to cause the reader a degree of trouble – imagining a genderless character is purposefully hard but not impossible.

Garréta's text reveals that language itself is a trap: language is creative and allows human beings to express themselves but this freedom is also restrictive because we are limited to the borders of our language, limited to what language allows us to do (see Spender 1998, 142 and Pinker 1994). Where there is freedom there is always constraint but where there is constraint there is freedom too. Livia seems to suggest that linguistic gender is immutable, that we cannot think of people without pronouns: if a person is not a "he" or a "she" they have to be an "it" but, while in English that might suggest something inanimate, it does not necessarily make a person non-human in other languages, as we saw with "young lady" in German which, grammatically, is not a feminine noun but a neuter one. What Garréta shows is that a category beyond "he" or "she" can be human and we *can* modify or question the structures we have already created in language.

Livia (2001, 37) is determined to find gender in *Sphinx* and she considers it to be a lesbian novel. Most reviewers of the novel seem sure it is a homosexual text, though they cannot agree if it is gay or lesbian. While the genders of A*** and *je* are always undecidable, we do know that one of A***'s lovers is male: he is A***'s "dernier amant en date" (Garréta 1986, 71) [last(m) lover(m) to date]. As we shall see below with *Written on the Body*, many critics are eager to write the possibility of bisexuality out of these texts, which is what those who see both *je* and A*** as lesbians must do. Bisexuality indicates yet more undecidability, in sexuality as well as in sex.

Many critics take Winterson's use of gendered language like "schoolgirl" or "boy scout" to prove that the narrator is a woman or a man, and ignore whichever references do not fit their interpretation. For example, Andrea Harris (2000, 130) argues that Winterson "depicts a nearly featureless narrator [...] and gives us no clear signals as to its gender such as gendered pronouns or a name. Despite this refusal to mark gender, at the same time the novel offers many hints that 'it' is in fact a she." Harris reads through the concealment of gender, seeing it as a trick to be uncovered. She justifies this argument by saying that she cannot imagine the narrator's radical feminist girlfriend, Inge, as anything but a lesbian and that, as Winterson is a lesbian, her narrator must be one too (143–144). By assuming the narrator is a lesbian, Harris ignores hir relationships with men – "I had a boyfriend once" (Winterson 1993, 92) – just as Livia ignores A***'s relationship with a man to make hir and *je* lesbians. They both read out bisexuality.

Both Gregory Rubinson and Brian Finney have conducted studies on the reception of *Written on the Body*, much as Livia did with *Sphinx*. Rubinson (2001, 219) concludes that many reviewers do the same as Andrea Harris and associate the narrator with Winterson, assuming ze is female, though he does find one critic who labels the narrator male. Finney (2002, 25) also discovers that the reviews by *The Sunday Telegraph*, *The Independent*, *The Times* and *The Financial Times* all conclude that *Written on the Body* is a lesbian novel. Livia herself looks at Winterson's work and appears to side with those who see the narrator as oscillating between genders; she feels that "the narrator of *Written on the Body* seems more hermaphroditic, alternating between the sexes. In this, Winterson's project seems to echo Garréta's, promoting gender fluidity as social progress" (Livia 2001, 80). However, just as she negates the fluidity she first sees in *Sphinx* by deciding *je* is a lesbian, she negates the "hermaphroditism" of "I" by also seeing hir as a lesbian: "Although Winterson never states that the relationship between Louise and the narrator is lesbian, this is powerfully suggested by the parallels between *Written on the Body* and [Wittig's] *The Lesbian Body*" (81). These reviewers actively ignore the undecidability of the text.

It is an undecidability that can be seen through a close reading. Louise, the narrator's lover, says: "I thought you were the most beautiful creature male or female I had ever seen" (Winterson 1993, 84) and, in another act of identification, on the following page ze is "like Puck sprung from the mist" (85). In Act II scene I of *A Midsummer Night's Dream* Puck is referred to with the pronoun "he" but the character is nonhuman: a "sprite" and a "hobgoblin" (Shakespeare 1958, 143). For me, Puck is undecidable and agender. If identification is the assimilation of an attribute of the other whereby the identifier is transformed after the model the other provides (Laplanche and Pontalis 198, 205) then here the narrator becomes undecidable:

> Sometime a horse I'll be, sometime a hound,
> A hog, a headless bear, sometime a fire;
> And neigh, and bark, and grunt, and roar, and
> burn,
> Like horse, hound, hog, bear, fire, at every turn.
>
> (Shakespeare 1958, 147)

By having her narrator identify with Puck, Winterson is suggesting that they are becoming and unbecoming, in a constant state of metamorphosis, unconfined to the human form. The narrator is, like Puck, always without a gender identity and anyone who gives the narrator a definitive identity must make their decision based on gender stereotypes. This reliance on stereotypes is borne out by the fact that in determining *Je* and A*** as lesbians Livia (2001, 32) feels that the reader must "adopt a working hypothesis about the gender of the narrator and the beloved based on social or cultural clues in the absence of grammatical ones".

Rubinson believes that *Written on the Body* must be left as open as possible and he is not the only one (see Finney 2002, 23; Morrison 2006, 173; McAvan 2011, 434; Leonardi 2013, 66). On the other hand, Jennifer Smith (2011, 414–6) does not see the narrator as having no gender but as being transgender. For Smith (425), "Winterson forces the reader to question the efficacy of the gender binary, once s/he realizes that his/her attempts to fill in the gap of the narrator's 'real' gender identity will be forever thwarted." The reader must realize not only that attempts will forever be thwarted but that the point of the text is to discourage the reader from making these attempts; though, of course, even attempts to see the narrators as neither masculine nor feminine (rather than both) still rely on the concept of the binary. Undecidability is still rooted in the binary gender system; everything is couched in this binary. By attempting to overthrow it we must still admit that it exists, and this is something I shall discuss further below.

While most of the reviews written for *Sphinx* chose a gender for Garréta's characters, the genderless nature of the text has also received much theoretical attention – though, as we shall see, genderless here seems to mean both man and woman, not neither. Despite the fact that Gill Rye (2000, 532) believes that both je and A*** have uncertain genders, both she (534) and Lauren Elkin believe that *je* and A*** move between being a man and a woman: "Just as the novel is genderless, it is also gender*full*, as the narrator's and A***'s sexes reconfigure and reform [...]; one minute you're sure A*** is a man, the next the narrator is definitively a woman, then the other way around" (Elkin 2015). I argue that in these texts we have an *Aufhebung* of gender, where gender is both abolished and preserved: just as Elkin sees *Sphinx* as "genderfull," Livia (2001, 56) considers it the novel's main achievement to "show how crucial gender is."

This *Aufhebung* does not mean that the narrators are both masculine and feminine but that by erasing gender we are immediately and contradictorily emphasizing the gender categories we live by because they are noticeably missing. Neither Garréta nor Winterson can deny that we live in a gendered world and, indeed, other characters in their novels are not genderless. But fiction gives us the space to see through the division of the world into male and female, to escape from the trap of language which has enchained us into seeing the world as always constructed on binary lines. Giving the reader this space to construct the world differently appears to be a primary aim of texts which play with the erasure of gender; Allez does the same in *Dominique,* making it explicit that gender (and gendered language) is a trap: "Dominique refused to let go of the Empire that hir ambivalence had given hir. Not just on paper, but in life. Without really realizing, Dominique was panicking at the idea of suddenly being trapped in a gender" (Allez 2015, 257, my translation). The agender characters of all of these texts attempt to escape this entrapment through the language they use (or refuse to use), a language that marks them out as undecidable. Em McAvan (2011, 438) sees the narrator of *Written on the Body* as being trans, but not in the same sense as Smith: she declares that "it is this undecidability that marks the narrator's body out as transgendered in the poetic sense that Judith Halberstam suggests, an open possibility rather than a probability." "An open possibility" is an appropriate description not only of the non-binary characters in the texts but also of the texts themselves.

Textual Undecidability

While both texts relate the story of a love affair, neither can be described as a traditional romance, and in this section I will examine the generic undecidability of the texts which is compounded by abundant intertextuality, open endings and unreliable narrators. Even the title of *Sphinx* reflects the riddle of the text it represents because the legend of the Sphinx holds that it devoured anyone who could not answer its riddle (Garréta 1986). But, in fact, "sphinx" also refers directly to the gender problem of the text because in Greek myth the Sphinx has the body of a lion, the wings of a bird and the head of a woman while in Egyptian myth the Sphinx has the head of a man (see Livia 2001, 37). *Written on the Body*, whose title also suggests a certain amount of instability in the idea that the body can be read and re-read, written and re-written as if a blank page (see Carpenter 2007, 71), is considered by Ina Schabert (2010, 89) to be an "English re-creation of Garréta's *Sphinx*" and equally difficult to categorize.

Written on the Body is particularly hard to categorize given Winterson's switch to scientific discourse when the narrator discovers that Louise has leukemia. In having the narrator scour medical textbooks for an answer, Winterson permeates scientific discourse with undecidability, precisely because there is no answer to be found. This is striking because science is often seen as the search for definitive answers while literature, especially romance literature that aims to understand love, is concerned with a far more nebulous quest (Rubinson 2001, 221). In *Middlesex*, as we saw in chapter five, Eugenides uses medical textbooks and notes to highlight how the medical establishment, in terms of sex and, consequently, gender, is built on sand. Winterson, like Eugenides, questions the power of science to dictate gender as something binary and biological. Here Winterson is also questioning the power of medicine which fails to provide the narrator with a cure for Louise.

In confusing the genre of her text, Winterson is exaggerating the fact that all texts are a mixture of genres and discourses and that the confusion they provoke is impossible to avoid. Winterson's text is multivocal, as all novels are according to Bakhtin (1981). Winterson uses discourses taken from a diversity of languages: from the Bible, travelogues, anatomical texts, epistolary fiction and drama (Finney 2002, 23). In her text, Winterson alludes to *Alice in Wonderland* (1993, 10), *A Midsummer Night's Dream* (85), *Romeo and Juliet* (81), *The Tempest* (16), *Jane Eyre* (17), *Madame Bovary* (17), the Bible (18, 91), *Anna Karenina* (75, 183), *Portrait of the Artist as a Young Dog* (162) and *Great Expectations* (163) as well as films (60, 79) and paintings (54).

All of these discourses are juxtaposed and bring their own contradictory and complementary world views and meanings to make the text undecidable. By juxtaposing scientific discourse with a plethora of references to romance stories, Winterson is challenging the factual basis of science – science is as much a set of constructed stories as fiction – and also challenging "traditional" romance (see Rubinson 2001, 225). According to Diane Elam (1992, 3), "romance" as a genre is always postmodern, and is therefore a challenge to what is "true". In my previous chapters the undecidability of the genre of "autobiography" led me to question the idea that any one text can belong only to one genre – as we have seen throughout, all texts are undecidable. Elam (7) argues that romance draws attention to this undecidability: "Romance seems in excess of itself, stepping beyond the lines which have always limited its definition." A text like *Written on the Body* makes us uncomfortable (as we saw above, the aim of novels like Winterson's or Garréta's is to defamiliarise, to cause the reader trouble) and romance, like autobiography I suggest, specifically draws the reader's attention to "reality" as something that is constructed by the author. Reality is not a "'natural' state of existence to which we all naturally, textually, refer" (Elam 1992, 8). The autobiographer can never relate the story of a true and unmediated 'reality' that is past. Indeed, autobiography questions the idea that what appears to be past is really "past" at all and romance does the same (12). All of the writers I have examined so far, including the ones in this chapter, challenge the idea that the past is something that we wholly grasp as a sequential series of events, events which are definitively over and which we can objectively represent in writing.

Winterson's narrator is unreliable, and she wants the reader to know it: "I can tell by now that you are wondering whether I can be trusted as a narrator" (Winterson 1993, 24). Winterson draws attention to the fact that no writer can adequately remember their own past. She makes the reader question what they know. Making one's narrator unreliable is not a new technique, which Winterson (17) also points out: "Have I got it wrong, this hesitant chronology? Perhaps I should call it Emma Bovary's eyes or Jane Eyre's dress." This is firstly a reference to the fact that

Emma Bovary's eyes change from brown to black (Flaubert 2001, 62) to blue (315) over the course of *Madame Bovary*. It is secondly a reference to a review made of *Jane Eyre* by Elizabeth Rigby in 1848 (when Currer Bell was the only known author) which accused the narrator of being wrong about clothes that ladies wore. This supposedly revealed the author as either being a man or a woman who had "long forfeited the society of her own sex" (Rigby 1848, 93–94).

Winterson's narrator picks up on things that "ordinary" readers might not. The point is that "I" is a close reader (but that goes without saying because ze is a translator) as well as an unreliable narrator whose unreliability makes the reader question what is true and what is not and whether the "truth" really matters. By admitting that ze cannot remember the past the narrator exposes all those who write about the past (including memoirists) as fiction writers and suggests that remembering the past accurately is not easy to do. We begin to doubt our own memories.

Historical knowledge is shown to always be narrative knowledge which cannot help us understand past events (Elam 1992, 11). With these texts "there is a loss of credulity in master narratives" (ibid.), the "master" narrative of science, for example. Trans writing shines a light on discourses of power and knowledge as constraining: knowledge is not natural (Elam 1992, 142; Foucault 1978, 95–100). Winterson makes a point in her novels of questioning (masculine) master narratives. Francesca Maioli (2009, 154) accuses Winterson of being incapable of describing a female body via a genderless narrator because the narrator "speaks like the male writers that s/he quotes." However, Winterson quotes these male writers to bring into question the androcentric literary canon, which, like language in general, has been constructed by men; this is a point she also makes in *Oranges are Not the Only Fruit* where her main intertext is the Bible (the chapters are named after books of the Old Testament (Winterson 2014). The literary canon was made by men and it makes women mute and invisible; this invisibility furthers the patriarchy. In his 1994 work *The Western Canon: The Books and School of the Ages*, Harold Bloom discusses twenty-six authors that he considers central to the Western canon, and of the twenty-six, only four are women: Jane Austen, Emily Dickinson, George Eliot and Virginia Woolf. Even when he considers those he has left out we see only a list of twenty-three men from Petrarch to D. H. Lawrence (Bloom 1994, 2). That Winterson's narrator quotes mainly male writers does not mean the narrator is male; instead it shines a spotlight on literature as exclusive and mocks that exclusivity.

Winterson juxtaposes incongruous texts to confuse the genre of her novel, and Garréta does the same. Intertextuality in *Sphinx* has received much less theoretical attention and this may be because most readers cannot see past the "gimmick" of concealed gender. Garréta references Greek and Egyptian mythology in her title and within the text she references the Myth of Sisyphus (1986, 28), Proust's *À la recherche du temps perdu* (55) [In Search of Lost Time], an English song entitled *Sphinx* (80), *La Chute* (109) [The Fall] by Albert Camus, *La ville inconnue* (87, 123) [the unknown town], an Edith Piaf song, the Bible (124), *Come in from the Rain* (139), a 1975 song, and Stéphane Mallarmé's untitled sonnet which begins *Le vierge, le vivace et le bel aujourd'hui* (156) [literally: the virgin, the lively and the beautiful today]. All of these allusions add to the themes of loneliness, memory, fragmentation and peripateticism that pervade the novel; in *Sphinx* (the song) the singer wishes to be rid of their past and despairs of the fake declarations of love they have received. These insincere words mirror the idea that the narrator's love for A*** really only exists in hir head; this is also echoed in the reference to Proust. When the narrator's friends are warning hir off A*** they tell hir that ze is not "«son genre»" (Garréta 1986, 55) [his/her type], ostensibly referring to the fact that A*** is black while *je* is white but also referencing the end of Proust's "Un amour de Swann": "Dire que j'ai gâché des années de ma vie, que j'ai voulu mourir, que j'ai eu mon plus grand amour, pour une femme qui ne me plaisait pas, qui n'était pas mon genre!" (Proust 1919, 150) [to say that I ruined years of my life, that I wanted to die, that I gave my greatest love, for a woman who I did not like, who was not my type!]. The allusion to Swann's realization that he was more in love with his memories of Odette than Odette herself presages the breakdown of the narrator's relationship with A***.

Piaf's song is about an unknown town with interminable streets in which the singer, who wants to sleep with her memories of love, is always getting lost. *Come in from the Rain*, while more traditionally romantic, is about being alone and far from home (Garréta 1986, 139) and *Le vierge, le vivace et le bel aujourd'hui* (translated by Blackmore and Blackmore (2006, 66) as 'This virginal long-living lovely day'), which I shall analyze in more detail later, is a sonnet which, like all of Mallarmé's poems, makes the reader "grapple with [...] existential doubt, strangeness, and uncertainty; [...] and thoughts that seem to escape being fixed into any one interpretation" (McCombie 2006, ix). The most widespread influence on Garréta, though, is the *roman noir* style and her text parodies crime writers like Raymond Chandler and Dashiell Hammett (see Livia 2001, 35). By telling what is purportedly a love story through the *roman noir* style Garréta makes her text anti-romantic (or questions what "romance" really is), just as Winterson does with hers through scientific discourse.

Both Winterson and Garréta make their texts a challenge to read, and they both produce what Barthes (1974, 4) would term "writerly" texts which are constantly aware that they are to be read and in being read by an active reader, re-written. "Readerly" texts, on the other hand, are "products (and not productions)" (5), read passively. This is evident in *Written on the Body* from the fact that the narrator is a translator.

The translator traditionally represents someone who has to decide, to make a decision on a text – the translator chooses one strand to follow at the expense of others because both readers (and translators) select meanings from the multiple choices within every text. Winterson makes manifest the idea that all texts are multiple by ensuring that neither the narrator nor the reader can sacrifice polysemy. Her translator, and the translator in literature more generally, is not always someone who can decide,

who is sure of him or herself: it can be a metaphor for one who is displaced, who does not belong, who is an image builder and who is both deceitful and manipulative (Strümper-Krobb 2003, 121). The translator of *Written on the Body* certainly grapples with these questions of belonging, identity and truth.

Winterson suggests that the body is a text to be read and written like a novel: "Written on the body is a secret code only visible in certain lights; the accumulations of a lifetime gather there. In places the palimpsest is so heavily worked that the letters feel like braille" (Winterson 1993, 89). Both Winterson's and Garréta's texts are like palimpsests because they play with intertextuality, but the bodies in their texts are palimpsestuous too, constantly being read and re-read by the reader, constantly becoming and unbecoming. Both texts rely on liminality and this can be seen most strongly in their endings which again direct the reader to an anti-romantic reading of the texts: there is no happily-ever-after. This liminality evokes the becoming of the narrators, the transitional phase of the process of their becoming.

The endings of both texts are surreal and spectral. At the end of *Sphinx*, A*** has died and *je* is visiting A***'s mother in New York when ze is attacked by two men; while the men harass hir, ze is haunted by lines from Mallarmé's poem *Le vierge, le vivace et le bel aujourd'hui*: 'ces vers qui tournoient dans mon esprit m'obsèdent' (Garréta 1986, 156) [these lines which turn in my mind obsess me]. Ramadan (2015, 119) translates "m'obsèdent" with "I am haunted". Further on from the only two lines *je* can remember, Mallarmé's (2006, 66) poem talks of a frozen lake; the lake has forgotten something that is haunting beneath the frost. What is trapped is a swan and this could be read as an analogy for the trapped poet, impotent and incapable of expression. The homophony of "cygnet" [swan] and "signe" [sign] further suggests that the sign is as trapped as the swan. However, according to Elizabeth McCombie (2006, xxv), this reading is too simplistic because the poem teems with paradoxical allusions. That this sonnet is so paradoxical shows how a huge variety of expressive possibilities can be found within culturally-inherited formal constraints; the constraints of rhythm and rhyme encourage the poet to be inventive and flexible. The idea that constraints bring new perspectives or encourage creative thinking is something Garréta exploits.

The end of Mallarmé's sonnet and the fate of the swan is open because there are simultaneous yet competing readings to be made. The same confusion can be seen at the end of Garréta's text. According to Ramadan (2015, 120), the narrator is "carried far away at the whim of those two lines in search of that symmetrical fragment which has disappeared into oblivion, the whole thus robbed of its meaning and harmony." But I would argue that "the whole," which is presumably the sonnet in its entirety which *je* cannot remember, never has unequivocal meaning or harmony because of its competing meanings (see also Bowie 1978, 12). *Je* is therefore on a quest for something which can never bring closure, can never be fully grasped, in the same way that the rest of the poem eludes hir. The fact that *je* cannot remember it is fitting, for the poem itself meditates on "the role of memory and the intrusion of the past into the present, to a re-interpretation of the present in the light of that past and of an immediate as well as hypothetical and eternal future" (Stafford 2000, 38).

Je's future is both hypothetical and eternal – on page 157 ze is thrown into the frozen canal: "Tandis que j'agonize et que de mon dos ruisselle et s'évade le sang à flots, je me sens m'envoler. Eblouissement d'un instant dans la chute d'une ténèbre où je somber et m'abîme" (Garréta 1986, 157) [while I am dying and while blood flows from my back and escapes in waves, I feel myself fly away. A moment's bedazzlement in the fall of a darkness where I sink and lose myself]. Is *je* dead? The reader cannot know and therefore hir future becomes hypothetical because it is whatever the reader wants it to be and eternal because this dénouement involves no definitive answers. Translation as a continuation of the source text's life, as an "unfinishing" of the source text is the perfect medium to ensure that readers, like *je*, never find closure.

The ending to Winterson's text is also surreal and open to possibilities. "I" describes seeing Louise, but we can never know if this is the real Louise or a ghost: "From the kitchen door Louise's face. Paler, thinner, but her hair still mane-wide and the color of blood [...] Am I stark mad? She's warm" (Winterson 1993, 190). Louise is both deathly white and vibrantly red. Just as Garréta's narrator flies away, Winterson's narrator and Louise are endowed with supernatural powers, able to sling the sun under their arms: the narrator "stretch[es] out [hir] hand and reach[es] the corners of the world" (190). This final paragraph is almost feverish or dream-like, and the last line – "I don't know if this is a happy ending but here we are let loose in open fields" (190) – brings to mind the Elysian fields which are first mentioned by Homer (2003, 55) in *The Odyssey* as a place where men go after death. Winterson's text is open-ended. We could also ask if the ending is a happy release or if it is empty and meaningless: has Louise come back to "I," is "I" dreaming, is "I" seeing Louise's ghost or is "I" perhaps also a ghost? "I" is talking with Louise's ghost, even if Louise is not dead; this conversation is as much with the narrator hirself and hir own specters as it is with Louise.

The dénouement of both texts is elusive and this is important because, as we saw in chapter five, the ending of a text is most often where the reader looks for answers to his or her questions (see Bennett and Royle 2004). One could claim that the ending of *Dominique* is where the "trick" is finally revealed, where the reader finally learns of Dominique's gender. As I used textual evidence to argue against the ending as a place of revelation where everything is neatly tied-up in *Middlesex*, I do the same here. Throughout *Dominique* there are hints that we will discover the "truth:" "Gabriel et France inviteraient Dominique à un entretien très sérieux afin de lui révéler son appartenance formelle à l'un des deux sexes" (Allez 2015, 224) [Gabriel and France would invite Dominique to a very serious interview to reveal to him/her his/her formal membership of one of the two sexes]. At the age of seven Dominique discovers hir sex, though ze continues to pretend ze does not know what it is. At the age of eleven Dominique agrees to acknowledge it when ze goes to school but the reader is still in the dark. On the very last page we are told Dominique's sex in the reproduction of a police report detailing the fact that Dominique has gone missing. Dominique's sex is revealed by an official document showing that sex always matters and we cannot do without it when being interpellated by institutions of power such as the police. Despite this, because Dominique has continued to be "un être irréductible à un H ou à un F" (Allez 2015, 258) [a being irreducible to an M or an F] and because ze runs away wearing a "tee-shirt blanc où l'on peut lire NO FUTURE" (259) [a white t-shirt on which can be read NO FUTURE], the revelation of Dominique's sex is a moment of anti-climax. It does not matter what Dominique's sex is, it clearly means nothing to Dominique hirself.

Dominique is unveiled but an act of unveiling is also a covering up; the model who disrobes for a photograph is "an allegory of truth itself in its movement of veiling and unveiling: the origin of light, the visibility of the visible, that is, the black night, that which, letting things appear in the light [*la clarté*], by definition hides itself from view" (Derrida 2010, 172). Following Heidegger, Derrida names the photographic model "Aletheia;" for Heidegger (2010, 210), *Aletheia* is "truth in the sense of discoveredness (unconcealment)" where the truth is revealed through sight: "to let things *be seen* in their unconcealment (discoveredness), taking them out of their concealment" (2010, 210, my emphasis). But there is no hidden truth, no state of unconcealment, to something that is undecidable. This suggests that there can be more than one truth just as the revelation of Dominique's sex is only one version of the "truth," a truth Dominique chooses not to follow. What we see with our eyes is not always the truth and this is something that literature can take advantage of.

In literature, we can identify with someone who is nothing like we are and perhaps this is because there is no visual element outside of the reader's head to confirm or deny what we imagine. We can undo the privilege of sight through literature because literature allows trans-gender identification. If the reader of the source texts embraces undecidability in all its manifestations, these texts can help us to question dominant ideology. As a rewriting of the source text and a continuation of its life, a translation is uniquely placed to work on the issues that said source text brings to light and to bring those issues to a new audience in a new time and place. It now remains to be seen whether the translators of these texts have embraced this unsettling undecidability or if they have written it out.

Translating *Sphinx*

In this section I will look in close detail at the 2015 English translation of *Sphinx* by Emma Ramadan and also discuss what it is about the source text which makes its translation so challenging. Gerald Prince (2014, 24–5), thinks that it is easier to write a genderless narrator in English than in French. However, Prince (25) also argues that "what constitutes a tour de force in French may require less linguistic virtuosity in English and may thus prove less striking and less efficient in suggesting, say, that love transcends sexual and gender difference." Emma Ramadan (2015, 124) might not agree that her translation required "less linguistic virtuosity." Instead, it required a different kind of linguistic virtuosity, as she says: "I broke Garréta's code by creating a new one." English does not gender past participles or adjectives but it does gender possessive adjectives, something French does not do. Both English and French are capable of (and resist) epicene narration but in different ways (see Schabert 2010, 75).

I will now examine some specific examples from *Sphinx* which demonstrate how Garréta conceals gender in French and consider Ramadan's translation solutions. Ramadan appears to be of the opinion that the removal of gender is not merely a gimmick, for her: "Garréta both reveals and undermines sex-based oppression, demonstrating that gender difference is not an important or necessary determinant of our [...] identities but is rather something constructed purely in the realm of the social" (Ramadan 2015, 123). Garréta avoids using past participles by writing the text using the imperfect and past historic tenses. The imperfect text is used for a past action that was habitual or repeated. This means that je is a character who has many habits. The use of the past historic, or *passé simple*, is unusual, it is mostly used in literary texts and is therefore a very formal tense, it does not exist in English (125).

To incorporate the use of the *passé simple* into her text, Garréta makes *je* the kind of pretentious, bourgeois character who might just use it in a memoir. Ramadan tackles the lack of such a formal tense in English by "accommodating elevated or unusual vocabulary when possible to keep the tone and register the same in English as in French" (126). This elevated vocabulary is often achieved by keeping the closest English word to the French, which is often a cognate: for example, "parure" (Garréta 1986, 19) [finery, jewelry] in French remains "parure" in English (Ramadan 2015, 7), or "congénères" (Garréta 1986, 56) [fellow creature, peer, contemporary] becomes "congeners" (Ramadan 2015, 37). Or by using another foreign word which is untranslated in English: "le contraste de clair et d'obscur" (Garréta 1986, 44) [the contrast of the light and the dark] becomes "the chiaroscuro" (Ramadan 2015, 26), "mélancolie" (Garréta 1986, 16) [melancholy] becomes "ennui" (Ramadan 2015, 5). The main way Garréta avoids gender is to only ever use invariable adjectives and nouns to refer to both *je* and A***, and this is not a problem in English: for example, "mon amour, mon enfant" (Garréta 1986, 15) becomes "my love, my child" (Ramadan 2015, 4). In the French text where *je* is referred to as "mon oiseau" (Garréta 1986, 14), Ramadan (2015, 3) avoids "my bird" which is gendered in English, as "bird" is a slang term for a woman, and translates with "my pet".

For a French writer wishing to achieve epicene narration, the use of gendered nouns in French is an obstacle; this is not a problem for translation into English. What makes French epicene narration easy, epicene possessive adjectives, presents an obstacle for English translation. It is not strictly true, however, that possessive adjectives are epicene. The possessive adjective is masculine or feminine in French depending on the gender of the relevant noun and not depending on the gender of the person it refers to. It is "sa jambe" as opposed to "son jambe" because "jambe" is feminine. This means that "sa," which is the feminine third person singular possessive adjective, does not indicate that the person who the leg belongs to is a woman. This reminds us that French genders inanimate objects. Garréta's text does not play with the gendering of inanimate objects, but what it does do is highlight how prevalent the gender binary is.

According to Schabert (2010, 89), to deal with these possessive adjectives, "the translator would certainly have to resort to creative solutions such as the you-narrative which Angela Carter used for epicene references to a third person." In *The Passion of New Eve,* Carter uses the second-person for a character whose gender is complicated (Carter 1982, 110). Ramadan never refers to A*** using "you" and she actively avoids epicene pronouns because "that approach just seemed very out of place for this book, because these aren't people who are choosing not to discuss gender, they're just people whose genders we happen not to know" (Ramadan in Hayes 2016). This attitude suggests that she sees the gender concealment as a trick. Indeed, she cannot avoid gendering A***: "I thought A*** was a woman. And when I was translating, I was trying really hard not to insert any "hers" [...] when I got the final proof, I suddenly found a "her" still in the text that nobody had caught. Like *five people* had read the text at this point and not one had caught it because they all thought A*** was a woman" (Ramadan in Hayes 2016). Despite this, her translation is devoid of gender markers and she explains in her translator's note that she tackled the problem of possessive adjectives four different ways: "using a demonstrative, dropping the article altogether, pluralizing, or repeating A***'s name [...]" elsewhere, she rewrites sections entirely to avoid personal pronouns (Ramadan 201, 124).

I will now discuss Ramadan's solutions in more detail to question how agender characters can be represented both in 'original' writing and in translation. By discussing Ramadan's translation techniques it will become clear that translation is the perfect medium through which to think through problems of gender in language and consider how gender might be kept out of a new translation concerned not just with gender as an aesthetic problem but as a political one, too, one that goes beyond pronouns. In the below example, Ramadan avoids difficulties with possessive adjectives by using A***'s name and shortening the passage:

> Je lui reprochai sa froideur, son manque de compassion à l'égard de mes états d'âme. Je l'accusai en vrac d'indifférence et de narcissisme coupable, d'égoïsme aussi.
>
> (Garréta 1986, 98)

> [I reproached him/her for his/her coldness, his/her lack of compassion regarding the states of my soul. I haphazardly accused him/her of indifference and guilty narcissism, selfishness too.]

> I haphazardly reproached A*** for being too cold and uncaring, for being shamefully narcissistic too.
>
> (Ramadan 2015, 72)

Here, Ramadan has avoided the gender of the "lui" in "lui reprochai" and of the "le" which has been contracted in "l'accusai" by merging the two into "I haphazardly reproached A***". In the source text, A*** is constantly referred to by hir body parts and Livia (2001, 47) considers that this constant referral to A***'s body parts fragments hir identity. These body parts are impersonal because they are shared with every other person, they cannot be specific because they must not reveal gender information; and because of this the reader cannot feel empathy for A***. When Ramadan drops the article this rather objectifies A***: "ses mains pendaient, poignets lâches, abandonnés, son regard perdu" (Garréta 1986, 81) becomes "hands dangling, wrists slack, gaze abandoned and lost" (Ramadan 2015, 58). The use of a demonstrative to get around things like "ses bras" (Garréta 1986, 12) [his/her arms] also rather cuts A*** out: Ramadan (2015, 1) uses "those arms". She also uses the indefinite article in this example: "l'empreinte résiduelle, à peine sensible, de son épaule" (Garréta 1986, 59) becomes "the residual imprint, barely there, of a shoulder" (Ramadan 2015, 40). This use of "a shoulder," which could belong to anyone, removes A*** from the text in translation even more so than in the source text.

I consider that A*** is meant to be an elusive, spectral figure and hir fragmentation merely mirrors the self-fragmentation the narrator undergoes throughout the text. Ramadan (127) also believes that A*** is deliberately absent: "A***'s character barely exists in the novel; A*** almost never speaks in his or her own words and doesn't have a developed personality [...] Garréta doesn't gloss over this, but rather makes it the focal point of the novel." Throughout the text *je* is in love with the image of A*** and not A*** hirself to the extent that *je* pushes the real A*** away to enjoy the imagined A*** better. *Je* drains the blood from hir relationship with A*** in an unconscious act of self-sabotage and A*** becomes more and more spectral until hir death.

Livia (2001, 44) also sees the constant repetition of A***'s name instead of the use of a subject pronoun as preventing the reader from identifying with A*** and as creating a "loose and disconnected" text. However, I believe that a fragmented, disjointed text is exactly what Garréta was hoping to create; Livia is imposing an aesthetic critique on a text which is using aesthetics to make a political critique. Does it matter that the text is disconnected if the reader is given a glimpse of a world without gender? It could be argued that Garréta's text is only an aesthetic achievement and not a political one because the power of the text is only wielded over a linguistic domain (see Ruby 2016), but we have already established the power of literature to make its readers think about the world around them.

As we can see from Ramadan's list of strategies above, she keeps the repetition of A***'s name in her translation.[1] On page 43 of Ramadan's translation "A***" or "A***'s" is repeated eleven times over twenty-eight lines. It is helpful here to see what Cookie Allez has done with *Dominique* to ascertain whether another French text (written in a language which normally shuns repetition (see Berman 2012, 244)) is prepared to repeat a first name and have politics trump style. Allez constantly repeats "Dominique," "Do" or "Sweetie" to refer to the child. This can be seen in the following extract where Dominique's mother, France attempts to get hir to choose a gender:

> Et toi, *Sweetie*, reprit France, surprise par le silence de son mari, tu sais qui tu es? Garçon ou fille? Non! Do ne savait pas. Et n'aimait pas cette question. Du reste, Do s'en fichait complètement. C'était pas son problème. On verrait plus tard, quand on serait grand [...] Do ferait tout pour devenir un être différent des autres.
>
> (Allez 2015, 232)

> [And you, Sweetie, France carried on, surprised by her husband's silence, do you know who you are? Boy or girl? No! Do didn't

> know. And didn't like that question. As for the rest, Do didn't care at all. It wasn't his/her problem. We would see later on, when we would be grown up [...] Do would do anything to be different from everyone else]

Allez (ibid.) does, however, introduce an epicene pronoun into her text by having Dominique's parents use the Swedish "hen:" "Do ira à l'école quand hen aura l'age d'entrer en sixième?" [Do will go to school when hen is eleven?]. However, the use of the epicene pronoun is very short-lived: "They still had to struggle, as they had for the past three years, to ban gendered adjectives from their vocabulary, and so this *hen* didn't bring them much" (146, my translation).

Garréta uses invariable adjectives to hide gender, and Allez (149) does the same: "Avant que lui soit révélé – assez prochainement sans doute – son sexe de naissance, Dominique ne sera jamais gentil ou gentille: Dominique sera sage, docile, calme, agréable ou tendre." To highlight that these adjectives have been specifically chosen because they are invariable in French, the gendered font I explored in chapter three could be used in an English translation (Figure 8.1).

Dominique is a text that is reflexively about translation: this translation is intralingual where Gabriel and France must translate gendered French into ungendered French but also interlingual in that other languages and gender systems provide a contrast. When Dominique is born, hir English grandmother thinks ze is a boy because ze is referred to as "le bébé" [the baby]; indeed, Allez (2015, 55) makes a point out of the fact that all the words one can use to refer to a new-born baby in French are masculine.

There is also a part of Garréta's text which is gendered simply because of the fact that the masculine is taken as the universal in French: at one point *je* describes hirself as "travelo en intellection, gigolo en énamorations" (Garréta 1986, 116). "Travelo" [transvestite] and "gigolo" take the masculine gender but do not reveal *je* to be male. According to Rye (2000, 533), "in this text where gender and gender attributes are always uncertain, because of the figurative use of the terms and also because no feminine equivalents for them exist, they cannot be accepted as unquestionably

Before Dominique discovered hir birth sex – which would undoubtedly be quite soon – ze would never be kind or kind: Dominique would be wise, sweet, calm, agreeable or tender.

Figure 8.1 An excerpt from *Dominique* (Allez 2015, 149, my translation) translated with my gendered font.

masculine signifiers." Ramadan (2015, 87) translates this phrase as "drag queen of intellection, gigolo of enamoration". In English we have two terms which, I suggest, are masculine signifiers.

In *Dominique*, Dominique's father, Gabriel notes that "it would be necessary to reform the entire French syntax to reach the extreme simplicity of the British system where nothing agrees because nothing has gender! Except the subject one is speaking of: *il ou elle*, he or she ..." (Allez 2015, 147, my translation). My discussion of Ramadan's translation of a genderless text into English serves to prove that things are not as simple as Gabriel assumes in English. While it is true that nothing agrees grammatically – except loanwords from French like blond(e) or fiancé(e) – it is not true that nothing has gender as we can see above with terms like "drag queen" or "drag king," "prostitute" or "gigolo". This is something which will become even more apparent when we look at how genderless narrators have been received in English-language texts.

Translating *Written on the Body*

Written on the Body is not the first English-language text to feature a genderless narrator and it is useful to consider how early translations of Virginia Woolf's *Orlando* into French dealt with a briefly genderless Anglophone protagonist to see if translators of *Written on the Body* had a precedent to follow. Although Orlando switches from a male protagonist to a female protagonist during the text, for a short while Orlando's sex is indeterminate. Between pages 86 and 87, Woolf ([1928] 2004, 87) does not use any pronouns and only uses the name "Orlando" to refer to her protagonist. After this, Woolf (87) continues to use masculine pronouns even though "he was a woman". Woolf (ibid.) then uses the epicene pronoun "they" to refer to both the masculine and the feminine Orlando at once: "The change of sex, though it altered their future, did nothing whatever to alter their identity". Orlando's name, for example, does not change to Orlanda. Woolf uses "their" three times before starting to use feminine pronouns.

This episode can be translated into French with the use of possessive adjectives (Pappo-Musard 1993, 136). In the French, Orlando remains without a precise gender for longer than in the original; between Orlando's waking and the use of the epicene "they," Woolf uses "he" to refer to Orlando five times, Catherine Pappo-Musard removes at least three of these references to masculine gender (see Schabert 2010, 83). For Schabert (ibid.), French is better suited in this instance to epicene narration. This section is crucial in the text because for the briefest of moments, Orlando is truly undecidable and French is equipped to deal with this undecidability.

I will now examine specific examples from *Written on the Body* where the narrator's gender is undecidable and consider how the French translator, Suzanne Mayoux, and the Spanish translator, Encarna Castejón, have dealt with these moments of undecidability. According to Schabert (90), "Mayoux had a much harder task [than Winterson] to recreate the sexually indeterminate narrator-protagonist." She rewrites passages to avoid using gendered past participles, for example "Louise and I were held by a single loop of love" (Winterson 1993, 88), becomes "c'était une simple boucle d'amour qui nous liait" (Mayoux 1993, 111) [it was a simple loop of love that linked us] to avoid writing "nous étions lié(e)s …" [we were linked …] which requires a gender marker on the past participle.

Both Mayoux and Castejón transpose verbs for nouns to avoid gender: for example, when "I" says "By morning I was bad tempered and exhausted" (Winterson 1993, 31), Castejón (1994, 38) writes "me caía de cansancio" [I was falling over with tiredness] instead of using "cansado/a" [tired]; and Mayoux (1993, 38) writes "ma fatigue se voyait" [my fatigue was visible] instead of using "fatigué(e)" [tired]. On page 52 the narrator says "I'm not married" (Winterson 1993). Castejón (1994, 63) has the narrator say that they don't have a marriage certificate and Mayoux (1993, 65) has "Je n'ai pas commis l'erreur de me marier" [I have not committed the mistake of marrying]. Mayoux's narrator gives an explicit value judgment on marriage where Winterson's narrator (who, admittedly, clearly lambasts marriage elsewhere in the text) does not. Just as Garréta's avoidance of gendered language creates a certain kind of character, so Mayoux's translation gives Winterson's narrator a different character because circumlocution is necessary to avoid gendering. Where Winterson's narrator was direct, Mayoux's is literary and verbose: "I want to be sure" (Winterson 1993, 84) becomes "je veux avoir des certitudes" (Mayoux 1993, 106) [I want to have certainties] or "Am I stark mad?" (Winterson 1993, 190) becomes "Ai-je sombré dans la folie?" (Mayoux 1993, 241) [have I sunk into madness?]. Mayoux's narrator becomes much like Garréta's narrator: old-fashioned, self-important and pedantic. We have two genderless characters in French who both use a specific kind of discourse. Whether all genderless characters in French necessarily use discourse in the first person is yet to be fully proven but we return to the problem of discourse as gendered.

Schabert (2010, 91) believes the narrator's new character is why, despite Mayoux's removal of grammatical gender from the text, "reviewers of the French version insisted on reading the narrator as male." This interpretation cannot have been helped by the back cover of the translation which declares that: "Au travers des élans du corps et du coeur de deux amants, il dresse une minutieuse cartographie du désir" (1993) [through the impetus of the body and the heart of the two lovers(m), [the book] raises a meticulous cartography of desire]. The "deux amants" can only refer to two men or a man and a woman as "amant" is in the masculine; as Louise is clearly a woman, the latter is the only option.

Camille Fort has also considered why the narrator is most often seen as a man in French and, like Schabert, thinks the problem is with the narrator's discourse. Fort considers that the grammatical neutrality of the text suggests masculinity because what is neutral is masculine, but that Winterson gets around this by suggesting femininity through rhythm and lexical values: "A fluid and fluctuating discourse where traits culturally associated with the masculine word – assertion, brevity, the constative mode – alternate with parts taken from writing which evokes the feminine: syntactic disconnection, longer sentences, importance of silence" (Fort 2008, 57, my translation). Fort (58) considers that Mayoux can only make her text grammatically neutral and cannot also reproduce the lexical values and rhythm of the text.

Fort's (56) criticism arises because she believes that the narrator is meant to oscillate between being a man and a woman and is not meant to be neither. Indeed, she thinks "neither" is not possible because in French, the neutral represents the masculine. In this view, Mayoux fails *because* her narrator is neutral, and is therefore really male (see also Maioli 2009, 144). Mayoux's text, however, is not entirely neutral in the grammatical sense. As with the translators of *Middlesex*, neither Mayoux nor Castejón is completely consistent in keeping their text free of grammatical gender. There are plenty of examples where they both keep out gender as we have seen above but alongside attempts to be gender neutral come instances where gender creeps in. For example, the narrator has conversations with a friend about hir penchant for married women. This friend has no gender in Winterson's (1993, 32) text yet in French they are female ("amie") (Mayoux 1993, 38) and in Spanish they are male ("amigo") (Castejón 1994, 39). While this does not gender the narrator, there are genderless options: for example, "pote" [pal, mate, buddy] in French, while informal, is invariable and similarly "colega" [friend, mate, buddy] is invariable in Spanish. When Louise and the narrator are together gender marking still has to be avoided on adjectives and past participles, as noted above with the mistake on the French back cover. In the English text the narrator goes to Louise's house and they "went down the hall together" (Winterson 1993, 30). In the Spanish the word for "together" must be gendered: "juntos/as" and Castejón (1994, 36) chooses the feminine plural which can only refer to two women.

In French, "I felt like a thief with a bagful of stolen glances" (Winterson 1993, 49), becomes "je me sentais comme un cambrioleur, avec mon baluchon d'images volées" (Mayoux 1993, 62). "Cambrioleur" is not invariable but is the masculine form of thief, for which there is a feminine alternative, "cambrioleuse". Though a slightly different word, the invariable "escroc" [crook] could have been used. Similarly, in the Spanish, Castejón (1994, 60) uses "ladrón" [thief] which does have a feminine equivalent "ladrona". Again, "mangante" [petty thief/swindler], albeit with different connotations, is invariable and could have been used to preserve the neutrality. Whilst I disagree with Fort above, where she argues that Mayoux does not, but should, represent the narrator's femininity discursively, I do agree that both Mayoux and Castejón rely on grammatical masculinity to represent universality.

Conclusions

The masculine is used to represent neutrality but, as we have seen, the feminine appears in these translations where it should not (even Ramadan wanted A*** to be feminine), suggesting that the idea that these are lesbian texts (especially *Written on the Body*) is pervasive. The Italian translator also makes Winterson's narrator feminine at least once; Leonardi (2013, 73) notes that this is an odd slip which is in no way influenced by the source text in a translation which endeavors to avoid gender markers and could have been easily avoided. Oriana Palusci, on the other hand, who has also analyzed Giovanna Marrone's Italian translation of *Written on the Body*, feels the same way about the Italian translation as Camille Fort does about the French translation. She believes that the narrator is meant to be both male and female and that "the Italian translation analyzed fail[s] to reproduce the appropriate gender markedness of the source text" (Palusci 2013, 30). She also makes it very clear that whether "I" is male *or* female is not the question readers should ask. Her point is that to make the text genderfull rather than genderless, is to dare the reader to see both masculine and feminine gender markers and yet believe that these attributes can be held by the same person (22). This is important but I also think that this text has more to offer about genderless identities, even more in translation than in the original English. In chapter nine I will consider exactly how we can use translation to ensure that gender remains something that is missing from these texts.

Note

1 Ramadan also keeps the asterisks and is not tempted to use a unisex name in English such as Alex. Elkin (2015) admits that she was tempted to fill in this name when reading.

9 The Lipogram and the Cut-Out Technique

The English *Sphinx*, the French *Écrit sur le corps* and the Spanish *Escrito en el cuerpo* may have more to say about genderless identities and texts in translation than their originals do because translating these texts comes with extra constraints. Every translation is constrained – the translator is tied (though of course not slavishly) to the source text – and these texts offer an extra element of constraint in the genderless narrator. In this chapter I will consider how translation is always constrained by looking at two radical texts which deconstruct their originals. I will return to ideas of both the palimpsest and the hypertext by looking at Tom Phillips' *A Humument* (1980) and Jonathan Safran Foer's *Tree of Codes* (2010). Both texts deconstruct their "originals," highlight the materiality of the book and suggest ways to experiment with erasure, undecidability, loss, haunting and deception in translation. I will finally consider how embracing the creativity inherent in working under constraints can suggest new ways of translating trans texts by exploring the ideas and work of some of the members of the Oulipo, of which Garréta is a member. My translation techniques create fragmented and surreal texts. These texts draw the reader's attention to the book and to their own part in the writing process, just as Garréta's and Winterson's texts do.

Translation Possibilities: Erased and Constrained Texts

Tom Phillips' *A Humument* shows how self-imposed constraints help authors find creativity, how the book can be emphasized as a material object but also how translation has limits. This artist's book is an intralingual translation as Phillips has taken a forgotten English text and, though leaving it in English, "treated" it to make a completely new text. Phillips (1980) imposed rules on his search for a book to treat: he chose the first sensible book that he came across which cost threepence. This book was W.H. Mallock's Victorian novel *A Human Document*. His first technique was to score out unwanted words with pen and ink, then he used acrylic paint, typing and cut out and stuck in parts from other pages in the book. He made it a rule that he could not use any work other than the book itself (Phillips 1980). He considers himself as in collaboration with Mallock, a collaboration he sees as incongruous. Indeed, he calls this an "unwriting" project (Phillips 1980). That this is "unwriting" instead of "rewriting" may point to how much of Mallock's text is erased. Because Phillips unwrites Mallock's text, *A Humument* becomes what Barthes (1986, 165) might term a perverse palimpsest: what is written and what is unwritten remain superimposed, one text effaces another "but only, one might say, to show that effacement: a veritable philosophy of time".

A Human Document is a story about an upper-class philosopher who falls in love with the already-married but possibly soon-to-be widowed Irma, and Mallock's narrator claims to have pieced the story together from old diary entries and notes. Phillips, therefore, effectively returns *A Human Document* to the fragmented state in which it supposedly started (see Maynard 2003, 84); Phillips leaves only clusters of original text visible and these clusters are connected by "rivers" of white lines running between words. Like *Written on the Body* and *Sphinx*, *A Humument* is both a mixture of many discourses, genres and media and a demonstration of how texts can point to other texts and writers that have come before and those that are still to come (Phillips references books which are long after Mallock's time (Pfahl 2015, 409)). In doing this, Phillips makes the reader think about originality through fragmentation and creativity; his text is entirely made up of other people's words in the same way that many other texts are made up of words that have come before and been said by somebody else first. A prototypical example of the genre that Phillips follows is Charles Reznikoff's Holocaust. Reznikoff uses government records and transcripts: "the material of this affectual contract consists of found text from corporate, governmental, and/or institutional archives. The text is typically reorganized and scored, then juxtaposed with more figurative language to narrate and excavate 'diverse constituencies:' alternative discourses, emotions, and social injustices from within the unspoken or silenced voices that linger in the historical record" (Belflower 2017). Reznikoff's work evinces the idea that working closely on a source text is a type of excavation. He also exemplifies the fact that writers cannot originate all of their work. Winterson's (1993, 10, 155) text is concerned with originality and declares multiple times that "it's the clichés that cause the trouble". This declaration could be neatly linked to the stereotypical ways men and women are meant to "be" in the world; there the clichés really do cause trouble. With the decrease in the power of the author comes the increase in the power of the reader; Hayles (2002, 81) sees *A Humument* as a form of print hypertext because one can follow Phillips' rivers in many different ways and the reader must actively participate in the construction of the story.

A Humument is invasive; the Art Libraries Society of the United Kingdom and Ireland considers an artist's book to be an object "in which an artist has had a major input beyond illustration or authorship: where the final appearance of the book owes much to the artist's interference/participation" (Bettley 2001, 164–5). It is a creative defacement only less violent than the "malicious damage" involving pasting pictures on book jackets and rewriting blurbs done to library books by Joe Orton and Kenneth Halliwell in 1959 (Hoare 2013) because Phillips paid for the book. Phillips interferes in Mallock's text beyond the idea of being just the author/editor or the illustrator. In this text, as in *Sphinx* and *Written on the Body*, what is absent is brought into view precisely because it is absent; Phillips draws attention to "the book" as an artifact not only by removing the plot, characters and description but also by covering over paragraph breaks, chapter breaks and linearity.[1] Phillips' text is what Hayles (2002, 26) might term a "technotext:" texts that "bring into view the machinery that gives their verbal constructions physical reality". The way that novels are organized, set out, presented and read is shown to be unnatural, an agreed-upon construction. Both Garréta and Winterson reorient their reader's attention to the body as a frame for the construction of meaning and subjectivity. They draw attention to the sexed body precisely by removing it from their texts. Both sex and gender are constructions because they can be erased (and yet the body still exists), just as plot or conventional page-layout are constructions because they too can be erased (and yet the book still exists).

Cutting the Page – The Book as a Sculpture

A Humument may have inspired John Eric Broaddus' artist's book *Above the Trees: A Short Novel* (1985) which treats Edward J. Bohan's 1982 novel *The Descension* in very similar ways, though it goes further than Phillips' work by including extraneous material and cutting the page with a scalpel to create shapes (Bettely 2001, 173). This idea of cutting is carried even further by Jonathan Safran Foer who also references trees in the title of his work, perhaps suggesting that by focusing on the paper that makes up a book we return to the origin of the page: the tree. This reminds us that books are constructions, they do not spring straight from the author's imagination but are physically cut, bound and packaged for the reader.

Like *A Humument*, *Tree of Codes* is a performance of a book. It also takes its lead from Phillips and his technique of unwriting novels written by somebody else (Brillenburg Wurth 2011, 5). Foer creates a paper sculpture out of an English translation of Bruno Schulz's Polish novel *The Street of Crocodiles* by cutting out whole sentences with a knife – it is a sculpture to be read but also to be admired. If you read the words of Foer's text out loud, ignoring the gaps, you get a similar "nonsense" to that produced by the Dadaist Tristan Tzara in the opening scene of Tom Stoppard's *Travesties* (1975). But this is a joke made at Tzara's expense because his nonsense can be made to make sense. Tzara cuts his writing word by word, puts the pieces in a hat and then reads what he picks out. What is just a series of unconnected words and sounds in English is actually a homophonic translation for the following French lines: "Il est un homme, s'appelle Tzara/Qui des richesses a-t-il nonpareil" (Demastes 2013, 71) [he is a man called Tzara who has unparalleled talent]. Sense can come from apparent gibberish – indeed the opening of the play is entirely based around this idea: the three characters Joyce, Lenin, and Tzara appear to be speaking incomprehensibly but in actual fact while Tzara's words can be made to make sense in another language, "Joyce is dictating abstruse lines from his masterpiece *Ulysses* to his assistant, and Lenin is dictating in Russian to his secretary" (ibid.). In two of these examples translation is the key to making sense. New meanings can be found in all texts that are out of the author's control by readers and translators. The cut-out technique means that a finite series of words can be put in an almost infinite order, something Queneau takes advantage of in his *Cent Mille Milliards de Poèmes* [One Hundred Trillion Poems]. Instead of cutting words he cuts lines: each line of each sonnet is cut into a strip which can be moved to show a different line underneath, and according to Queneau (1961) himself, it would take 190,258,751 years of reading all day every day to read every combination. This exemplifies the fact that one text can make multiple meanings.

Foer's cutting is at once a record of a very close reading by Foer himself (which suggests that all adaptations, including translations, are records of a reading) and also a way of making the reader slow down: "the whites and holes halting our reading: we become aware of those blank spaces in between the words – spaces once full and inhabited and now wrecked, as if constantly reminding us of an irreparable loss" (Brillenburg Wurth 2011, 3). What is lost is lost forever (unless you find a whole version of the original translation, of course) but this is not sanitization or censure meant to put the reader in a position of ignorance; what is removed is less important than the fact that it has been removed.

By erasing words is Safran Foer erasing the possible meanings that words, and therefore whole sentences, may have, or is he emphasizing *différance*? In *A Humument,* Phillips' erasures are mostly illegible but some are still legible because they are crossed through rather than covered up (Phillips 1980, 99, 153). This brings to mind Derrida's "sous rature:" following Heidegger he crosses through words allowing them to remain legible (Derrida 2016, 24); in doing this he suggests a simultaneous presence and absence. For Derrida, however, a presence never really existed in the first place and erasure demonstrates this (see Strysick 2001). Erasure demonstrates the impossibility of the presence of meaning, of Truth. In Heidegger's unconcealment model of truth, presence, or "Dasein," "is equiprimordially in truth and untruth" (Heidegger 2010, 214). For Heidegger, to be human, to exist, one must fight this permanent contradiction:

> To be human (or Dasein, to use Heidegger's term of art) is to find yourself always already confronted with a world of meaning that you have not made and that is constantly presenting you with interpretive decisions about how you are to go about being in it. While you cannot exist in a world without a given structure, since this is how meaning happens to us, you can either accept the structure of meaning as given and go with the flow, or you can confront that structure and beat a course within it. For Heidegger, [...] the latter route is the proper burden of being human: to enter into a polemic with Being.
>
> (Fried 2006, 158)[2]

The translator confronts a structure and beats a course within it: when a translator translates a proposition, they are translating an articulation made up of elements in a structure. They cannot translate the elements alone and they make a choice between similar yet competing propositions with similar yet competing meanings, but every sign carries the trace of other signs, unchosen, invisible, out of reach, never present: "since the trace is not a presence but the simulacrum of a presence that dislocates itself, displaces itself, refers itself, it properly has no site – erasure belongs to its structure" (Derrida 1982, 24). Derrida points to the undecidability of words, the undecidability of meaning and truth because meaning and truth are always deferred; the text has no authority, the original is merely a trace, meaning has no primacy and the critic has no control (see Spivak 2016, xxxvi-c).

For Safran Foer (2010, 138), the erasure of *The Street of Crocodiles* is another layer prolonging the life of the text. It is what Foer (ibid.) long wanted to create a text that has been exhumed from another text. Indeed, he talks of *The Street of Crocodiles* as a gravestone and *A Tree of Codes* as the rubbing made of that gravestone (139). The language used to describe this creation centers around the ideas of death, loss, resurrection, the idea of one text representing the ghost of another. The idea of "exhumation" also works well with *A Humument*, more than phonologically, for it is an exhumation of Mallock's text. Given that both *Sphinx* and *Written on the Body* are meditations on loss and a descent into unreality due to this loss, *Tree of Codes* would appear to be a good place to look for translation ideas.

Safran Foer's adaptation of *The Street of Crocodiles* is an intralingual translation of a translation and not an "original" text. In his author's afterword, however, Safran Foer does not once acknowledge the fact that what he cut was a translation. He talks of how he felt that *The Street of Crocodiles* was itself exhumed from something else (Foer 2010, 139). What Safran Foer cuts is, of course, the product of an exhumation; an exhumation done by the translator, Celina Wieniewska, of Schulz's "original" text.

These "translations" are not generally considered translations: *Tree of Codes* is an "adaptation" (Brillenburg Wurth 2011, 3) and *A Humument* is "an artist's book" (Hayles 2002, 6), "a text" and a "book" (Pfahl 2015, 413), though Maynard (2003, 82) does call it "a radical translation". However, they demonstrate that the line between original writing and translation is very thin. Translation reveals the constraints under which writing always happens, though the translator works with the very obvious constraint of the source text; translation itself is therefore an Oulipian activity because it is writing under constraint, and Oulipian works often point to the "presence of the translator as writing subject, and the impossibility of a pure, unmediated relationship between a translation and its original" (Duncan 2011, 12).

Oulipian Translation

The Oulipo (OUvroir de LIttérature POtentielle [workshop of potential literature]) takes its name from the potentiality of literature, and Garréta sees potentiality in the freedom from everyday rules (such as grammatical gender) which offers a form of play or invention, a way to preserve new ways of reading signs and bodies and a way to mobilize acts differently (Garréta 2009). Garréta has been a member of the Oulipo since 2000 and, though written fourteen years previously, *Sphinx* is listed in *The Oulipo Compendium* (2005) as an Oulipian text because Garréta removes grammatical gender markers from her text (Mathews and Brotchie 2005, 153).

While Garréta attempts to free herself from the rules of grammatical gender in her work (or at least rules pertaining to the gendering of animate objects if not inanimate ones), following the rule of removing grammatical gender is a *sine qua non* of her text. Being rule-bound is a condition of Oulipian writing but it is not their sole *raison d'être*, as Jacques Roubaud (2004, 100) explains: the aims of the Oulipo are often erroneously thought to be to discover constraints and then produce texts using said constraints, but in actual fact "*writing under constraint* is not the primary aim of the Oulipo; it is merely one of the strategies employed to attain its goal [...]: Potentiality." Potentiality is contrasted with actuality; here this means keeping gender fluid until disclosure becomes necessary (which it always does outside of literature) but even this disclosure, as we have seen, is one truth among many.

Constraint brings freedom, the freedom of potentiality and multiplicity, and there is a dialectic of freedom and constraint in every Oulipian work, as there is, I would argue, in every translation. Raymond Queneau, one of the founding members of the Oulipo, attended Kojève's lecture series on Hegel (see Tufail 1999, 122) and is influenced by him as I am here, by the concepts of freedom in constraint and the *Aufhebung*. For Queneau, to experiment with a text in an Oulipian manner is to give more balance to the collaboration between writer and reader by giving the reader more to do than simply read the words on the page (see Shorley 1985, 2). By presenting the reader with a text that has been worked on using a constraint, Queneau exposes reading as a deliberate and careful act: it is not casual or passive, not "readerly" in Barthes' (1974, 4) sense. Winterson often strives for this exposition in her works as well: books only become alive when someone is reading them. Reading, rather than writing, creates the text (see Carpenter 2007, 69).

As we saw above, *Tree of Codes* was influenced by *A Humument* and one of the consequences of working under a constraint is how the same constraint can offer its own potentialities: "It bears the seeds of *variations* and *extensions* that subsequent work on that constraint will ferret out" (Roubaud 2004, 109). A single text written or translated using a constraint holds within it the promise of other attempts and experiments. Scott (2012, xi) advocates a translational practice that moves from "the single towards the multiple (the endless variations and modulations of ongoing, living response)" and that multiple response to a (not-so-)single source text is what I have tried to achieve so far and will also look at here.

Constraints are often described in terms of loss and violence, for some perhaps a negative loss of creativity or literary quality; they are treated as something monstruous that has been done to both language and writing (Perec in Tufail 1999, 125). Here the monstrously constrained work is seen as the antithesis of the "unconstrained" work (as if there were such a thing) just as the monstrously intersexual body is seen as the antithesis of the normally-sexed body (and, as we saw in chapter four, this does not exist either). For others, constraints are a representation of the loss, or the absence, that is present in all writing and the violence that is done to all language by writers. While writing poetry under the constraint of rhyme or verse form is considered creative, writing under other kinds of constraints is sometimes considered uncreative writing because the writer merely sets the constraint to work: uncreative writers "are more likely to determine pre-established rules and parameters – to set up a system and step back as it runs its course – than to heavily edit or masterfully polish" (Dworkin 2011, xliv).

This stepping back, however, can lead to more creativity, more authorial input and not less. Craig Dworkin (xlvii) uses the analogy of Echo who is forever condemned to repeat the last thing she hears to explain this; Echo is "continuing to communicate in her restricted state with far more personal purpose than her earlier gossiping, turning constraint to her advantage, appropriating others' language to her own ends, 'making do' as a verbal *bricoleuse*." Echo is a builder using elements of the language structure (here single words) as her tools and this is what translators do – they echo the source text for their own ends. In terms of creative uncreative writing, perhaps less is more. Like Echo who repeats what has come before, Jorge Luis Borges' character Pierre Ménard repeats and re-creates *Don Quijote* in what Borges (1998, 90) describes as a work with no likeness. Of course, the work does have its likeness in Cervantes' text, but though it is a word-for-word replica it is not a copy (see Bush 2006, 216). Ménard uses the words in a different time and place and they are invested with different meanings because of it.

One of the best known Oulipian texts is Georges Perec's *La Disparition* which involves a lipogram of the letter "e;" he writes the whole novel without once using the letter "e". The text, therefore, evidently involves a loss, but this loss creates gains elsewhere. With this invention the author must manipulate the text's style and content to avoid the "e," Perec is forced to write in a way he might not have done without the constraint. Dennis Duncan (2011, 7) looks at translations of *La Disparition* in his PhD thesis and what he finds interesting is not the inevitable fact that the French and English versions are different but the degree to which they are different. *La Disparition* is almost the poster-child for literary translation itself because it makes patently clear what makes translation so difficult: "some formal property of the original which roots the text deeply in the humus of its home language has to be replicated within a wholly different but equally arbitrary structure of letters and sounds" (8). The formal yet arbitrary structures of language that we are most concerned with here are gender codes which are more prevalent in French and Spanish than in English.

The fragmentation of *La Disparition*, due to the lack of the letter "e," creates a text which is disjointed and surreal. According to Jacques Neefs (2007, 72), it works like memory, or like a dream. The same could be said for *Sphinx* and *Written on the Body*: the loss of gender creates surreal, fragmented, and, therefore, undecidable texts. But can translators, in striving to keep the constraint, also keep the haunting, elusive, fragmented quality of the texts? Gilbert Adair's (1995) translation of *La Disparition*, *A Void,* is doubly constrained because he has to not only remove the letter "e" but represent the source text's story, characters and style: as he has chosen to honor the lipogram, it is not surprising that the representation of the story, characters and style often falters.

While Neefs (2007, 60) feels that "the rules, whether they be given, received, adapted, stolen or specially worked out, cannot be the center of attention of the text or the work of art," it is right for Perec's translators to replicate the constraint he placed on his text – the lipogram is by far the most interesting thing about the text which would otherwise be just another crime novel – even if this means giving the target audience a text which is very different in every other respect. Mayoux certainly presents the reader with a different narrator to Winterson's to erase gender, but even if she had focused less on removing gender and more on giving the French reader a narrator of similar character, it would still be a totally different narrator from Winterson's. Above, Livia disparages Garréta's work for not following novelistic conventions (it is fragmented and disjointed with characters we cannot sympathize with) but whether it is "well written" with an exciting plot and well-rounded characters is not the point and the same could be said for *La Disparition.*[3] Translation between different languages will always produce different texts, with or without added constraints, and sometimes it is necessary for translators to break the original author's code by creating a new one as Ramadan (2015, 124) does, since this is the only way potentiality can be released. Ramadan makes use of the constraints of Garréta's text to play with the concepts of translation and writing just as Garréta made use of the constraints of grammatical gender to play with the cultural concepts of binary sex and gender. We can never do without the constraints of sex or gender and we can never do without the constraints of writing but it is these very constraints which give us the freedom to see sex, gender and writing in a different light. Garréta (2009, my translation) believes that "to be Oulipian is to be queer and, to be queer, that is to participate in the possible." *Sphinx* experiments with what is possible – that is what makes it a queer project and also an Oulipian project.

A 'Lipogrammic' Translation

Queer "is in the business of deliberate proliferation" and translation is a breeding ground for this proliferation: "Queer and its translation insist on the importance of seepage and contamination, hybridity, in-betweenness and indeterminacy" (Epstein and Gillett 2017, 4). Palimpsestuous, hypertextual translation is a celebration of in-betweenness and indeterminacy. I wanted any translation method for *Sphinx* and *Written on the Body* to celebrate this in-betweenness and indeterminacy as well, to be experimental, to encourage the reader to be a player in the text and to maintain the undecidability of both the texts and their protagonists.

Given Neefs' (2007, 72) consideration that the removal of the letter "e" makes *La Disparition* read like a dream or a memory, a lipogram is a good translation method for *Sphinx*: I decided to remove the letter "i" from my translation. Throughout this book we have come up against issues of the masculine standing for the universal, or the neutral or vice versa. This deletion of "i" from my translation is not meant to suggest that agender identity is not worthy of proper representation but is inspired by Monique Witting and Judith Butler. It is meant to undo the fact that gender is present in the pronoun je, something Wittig bemoans in "The Mark of Gender" and also the idea that "there is no 'I' who stands *behind* discourse and extends its volition or will *through*discourse" (Butler 1997b, 12). The concept of subjectivity is a discursive construct; no subject has total authority over what they say and the removal of "i" mirrors this. It is meant to expose the fact that "language casts sheaves of reality upon the social body, stamping it and violently shaping it" (Wittig 1985, 4). Butler (2016a, xxiv) warns that danger does not lie in discovering "that we are the passive dupes of an all-powerful writing; on the contrary, it is the resistance to reading that is the greatest risk, for it leaves us clutching forms of knowledge and language that are the sign of our unknowingness. Better to tarry attentively with the unknowable." Better to acknowledge and work against our ignorance, no matter how futile, than to wallow in it. And the best tool to fight the power of language and of writing is translation.

This deletion of the "i" in a translation of *Written on the Body* may also go some way to preventing readers from assuming the narrator is Winterson herself. The fact that "I" is something complicated and multiple is also attested to by Derrida, for the "I" that addresses the reader is: "An 'I' that, functioning as a pure passageway for operations of substitution, is not some singular and irreplaceable existence, some subject or 'life', but only, moving between life and death, reality and fiction, etc., a mere function or phantom" (Derrida 2004, 357). The "I" of the narrator only represents one moment of their existence, an existence that is haunted and constantly mobile, becoming and unbecoming.

We saw in chapter eight that we can identify with something or someone that is nothing like we are: the "I" is something trans-gender. Everyone who reads a text like *Jane Eyre* has a "female" "I" in their heads, replacing their own "I," including an anonymous critic of the time in 1849: "But as we read on we forgot both commendations and criticism, identified ourselves with Jane in all her troubles, and finally married Mr Rochester about four in the morning" (Allott 1974, 152). As we saw in the above section, Winterson's narrator is unreliable and Jennifer Hansen (2005, 367) suggests that "what happens when we cannot make this character into an object with clear boundaries is that we are invited to occupy the space of the protagonist ourselves." All writing invites the reader to do this, even if the narrator is clearly gendered, and therefore, all reading is trans as I noted above. Female writers write male protagonists and male writers write female protagonists. The writer occupies the position of the character they are writing, regardless of their gender. According to Francis Steegmuller (1968, 283), by the time he was halfway through *Madame Bovary,* Flaubert was modeling Emma Bovary on himself: "'I am Madame Bovary' – 'Madame Bovary, c'est moi!'" (see also Steegmuller 2001, 320).

Writing and reading a character is not writing and reading a gendered experience. As we have seen with Puck, we can read characters who are neither female nor male nor even human. And reading is an important means of identification because in reading we always form our identities:

> Whenever I read, I mentally pronounce an *I*, and yet the *I* which I pronounce is not myself [...] as soon as something is presented as *thought*, there has to be a thinking subject with whom, at least for the time being, I identify, forgetting myself, alienated from myself. [...] Another *I* [...] has replaced my own, and [...] will continue to do so as long as I read.
>
> (Poulet 1970, 60)

With Garréta's and Winterson's texts, the power of the genderless narrator is that I, the reader, can see myself as undecidable.

The constraint I placed on myself to remove the letter "i" required much thought. It meant that I could not use the present continuous, something the narrator uses frequently in French to avoid past participles. Without it sentences become fragmented – *Je* becomes a lazy writer, unconcerned with full sentences. "A*** dansait: j'ai passé des soirées à guetter son apparition sur la scène de L'Eden" (Garréta 1986, 12) [A*** danced: I passed nights watching hir appearance on the stage of the Eden], becomes: "A*** danced: me at dusk, on hold for per appearance on the stage of *the Eden*". I cannot use "hir" or "their" because they contain the letter "i," "per" is another epicene pronoun (see Chak 2015). Descriptions become like snapshots. In Garréta's text the narrator is someone of habitual actions because of the prevalence of the imperfect tense; in my translation ze is less obsessive and more instinctive, less measured and flightier:

> These thoughts sadden me even now, all these years later. How many exactly, not sure. Ten or a few more perhaps. And why force myself to endure only through memory? My soul wants a body. But the soul, already heavy from too much knowledge or the body exhausted from thoughtfulness and lack of power, so caught up by a fevered boredom that naught, or almost naught, can occupy me anymore. Suppose that memory serves: back then, to me, the world was a theatre where corpses danced at a macabre ball of urges. Contempt and outcry couldn't keep me, however, from my craze for the waltz and her decay to a dance of love. Languorous darkness floats at the mercy of syncopated rhythms, short beats; the road to hell sparkled with deaf lanterns; the bottom of the abyss drew ever closer. On the smooth walls of the tornado that moved me forward, deformed forms of overjoyed cadavers presented themselves to me; tortured flesh, they gave off a hoarse death rattle.
>
> (Garréta 1986: 11, my translation)

The present tense replaces the "ing" of continuous action: "un souterrain travail commença à s'opérer, creusement, percée de mine dans mon esprit" (12) [an underground work started to operate, digging, opening a mine in my spirit]. I translate this digging as an action without a subject:

"an underground work started to operate: gouge, gouge at my soul." The present tense also replaces the past historic: "Après l'avoir dépassé, je me retournai pour verifier sans doute le detail de sa mise" (13) [After having passed her, I turned back to check beyond doubt the detail of her appearance]: "Pass her. Turn back. Check beyond doubt the features of her appearance." Sentences become short; it is as if the narrator is giving hirself instructions, living in the moment of the recollection and this, in its own way, suggests an obsession with the past.

A Cut-Out Translation

To consider the text as an artwork I look to *Tree of Codes* and use Foer's cut-out technique to remove the letter "i" from Ramadan's translation; here language becomes a sculptural material. Foer's *Tree of Codes*, as an imposing physical object, makes you, as the reader aware of reading as something physical, you hold the book, you turn the pages but you also engage with the book and intervene in it.

I cut out words including the letter "i" à la Foer to mirror the erasure of gender in the text with the physical erasure of the text itself (see Figure 9.1).

The use of such a radical technique serves not only to make the text unfamiliar and to show how language deceives as it controls but also to show that all translation is mediated. Brillenberg-Wurth (2011, 4) calls

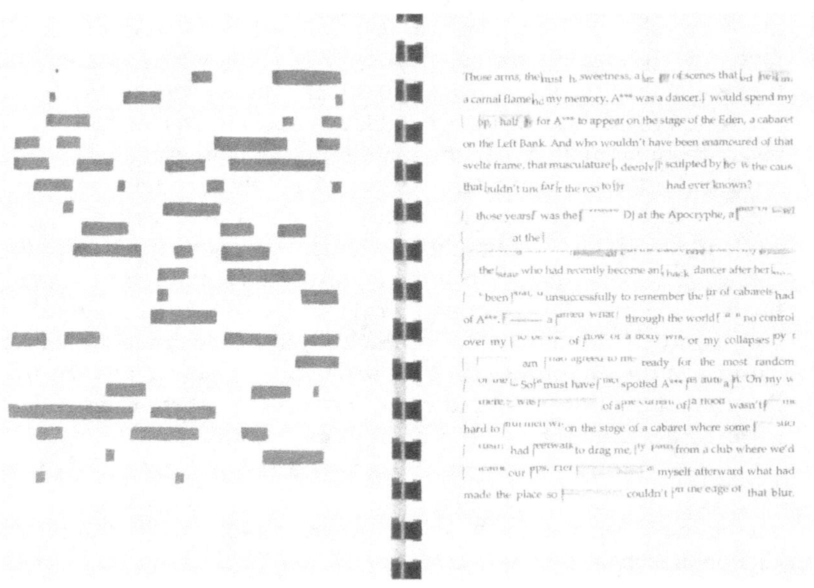

Figure 9.1 Page one of my cut-up of Ramadan's translation (Ramadan 2015, 1).

Foer's adaptation of *The Street of Crocodiles* a verbal-visual commentary of the text. This translation is a verbal-visual commentary on Garréta's text via Ramadan's translation, demonstrating that translation (that writing) is never a completed act, that the text can always be worked upon by the reader. Translation is the written exemplification of loss but the loss does not occur in the act of translation because that would imply that the original was whole and therefore untranslatable (Butler 2016a, x). Translation is a work of mourning and of ruin: "ruin is perhaps its vocation and a destiny that it accepts from the very outset" (Derrida 2001b, 181). By cutting away sections of the text we dramatize and celebrate the incompleteness of translation, its inevitable ruin and its status as something different from its source.

Conclusions

In my previous sections I have explored how translation can deal with two particular kinds of undecidability, one based on oscillation and one based on (inter-)sex. Here I have considered the undecidability caused by rejecting the gender binary. To be gender neutral is often considered to be an impossibility: "There is no such thing as gender-neutral, in language or in reality" (de Lotbinière-Harwood 1991, 100). In the vein of those who cannot read our narrators as genderless, de Lotbinière-Harwood (ibid.) believes that the "translating subject's position is necessarily a gendered position". It is true that to attempt to remove oneself from the gender spectrum involves effort, an effort which is often thwarted in real life by such establishments as hospitals, schools, workplaces and publishers. Where one can be gender neutral is within the pages of a book and we have seen in chapter eight that it *is* possible for translation to echo the gender neutrality of the source text (and it is possible for the translator to leave their own gender out of the equation) even if the target language treats gender differently from the source language. Indeed, I argue that because translation requires such close reading at the level of the text and because it brings up questions of linguistic gender, it is more illuminating to look at translations of agender texts than it is to look at "original" texts. Translation shows us something important about sex, gender and forms of transness: the translations of these particular agender texts allow us to consider agender lives more fruitfully; but they also expose the gender masquerade (that we all have one and that it is always only one of two choices) and the masquerade of original writing (that writers are in control of their texts and originate all the words and ideas they use).

Both Winterson and Garréta have written highly intertextual novels, showing that all texts are influenced by other texts. Once we see that "original" writing is as much a copy as translation is we can start to question the whole concept of "the original". Translation does not come after the source text but predates the original which is not the beginning: "without the derivative there is no original" (Butler 2016a: x); the original text relies on the translation to give it continued life. Translation "guarantee[s] the *survival* of the body of the original (*survival* in the double sense that Benjamin gives it in 'The Task of the Translator,' fortleben and überleben; prolonged life, continuous life, *living on*, but also life after death)" (Derrida 2001b, 199). The death of the original is not final, it continues to ghost. Derrida takes this Hegelian idea to think about the trace: a "double movement of occultation (or erasure) and retroactive constitution" (199). And "the trace is the means through which what is prior is marked [...] it is at once lost and found in the course of that marking" (ibid.).

Translation is the trace of the original and it marks the original *as* original but "origins are instituted, and in such a way that involves both an erasure and a deferral of the origin itself" (Butler 2016a, xxii). The "origin" of translation and of the transgender body is erased and deferred but forever lingers on as a ghost. Translation is the record of a reading, but of multiple readings by both the author and the translator, readings of the process that haunt the "final" product, these hauntings coming from the past but not properly belonging only to the past. The specter is always there looking at us, and we can feel its look, it is always already present (Derrida 2006, 7). Translation acknowledges this look and returns the gaze; it can exemplify the presence of texts and bodies that came before. It is the perfect medium through which to explore ideas of textual and sexual undecidability.

Notes

1 That Phillips reveals by concealing goes against received ideas on *A Humument* as most critics feel that he draws attention to the materiality of the book by making things like textblocks, running titles and page borders visible (see Hayles 2002; Maynard 2003; Pfahl 2015). Brillenburg Wurth (2011: 5) does consider, however, that *A Humument* "shows how the meaning, the physical state of a text, is determined by what it reveals and conceals at the same time".

2 It should be noted that Heidegger takes his ideas from Greek philosophical thought (Hyland 2006: vix) but that "for the professional classicist, there is almost nothing at all of interest in Heidegger's work on Greek philosophy and poetry" (Most 2002: 96). This is not to say that Heidegger's work is without value but that "Heidegger's Greeks are Germans" (ibid.).

3 What "well written" means is debateable – both texts are well written because they remove gender and the letter "e" (they are clever and yet still readable) and many books which are lauded as classics of literary fiction involve characters who are hard to understand or plots that are difficult to follow – James Joyce's *Finnegans Wake* (2015 [1939]), for example.

Conclusion

An Open Ending

Translation is often seen as a "carrying across" (Bellos 2012, 26). The translator acts as the one who carries a text from one culture and one language into another. They cross a river like Ali Smith's reader in *Girl Meets Boy* who can cross any river with the aid of a story; these stories are the ones that must be told, that cannot be silenced and they act like tightropes: the reader must balance bravely above the abyss but it is precisely the story that enables them to carry out this balancing act and the story and this process inevitably and irrevocably changes the reader (Smith 2007, 160). What is problematic about the "carrying across" metaphor, though, is its suggestion that transfer only goes in one direction. As we have seen, drawing on Benjamin's concept of the "afterlife," the source text is as much changed by the translation as the translation is by the source text. Maria Tymoczko (2007, 7) also notes that "Western conceptualizations of translation can be associated with the metaphor of the translator as standing 'between' in the transfer process. The metaphor of between suggests that the translator is neutral, above history and ideology". However, throughout this book, I have read the position of being as a position of power. The trans person is in-between bodies, trans writing is in-between genres and the translator is in-between texts.

While Tymoczko criticizes the metaphor of being "in-between" as suggesting a neutrality – where the translator is, impossibly, neither on the side of the source nor of the target – Smith's acrobat balancing in-between a crevasse looks at the metaphor from a different angle. Smith suggests that to be in-between is not about being unbiased but about how difficult it is to be in the middle; there is something important in the process of balancing, not just in reaching the other side. The crossing is a space of undecidability: "this disruptive, subversive space of indeterminacy between source and target languages, the space of *l'intraduisible*, is a queer space, one that challenges any normative idea of straightforward, untroubled translatability" (Spurlin 2014, 207).

In his 1680 preface to his translation of Ovid's *Epistles*, John Dryden (1992, 103) likened attempting to metaphrase or imitate a source text to "dancing on ropes with fettered legs: a man may shun a fall by using caution; but the gracefulness of motion is not to be expected; and when we have said the best of it, 'tis but a foolish task". If translation that imitates cannot be smooth or elegant then the translator would do better to throw caution to the wind and remove the fetters that chain him or her to the source. This may not result in a graceful motion, however, or reduce the risk of a fall. But I do not think that a gracefulness of motion is the end goal of queer translation. Translators only undertake such difficult crossings for stories that need telling. Trans stories need telling and they need translating and queer translation looks to make the crossing just as perilous for the reader as it was for the translator.

As I noted in my introduction and in chapter four where I listed the titles of twentieth-century intersex novels, more trans texts are being written than ever before and there has recently been an explosion of visibility around the question of being trans. In May 2014, *TIME magazine* announced that we had reached the "transgender tipping point" (Steinmetz 2014): "'We are in a place now,' [Laverne] Cox tells TIME, 'where more and more trans people want to come forward and say, 'This is who I am'. And more trans people are willing to tell their stories. More of us are living visibly and pursuing our dreams visibly'" (ibid). In May 2016, Jacqueline Rose (2016) wrote in the *London Review of Books* that "today, trans people – men, women, neither, both – are taking the public stage more than ever before". However, both Rose and Steinmetz know that there is still a long way to go. Rose writes, as I do, "from the position of a so-called 'cis' woman" (Rose 2016), and while some may argue that cis people are not best placed to write about trans issues, what Rose makes clear is that to write about trans issues is to reveal that being "cis" is not unproblematic, it is not without issues, too. Douglas Robinson also asks why "cisnormative translation scholars [should] care about translation and transgender" (2020, xxix) in his 2020 book, *Transgender, Translation, Translingual Address*. For him, "it's worth our cis-/transgendered while to pay attention to the complexities of our reality, and especially [...] to the phenomenological complexity of our lived reality. It's good to pay attention to how it feels to be alive in the body" (ibid.). What I want to make clear is that being "cis" can also be something undecidable and that, at the end of the day, no matter how someone chooses to live their life and embody their identity, cis bodies and trans bodies are all human bodies.

This topic is more significant than ever now as President Trump undid much of the work started by Barak Obama. In February 2017 the Trump administration revoked Obama's guidelines on transgender bathrooms (*Telegraph* 2017) and in July 2017 Trump announced a ban on transgender individuals serving in the US military (Green, 2017) – this was put into effect in April 2019 (see National Center for Transgender Equality 2020). In May 2018 the Bureau of Prisons rolled back laws that prevented transgender prisoners from being abused; transgender prisoners would also be placed according to their "biological sex" (Hayes 2018). And in May 2019 Trump announced a proposal to allow health care providers and insurers to legally discriminate against transgender patients (Rosenbaum 2019). This proposal was finalized as a regulation on June 12th 2020 meaning that "the federal government no longer recognizes gender identity as an avenue for sex discrimination in health care" (Sanger-Katz and Weiland 2020). Trans people are still discriminated against all over the world. In the UK there have been fears that leaked plans indicate a change to the Gender Recognition Act, meaning that transitioning will become more difficult for trans people (Hunte 2020). This book begins to tackle the injustices done to trans people by coming at this particular topic from the question of literature and translation, thinking about how trans people are and can be seen through what is arguably a very private yet powerful undertaking: reading. I have considered how to make individual voices heard in translation, whether that be the voice of the trans author or the trans protagonist, but also how to acknowledge that these voices, these struggles, are never just "individual". It is translation itself that helps to suggest multivocality because the translator's voice always includes the author's voice and both of these voices are marked by the voices of those who influence them.

While trans issues are becoming a prevalent area of discussion in fiction and politics, they are also becoming more topical in scholarship. In this book I have placed translation and transgender identity together; I am not the first to do this and as this topic continuously gathers momentum I will certainly not be the last. My own work follows on from research on translating gender, or more specifically on translating women, where feminist translators have suggested that the source text is not sacrosanct, that it can and should be "hijacked" (von Flotow 1997, 82) if it does not fit with the translator's agenda. The power of the translator is emphasized. This book considers how trans people can be shown to "belong" in literature and across literatures and therefore in the world, and translators open up the world to new readers; as Edith Grossman (2010, 14) puts it, translation matters because it

> expands our ability to explore through literature the thoughts and feelings of people from another society or another time. It permits us [...] for a brief time to live outside our own skins, our own preconceptions and misconceptions. It expands and deepens our world, our consciousness, in countless, indescribable ways.

In the particular instance of trans source texts, translation shows (and my translations aim to show) that in a world divided into "cis" and "trans" there is actually more that unites us than divides us.

Findings

As set out in the introduction, this book began with one question:

> What does considering how to translate shifting gender identity reveal about the act of translation and/or about gender and how we present our gender identity (or identities) to the world?

A close reading of six texts whose protagonists have shifting gender identity confirmed my premise that undecidability is an inherent characteristic of texts written by or about trans people: these are all undecidable texts with undecidable protagonists. It is important that no precise conclusions be drawn about the genre of these texts or the characters they present. This means that what the translator chooses to do with the text comes with high stakes.

I noted in my introduction that some of these texts, though widely researched, have been undervalued as texts which help us to think through what it means, and has meant, to be trans and, by extension, what it means, and has meant, to be human (as we have seen, this is not a fixed definition throughout time). This book has aimed to give value to these texts, not just as texts which tell us about being trans or being human, but also as texts whose translations show us that while translating transness requires particular care, translating a trans experience is translating a human experience just as reading a trans text is reading a human experience.

Undecidability is heightened in trans texts and I also asked:

> How can translation deal with sexual and textual undecidability?

The textual and the sexual cannot be separated from one another here. Undecidability is produced by the particular blend of form and content, writer and text. This is why my research does not simply consider how to translate grammatical gender (or a lack of it), though, of course, this is something I do look at. As I have suggested in reference to *Sphinx* and *Written on the Body*, it is not enough to argue that these characters' gender transgressions are a linguistic gimmick. In order to represent these gender transgressions in translation this book brings to bear an eclectic critical approach. This eclectic approach not only reflects the nature of translation studies as a field which must look outside itself in order to expand, but also reflects a transdisciplinary methodology. My research is informed by postmodernism, literary theory, translation theory, transgender theory and queer theory: it is multi-faceted like the texts it discusses. In turn, my translation practice mimics the discourses I am analyzing – it is fragmented and hybrid; it involves close reading, undoing the source text and creating several new becomings which will inevitably themselves "unbecome" eventually. I use experimental translation methods to queer both writing and gender.

My first section presented the idea that translation is an active intrusion on the source text: the source text is not a museum exhibit, never to be touched or questioned, even when it is literally kept in archives, available only to a select few. Indeed, the source's unavailability (d'Eon's French text has never been published, for example) makes its translation even more important. In chapter three I discussed the idea that translation and transgender identity are formed of grafts, built up of layers of previous identities or drafts. This was especially apt for Erauso's text which is itself split into four versions, two of which I used to form the layers of a palimpsestuous translation which also included a layer of my own translation. It is possible, however, to create a palimpsestuous translation with source texts whose "original" versions seem to be (but are anything but) singular by using layers of translator's drafts or by picking out intertexts from the source. All of the writers I translate (and all writers *tout court*) draw heavily on previous texts in their writings.

In chapter six I developed this concept of layering further by looking at translation and transgender identity as characterized by various hauntings or specters. Intersex bodies are haunted by medical decisions, by past conceptualizations of gender and what "male" and "female" "should" look like. Both Barbin and Cal/lie are forever haunted by the sex that they thought they were while struggling to fit into the sex that they have been reassigned. In order to think about the idea of being constantly in-between two sex assignments, both forced upon our characters by the medical establishment, I looked to the hypertext as something which can display multiplicity and plurivocality. Barbin and Cal/lie are caught between their past and future selves. Websites and other media such as videos haunt the main blog posts. While the hypertext is not perfect (it does not live up to much of the hype that first surrounded it), it serves its purpose as a translation method that can keep the source text visible.

Section three continued this line of thought by considering the question of how translation brings out the potentiality or the future possibilities of any text or body. I moved on from the idea of layers that I started with and focused more fully on how the concept of hauntings is prescient for the translation of my texts in particular and trans writing in general. The hauntings now include future possibilities as well as past embodiments. I analyzed how the in-between and the hybrid can be represented through a queer type of translation, translation that is ludic and experimental. This brought the book full circle, from the palimpsest to the perverse palimpsest, back to the idea of the source text as a living body of words; it is not just that it is possible to change the source text but that it is preferable to do so. The source text wants to be worked on because this ensures its afterlife. I have shown that all texts and all bodies, "trans" or not, "translations" or not, are unstable and undecidable. Texts erased using a cut-out technique can reflect an erased gender identity where, as in what is truly undecidable, concealment is without hidden truth.

The Future

My work aims to form part of a much wider potential research agenda on translating transness and to serve as a building block for further work in this area. As I mentioned above, scholarship in the areas of trans fiction and translating transness has moved on in the years since I began my research. Edited collections and special journal issues are being dedicated to the translation of queer and transgender identity but monographs on the topic of translating transgender works of literature are scarce: Douglas Robinson looks at Finnish literature in his 2020 book. Academic inquiry into this area has moved at an alarming pace recently and other theorists are already looking at case studies of translated trans texts (Baer 2016; Gabriel 2016) and writing about their own translation practice in connection to trans texts as I do (Concilio 2016; Larkosh 2016; Heinrich and Dowd 2016).[1]

I chose to focus on three types of trans identity and three languages, and more work could now be done that is not limited by categories or by languages. What many trans memoirs appear to have in common is an interference from an editor, or as we shall see below, a co-writer, and this is an angle that could be taken further to think about how the translator is also an intruder on the source text: Lili Elbe's Danish memoir *Man into Woman* is an example of a memoir that has been heavily edited in a similar vein to Barbin's (see Gailey and Brown 2016); indeed, as with the English translation of Barbin where Foucault takes center stage, Elbe is not credited on the front cover as the author (Hoyer 2004): it is a portrait *of* Lili Elbe, not *by* her.

There are also trans autobiographies, biographies and works of fiction appearing in languages from beyond Western Europe suggesting that trans issues are starting to be accepted in many societies. *Last Words from Montmartre*, an experimental Chinese text by Taiwanese author Qui Maiojin with a narrator whose "name and gender [...] seem to shift over the course of the book" (Heinrich and Dowd 2016, 569), was published as early as 1996 but only translated into English in 2014. This publication did not pave the way for more of its kind, however. *Life Beyond my Body: A Transgender Journey to Manhood in China* (2016), which was billed as "the first memoir by a trans man from China" (Ming and Frazey 2017), was never published in Chinese: it had to be written in English by Lei Ming with a ghost-writer, Lura Frazey. Similarly, the 2010 Arabic memoir of Randa, *Mouzakarat Randa al-Trans* [The Memoirs of Randa the Trans], was co-written in Lebanon by journalist Hazem Saghieh (*Independent* 2010) because Randa had to flee Algeria in order to find acceptance (Whitaker 2016). This memoir is, again, an exception because trans people are still invisible in the Middle East: while transwoman Abu Hanna won the Miss Trans Israel pageant in 2016 (Hadid 2016), "most [trans people] remain anonymous and if they come to public attention it's usually through conflict with the law" (Whitaker 2016). This is despite the fact that "the study of gender, sex, and sexuality in Islamic societies has been growing in caliber and intensity" (Almarri 2016, 578).

It is still very early days for the public dissemination of trans texts in many parts of the world with people from transphobic countries or cultures having to cross geographical and/or linguistic borders to get their voices heard, but the publication of these texts seems to be representative of what is slowly becoming a global trend. In Japan the Manga series *Wandering Son* by Shimura Takako which ran from 2002 to 2013 featured multiple trans characters and has been translated into English by Matt Thorn, the first volume being published in translation in 2011. In 2016 *Major i Helena: Priča o vojniku koji se nije predao* [Major and Helena: The Story of a Soldier who has not Surrendered], a biography by Maja Bekčić Petrović, came out in Serbian. In India there has been a small but significant advent of autobiographical texts written by hijras and transwomen: in 2010 *The Truth About Me: A Hijra Life Story* by A. Revathi was published in Tamil and translated into English by V. Geetha. In 2015 Laxmi Narayan Tripathi wrote *Me Hijra, Me Laxmi* in Marathi. It has already been translated into English. Again in 2016 "Malayalee transgender [woman] Sheetal Shyam was approached to write her story soon after Kerala became the first Indian state to adopt a transgender policy" (Gupta 2017) and a memoir written by India's first transgender head teacher Manabi Bandopadhyay was released in February 2017 (Gupta 2017).

As I discussed in the Introduction, I have analyzed transgender, intersex and agender texts for the sake of a coherent structure. My focus was on languages that either showed masculine and feminine grammatical gender and that allowed their users to switch linguistically or that did not show masculine and feminine grammatical gender and allowed their users to hide linguistically. There is no reason why future research, resulting from my work, into the translation of trans fiction and non-fiction must look to books whose protagonists also switch or hide linguistically. It is possible to be undecidable in more subtle ways. As we saw in chapter three, there is a period in Woolf's *Orlando* ([1928] 2004, 87) where Orlando is briefly truly linguistically undecidable with the use of "they". But even in the parts of the narration where Orlando is gendered through third person pronouns, "she" is still undecidable: "Whether, then, Orlando was most man or woman, it is difficult to say and cannot now be decided" (122). My aim has been to show that translating transness reaches beyond the matter of grammatical gender.

My translation methods are extreme: they play games with the source text in an attempt to suggest that the source text is not a perfect, unadulterable body of words that must remain the same under different clothes but is a living body that is open to change. These methods may not be widely accepted by publishers and, as I have said, I do not intend for them to be used as a guide for how to translate trans literature; my methods are not intended as prescriptive instructions. By thinking about my own translation practice I engage with the source texts extremely closely and by opening up a discussion using experimental translation I pave the way for translations which can find a compromise between being radical and being publishable. There is no easy "one size fits all" solution as I have demonstrated with my three different translation techniques for three different types of identity. My structure might be taken to suggest that it could be appropriate to translate all intersex texts using the hypertext or all transgender texts using the palimpsest, but this would be a rather simplistic outlook not least because there is no one way to tackle "trans" texts. Everybody's conception of their own gender identity is different; no two people who identify as "transgender" or "agender" or even "cisgender" will feel the same about their bodies. My aim is to encourage both the translator and the publisher to acknowledge that a trans text is more undecidable than most, that this undecidability is something the target text reader deserves to be aware of.

Catalina de Erauso, François-Timoléon de Choisy, or Herculine Barbin all have texts which are complicated, and while they all wrote for an audience, none of them wrote for publication, let alone translation. This does not mean, however, that we can be lax with their texts. I have suggested that they have not been translated in a manner which makes the most of their transgressive voices. I hope this book will galvanize retranslations: translations which help us to see that being trans is being human, that translation is creative writing and that trans people, translators and translations occupy a position in-between. A between that shows that people and texts are constantly evolving and becoming: they are never perfect, never too precious to be changed.

Translation is an apt medium through which to think about the past, present and future ghosts of the text and the body that are always captured within the source text; "captured" as one moment in time that is mercurial, that has changed as soon as the reader looks away. Translation is a record of multiple readings and these readings haunt the translation which is itself mercurial; it represents becomings, ghosts, while simultaneously and endlessly creating more. Through writing, trans people and translators expose and celebrate the fact that texts and bodies are anything but "finished;" they both articulate a state of becoming, of undecidability.

Note

1 Whilst I consider what I do to be queer translation, I do not include work on translation analysis or practice for homosexual texts in this review of recent literature.

Appendices

Appendix I selected pages from Seville M-1 and Seville M-2 held in the Institución Colombina of the Cathedral of Seville: ACS, Fondo Capitular, Sec. IX, sign.: 11.313, Monja alférez, M-1 (h. 1–3) y M-2 (h. 1–3). All pages reproduced with permission of the Archivo de la Catedral de Sevilla

Appendix II my translation of*Sphinx*(Garréta 1986: 11–14) without the letter "i"

These thoughts sadden me even now, all these years later. How many exactly, not sure. Ten or a few more perhaps. And why force myself to endure only through memory? My soul wants a body. But soul already heavy from too much knowledge, body exhausted from thoughtfulness and lack of power, so caught up by a fevered boredom that naught, or almost naught, can occupy me anymore. Suppose that memory serves: back then, to me, the world was a theatre where corpses danced at a macarbre ball of urges. Contempt and outcry couldn't keep me, however, from my craze for the waltz and her decay to a dance of love.

Languorous darkness floats at the mercy of syncopated rhythms, short beats; the road to hell sparkled with deaf lanterns; the bottom of the abyss drew ever closer. On the smooth walls of the tornado that moved me forward, deformed forms of overjoyed cadavers presented themselves to me; tortured flesh, they gave off a hoarse death rattle.

But my fall was constant, my fate of enchanted escape couldn't be abandoned. A betrayal to deny grace there where grace couldn't be, not to me at least? Heresy to hold that the sober journey to hell be the nonstop road to atonement? "You would not look for me had you not already found me; you would not long for me had you not once held me between your arms."

Per arms, sweet fervour, carnal scenes, one after the other rouse my memory. A*** danced: me at dusk, on hold for per appearance on the stage of the Eden, tasteful cabaret on the Left Bank. And who would not have fallen for that svelte frame, for that musculature almost sculpted by one of the greats, for that soft touch that naught from the past can ever emulate? For most of the week my job was DJ at the Apocryphe, popular club, back then.

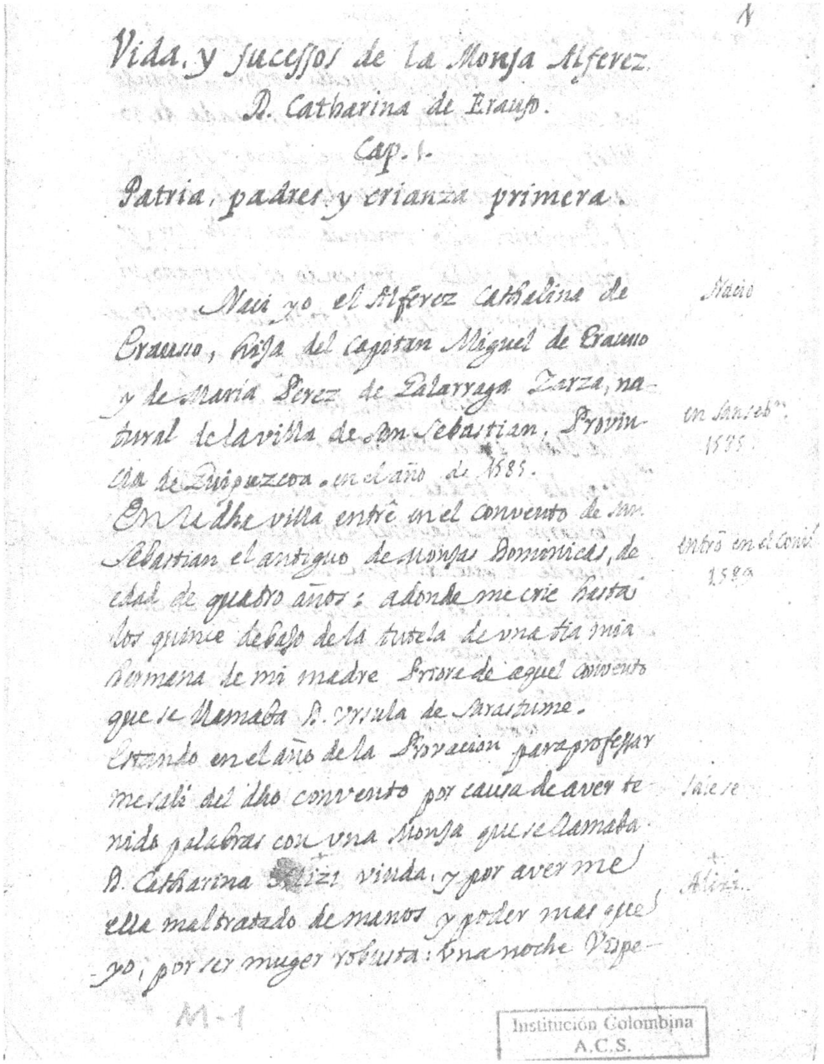

Vida, y sucessos de la Monja Alferez.
D. Catharina de Erauso.
Cap. 1.
Patria, padres, y crianza primera.

Naci yo el Alferez Cathalina de Erauso, hija del capitan Miguel de Erauso y de Maria Perez de Galarraga y Arza, natural de la villa de San Sebastian, Provincia de Guipuzcoa, en el año de 1585.
En dicha villa entré en el convento de San Sebastian el antiguo de monjas Dominicas, de edad de quatro años: adonde me crie hasta los quince debaxo de la tutela de una tia mia hermana de mi madre Priora de aquel convento que se llamaba D. Ursula de Sarastume.
Estando en el año de la Provacion para professar me sali del dho convento por causa de aver tenido palabras con una Monja que se llamaba D. Catharina Aliri viuda, y por aver me ella maltratado de manos y poder mas que yo, por ser muger robusta: Una noche Vispe-

M-1

Figure A1 The beginning of chapter I of M-1, page 1 recto.

Can't remember the moment my eyes saw A***. My lethargy, a sort of abandonment of the world, a world that offers me no outbursts of joy, no collapses of despondency, that has always left me every freedom for the most absurd rootlessness and jaunts. The start with A*** must've been at the sad and ghastly study of a ballet of forms, confused on the stage of a cabaret where we'd suffused our setbacks.

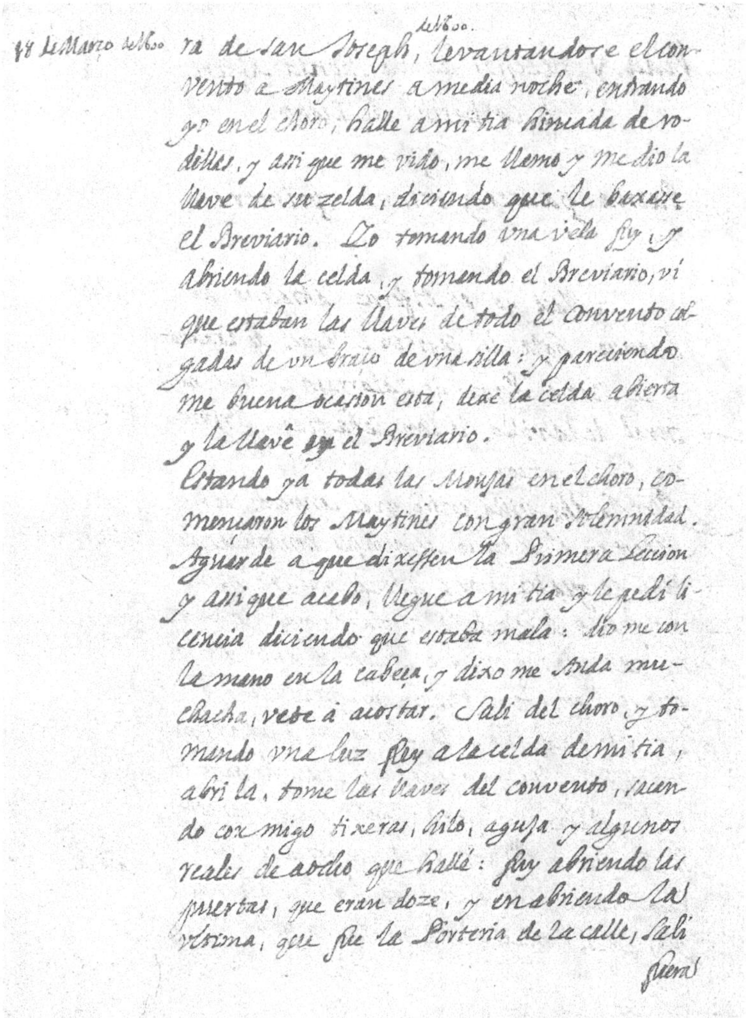

18 de Marzo del 600 ra de san Joseph, levantandose el convento a Maytines a media noche, entrando
yo en el choro, halle a mi tia hincada de ro-
dillas, y assi que me vido, me llamo y me dio la
llave de su zelda, diciendo que le baxasse
el Breviario. Yo tomando una vela fuy, y
abriendo la celda, y tomando el Breviario, vi
que estaban las llaves de todo el convento colgadas de un braço de una silla: y pareciendo
me buena ocasion esta, dexe la celda abierta
y la llave en el Breviario.
Estando ya todas las Monjas en el choro, començaron los Maytines con gran solemnidad.
Aguarde a que dixessen la Primera Lecion
y assi que acabo, llegue a mi tia y le pedi licencia diciendo que estaba mala: Dio me con
la mano en la cabeça, y dixo me Anda mu-
chacha, vete a acostar. Sali del choro, y tomando una luz fuy a la celda de mi tia,
abri la, tome las llaves del convento, sacan-
do conmigo tixeras, hilo, aguja y algunos
reales de a ocho que halle: fuy abriendo las
puertas, que eran doze, y en abriendo la
ultima, que fue la Porteria de la calle, sali
fuera

Figure A2 Page 1 verso.

When the blurred tableau went on, only just heeded by me, my eye must have been caught: after the shock of a fragment seen, an underground work started to operate: gouge, gouge at my soul. What made the place pleasurable? Couldn't say. A body, only one nameless to me, had offered the place an allurement that lasted to the extent that the cause was unknown, the root unfound.

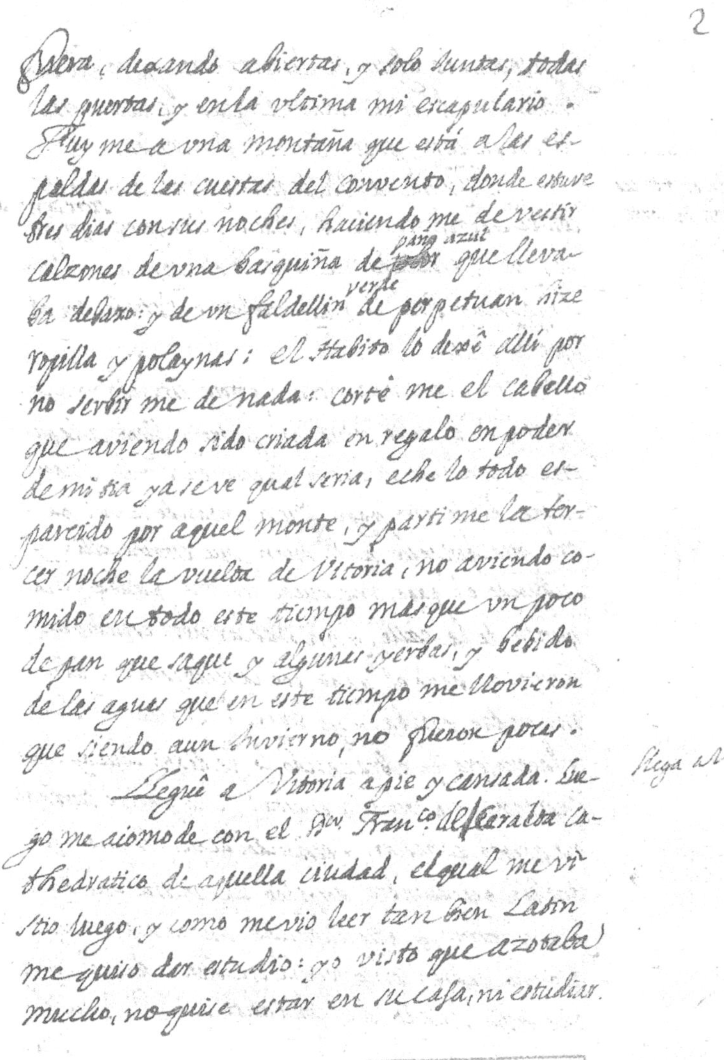

2

fuera, dexando abiertas, y solo juntas, todas
las puertas, y en la ultima mi escapulario.
Fuy me a una montaña que está a las espaldas de las cuestas del convento, donde estuve
tres dias con sus noches, haciendo me de vestir
calzones de una basquiña de paño azul que llevaba debaxo: y de un faldellin verde de perpetuan hize
ropilla y polaynas: el Habito lo dexê alli por
no servir me de nada: cortê me el cabello
que aviendo sido criada en regalo en poder
de mi tia ya se ve qual seria, eche lo todo es-
parcido por aquel monte, y parti me la tercer noche la vuelta de Vitoria, no aviendo comido en todo este tiempo mas que un poco
de pan que saque y algunas yerbas, y bebido
de las aguas que en este tiempo me llovieron
que siendo aun Invierno, no fueron pocas.
Lleguê a Vitoria a pie y cansada. Lue- Llega a Vitoi
go me acomode con el Dor. Franco. de Ceralta Cathedratico de aquella ciudad, el qual me vistio luego, y como me vio leer tan bien Latin
me quiso dar estudio: yo visto que azotaba
mucho, no quise estar en su casa, ni estudiar.

Figure A3 Page 2 recto.

Not long after that foray to the Eden, one of my mates from back then, Ty, who became a burlesque dancer after she was an acrobat, dragged me on her round of cabarets. She eventually accorded me a favour: to be the shadow of a body whose own was stolen by that beam of yellow on

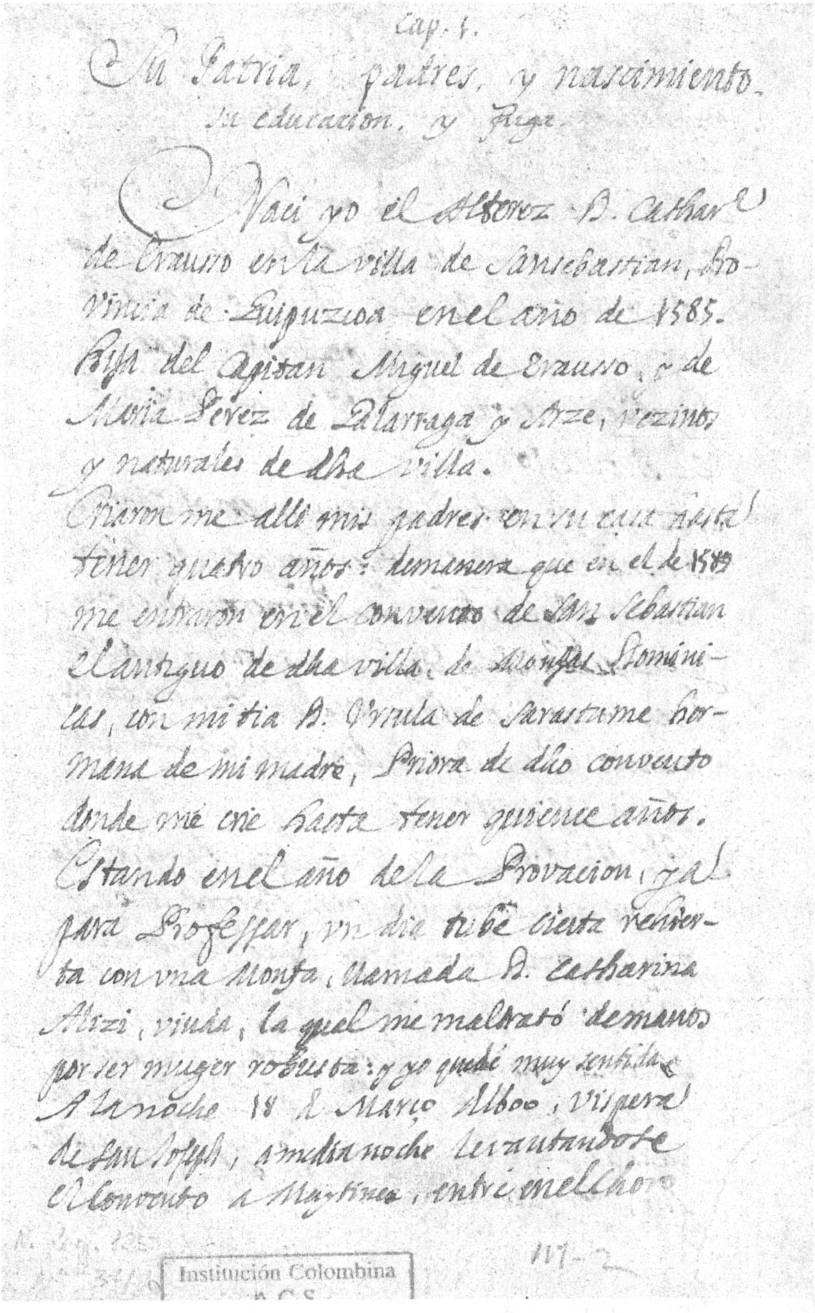

Cap. 1.
Su Patria, padres, y nascimiento.
su educacion, y fuga.
Naci yo el Alferez D. Cathar[ina]
de Erauso en la villa de Sansebastian, Provincia de Guipuzcoa en el año de 1585.
Hija del Capitan Miguel de Erauso, y de
Maria Perez de Galarraga y Arze, vezinos
y naturales de dha villa.
Criaron me alli mis padres en su casa hasta
tener quatro años: demanera que en el de 1589
me entraron en el convento de San Sebastian
el Antiguo de dha villa, de Monjas Dominicas, con mi tia D. Ursula de Sarastume hermana de mi madre, Priora de dho convento
donde me crie hasta tener quince años.
Estando en el año de la Provacion, ya
para Professar, vn dia tube cierta reñer-
ta con vna Monja, llamada D. Catharina
Alrzi, viuda, la qual me maltrató de manos
por ser muger robusta: y yo quedé muy sentida.
A la noche 18 de Março 1600, vispera
de San Joseph, a media noche levantandose
el Convento a Maytines, entré en el choro

Figure A4 The beginning of chapter I of M-2, page 1 recto.

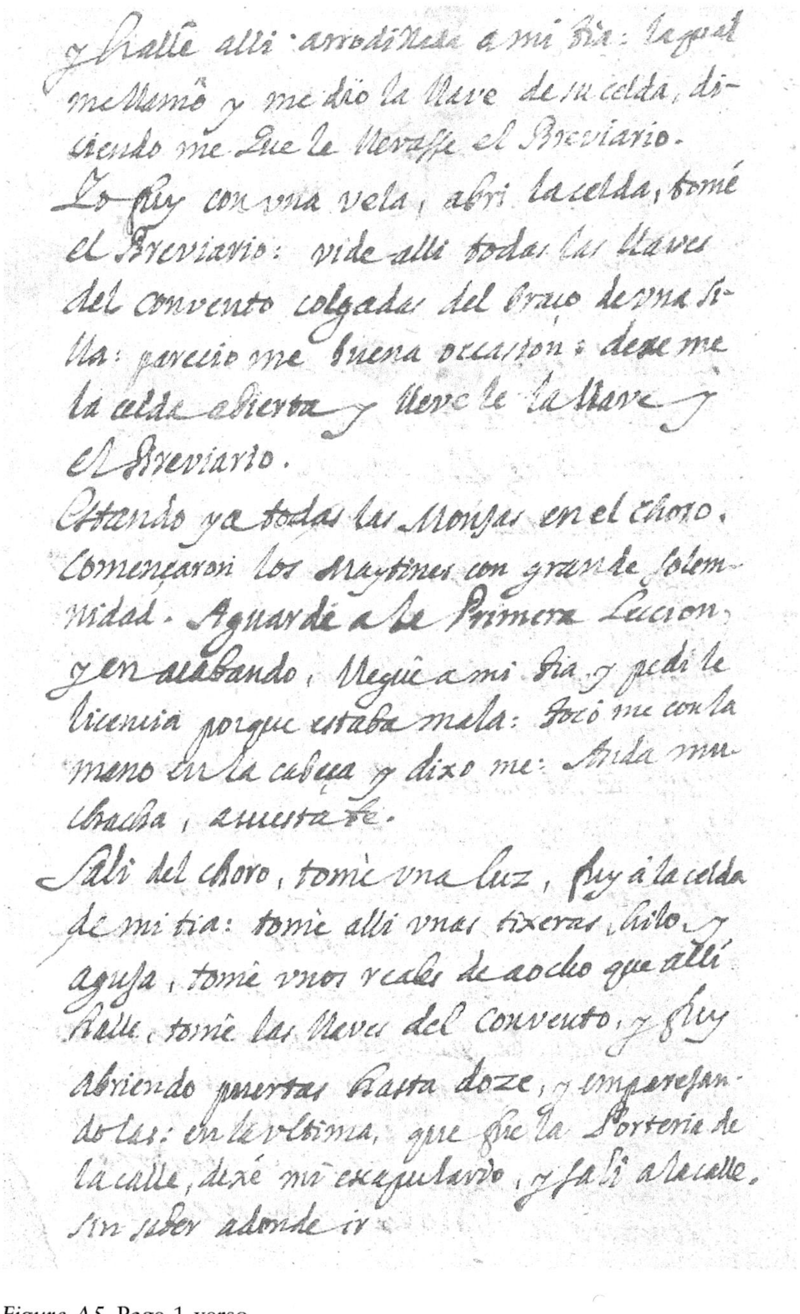

y hallé alli arrodillada a mi tia: la qual
me llamó y me dio la llave de su celda, diciendo me que le llevasse el Breviario.
Yo fuy con vna vela, abri la celda, tomé
el Breviario: vide alli todas las llaves
del convento colgadas del braço de vna silla: pareciome buena ocasion: dexe me
la celda abierta y lleve le la llave y
el Breviario.
Estando ya todas las Monjas en el choro.
Començaron los Maytines con grande solemnidad. Aguardé a la Primera Leccion,
y en acabando, llegué a mi tia, y pedi le
licencia porque estaba mala: tocó me con la
mano en la cabeça y dixo me: Anda mu-
chacha, acuesta te.
Sali del choro, tomè vna luz, fuy á la celda
de mi tia: tomè alli vnas tixeras, hilo, y
aguja, tomè vnos reales de a ocho que allí
halle, tomè las llaves del Convento, y fuy
abriendo puertas hasta doze, y emparejan-
dolas: en la vltima, que fue la Porteria de
la calle, dexé mi escapulario, y salí a la calle.
sin saber adonde ir

Figure A5 Page 1 verso.

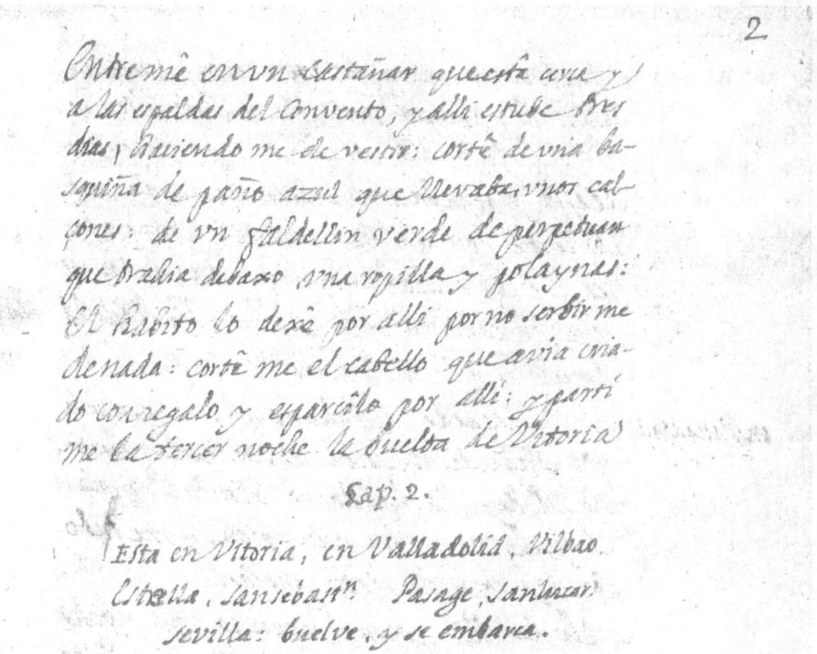

2

Entreme en vn castañar que esta cerca y a las espaldas del Convento, y alli estube tres dias, haciendo me de vestir: corte de vna basquiña de paño azul que llevaba, vnos calçones: de vn faldellin verde de perpetuan que traia debaxo, vna ropilla y polaynas: El habito lo dexe por alli por no servir me de nada: corte me el cabello que avia criado con regalo y esparcilo por alli: y parti me la tercer noche la buelta de Vitoria

Cap. 2.

Esta en Vitoria, en Valladolid, Vilbao, Estella, Sansebastn. Pasage, Sanlucar, Sevilla: buelve, y se embarca.

No aviendo comido en dhos tres dias mas que vn poco de pan que saque del convento y algunas yerbas, y bebido de la mucha agua que entonces llovio, llegue a Vitoria a pie, y cansada. — en Vitoria

Acomode me alli luego con el Dor. Franco. de Ceralta cathedratico de aquella ciudad. el qual me vistio luego, sin conocer me: era casado con prima hermana de mi madre.

Figure A6 Page 2 recto.

the stage. We'd arranged to meet around ten, one of the huge cafés of the Place at the foot of Montmartre. Autumn. On the way to my rendezvous, the wrong way among a fast flow of men – what was the rush?.

Watchful men, careful step. An amazon, harnessed by garters and leather straps, crossed my path. Her body was bound by black leather fastened by metal buckles. On the edge of the pavement where she started her peacock ballet, she seemed a combatant, or, better, some harnessed beast. Pass her. Turn back. Check beyond doubt the features of her appearance. All along the boulevard, regularly spaced, one sees these shops, half sex shop, half sexy underwear shop, that offer the ensemble of such a get-up. Just further on, stop. Before the half-obscured front of one of these shops. Do women wear those blood-red basques shown between a purple suspender belt and a sheer lace thong?.

Bibliography

Adair, Gilbert, trans. 1995. *Georges Perec: A Void*. London: Harvill.

Allez, Cookie. 2015. *Dominique*. Paris: Buchet et Chastel.

Allot, Miriam, ed. 1974. *The Brontës: The Critical Heritage*. London: Routledge & Kegan Paul.

Almarri, Saquer A. 2016 "'You Have Made Her a Man Among Men': Translating the *Khuntha*'s Anatomy in Fatimid Jurisprudence." *Translation Studies Quarterly 3* (3–4): 578–586.

Apps, Aaron. 2015a. *Intersex: A Memoir*. Grafton: Tarpaulin Sky Press.

Apps, Aaron. 2015b. *Dear Herculine*. Boise: Ashata Press.

Aresti, Nerea. 2007. "The Gendered Identities of the 'Lieutenant Nun:' Rethinking the Story of a Female Warrior in Early Modern Spain." Translated by Rosemary Williams. *Gender & History*, *19* (3): 401–418.

Athanassakis, Yanoula. 2011. "'The American Girl I had Once Been': Psychosomatic Trauma and History in Jeffrey Eugenides' *Middlesex*." *European Journal of American Culture 30* (3): 217–230.

Baer, Brian James. 2016. "Translation, Transition, Transgender: Framing the Life of Charlotte von Mahlsdorf." *Transgender Studies Quarterly 3* (3–4): 506–523.

Baer, Brian James, and Klaus Kaindl. 2017. *Queering Translation, Translating the Queer*. London: Routledge.

Baker, Catherine. 2017. "Yes Gender is a Spectrum and Yes, Trans Women are Women Full Stop: Why Both these Things are True at the Same Time." *Catherine Baker*, March 5. https://bakercatherine.wordpress.com/2017/03/05/yes-gender-is-a-spectrum-and-yes-trans-women-are-women-full-stop-why-both-these-things-are-true-at-the-same-time/ (accessed 05 March 2017).

Bakhtin, Mikhail M. 1981. *The Dialogic Imagination: Four Essays*. Translated by Caryl Emerson and Michael Holquist, edited by Michael Holquist. Austin: University of Texas Press.

Baldick, Robert. 1970. "Introduction." In *The Memoirs of the Chevalier d'Eon*, by Frederic Gaillardet, xix–xx. London: Anthony Blond.

Baranowski, Maciej. 2002. "Current Usage of the Epicene Pronoun in Written English." *Journal of Sociolinguistics* 6 (3): 378–397.

Barbin, Herculine. 1874. "Mes souvenirs." In *Question médico-légale de l'identité dans les rapports avec les vices de conformation des organes sexuels*, edited by Ambroise Tardieu, 63–174. Paris: Librarie J.B. Baillière et Fils. http://gallica.bnf.fr/ark:/12148/bpt6k76971v/f9.item (accessed 28 January 2017).

Barbin, Herculine. 2014 [1978]. *Herculine Barbin dite Alexina B*. Edited by Michel Foucault. Paris: Editions Gallimard.

Baron, Dennis. 2010. "The Gender-Neutral Pronoun: After 150 Years Still an Epic Fail." *The Web of Language*, August 2. https://illinois.edu/blog/view/25/31097 (accessed 06 May 2015).

Barthes, Roland. 1970 [1957]. *Mythologies*. Paris: Seuil.

Barthes, Roland. 1974. *S/Z*. Translated by Richard Miller. London: Cape.

Barthes, Roland. 1977. *Image Music Text*. Translated by Stephen Heath. London: Fontana Press.

Barthes, Roland. 1986. *The Responsibility of Forms: Critical Essays on Music, Art and Representation*. Translated by Richard Howard. Oxford: Basil Blackwell.

Barthes, Roland. 1989. *The Rustle of Language*. Translated by Richard Howard. Berkeley: University of California Press.

de Beauvoir, Simone. 2009 [1947]. *The Second Sex*. Translated by Constance Borde and Sheila Malovany-Chevallier. London: Jonathan Cape.

Bekčić Petrović, Maja. 2016. *Major i Helena: Priča o vojniku koji se nije predao*. [s.l.] AMP Print.

Belflower, James. 2017. "The Unsettled Surface of the Document: Seams, Erosion, and After-images in Charles Reznikoff's Holocaust." *Postmodern Culture 28* (1).

Bellos, David. 2012. *Is That a Fish in Your Ear? The Amazing Adventure of Translation*. London: Penguin Books.

Benjamin, Walter. 2012 [1923]. "The Translator's Task." Translated by Steven Rendall. In *The Translation Studies Reader*, 3rd edition, edited by Lawrence Venuti, 75–83. London and New York: Routledge.

Bennett, Andrew, and Nicholas Royle. 2004. *An Introduction to Literature, Criticism and Theory*. Harlow: Pearson Education Limited.

Berman, Antoine. 2012. "Translation and the Trials of the Foreign." Translated by Lawrence Venuti. In *The Translation Studies Reader*, 2nd edition, edited by Lawrence Venuti, 240–253. London: Routledge.

Bernau, Anke. 2012. "Medieval Antifeminism." In *The History of British Women's Writing, 700-1500: Volume One* edited by Liz Herbert McAvoy and Diane Watt, 72–84. Basingstoke: Palgrave Macmillan.

Bettley, James, ed. 2001. *The Art of the Book: From Medieval Manuscript to Graphic Novel*. London: V&A Publications.

Bhabha, Homi. 2004 [1994]. *The Location of Culture*. Abingdon: Routledge.

Birdsall, Bridget. 2014. *Double Exposure*. New York: Sky Pony Press.

Blackmore, E. H., and A. M. Blackmore, trans. 2006. *Stéphane Mallarmé: Collected Poems and Other Verse*. Oxford: Oxford University Press.

Bloom, Harold. 1994. *The Western Canon: The Books and School of Ages*. New York: Harcourt Brace and Company.

Boase-Beier, Jean. 2011. *A Critical Introduction to Translation Studies*. London: Continuum.

Bohan, Edward J. 1982 *The Descension*. Pittsburgh: Dorrance Publishing Company.

Borges, Jorge. 1998. *Collected Fictions*. Translated by Andrew Hurley. New York: Viking.

Boroditsky, Lera, and Lauren A. Schmidt. 2000. "Sex, Syntax, and Semantics." *Proceedings of the Cognitive Science Society* 22: 42–47.

Bourdieu, Pierre. 1993. *The Field of Cultural Production: Essays on Art and Literature*. Cambridge: Polity Press.

Bowie, Malcolm. 1978. *Mallarmé and the Art of Being Difficult*. Cambridge: Cambridge University Press.

Brent Plate, S. 2015. "Marginalia and its Disruptions." *Los Angeles Review of Books*. December 16. https://lareviewofbooks.org/article/marginalia-and-its-disruptions/#! (accessed 28 August 2019).

Brillenburg Wurth, Kiene. 2011. "Old and New Medialities in Foer's *Tree of Codes*." *CLCWeb: Comparative Literature and Culture 13* (3): 2–8.

Broaddus, Eric. 1985. *Above the Trees: A Short Novel*. Tenterden: The Artist.

Brugman, Alyssa. 2013. *Alex as Well*. Melbourne: The Text.

Burke, Seán. 1998. *The Death and Return of the Author: Criticism and Subjectivity in Barthes, Foucault and Derrida*. Edinburgh: Edinburgh University Press.

Burrows, Stephen, Jonathan Conlin, Russell Goulbourne, and Valerie Mainz. 2010 "Introduction." In *The Chevalier d'Eon and his Worlds: Gender, Espionage and Politics in the Eighteenth Century*, edited by Stephen Burrows, Jonathan Conlin, Russell Goulbourne, and Valerie Mainz, 1–11. London: Continuum.

Bush, Peter. 2006. "Intertextuality and the Translator as Story-Teller." *Palimpsestes 18*: 213–229.

Butler, Judith. 1994. "Gender as Performance: An Interview with Judith Butler." *Radical Philosophy*, 64: 32–39.

Butler, Judith. 1997a. *Excitable Speech: A Politics of the Performative*. New York: Routledge.

Butler, Judith. 1997b. "Critically Queer." In *Playing with Fire: Queer Politics, Queer Theories*, edited by Shane Phelan, 11–29. New York: Routledge.

Butler, Judith. 2004a. "Imitation and Gender Insubordination: On the Being of Gayness as Necessary Drag." *The Judith Butler Reader*, edited by Sara Salih, 127–135. Oxford: Blackwell.

Butler, Judith. 2004b. "Changing the Subject: Judith Butler's Politics of Radical Resignification." *The Judith Butler Reader*, edited by Sara Salih, 325–356. Oxford: Blackwell.

Butler, Judith. 2004c. *Undoing Gender*. New York: Routledge.

Butler, Judith. 2006 [1990]. *Gender Trouble: Feminism and the Subversion of Identity*. New York: Routledge.

Butler, Judith. 2011 [1993]. *Bodies That Matter: On the Discursive Limits of "Sex"*. New York: Routledge.

Butler, Judith. 2014. "Gender Performance: The Transadvocate interviews Judith Butler." *The Transadvocate*, 1 May. http://transadvocate.com/gender-performance-the-transadvocate-interviews-judith-butler_n_13652.htm (accessed 25 January 2017).

Butler, Judith. 2016a. "Introduction." In *Of Grammatology, 40th Anniversary edition, by Jaques Derrida, translated by Gayatri Chakravorty Spivak*, vii–xxiv. Baltimore, MD: Johns Hopkins University Press.

Butler, Judith. 2016b. *Gender in Translation: On the Limits of Monolingualism*. [Lecture presented as the Diane Middlebrook and Carl Djerassi Visiting Professorship Lecture for the University of Cambridge Centre for Gender Studies]. 17 October.

Callahan, Gerald N. 2009. *Between XX and XY: Intersexuality and the Myth of Two Sexes*. Chicago: Chicago Review Press.

Carpenter, Ginette. 2007. "Reading and the Reader." In *Jeanette Winterson: A Contemporary Critical Guide*, edited by Sonya Andermahr, 69–81. London: Continuum.

Carroll, Lewis. 2010 [1865]. *Alice's Adventures in Wonderland and Through the Looking Glass*. London: Bloomsbury.

Carroll, Rachel. 2010. "Retrospective Sex: Rewriting Intersexuality in Jeffrey Eugenides's *Middlesex*." *Journal of American Studies* 44 (1): 187–201.

Carter, Angela. 1982. *The Passion of New Eve*. London: Virago.

Casagranda, Mirko. 2013. "Bridging the Genders? Transgendering Translation Theory and Practice." In *Bridging the Gap between Theory and Practice in Translation and Gender Studies*, edited by Eleonora Federici and Vanessa Leonardi, 112–121. Cambridge: Cambridge Scholars Publishing.

Castejón, Encarna, trans. 1994. *Jeanette Winterson: Escrito en el cuerpo*. Barcelona: Anagrama.

Castro, Olga, and Emek Ergun. 2017. *Feminist Translation Studies: Local and Transnational Perspectives*. New York: Routledge.

Castro, Olga. 2013. "Introduction: Gender, Language and Translation at the Crossroads of Disciplines." *Gender and Language* 7 (1): 5–12.

Chak, Avinash. 2015. "Beyond 'he' and 'she:' The Rise of Non-Binary Pronouns". *BBC News*, 7 December. http://www.bbc.co.uk/news/magazine-34901704 (accessed 21 April 2016).

Chamberlain, Lori. 2012. "Gender and the Metaphorics of Translation." In *The Translation Studies Reader*, 3rd edition, edited by Lawrence Venuti, 254–268. London and New York: Routledge.

Chambers. 2001. *Dictionary of Etymology*, edited by R. K. Barnhart. Edinburgh: Chambers Harrap Publishers Ltd.

Champagne, Roland A., Nina Ekstein, and Gary Kates, trans. 2001. *Charles d'Eon de Beaumont: The Maiden of Tonnerre: The Vicissitudes of the Chevalier and the Chevalière d'Eon*. Baltimore, MD: Johns Hopkins University Press.

Chesnet. 2014 [1860]. "Question d'identité; vice de conformation des organes génitaux externes; hypospadias; erreur sur le sexe" in, *Herculine Barbin dite Alexina B*, by Herculine Barbin, 147–150. Paris: Gallimard.

de Choisy, François-Timoléon. 1995. *Mémoires de l'abbé de Choisy habillé en femme*. Toulouse: Ombre.

Cholodenko, Marc, trans. 2003. *Jeffrey Eugenides: Middlesex*. Paris: Éditions de l'Olivier.

Chrisman-Campbell, Kimberley. 2010. "Dressing d'Eon." In *The Chevalier d'Eon and his Worlds: Gender, Espionage and Politics in the Eighteenth Century*, edited by Stephen Burrows, Jonathan Conlin, Russell Goulbourne, and Valerie Mainz, 97–112. London: Continuum.

Chucky Tate, Charlotte, Ella Ben Hagai and Faye J. Crosby. (2020) *Undoing the Gender Binary*. Cambridge and New York: Cambridge University Press.

Clune-Taylor, Catherine. 2019. "Securing Cisgendered Futures: Intersex Management Under the 'Disorders of Sex Development' Treatment Model." *Hypatia 34* (4): 690–712.

Cohen, Samuel. 2007. "The Novel in a Time of Terror: *Middlesex*, History and Contemporary American Fiction." *Twentieth-Century Literature 53* (3): 371–393.

Collins. 2017. *The Collins English Dictionary*. https://www.collinsdictionary.com (accessed 23 January 2017).

Collins. 2020. "Neutrois: New word suggestion." *The Collins English Dictionary.* https://www.collinsdictionary.com/submission/12615/Neutrois (accessed 25 June 2020).

Concilio, Arielle A. 2016. "Pedro Lemebel and the Translatxrsation: On a Genderqueer Translation Praxis." *Transgender Studies Quarterly* 3 (3–4): 462–484.

Conlin, Jonathan. 2010. "The Strange Case of the Chevalier d'Eon." *History Today 60* (4): 45–51.

Connors, Clare. 2010. *Literary Theory: A Beginner's Guide*. London: Oneworld Publications.

Corbett, Greville G. 2013. "Sex-Based and Non-Sex-Based Gender Systems." In *The World Atlas of Language Structures Online*, edited by Matthew Dryer and Martin Haspelmath. Leipzig: Max Planck Institute for Evolutionary Anthropology. http://wals.info/chapter/31 (accessed 11 February 2018).

Couser, G. Thomas. 2012. *Memoir: An Introduction*. Oxford: Oxford University Press.

Creighton, Sarah. 2001. "Surgery for Intersex." *Journal of the Royal Society of Medicine 94* (5): 218–220.

De Boever, Arne. 2012. *States of Exception in the Contemporary Novel: Martel, Eugenides, Coetzee, Sebald*. New York: Continuum.

Deleuze, Gilles. 1990. *The Logic of Sense*. Translated by Mark Lester with Charles Stivale, edited by Constantin V. Boundas. London: Continuum.

Demastes, William. 2013. *The Cambridge Introduction to Tom Stoppard*. Cambridge: Cambridge University Press.

D'Eon de Beaumont, Charles. 1785. *La Pucelle de Tonnerre: Les Vicissitudes du Chevalier et Chevalière d'Eon [manuscript] Brotherton Collection. BS MS Chevalier d'Eon/01*. Leeds: Brotherton Library.

D'Erasmo, Stacey. 2011. "Announcing Her Existence." *The New York Times Sunday Book Review*, January 7. http://www.nytimes.com/2011/01/09/books/review/DErasmo-t.html (accessed 18 November 2015).

de Erauso, Catalina. No Date. *Copia manuscrita de la autobiografía de la monja Catalina de Erauso [manuscript] Sección Fondo Historíco General. 34*. Seville: Cathedral Archive of the Colombina Institute.

de Erauso, Catalina (1784) *Vida i Sucesos de la Monja Alférez o Alférez Catarina, doña Catarina de Araujo doncella, natural de San Sebastián, Provincia de Guipúzcoa. Escrita por ella misma en el 18 de Septiembre 1646 volviendo de las Indias a España en el Galeón San Josef, Capitán Andrés Otón, en la flota de Nueva España, General D. Juan de Benavides, General de la Armada Tomás de la Raspuru, que llegó a Cádiz en 18 de noviembre de 1646 [manuscript]. Muñoz Collection. 9/4807*. Madrid: Royal Academy of History.

de Erauso, Catalina (1829) *Historia de la Monja Alférez, Doña Catalina de Erauso, escrita por ella misma*, edited by Joaquín María Ferrer. Paris: Julio Didot. http://www.libros.uchile.cl/files/presses/1/monographs/70/submission/proof/index.html#/1/ (accessed 8 April 2015).

de Erauso, Catalina (1992) *Vida i sucesos de la Monja Alférez*. Edited by Rima de Vallbona. Tempe: Center for Latin American Studies, Arizona State University.

de Erauso, Catalina (1995) *La Monja Alférez: Doña Catalina de Erauso, dos manuscritos inéditos de su autobiografía conservados en el archivo de la Santa Iglesia Catedral de Sevilla*, edited by Pedro Rubio Merino. Seville: Cabildo Metropolitano de la Catedral de Sevilla.

Derrida, Jacques. 1979. "Living On/Border Lines." Translated by J. Hulbert, In *Deconstruction and Criticism*, edited by Harold Bloom, Paul de Man, Jacques Derrida, Geoffrey Hartmann and Joseph Hillis Miller, 75–176. New York: Continuum.

Derrida, Jacques. 1980. "The Law of Genre." Translated by Avital Ronell, *Critical Inquiry* 7 (1): 55–81.

Derrida, Jacques. 1982. *Margins of Philosophy*. Translated by Alan Bass. New York: Harvester Wheatsheaf.

Derrida, Jacques. 2001a. *Writing and Difference*. Translated by Alan Bass. London: Routledge.

Derrida, Jacques. 2001b. "What is 'Relevant' Translation?" Translated by Lawrence Venuti, *Critical Inquiry* 27 (2): 174–200.

Derrida, Jacques. 2004 [1981]. *Dissemination*. Translated by Barbara Johnson. London: Continuum.

Derrida, Jacques. 2006 [1994]. *Specters of Marx: The State of the Debt, the Work of Mourning, and the New International*, translated by Peggy Kamuf. New York: Routledge.

Derrida, Jacques. 2010. "Aletheia." Translated by Pleshette DeArmitt and Kas Saghafi, *The Oxford Literary Review* 32 (2): 169–188.

Derrida, Jacques. 2016 [1976]. *Of Grammatology. Translated by Gayatri Chakravorty Spivak*. Baltimore: Johns Hopkins University.

de Vallbona, Rima. 1992. "Introducción: Historia y ficción en *Vida i sucesos de la Monja Alférez*." In *Vida i sucesos de la Monja Alférez* by Catalina de Erauso, 1–32. Tempe: Arizona State University.

de Vaugelas, Claude F. 1647 *Remarques sur la langue françoise: utiles à ceux qui veulent bien parler et bien escrire [online]*. Paris: Vve J. Camusat et P. Le Petit. http://gallica.bnf.fr/ark:/12148/bpt6k84316s/f230.image (accessed 23 January 2015).

Dick, Maria-Daniella and Julian Wolfreys. 2013. *The Derrida Wordbook*. Edinburgh: Edinburgh University Press.

Dillon, Sarah. 2007. *The Palimpsest: Literature, Criticism, Theory*. London: Continuum.

Ditum, Sarah. 2018. "Genderquake failed. Now for a proper trans debate". *The Guardian*. https://www.theguardian.com/commentisfree/2018/may/13/genderquake-failed-now-for-a-proper-trans-debate (accessed 10 August 2019).

Dreger, Alice. 1998 *Hermaphrodites and the Medical Invention of Sex*. Cambridge: Harvard University Press.

Dryden, John. 1992 [1680]. "Extracts from the Preface to his Translation of *Ovid's Epistles* Published in 1680." In *Translation, History, Culture: A Sourcebook*, edited by André Lefevere, 102–105. London: Routledge.

Duncan, Dennis. 2011. *Tropes of Translation and Conceptions of the Subject in the Work of the Oulipo*. PhD. Birkbeck University. http://ethos.bl.uk/OrderDetails.do?uin=uk.bl.ethos.615322 (accessed 28 January 2017).

Dworkin, Craig. 2011. "The Fate of Echo." In *Against Expression: An Anthology of Conceptual Writing*, edited by Craig Dworkin and Kenneth Goldsmith, xxiii–liv. Illinois: Northwestern University Press.

Dworkin, Craig, and Kenneth Goldsmith, eds. 2011. *Against Expression: An Anthology of Conceptual Writing*. Illinois: Northwestern University Press.

Easton Jr., Roger L., and William Noel. 2010. "Infinite Possibilities: Ten Years of Study of the Archimedes Palimpsest." *Proceedings of the American Philosophical Society 154* (1): 50–76.

Elam, Diane. 1992. *Romancing the Postmodern*. London: Routledge.

Eliot, Thomas Stearns. 2013 [1922]. *The Waste Land*. New York: Liveright Publishing Corporation.

Elkin, Lauren. 2015. "*Sphinx* by Anne Garréta, Translated by Emma Ramadan." *BookForum*, July 10. www.bookforum.com/review/14775 (accessed 14 December 2015).

Ellis, Havelock. 1928. *Studies in the Psychology of Sex, Volume* 2. New York: Random House.

Epstein, B. J., and Robert Gillett. (2017) *Queer in Translation*. London: Routledge.

Epstein, B. J., and Robert Gillett. 2017. "Introduction." In *Queer in Translation*, edited by B. J. Epstein and Robert Gillett, 1–7. London: Routledge.

Eugenides, Jeffrey. 2002. *Middlesex*. London: Fourth Estate.

Eugenides, Jeffrey. 2007a. "A Conversation with Jeffrey Eugenides." http://www.oprah.com/oprahsbookclub/A-Conversation-with-Middlesex-Author-Jeffrey-Eugenides (accessed 18 June 2015).

Eugenides, Jeffrey. 2007b. "Q & A with Jeffrey Eugenides." http://www.oprah.com/oprahsbookclub/Middlesex-QA (accessed 19 June 2015).

Fassin, Eric. 2014. "Postface, Le Vrai Genre." In *Herculine Barbin dite Alexina B*, by Herculine Barbin, 221–258. Paris: Gallimard.

Fausto-Sterling, Anne. 2000 *Sexing the Body: Gender Politics and the Construction of Sexuality*. New York: Basic Books.

Federici, Eleonora, and Vanessa Leonardi, eds. 2013. *Bridging the Gap between Theory and Practice in Translation and Gender Studies*. Cambridge: Cambridge Scholars Publishing.

Federici, Eleonora, and Vanessa Leonardi. 2013. "Introduction." In *Bridging the Gap between Theory and Practice in Translation and Gender Studies*, edited by Eleonora Federici and Vanessa Leonardi, 1–3. Cambridge: Cambridge Scholars Publishing.

Feinberg, Leslie. 1996. *Transgender Warriors: Making History from Joan of Arc to RuPaul*. Boston: Beacon Press.

Féret, René. dir. 1985. *Mystère Alexina*. Brussels: Les Cinéastes Associés.

Ferrer, Joaquín María. 1829 "Prologo del Editor." In *Historia de la Monja Alférez, Doña Catalina de Erauso, escrita por ella misma* by Catalina de

Erauso, v–xlxi. Paris: Julio Didot. http://www.libros.uchile.cl/files/presses/1/monographs/70/submission/proof/index.html#/2 (accessed 28 January 2017).

Finney, Brian. 2002. "Bonded by Language: Jeanette Winterson's *Written on the Body*." *Women and Language 25* (2): 23–31.

Fitzgerald, Des, and Felicity Callard. 2014. "Social Science and Neuroscience beyond Interdisciplinarity: Experimental Entanglements." *Theory, Culture and Society 32* (1): 3–32.

Fitzmaurice-Kelly, James. 1992 [1908]. "The Nun Ensign." In *Vida i Sucesos de la Monja Alférez by Catalina de Erauso*, edited by Rima de Vallbona, 192–222. Tempe: Center for Latin American Studies, Arizona State University.

Fitzpatrick, Kevin. 2019. "'I Am Not Male or Female': Sam Smith Comes Out as Non-Binary". *Vanity Fair*. https://www.vanityfair.com/style/2019/03/sam-smith-non-binary-genderqueer (accessed 17 July 2019).

Flaubert, Gustave. 2001. *Madame Bovary*. Paris: Gallimard.

Fort, Camille. 2008. "Traduire le Neutre sans Neutraliser le Littéraire: *Written on the Body* de Jeannette Winterson et *In Transit* de Brigid Brophy." *Palimpsestes 21*: 55–73.

Foucault, Michel. 1978. *The Will to Knowledge, The History of Sexuality: Volume 1*. Translated by Robert Hurley. London: Penguin.

Foucault, Michel. 1979 [1969]. "What is an Author." Translated by Donald F. Bouchard, *Screen 20* (1): 13–34.

Foucault, Michel. 1985. *The Use of Pleasure, The History of Sexuality: Volume 2*. Translated by Robert Hurley. London: Penguin.

Foucault, Michel. 1986. *The Care of the Self, The History of Sexuality: Volume 3*. Translated by Robert Hurley. London: Penguin.

Foucault, Michel. 1994. "Self Writing." In *Ethics: Subjectivity and Truth*. Edited by Paul Rainbow and translated by Robert Hurley and others, 207–222. London: The Penguin Group.

Foucault, Michel. 2014 [1978]. "Préface." In *Herculine Barbin dite Alexina B*, edited by Michel Foucault, 9–21. Paris: Gallimard.

Fournier, Nathalie. 1998. *Grammaire du français classique*. Paris: Belin.

Franklin, Leanne. 2012. *Gender*. Basingstoke: Palgrave Macmillan.

Freely, John. 2014. *A Travel Guide to Homer: On the Trail of Odysseus Through Turkey and the Mediterranean*. London: I. B. Tauris.

Freid, Gregory. 2006. "Back to the Cave: A Platonic Rejoinder to Heideggerian Postmodernism." In *Heidegger and the Greeks: Interpretive Essays*, edited by Drew A. Hyland and John Panteleimon Manoussakis, 157–176. Bloomington: Indiana University Press.

Freud, Sigmund. 2003. *The Uncanny*. Translated by David McLintock. London: Penguin.

Froneman, Willemein. 2010. "Composing According to Silence: Undecidability in Derrida and Cage's 'Roratorio'." *International Review of Aesthetics and Sociology of Music 41* (2): 293–317.

Frow, John. 2006. *Genre*. London: Routledge.

Fuss, Diana. 1989. *Essentially Speaking*. New York: Routledge.

Gabriel, Kay. 2016. "Untranslating Gender in Trish Salah's *Lyric Sexology Vol. 1*." *Transgender Studies Quarterly 3* (3–4): 524–544.

Gaillardet, Frédéric. 1970. *The Memoirs of the Chevalier d'Eon*. Translated by Antonia White. London: Anthony Blond.

Gailey, Nerissa and Alan D. Brown. 2016. "Beyond Either/Or: Reading Trans* Lesbian Identities." *Journal of Lesbian Studies* 20 (1): 65–86.

Garber, Marjorie. 1992. *Vested Interests: Cross-Dressing and Cultural Anxiety*. London: Penguin.

Garber, Marjorie. 1996. "Foreword." In *Lieutenant Nun: Memoir of a Basque Transvestite in the New World by Catalina de Erauso*, translated by Gabriel and Michele Stepto, vii–xxiv. Boston: Beacon Press.

Garréta, Anne. 1986. *Sphinx: Roman*. Paris: Bernard Grasset.

Garréta, Anne. 2009. "Eros Mélancolique: Interview de Anne F. Garréta." *Têtu.com*, March 18. www.univers-l.com/eros_melancolique_interview_anne_garreta.html (accessed 14 December 2015).

Genette, Gérard. 1997. *Palimpsests: Literature in the Second Degree*. Translated by Channa Newman and Claude Doubinsky. Lincoln: The University of Nebraska Press.

Giffney, Noreen. 2009. "Introduction: The 'Q' Word." In *The Ashgate Research Companion to Queer Theory*, edited by Noreen Giffney and Michael O'Rourke, 1–16. Farnham: Ashgate.

Gilbert, Ruth. 2002. *Early Modern Hermaphrodites: Sex and Other Stories*. Basingstoke: Palgrave.

Glover, David, and Cora Kaplan. 2009. *Genders*. Abingdon: Routledge.

Gómez Ibañez, Benito, trans. 2003. *Jeffrey Eugenides: Middlesex*. Barcelona: Anagrama.

Gomolka, C. J. 2012. "Lost in (Trans)lation: The Misread Body of Herculine Barbin." *Synthesis 4*: 62–82.

Goujon, E. 2014 [1869]. "Étude d'un cas d'hermaphroditisme imparfait chez l'homme." In *Herculine Barbin dite Alexina B* by H. Barbin, 151–164. Paris: Gallimard.

Graham, Sarah. 2009. "'See Synonyms at Monster:' En-Freaking Transgender in Jeffrey Eugenides' *Middlesex*." *ARIEL 40* (4): 1–18.

Gramling, David, and Aniruddha Dutta. 2016. "Introduction." *Transgender Studies Quarterly 3* (3–4): 333–356.

Green, Emma. 2017. "Trump's Transgender Ban Could Force Out Thousands of Service Members." *The Atlantic*. 26 July. https://www.theatlantic.com/politics/archive/2017/07/trump-bans-transgender-americans-from-serving-in-the-military/534939/ (accessed 29 June 2020).

Greenblatt, Stephen. 2005. *Renaissance Self-Fashioning: From More to Shakespeare*. Chicago: The University of Chicago Press.

Gregorio, I. W. 2015. *None of the Above*. New York: Balzer & Bray.

Grossman, Edith. 2010. *Why Translation Matters*. New Haven: Yale University Press.

Grosz, Elizabeth. 2005. "Bergson, Deleuze and the Becoming of Unbecoming." *Parallax 11* (2): 4–13.

Guardian, The. 2017. "Muxes: gender-fluid lives in a small Mexican town." 27 October. https://www.theguardian.com/news/2017/oct/27/muxes-documentary-gender-fluid-lives-in-a-small-mexican-town (accessed 29 June 2020).

Gupta, Kanishka. 2017. “These Books Are (Not) Lost in Transgender.” March 15. http://www.dnaindia.com/lifestyle/report-these-books-are-not-lost-in-transgender-2352793 (accessed 6 September 2017).

Hadid, Diaa. 2016. “A ‘Seed of Hope’ for Transgender People in Arab Communities.” *The New York Times*, July 29. https://www.nytimes.com/2016/07/30/world/middleeast/a-seed-of-hope-for-transgender-people-in-arab-communities.html (accessed 6 September 2017).

Halberstam, Judith. 1998. *Female Masculinity*. Durham: Duke University Press.

Halberstam, Judith. 2005. *In a Queer Time and Place: Transgender Bodies, Subcultural Lives*. New York: New York University Press.

Halberstam, Judith. 2011. *The Queer Art of Failure*. Durham: Duke University Press.

Hansen, Jennifer L. 2005. “Written on the Body, Written by the Senses.” *Philosophy and Literature 29*: 365–378.

Harris, Andrea L. 2000. *Other Sexes: Rewriting Difference from Woolf to Winterson*. New York: State University of New York Press.

Harris, James C. 2013. “Joan of Arc.” *Jama Psychiatry 70* (1): 6–7.

Harris, Joseph. 2005. *Hidden Agendas: Cross-Dressing in 17th-Century France*. Tübingen: GNV.

Harris, Joseph. 2010. “Transvestite Traditions and Narrative Discontinuities: d’Eon and the abbé de Choisy.” In *The Chevalier d’Eon and his Worlds: Gender, Espionage and Politics in the Eighteenth Century*, edited by Stephen Burrows, Jonathan Conlin, Russell Goulbourne, and Valerie Mainz, 177–186. London: Continuum.

Hayes, Christal. 2018. “Trump rolls back Obama rules that helped transgender prisoners”. *USA Today*. https://eu.usatoday.com/story/news/2018/05/11/trump-obama-rules-protecting-transgender-inmates/603904002/ (accessed 17 July 2019).

Hayes, Stephanie. 2016. “The Challenges of Genderless Characters.” *The Atlantic*, May 11. www.theatlantic.com/entertainment/archive/2016/05/the-challenge-of-genderless-characters/482109/ (accessed 26 October 2017).

Hayles, N. Katherine. 2002. *Writing Machines*. Cambridge and London: The MIT Press.

Hayles, N. Katherine. 2008. *Electronic Literature: New Horizons for the Literary*. Notre Dame: University of Notre Dame Press.

Headlam Wells, Robin. 2005. *Shakespeare’s Humanism*. Cambridge: Cambridge University Press.

Hegel, Georg Wilhelm. 2010. *The Science of Logic*. Translated and edited by George Di Giovanni. Cambridge: Cambridge University Press.

Heidegger, Martin. 2010. *Being and Time*. Translated by Joan Stambaugh. Albany: State University of New York Press.

Heinrich, Ari Larissa and Eloise Dowd. 2016. “In Memoriam to Identity: Transgender as Strategy in Qiu Miaojin’s *Last Words from Montmartre*.” *Transgender Studies Quarterly 3* (3–4): 569–577.

Hird, Myra, and Jenz Germon. 2001. “The Intersexual Body and the Medical Regulation of Gender.” In *Constructing Gendered Bodies*, edited by Kathryn Backett-Milburn and Linda McKie, 163–178. Basingstoke: Palgrave.

Hirschfeld, Magnus. 1991. *Transvestites: The Erotic Drive to Cross Dress*. Translated by Michael A. Lombardi-Nash. New York: Prometheus Books.

Hoare, Philip. 2013. "Kenneth Halliwell: Lover, Killer ... Artist?" *The Guardian*, September 30. https://www.theguardian.com/stage/2013/sep/30/halliwell-orton-art-collage-library-books (accessed 26 October 2017).

Holmes, Morgan. 2008. *Intersex: A Perilous Difference*. Cranbury: Rosemont Printing and Publishing Corp.

Homer. 2003. *The Odyssey*. Translated by Emile Victor Rieu. London: Penguin.

Houlgate, Stephen. 2006. *The Opening of Hegel's Logic: From Being to Infinity*. West Lafayette: Purdue University Press.

Hoyer, Niels, ed. 2004. *Man into Woman: The First Sex Change, A Portrait of Lili Elbe*. Translated by James Stenning. London: Blue Boat Books Ltd.

Hsu, Stephanie. 2011. "Ethnicity and the Biopolitics of Intersex in Jeffrey Eugenides' *Middlesex*." *MELUS 36* (3): 87–110.

Huet, Pierre Daniel. 1992 [1683]. "Long Extracts from 'De optimo genere interpretandi' ('On the Best Way of Translating'), Book One of *De inierpretatione libri duo* ('Two Books on Translation')." In *Translation, History, Culture: A Sourcebook* edited by André Lefevere, 86–101. London: Routledge.

Hunte, Ben. 2020. "Gender Recognition Act: LGBT political group anger at trans law 'changes'." *BBC News*. 20 June. https://www.bbc.co.uk/news/uk-53101071 (accessed 26 June 2020).

Huston, Matt. 2015. "None of the Above." *Psychology Today 48* (2): 28–30.

Hyland, Drew A. 2006. "Preface." In *Heidegger and the Greeks: Interpretive Essays*, edited by Drew A. Hyland and John Panteleimon Manoussakis, ix. Bloomington: Indiana University Press.

Independent, The. 2010. "Transsexual's Memoirs Breaks New Ground in Arab World." July 3. http://www.independent.co.uk/arts-entertainment/books/transsexuals-memoirs-breaks-new-ground-in-arab-world-2018207.html (accessed 03 August 2017).

Intersex Society of North America, The. No Date. "What is Intersex?" http://www.isna.org/faq/what_is_intersex (accessed 5 April 2016).

Irigaray, Luce. 1985. *This Sex Which Is Not One*. Translated by Catherine Porter with Carolyn Burke. Ithaca: Cornell University Press.

Irigaray, Luce. 1993. *An Ethics of Sexual Difference*. Translated by Carolyn Burke and Gillian C. Gill. London: The Athlone Press.

Jackman, Josh. 2017a. "Canadian Baby Becomes First in the World to be Officially Identified as Agender." *Pink News*, July 3. http://www.pinknews.co.uk/2017/07/03/canadian-baby-becomes-first-in-the-world-to-be-officially-identified-as-agender/2/ (accessed 26 October 2017).

Jackman, Josh. 2017b. "Washington DC Has Become the First to Recognise Non-Binary People – and it Was No Big Deal." *Pink News*, June 29. http://www.pinknews.co.uk/2017/06/29/washington-dc-has-become-the-first-state-to-recognise-non-binary-people-and-it-was-no-big-deal/ (accessed 26 October 2017).

Jackman, Josh. 2017c. "Oregon Just Became the First State to Legally Recognise Non-Binary People." *Pink News*, June 16. http://www.pinknews.co.uk/2017/06/16/oregon-just-became-the-first-state-to-legally-recognise-non-binary-people/ (accessed 26 October 2017).

Jagose, Annamarie. 1996. *Queer Theory*. Victoria: Melbourne University Press.

Janés, Clara, trans. 1988. *Anne Garréta: Esfinge*. Barcelona: Tusquets.

Johnson, Barbara. 2004. "Translator's Introduction." In *Dissemination* by Jaques Derrida, translated by Barbara Johnson, vii–xxxv. London: Continuum.

Joyce, James. 2015 [1939]. *Finnegans Wake*. London: Penguin UK.

Juárez-Almendros, Encarnación. 2006. *El cuerpo vestido y la construcción de la identidad en las narrativas autobiográficas del Siglo de Oro*. Woodbridge: Tamesis.

Kates, Gary. 1991. "D'Eon Returns to France: Gender and Power in 1977." in *Body Guards: The Cultural Politics of Gender Ambiguity*, edited by Julia Epstein and Kristina Straub, 167–194. London: Routledge.

Kates, Gary. 1995. "The Transgendered World of the Chevalier/Chevalière d'Eon." *The Journal of Modern History* 67 (3): 558–594.

Khomani, Nadia. 2016. "I Thought it's Now or Never, Says Student Who Came Out as Non-Binary to Obama." *The Guardian*, April 24. www.theguardian.com/world/2016/apr/24/now-or-never-says-student-who-came-out-as-non-binary-to-obama (accessed 12 September 2016).

Kosofsky Sedgwick, Eve. 1994. *Tendencies*. New York: Routledge.

Kosofsky Sedgwick, Eve. 2008 [1990]. *Epistemology of the Closet*. Berkeley: University of California Press.

Landow, George P. 1994. "What's a Critic to Do?: Critical Theory in the Age of Hypertext." In *Hyper/Text/Theory*, edited by George P. Landow, 1–48. Baltimore: The Johns Hopkins University Press.

Landow, George P. 2006. *Hypertext 3.0: Critical Theory and New Media in an Era of Globalization*. Baltimore: The Johns Hopkins University Press.

Laplanche, Jean and J. B. Pontalis. 1988. *The Language of Psychoanalysis*. Translated by Donald Nicholson-Smith. London: Karnac Books.

Laqueur, Thomas W. 2012. "The Rise of Sex in the Eighteenth Century: Historical Context and Historiographical Implications." *Signs: Journal of Women in Culture and Society* 37 (4): 802–813.

Larkosh, Christopher. 2016. "Flows of Trans-Language: Translating Transgender in the *Paraguayan Sea*." *Transgender Studies Quarterly* 3 (3–4): 552–568.

Leavy, Patricia. 2011. *Essentials of Transdisciplinary Research: Using Problem-Centered Methodologies*. Walnut Creek: Left Coast Press.

Lee, P. A., C. P. Houk, S. F. Ahmed, I. A. Hughes and in collaboration with the participants in the International Consensus Conference on Intersex organized by the Lawson Wilkins Pediatric Endocrine Society and the European Society for Paediatric Endocrinology. 2006. "Consensus statement on management of intersex disorders." *Pediatrics* 118 (2): 488–500.

Lefevere, André, ed. 1992a. *Translation, History, Culture: A Sourcebook*. London: Routledge.

Leonardi, Vanessa. 2013. "Can we Translate Ambiguity?" In *Bridging the Gap between Theory and Practice in Translation and Gender Studies*, edited by Eleonora Federici and Vanessa Leonardi, 63–74. Cambridge: Cambridge Scholars Publishing.

Lester, C. N. 2017. *Trans Like Me*. London: Virago Press.

Livia, Anna. 2001. *Pronoun Envy: Literary Uses of Linguistic Gender*. New York: Oxford University Press.

de Lotbinière-Harwood, Suzanne. 1991. *The Body Bilingual: Translation as a Rewriting in the Feminine*. Toronto: Women's Press.

MacDougall, Richard, trans. 1980. *Herculine Barbin: Herculine Barbin: Being the Recently Discovered Memoirs of a Nineteenth Century French Hermaphrodite*. New York: Pantheon Books.

McAvan, Em. 2011. "Ambiguity and Apophatic Bodies in Jeanette Winterson's *Written on the Body*." *Critique 52*: 434–443.

McCombie, Elizabeth. 2006. "Introduction." In *Collected Poems and Other Verse*. Translated by E. H and A. M. Blackmore, ix–xxvii. Oxford: Oxford University Press.

Madden, Ed. 2008. *Tiresian Poetics: Modernism, Sexuality, Voice, 1888-2001*. Madison: Fairleigh Dickinson University Press.

Maioli, Francesca. 2009. "The Female Body as a Text in Jeanette Winterson's *Written on the Body*." *European Journal of Women's Studies 16* (2): 143–158.

de Man, Paul. 1984. *The Rhetoric of Romanticism*. New York: Columbia University Press.

Marrone, Giovanna, trans. 1993. *Jeanette Winterson: Scritto sul corpo*. Milan: Mondadori.

Mathews, Harry, and Alastair Brotchie, eds. 2005. *Oulipo Compendium*. London: Atlas Press.

Maynard, J. L. 2003. "'I Find/I Found Myself/and/Nothing/More than That:' Textuality, Visuality, and the Production of Subjectivity in Tom Phillips' *A Humument*." *The Journal of the Midwest Modern Language Association 36* (1): 82–98.

Mayoux, Suzanne, trans. 1993 *Jeanette Winterson: Ecrit sur le corps*. Paris: Plon.

Mendelsohn, Daniel. 2002. "Mighty Hermaphrodite." *The New York Review of Books*, November 7. http://www.nybooks.com/articles/archives/2002/nov/07/mighty-hermaphrodite/ (accessed June 15 2015).

Mendieta, Eva. 2009. *In Search of Catalina de Erauso: The National and Sexual Identity of the Lieutenant Nun*. Translated by Angeles Prado. Reno: University of Nevada.

Merton, Lee. 2010. "Why Jeffrey Eugenides' *Middlesex* Is So Inoffensive." *Critique 51* (1): 32–46.

Micah. No Date. "About Micah", *Genderqueer.Me*. Available at: https://genderqueer.me/about/ (accessed 20 July 2019).

Micah. 2013. "Explaining Genderqueer to those who are not". *Genderqueer.Me*. https://genderqueer.me/2013/04/17/explaining-genderqueer-to-those-who-are-not/ (accessed 20 July 2019)

Micah. 2013. "Reader Ramblings: Not-Binary, not Trans Enough". *Genderqueer.Me*. https://genderqueer.me/2013/10/30/non-binary-not-trans-enough/ (accessed 20 July 2019)

Ming, Lei, and Frazey, Lura. 2017. "Life Beyond My Body: A Transgender Journey to Manhood in China." http://www.lifebeyondmybody.com/ (accessed 6 September 2017).

Ming, Lei, and Frazey, Lura. 2016. *Life Beyond My Body: A Transgender Journey to Manhood in China*. Oakland: Transgress Press.

Morales, Ed. 2018. "Why I Embrace the Term Latinx." *The Guardian*, January 8. https://www.theguardian.com/commentisfree/2018/jan/08/why-i-embrace-the-term-latinx?CMP=share_btn_link (accessed 8 January 2018).

Morrison, Jago. 2006. "'Who Cares about Gender at a Time like this?' Love, Sex and the Problem of Jeanette Winterson." *Journal of Gender Studies 15* (2): 169–180.

Most, Glen A. 2002. "Heidegger's Greeks." *Arion 10* (1): 83–98.

Munir, Maria. (2016) "Why I Came Out as Non-Binary to Barack Obama". *The Telegraph*, 27 April. Available at: www.telegraph.co.uk/news/2016/04/27/why-i-came-out-as-non-binary-to-barack-obama (Accessed 12 September 2016).

Nanda, Serena. 1994. "Hijras: An Alternative Sex and Gender Role in India." In *Third Sex, Third Gender: Beyond Sexual Dimorphism in Culture and History*, edited by Gilbert Herdt, 373–417. New York: Zone Books.

Narayan Tripathi, Laxmi. 2015. *Me Hijra, Me Laxmi*. Translated by R. Raj Rao and P. G. Joshi. Oxford: University Press India.

National Centre for Transgender Equality. 2020. "Trump's record of action against transgender people". https://transequality.org/the-discrimination-administration (accessed 14 August 2019).

Neefs, Jacques. 2007. "Georges Perec: Distinctive Constraints, Textual Liberties." *Journal of Romance Studies* 7 (3): 59–74.

Nelson, Ted. 1965. "A File Structure for the Complex, the Changing and the Indeterminate." http://csis.pace.edu/~marchese/CS835/Lec3/nelson.pdf (accessed 08 January 2016).

Nietzsche, Friedrich. 1967. *The Portable Nietzsche*. Edited and translated by Walter Kaufmann. London: Penguin Books.

Noble, Jean Bobby. 2006. *Sons of the Movement: FtMs Risking Incoherence on a Post-Queer Cultural Landscape*. Toronto: Women's Press.

Intersex Human Rights Australia. 2012. "Intersex legislative Issues 2012 – a Brief Summary." https://ihra.org.au/21053/intersex-legislative-issues/ (accessed 29 June 2020).

Ovid. 2000. *Metamorphoses: Book IV*. Translated by A. S. Kline. http://ovid.lib.virginia.edu/trans/Metamorph4.htm (accessed 8 December 2017).

Oxford. 2017. *Oxford English Dictionary*. Oxford: Oxford University Press. http://www.oed.com/ (accessed 16 February 2017).

Oxford. 2003. *The Concise Oxford Dictionary of English Etymology*. Oxford: Oxford University Press. http://www.oxfordreference.com/view/10.1093/acref/9780192830982.001.0001/acref-9780192830982 (accessed 16 February 2017).

Palusci, Oriana. 2013. "Translating Dolls." In *Bridging the Gap between Theory and Practice in Translation and Gender Studies*, edited by Eleonora Federici and Vanessa Leonardi, 15–31. Cambridge: Cambridge Scholars Publishing.

Pappo-Musard, Catherine, trans. 1993. *Virginia Woolf: Orlando*. Paris: Le Livre de Poche.

Parsons, Vic. 2019. "Bre Kidman is the first out non-binary person to run for the US Senate". *Pink News*. https://www.pinknews.co.uk/2019/07/01/bre-kidman-first-out-non-binary-person-us-senate/ (accessed 03 August 2019).

Perec, Georges. 1969. *La disparition*. Paris: Lettres Nouvelles.

Pérez-Villanueva, Sonia. 2014. *The Life of Catalina de Erauso, the Lieutenant Nun: An Early Modern Autobiography*. Madison: Fairleigh Dickinson University Press.

Petitjean, Luc. 1991. "Un vieux casse-tête: l'accord du participe passé." *Mots 28*: 70–85.

Pfahl, C. A. (2015) "'After the/unauthor:' Fragmented Author Functions in Tom Phillips' *A Humument*." *Studies in the Novel 47* (3): 399–419.

Phillips, Tom. 1980. *A Humument: A Treated Victorian Novel*. London: Thames and Hudson Ltd.

Pinker, Stephen. 1994. *The Language Instinct*. New York: Penguin.

Plato. 2008. *The Symposium*. Translated by M. C. Howatson, edited by M. C. Howatson and Frisbee C. C. Sheffield. Cambridge: Cambridge University Press.

Pope, Rob. 2005. *Creativity: Theory, History, Practice*. London: Routledge.

Poulet, Georges. 1970. "Criticism and the Experience of Interiority." In *The Languages of Criticism and the Sciences of Man: The Structuralist Controversy*, edited by Richard Macksey and Eugenio Donato, 56–73. Baltimore: The Johns Hopkins University Press.

Prince, Gerald. 2014. "Narratology and Translation." *Language and Literature 23* (1): 23–31.

Proust, Marcel. 1919. *À la recherche du temps perdu: tome I, du côté de chez Swann*. Paris: Nouvelle Revue Française.

Prosser, Jay. 2006. "Judith Butler: Queer Feminism, Transgender and the Transubstantiation of Sex." In *The Transgender Studies Reader*, edited by Susan Stryker and Stephen Whittle, 257–280. New York: Taylor & Francis Group.

Qiu, Miaojin. 2014. *Last Words from Montmartre*. Translated by Ari Larissa Heinrich. New York: New York Review Books.

Queneau, Raymond. 1961. *Cent mille milliards de poèmes*. Paris: Gallimard.

Ramadan, Emma, trans. 2015. *Anne Garréta: Sphinx*. Dallas: Deep Vellum Publishing.

Randa and Hazem Saghieh. 2010. *Mouzakarat Randa al-Trans*. Beirut: Dar-Al Saqi.

Rettberg, Scott. 2011. "All Together Now: Hypertext, Collective Narratives and Online Collective Knowledge Communities." In *New Narratives: Stories and Storytelling in the Digital Age*, edited by Ruth Page and Bronwen Thomas, 187–204. Lincoln: University of Nebraska Press.

Rex, Cathy. 2016. "Ungendering Empire: Catalina de Erauso and the Performance of Masculinity." In *Women's Narratives of the Early Americas and the Formation of Empire*, edited by Mary McAleer Balkun and Susan C. Imbarrato, 33–46. Basingstoke: Palgrave Macmillan.

Revathi, A. 2010. *The Truth About Me: A Hijra Life Story*. Translated by V. Geetha. New Delhi: Penguin India.

Rickard, Peter. 1989. *A History of the French Language*. London: Unwin Hyman.

Rigby, Elizabeth. 1848. "A Review of *Jane Eyre* and *Vanity Fair*." *The London Quarterly Review CLXVII*: 82–99.

Roger, Alain. 1977. *Hermaphrodite*. Paris: Denoël.

Roscoe, Will. 1998. *Changing Ones: Third and Fourth Genders in Native North America*. New York: St Martin's Griffin.

Rose, Emily. 2016. "Keeping the Trans in Translation: Queering Early Modern Transgender Memoirs." *Transgender Studies Quarterly 3* (3–4): 485–505.

Rose, Emily. 2017. "Revealing and Concealing the Masquerade of Translation and Gender: Double-Crossing the Text and the Body." In *Queer in Translation*, edited by B. J. Epstein and Robert Gillet, 37–50. London: Routledge.

Rose, Herbert Jennings. 2005 [1928]. *A Handbook of Greek Mythology*. London: Routledge.

Rose, Jaqueline. 2016. "Who Do You Think You Are?" *London Review of Books 38* (9): 3–13.

Rosenbaum, S. I. 2019. "Trump wants to deny transgender rights on religious grounds. But what if gender identity, itself, is a matter of the soul?" *The Boston Globe*. July 5. https://www.bostonglobe.com/ideas/2019/07/05/trump-wants-deny-transgender-rights-religious-grounds-but-what-gender-identity-itself-matter-soul/A7VFzaO6rUCn3krlLum4tO/story.html (accessed August 03 2019).

Rossi, Andrea. 2013. "Herculine Barbin. *Mes Souvenirs, Histoire d'Alexina/Abel B.*" *Foucault Studies 15*: 187–189.

Roubaud, Jacques. 2004. "Perecquian OULIPO." Translated by Jean-Jacques Poucel, *Yale French Studies 105*: 99–109.

Roxie, Marilyn. 2011a. "What is Genderqueer?" www.genderqueerid.com/what-is-gq (accessed 31 March 2016).

Roxie, Marilyn. 2011b. "Genderqueer History." www.genderqueerid.com/gqhistory (accessed 31 March 2016).

Rubinson, Gregory L. 2001. "Body Languages: Scientific and Aesthetic Discourses in Jeanette Winterson's *Written on the Body*." *Critique 42* (2): 218–232.

Rubio Merino, Pedro. 1995. "Introducción." In *La Monja Alférez: Doña Catalina de Erauso, dos manuscritos inéditos de su autobiografía conservados en el archivo de la Santa Iglesia Catedral de Sevilla by Catalina de Erauso*, edited by Pedro Rubio Merino, 9–49. Seville: Cabildo Metropolitano de la Catedral de Sevilla.

Ruby, Ryan. 2016. "Know Thyself: The Riddles of Anne Garréta's *Sphinx*." *3 Quarks Daily*, June 27. http://www.3quarksdaily.com/3quarksdaily/2016/06/know-thyself.html (accessed 24 January 2017).

Rutter-Jensen, Chloe. 2007. "La transformación transatlántica de la monja alférez." *Revista de Estudios Sociales 28*: 86–95.

Rye, Gill. 2000. "Uncertain Readings and Meaningful Dialogues: Language and Sexual Identity in Anne Garréta's *Sphinx* and Tahar Ben Jelloun's *L'Enfant de Sable* and *La Nuit Sacrée*." *Neophilologus 84*: 531–540.

Safran Foer, Jonathan. 2010. *Tree of Codes*. London: Visual Editions Ltd.

Salih, Sara, ed. 2004. *The Judith Butler Reader*. Oxford: Blackwell Publishing.

Sanger-Katz, Margot and Noah Weiland. 2020. "Trump Administration Erases Transgender Civil Rights Protections in Health Care." *The New York Times*. June 12. https://www.nytimes.com/2020/06/12/us/politics/trump-transgender-rights.html (accessed 26 June 2020).

Schabert, Ina. 2010. "Translation Trouble: Gender Indeterminacy in English Novels and their French Versions." *Translation and Literature 19*: 72–92.

Scott, Clive. 2008. *"Experimenting with a Single String: Apollinaire's 'Chantre'."* In *Norwich Papers*, edited by Rosalind Harvey, Isabel Hempen and Marzenka Sieradzki, *16*: 72–87.

Scott, Clive. 2012. *Translating the Perception of Text: Literary Translation and Phenomenology*. London: Legenda.

Scott, Clive. 2014a. *Translating Apollinaire*. Exeter: University of Exeter Press.

Scott, Clive. 2014b. "Foreword." In *Literary Translation: Redrawing the Boundaries*, edited by Jean Boase-Beier, Antionette Fawcett and Philip Wilson, ix–xi. Basingstoke: Palgrave Macmillan.

Sedlmeier, Peter, Arun Tipanjan, and Anastasia Jänchen. 2016. "How Persistent are Grammatical Gender Effects? The Case of German and Tamil." *Journal of Psycholinguistic Research 45*: 317–336.

Shakespeare, William. 1958. "A Midsummer Night's Dream." In *The Complete Works of William Shakespeare* by William Shakespeare, 139–158. London: Spring Books.

Shapiro, Eve. 2010. *Gender Circuits: Bodies and Identities in a Technological Age*. New York: Routledge.

Shorley, Christopher. 1985. *Queneau's Fiction: An Introductory Study*. Cambridge: Cambridge University Press.

Shostak, Debra. 2008. "'Theory Uncompromised by Practicality:' Hybridity in Jeffrey Eugenides' *Middlesex*." *Contemporary Literature 49* (3): 383–412.

Simon, Sherry. 1996. *Gender in Translation: Cultural Identity and the Politics of Transmission*. London: Routledge.

Spender, Dale. 1998 [1980]. *Man Made Language*. London: Pandora Press.

Spivak, Gayatri Chakravorty. 1988. "Subaltern Studies: Deconstructing Historiography." In *Selected Subaltern Studies*, edited by Ranajit Guha and Gayatri Chakravorty Spivak, 3–32. New York: Oxford University Press.

Spivak, Gayatri Chakravorty. 2016. "Translator's Preface." In *Of Grammatology by Jacques Derrida*, translated by Gayatri Chakravorty Spivak, xxvii–cxi. Baltimore: Johns Hopkins University Press.

Spurlin, William J. 2014. "The Gender and Queer Politics of Translation: New Approaches." *Comparative Literature Studies 51* (2): 201–214.

Spurlin, William J. 2017. "Queering Translation: Rethinking Gender and Sexual Politics in the Spaces between Languages and Cultures." In *Queer in Translation*, edited by B. J. Epstein and Robert Gillett, 172–183. London: Routledge.

Smith, Ali. 2007. *Girl Meets Boy*. Edinburgh: Canongate Books.

Smith, Jennifer A. 2011. "'We shall Pass Imperceptibly through Every Barrier:' Reading Jeanette Winterson's Trans-formative Romance." *Critique 52* (4): 412–433.

Stafford, Hélène. 2000. *Mallarmé and the Poetics of Everyday Life: A Study of the Concept of the Ordinary in his Verse and Prose*. Amsterdam: Rodopi.

St. André, James. 2010a. "Translation and Metaphor: Setting the Terms." In *Thinking Through Translation With Metaphors*, edited by James St. André, 1–16. Manchester: St Jerome.

St. André, James. 2010b. "Passing Through Translation." In *Thinking Through Translation With Metaphors*, edited by James St. André, 275–294. Manchester: St Jerome.

Steegmuller, Francis. 1968. *Flaubert and Madame Bovary: A Double Portrait*. London: Macmillan.

Steegmuller, Francis. ed. 2001 *The Letters of Gustave Flaubert, Volumes I & II, 1830-1880*. London: Picador.

Steinmetz, Katy. 2014. "The Transgender Tipping Point." *The New York Times*, May 29. http://time.com/135480/transgender-tipping-point/ (accessed 1 August 2017).

Stepto, Michele. 1996. "Introduction." In *Lieutenant Nun: Memoir of a Basque Transvestite in the New World*, translated by Gabriel and Michele Stepto, xxv–xliv. Boston: Beacon Press.

Stepto, Michele and Gabriel Stepto, trans. 1996. *Catarina de Erauso: Lieutenant Nun: Memoir of a Basque Transvestite in the New World*. Boston: Beacon Press.

Stone, Sandy. 2006. "The Empire Strikes Back: A Posttranssexual Manifesto." In *The Transgender Studies Reader*, edited by Susan Stryker and Stephen Whittle, 221–235. New York: Taylor & Francis Group.

Stonewall. 2017. "Glossary of Terms." https://www.stonewall.org.uk/help-advice/faqs-and-glossary/glossary-terms#t (accessed 29 June 2020).

Stoppard, Tom. 1975. *Travesties*. New York: Grove Press.

Strümper-Krobb, Sabine. 2003. "The Translator in Fiction." *Language and Intercultural Communication 3* (2): 115–121.

Strysick, Michael. 2001. "Erasure." In *Encyclopedia of Postmodernism*, edited by Victor Taylor and Charles Winquist. London: Routledge. http://search.credoreference.com/content/entry/routpostm/erasure/0?searchId=f40d3635-e2ea-11e6-875b-0e58d2201a4d&result=0 (accessed 04 April 2016).

Sturges, Fiona. 2018. "Genderquake: Channel 4's nonbinary answer to Big Brother". *The Guardian*. https://www.theguardian.com/tv-and-radio/2018/may/05/genderquake-channel-4-trans-non-binary (accessed 20 July 2019).

Takako, Shimura. 2011. *Wandering Son: Volume One*. Translated by Matt Thorn. Seattle: Fantagraphics Books.

Tambling, Jeremy. 1990. *Confession: Sexuality, Sin, the Subject*. Manchester: Manchester University Press.

Tardieu, Ambroise. 1874. *Question médico-légale de l'identité dans les rapports avec les vices de conformation des organs sexuels*. Paris: Librarie J.B. Baillière et Fils. http://gallica.bnf.fr/ark:/12148/bpt6k76971v/f9.item (accessed 29 January 2017).

Tarttelin, Abigail. 2013. *Golden Boy*. New York: Atria.

Telegraph, The. 2017. "Donald Trump Revokes Barak Obama Guidelines on Transgender Bathrooms." February 23. http://www.telegraph.co.uk/news/2017/02/23/donald-trump-revokes-barack-obama-guidelines-transgender-bathrooms/ (accessed 01 August 2017).

Tidd, Ursula. 2000. "Bodily Dissymmetries and Masculine Anxiety: Herculine Has the Last Laugh." In *Body Matters: Feminism, Textuality, Corporeality*, edited by Avril Horner and Angela Keane, 75–84. Manchester: Manchester University Press.

Trans Media Watch. No Date. "Understanding Non-binary People: A Guide for the Media." http://transmediawatch.org/Documents/non_binary.pdf (accessed 14 April 2016).

Tufail, Burhan. 1999. "Oulipian Grammatology: La Règle du Jeu." In *The French Connections of Jacques Derrida*, edited by Julian Wolfreys, John Brannigan and Ruth Robbins, 119–134. Albany: State University of New York Press.

Twain, Mark. 2010 [1880]. "The Awful German Language." In *A Tramp Abroad*, edited by Roy Blount Jr., 374–392. New York: Library of America.

Tymoczko, Maria. 2007 *Enlarging Translation, Empowering Translators*. Manchester: St. Jerome.

Tytler, Alexander Fraser. 1992 [1790]. "Extracts from his *Essay on the Principles of Translation.*" In *Translation, History, Culture: A Sourcebook*, edited by André Lefevere, 128–135. London: Routledge.

Van Wyke, Ben. 2010. "Imitating Bodies and Clothes: Refashioning the Western Conception of Translation." In *Thinking Through Translation with Metaphors*, edited by James St. André, 17–46. Manchester: St Jerome.

Velasco, Sherry. 2000. *The Lieutenant Nun: Transgenderism, Lesbian Desire, and Catalina de Erauso*. Austin: University of Texas Press.

Velasco, Sherry. 2011. *Lesbians in Early Modern Spain*. Nashville: Vanderbilt University Press.

Venuti, Lawrence, ed. 1992. *Rethinking Translation: Discourse, Subjectivity, Ideology*. London: Routledge.

Venuti, Lawrence. 2000. "Translation, Community, Utopia." In *The Translation Studies Reader* edited by Lawrence Venuti, 468–488. London and New York: Routledge.

Venuti, Lawrence. 2013. *Translation Changes Everything: Theory and Practice*. New York: Routledge.

Viloria, Hida. 2017. *Born Both: An Intersex Life*. New York: Hachette Books.

Von Flotow, Luise. 1997. *Translation and Gender: Translating in the "Era of Feminism"*. Manchester: St Jerome.

Von Flotow, Luise. ed. 2011. *Translating Women*. Ottawa: University of Ottawa Press.

Von Flotow, Luise. 2013. "Postface, Gender and Translation, and Translation Studies: An Ongoing Affair." In *Bridging the Gap between Theory and Practice in Translation and Gender Studies*, edited by Eleonora Federici and Vanessa Leonardi, 163–164. Cambridge: Cambridge Scholars Publishing.

Wakefield, Lily. 2019. "Indigenous third gender person graces history-making cover of Vogue Mexico and Britain." *The Pink News*. 22 November. https://www.pinknews.co.uk/2019/11/22/vogue-mexico-britain-indigenous-third-gender-zapotec-oaxaca-cover-tim-walker-photo-shoot/ (accessed 29 June 2020).

Walker Rettberg, Jill. 2014. *Blogging*. Cambridge: Polity Press.

Ward Howe, Julia. 2004 [1846]. *The Hermaphrodite*. Lincoln: University of Nebraska Press.

Ware, Libby. 2015. *Lum*. Berkeley: She Writes Press.

Weininger, Otto. 2005 [1903]. *Sex and Character: An Investigation of Fundamental Principles*. Translated by Ladislaus Löb, edited by Daniel Steuer with Laura Marcus. Bloomington: Indiana University Press.

Whitaker, Brian. 2016. "Transgender Issues in the Middle East." *Al-bab.com*, February 8. http://al-bab.com/blog/2016/02/transgender-issues-middle-east-1 (accessed 6 September 2017).

White, Rachel R. 2012. "Neither Man Nor Woman: Meet the Agender." *The Cut*, August 20. https://www.thecut.com/2012/08/neither-man-nor-woman-meet-the-agender.html (accessed 31 March 2016).

Wilchins, Riki. 2002a. "It's Your Gender, Stupid." In *GenderQueer: Voices from Beyond the Sexual Binary*, edited by Joan Nestle, Clare Howell and Riki Wilchins, 23–32. New York: Alyson Books.

Wilchins, Riki. 2002b. "Changing the Subject." In *GenderQueer: Voices from Beyond the Sexual Binary*, edited by Joan Nestle, Clare Howell and Riki Wilchins, 47–54. New York: Alyson Books.

Wing, Nathaniel. 2004. *Between Genders: Narrating Difference in Early French Modernism*. Delaware: University of Delaware Press.

Winter, Kathleen. 2011. *Annabel*. London: Vintage.

Winterson, Jeanette. 2014. *Oranges are Not the Only Fruit*. London: Vintage.

Winterson, Jeanette. 1993 [1992]. *Written On the Body*. London: Vintage.

Wittig, Monique. 1985. "The Mark of Gender." *Feminist Issues 5* (2): 3–12.

Wolff, Charlotte. 1986. *Magnus Hirschfeld: A Portrait of a Pioneer in Sexology*. London: Quartet Books.

Woolf, Virginia. 2004 [1928]. *Orlando: A Biography*. London: Vintage.

Yaguello, Marina. 2002 [1978]. *Les mots et les femmes*. Paris: Petit Bibliothèque Payot.

Ziolkowski, Theodore. 2005. *Ovid and the Moderns*. Ithaca and London: Cornell University Press.

Index

For Product Safety Concerns and Information please contact our EU representative GPSR@taylorandfrancis.com
Taylor & Francis Verlag GmbH, Kaufingerstraße 24, 80331 München, Germany

www.ingramcontent.com/pod-product-compliance
Lightning Source LLC
Chambersburg PA
CBHW071109100726
47908CB00008B/2321

* 9 7 8 0 3 6 7 7 4 4 7 4 8 *